Among the Cinders

Maurice Shadbolt

ATHENEUM   NEW YORK

1965

AUTHOR'S NOTE
All the characters in this novel,
including the author,
are of course entirely fictitious.

Among the Cinders

For Sean and Brendan

CINDER . . . hard, crumbly substance which remains after the inflammable quality of coal, coke, wood has been destroyed by burning but when they have not yet been reduced to ashes.

H. C. WYLD, *Universal English Dictionary*

Among the Cinders

Chapter One

THERE'S NOTHING I LIKE BETTER THAN A YARN, SO I
might as well get down to business. My name is Nick Flinders,
and I plan to tell about this trip I made with my grandfather last
summer.

You might have heard about it. A lot of people have, one way
and another. I've decided to tell about it mainly because I want
to tell the real truth. There's truth and there's real truth, if you
know what I mean. People think they know the truth about that
trip. But no one is much interested in the real truth.

Even if you haven't heard about the trip, you've possibly
heard about the accident. Everything I've done lately has been
fairly well advertised. I mean the accident which accounted for
me getting together with my grandfather. There's a definite
connection between the accident and the trip, but it seems that
people don't want to see it. If you can't understand one, you
can't hope to understand the other, and all that happened after.

I've told my name. I'm not sure what else I should tell. My
age? I was sixteen last birthday. Not that it matters a hell of a lot
one way or the other. At least that's what I've just explained to
this character who is writing down the whole story for me. My
grandfather maintains that, strictly speaking, no one can be more
than seven years old. It seems he once read a book which said
that each cell in the human body is replaced every seven years.
"That's the statistical fact of the situation," he says. "I might be
five years old, and you might be two. Or it might even be the
other way round. You might be older than me. There's no way
of telling." Actually, he's all of eighty-six. That is, he might be
two years old or five, but he's been walking round the earth in
something like his present shape for eighty-six years.

What else? Well, I live in this little country place called Te Ika.
Even if you live in New Zealand, you're probably vague about

I

Te Ika. I don't blame you. I've been vague about it myself, at times. I'm prepared to admit that about three thousand people live here, for some reason. The town is near the middle of the North Island, about a hundred miles south of Auckland, in a pretty long but narrow valley with hills shooting up suddenly on each side. The sea is about twenty or thirty miles off, in a straight line, with sheep farms and rough bush country between the town and the coast. Inland there is more sheepland, more rough country, and then mountains. On the flat, above and below where Te Ika sits in the valley, there are dairy farms, stray dusty townships and butter factories, and wandering clay roads. Te Ika itself isn't exactly huge. There is a long and very wide main street with shops jammed along one side, and trees and lawns on the other; beyond the trees is the railway station and yards. At the north end of the main street you can find Te Ika's two schools, primary and secondary, built along a bend in the river. At the south end, hard against a hillside, is the local Maori meeting house; it is a fairly ornate and impressive place, bright red, and has a pallisade all round, with carved gods guarding the gateway. Most people live on the flat, somewhere near the banks of the Waipa river which loops through the town and is bridged in about a dozen places; a few houses straggle up the hillsides, half-hidden among punga fern and other native trees which still have a hold here and there on the steeper slopes. Apart from a kowhai or two, native trees have almost gone from the flat; you'll find poplar, oak, chestnut, sycamore and willow along the streets and riverbank, and the Waipa runs bright with their falling leaves in autumn. Some people think Te Ika is pleasant, others think it is a dead-end dump. I've held both views, in my time.

People have heard about Te Ika mainly because of a horrible murder case here a couple of years ago. Actually it's not quite fair to the town because the murders really took place about twelve miles away, in a lonely valley out towards the coast. These people had a farm. They could talk to each other or they could talk to the sheep. There wasn't another farm in sight, there was bush country on three sides, and the road out to town was often flooded in winter. You couldn't exactly blame them for being religious fanatics in a place like that. They sang hymns every evening of the week, and almost all day Sunday. One rainy winter Sunday the two sons of the family, aged fifteen and seventeen, took axes to their sleeping parents and three small sisters.

People round here said that kind of thing gave the district a bad name.

The trial was interesting. A lot of the trial was taken up with poetry. That's right: poetry. Both boys wrote it, screeds and screeds of the stuff. Full of gibbets and crucifixes, corpses and ghosts, and moreporks hooting lonely in the moonlight. It was all read aloud in court, to show the mental state of the boys at the time of the murders.

People round here bucked up a lot while the trial was on. They said New Zealand produced some weird and wonderful murders, but it took Te Ika to produce the weirdest of the lot. I mean they actually took a pride in it. As my father said, people round here have to take a pride in something.

Later they had second thoughts, though. The boys, you see, learnt about poetry at the school where my father teaches and where I still go. They'd never come across poetry before because their parents had only one book in the house, the Bible, and forbade all others. They were excited by it anyway, and this led to all sorts of wild thoughts.

I know my father, who actually teaches poetry, and taught both boys, was upset for a long time after. I don't blame him. How would you feel? And it didn't help him at all when letters appeared in the *Te Ika Gazette* demanding that poetry be removed from the school syllabus. The trial confirmed the fears of most parents in the district. Who could feel safe at nights with children learning poetry at school? People were always suspicious of poetry round here. Now it's actually a dirty word.

These letters eventually provoked a special meeting of the school committee. My father, who really isn't the happiest of men anyway, had to be present at the meeting. He did his best. He talked about Shakespeare and Milton and Keats and the glories of the English language. He did his best, he really did. But the chairman said he felt my father was getting away from

3

the point. That was awfully shattering for my father. How would you like to be told that your whole life was away from the point? That was what it amounted to.

This probably explains why my father lost his temper. I must say it takes some doing. To make him lose it, I mean. God knows I've tried hard enough. He infuriates me, the way he gets so reasonable and civilized when I do something wrong. "Now sit down, Nick," he says in a terribly pleasant voice, "now sit down and listen to me." It gets me, it really does. I mean another father would take his belt off and settle the whole thing in two minutes. But my father never does his block like that. He keeps telling me we have a special relationship. I suppose it's all on account of the way he was belted when he was a child. Grandfather Flinders used to make a point of knocking his eight boys down, one by one, for no special reason. Just as a warning, to remind them who was boss. From the way he tells stories like this, I guess my father never got over it. I don't suppose I would, either. But now I come to think of it, I wonder if I'll ever get over our special relationship? Perhaps I'll knock my future sons down, one by one, to show them I'm boss. It might be something in the family which comes out every second generation. Some things do; colour-blindness, for example. Grandfather Flinders is colour-blind. My father isn't, none of his brothers are. But I'm colour-blind, the only one of thirty-odd Flinders grandchildren. I can't say I'm at all grateful to Grandfather Flinders for this inheritance. I'm always asked the most maddening questions. "Can you only see black and white?" or "What is it you see, exactly?" It's hopeless trying to explain how colour-blindness is. How can you? People politely refuse to believe me when I say, "I see the same things as you. The same colours. Only different, that's all."

I mean, do they think I've got a weak mind too or something?

Anyway, about this meeting. After some discussion, one parent proposed that poetry classes be replaced with hymn-singing. My father must still have been on the boil. For he declared recklessly that in his opinion excessive hymn-singing rather than poetry had been responsible for the murders. Which

4

caused quite an uproar. Because everyone knew he was right, of course. But how could he come right out and say it? Someone actually said my father was rocking the very foundations of Te Ika. Roughly it was true, I suppose. Te Ika's foundations are shaky enough when you come to think about it. And the place did actually grow on hymn-singing. I mean the missionaries arrived here, with hymns and catechism, before the land-grabbers and the speculators. They wouldn't have stood much of a show if the missionaries hadn't got in first. The Maoris were too busy praying and singing hymns to notice how fast their land was vanishing. When they did wake up, they fought well enough. But it didn't make a terrible lot of difference. After the fighting, their land was confiscated anyway – as a punishment for fighting. They couldn't win whatever way you look at it.

You might have guessed, from all this, that my father teaches history at Te Ika school too; only not this kind. This is strictly for home consumption, when the logs are blazing on a frosty winter night. It worries me. Say he's telling the truth? What it amounts to is that we people with white skins haven't got any moral right to be here at all. And if we were even a damn bit honest, we wouldn't be here. If you can follow my argument. So if this is the real truth, it's no wonder people are uneasy round here. And no wonder either that people were so upset when my father criticized hymn-singing.

On the other hand, though, I don't know what to think about my father. If that's the real truth, why doesn't he come right out and say it? If you've got the real truth, isn't it your duty to come right out and say it? You're bound to feel a whole lot better afterwards, freer and cleaner. I'm sure my father would, because I know he felt a whole lot better after that school committee meeting where he lost his temper and said what no one else would say. Telling the real truth all the time, and not just when he loses his temper, wouldn't hurt him a bit. It's true that he wouldn't be terribly popular in Te Ika, and that he might even get run out of town. But at least he couldn't be in a worse state than he is now. With his muttering to himself, his forgetfulness, his bitterness about everything. You might think he's like this

5

just because he has the frustrating job of teaching country kids history and poetry. But it's not, believe me. It's because he's not really teaching them at all. What's real truth, anyway, when it has to be spoken quietly beside a warm fireside?

I suppose I'm actually arguing with myself now. The fact is, as I've said, there's truth and there's real truth. People can be happy enough with the truth sometimes – that is, with the facts. The fact that I'm colour-blind, for example. But when it comes to the real truth about colour-blindness, about how it feels to be colour-blind, they don't really want to hear. Or about that trip with my grandfather. Or the accident. Or about how we mightn't belong here, if we were honest with ourselves and could face the real truth. I'm still trying to sort these things out so I can fit them together again. You might be able to do it too. And see the same things, only different.

Chapter Two

NOW I HAVEN'T BEEN GETTING AWAY FROM THE POINT.
About those murders, say. I don't plan, though, to tell you any
more about the argument afterwards, except to say that the
school committee meeting ended in confusion. The letters in the
Gazette, saying that poetry caused unhealthy things like murder
and sex, dribbled away after a while; the town became almost
normal again.

No, the murders are quite important. Because it was across
that farm Sam Waikai and I walked when we went on our famous
hunting trip.

When I first met Sam, I didn't think too much about him
being Maori. Or half-caste, I should say; his father was
part pakeha, his mother nearly full Maori. We were friends
all through school from the time we were nine. It was quite
a while before I ever thought of him as anything more than
just another boy, a friend of mine. I suppose I changed when
my father started giving me a few clues about the real history
of this place. It was certainly then that I became careful about
what I said to Sam. I'd never been careful before. Perhaps
Sam noticed that I was sometimes uneasy with him. I don't
know.

Last year, after the football season ended, we borrowed a
couple of rifles, a ·303 and a ·22, for a hunting trip. Sam's older
brother Matthew ran us out of town in his truck after school on
a Friday; he took us up through the Ohemai gorge and into the
rugged country beyond. It was Labour weekend, and we had
three clear days ahead. The weather was sunny and warm, and
gorse and broom along the roadside were bright with spring.
Matthew dropped us at the foot of the valley where the murders
had taken place. He couldn't take us any farther; a bridge on the
road up to the farm had been washed out in a spring flood. Sam

and I fetched our packs off the back of the truck, and hoisted them on our shoulders.

"Don't forget," Matthew said. "We're expecting plenty of meat."

"Don't worry," Sam replied. "We'll be bringing plenty back."

"See you here, then," Matthew said, putting the truck into gear. "About the same time, Monday. All right?"

"Fine," we said.

And then, as his truck rumbled away out of sight, we hiked up through that valley, across the abandoned farm. I hadn't seen the place before. It looked murdering land, all right. A bleak, boggy valley with sick pasture. A few miserable, extra woolly sheep roamed the patchy grass. Their sad eyes seemed to say they knew the whole dreadful truth about the murders, and I began wondering if the boys had actually confided their plans to any of the sheep. It was possible; in court it was said that, among other things, the boys held lengthy conversations with sheep. One of the sheep seemed to guess what I was thinking, for it let out a long, melancholy baaaa.

To tell the truth, I jumped about a mile. Sam looked fairly shaken too.

"I feel like singing a hymn myself, right now," I told him.

He grunted. I realized I shouldn't have said that about singing a hymn. It sounded as if I was making fun of religion. Sam's folks were very religious; they sang a lot of hymns.

Soon every one of the sheep left on the farm had its eyes on us. They all began bleating. At least they were pretty unanimous in whatever it was they were saying.

In the yellowy late afternoon light, on the steep stripped slopes above the valley, patches of erosion showed up like great inflamed sores. There were still a few dead, half-burned trees around. They rose like skinny blackened claws among charred or shattered stumps.

We scrambled through a couple of fences, crossed a creek, and then the farmhouse appeared on a rise just ahead. Sam set off in a new direction, so that we would go wide of it.

"Can't we have a look?" I asked.

8

"What do you want to see?" he growled.

"I don't know. I'd just like to be able to say I'd seen the place." I knew this sounded unsatisfactory, but Sam didn't argue. He changed direction again.

Well, the house looked harmless enough, unlike the land. It was already as lonely and forgotten as other deserted farmhouses in the district. A crumpled sheet of roofing iron banged back and forward in the wind. A tap dripped by a smelly water-tank. There were rusting petrol drums, odd bits and tangles of fencing wire. Spring grass and weeds sprang high everywhere. The place itself was about twenty years overdue for a coat of new paint. Bricks had tumbled from the chimney on to the rusty corrugated roof. One or two windows had been broken – by local hooligans, I supposed. It was less than a year since the murders.

In my experience, which I admit doesn't amount to much, there's generally something sad about old falling houses. But I hadn't seen anything sadder than that place. It didn't look scary or haunted, especially; it just looked pathetic.

"Well," Sam said. "You seen enough?"

To have said yes would have been as good as confessing my morbid curiosity outright. As well as admitting disappointment.

"I'd just like to have a look inside," I told him, as I climbed the rickety steps and crossed the broken groaning boards of the veranda. I tried the front door. It was stiff, but swung in.

Sam stopped just short of the veranda. "What do you want to find?" he asked. "Blood?"

That unnerved me, I admit. The thought of all that blood having been splashed round. The police probably hadn't managed to clear up all the stains. It stood to reason.

"No," I said, very cool. "As a matter of fact" – I hesitated as the thought struck me – "I was wondering if this might be a decent place to bunk down for the night." I scared hell out of myself saying that, I really did. Yet I found I was almost serious too. I wondered how far I could go with something like that. "It's good shelter here," I argued. "Why not make use of it?"

Sam's eyes grew wide. "Are you crazy?"

"No. I mean it." I really was starting to mean it. Sometimes you need to find out how scared you can be; I could think of worse ways of testing myself. Besides, a night spent in a murder house would lend me, and Sam too, a certain amount of prestige when we returned to town.

But I was forgetting, of course. Sam wouldn't see it that way. He didn't need to test himself. I mean he probably knew already how scared he could be.

Thinking this, I hesitated at the door.

"Come on," he said. "Either you go in or you don't. Make up your mind and get it over with. We want to get up into the hills before it's too dark. So we can make an early start in the morning."

Well, he had a good point there. About the early start.

"Besides," he went on, "you don't really want to spend the night here." He sounded very damn sensible and very damn patient.

"No," I agreed at last, "I don't suppose I do, really. I mean I just thought it might have been interesting to spend the night here."

Sam looked baffled. "Interesting?"

"Yes. I just thought it might have been."

"You just think too much," Sam said. "Hurry up and make up your mind about going inside. If you're not too scared."

That settled it. I had to go inside anyway.

"Sure you don't want to have a look too?" I asked cheerfully.

"What for?" he said, and shook his head. "No thanks." He sat himself on the edge of the veranda to wait for me.

I turned and marched down the dim passage with my eyes strictly forward. I didn't peer into any of the rooms leading off; I guessed they were the bedrooms. The bedrooms where the parents and sisters slept while the boys crept softly through the house with their axes. I must say I would have felt a whole lot better if Sam had been with me; I had a terribly strange feeling in my knees. I pushed open another creaky door and got through to the kitchen.

That was what finished me. I couldn't get out of the place quick enough.

No, I didn't see any bloodstains. To tell the truth, I didn't see much at all. I might have seen a cobwebbed window and a sooty fireplace and perhaps a few sticks of furniture. But I wouldn't swear that on oath. The only thing I really saw was a little kid's potty-chair. Just sitting there all dusty on the floor. I've never seen anything more terrible in my life. I mean afterwards I could have described it exactly, though I only saw it for about one thousandth of a second. I could have told about all its chips and scratches, for instance, and about how the paint was peeling off the sides. And how spiders had spun a web across the little hole.

It was one of those things that gets passed along from child to child, for years. The boys probably used that chair when they were babies. Then their sisters. The youngest little girl was only about three years old when she was killed, so she must still have been using it. Right up to that Sunday.

Well, I started collecting myself as I roared back down the passage to where Sam was waiting. I came out on the veranda at a mere trot.

I was grateful for the fact that Sam wasn't looking in my direction. It gave me a short space to recover; my heart was knocking wildly. Sam was sitting comfortably on the edge of the veranda, his legs crossed, and for some reason was bent forward. I finally decided he was studying the condition of his boots.

"You were quick," he said. "You seen enough?"

"Yes," I replied. "I've seen enough, all right. To tell the truth, there wasn't a terrible lot to see in there."

Then I realized why he was bent forward. He wasn't studying his boots. He was chuckling to himself, almost convulsed. It didn't make me feel any better at all.

I still wish he hadn't laughed at me, that day.

We were dead lucky with the weather. It was a calm spring night with the moon floating high and bright. There was hardly a cloud at all, and the sky seemed solid with stars. The bush smelt damp and clean. We followed a track two or three miles into the hills. The moon helped us find the way. We finally bedded down for the night near some water which tinkled out of a limestone spring. Sam said it was a likely place for pigs or deer to drink early in the morning. So after a meal of cold sausages and boiled eggs, washed down with cold water, we settled down with our rifles beside us.

Nothing came, though. We were up early in the morning, folding our sleeping bags, munching down a quick breakfast, and then working slowly through the bush with our rifles loaded. The orange sunlight drifted through the tall bronze trees as we stumbled through fern and undergrowth and untangled ourselves from supplejack. It was rough going, most of the time. I still thought the bush a good place to be, though. Even when, after three hours' searching, we hadn't seen anything worth a shot. We found clearings warm with sunlight where wild pigs had once basked and rooted, and argued about whether the marks were fresh. The odd fat wood-pigeon lumbered away on squeaking wings, and fantails darted chittering round our heads.

"I reckon this place must have been shot out by someone," Sam said. "Just lately, the last month or two."

"It looks that way," I agreed unhappily. It had been my idea to try this part of the country on Labour weekend. I'd had to talk hard to convince Sam that something new was worth a try. We usually went shooting near a farm belonging to one of his brothers. "I suppose we should have stuck to our old place."

"Always stick to what you know," Sam said. "You're safe, that way. We're liable to finish up with nothing to show for the weekend."

"We could try the other side of the camp," I suggested.

"Yes," Sam said sadly. "We could try."

No one was going to be able to say we didn't try.

On our way back through the camp we feasted on cold sausage again. It was beginning to taste like sawdust. We should by rights have had fresh meat already.

Then we explored new hills. To tell the truth, Sam was getting pretty surly. He made it clear, one way and another, that the lack of game was my fault. I mean he didn't get a kick out of just being deep in the bush, as I did. He said he'd had a gutsful of the bush when he was younger, when he lived with a timberworker brother for a while. Anyway, I was damn glad when he clobbered an opossum first shot. It was high in a tree, and a small target. He squinted through the sight of the ·22, squeezed the trigger, and the opossum dropped like a ripe apple. We exchanged rifles and a few minutes later I shot an opossum too, so we both felt slightly better.

We were up high, very high, and when we entered a clearing, a place so rich with sunlight you could almost taste it on your tongue, we could view the sea, calm and silver, about twenty miles away. In the opposite direction, inland, we saw the volcanoes still bright with winter snow. Right then, as we sat taking a breather with our opossums and rifles beside us, I decided there couldn't be a better place in the world to relax. In fact I told Sam this.

"You reckon?" he said casually. Then he lay back with his hands behind his head and looked up at the sky. "Well, I don't know. There could be worse places."

I mean he was being enthusiastic; as enthusiastic as he could ever be about anything.

There was hardly a sound anywhere. Not unless you count the birds, which grew pretty quiet at that time of day, anyway. Or the gently sucking noise which a light wind made through wet foliage up there high. Water splashed on rocks somewhere distant, and some cicadas, woken from winter, were starting to celebrate the return of warmth to the sun.

No, I couldn't think of a better place, not anywhere in the world. I didn't want to move. I just wanted to stay there, dreamy, and let the sun warm me forever. To tell the truth, I no longer much cared about what we shot and what we didn't. It was all the same to me. We had opossum stew for dinner. What more did we want? Feeling so content and lazy, I must have dozed off. Then I heard Sam say, "I haven't heard another shot all day. Everyone must know this place is shot out. Except us."

He sounded more bitter than ever. It depressed me.

13

"It's all right for you," he went on. "Snoring like an elephant. But I promised to take some meat home."

I suppose I needed a jolt like that to stop me dreaming the rest of the day. I saw I needed a friend like Sam. But I wished he didn't make me feel quite so guilty. Because he did. I hadn't promised my parents anything at all.

It was cold and gloomy in the bush after being in the sun so long. We split up and, walking about thirty yards apart, did a wide sweep along the side of a hill. I could hear Sam, on my right, cracking and crunching along, and swearing now and then. In his present sour mood, he was bound to scare hell out of something in the end.

Then, just ahead, there was uproar in the bush. "Pigs!" Sam yelled, racing forward as the sound faded. It was his own stupid fault if we missed them. He'd been too damn noisy.

Just when I thought we'd dipped out altogether a young boar, looking pretty baffled, staggered into a small clearing just ahead. It was obvious, the way he twitched, that he could smell one or both of us on each side of him. But the sudden sunlight seemed to dazzle him, to slow him up. He hesitated just long enough for the dinner table. I didn't like the look of his tusks, even if they were small; I wished we had a dog to bail him up. He could do a lot of damage to us if we missed.

We flicked back our safety catches and fired at the same moment. Then there was a huge silence. The pig just swayed, looking a bit troubled, as our bolts clicked. Then it charged blind before we could get our second shots in. My shot went wild, kicking up dirt in front of the boar as it came. I saw dimly that it was heading straight for me. All confused, I tried to slam it with the butt of my rifle. Then I went down and it was all over me. I heard my shirt rip. I couldn't even get at my sheath-knife. All I could think of was that Sam's second shot – I hadn't heard it – might go into me instead of the pig.

Chapter Three

ABOUT TWO THOUSAND YEARS LATER I SEEMED TO BE
all right. There was a thin, frantic squeal which for a dizzy
moment I thought came from my mouth, since I'd yelled too.
Like a stuck pig, and it was a stuck pig. With Sam astride it,
slashing. The boar shrank like a balloon as the blood spouted.
Soon we both dripped with it. Then the ripped carcass lay there
at our feet. It was only a little fellow, really.

"We got our second shots in together too," Sam explained.
"You missed. I hit. But it just kept on going."

"You must have moved damn quick."

"I just dropped my rifle and grabbed my knife. It was nearly
dead anyway, by the time I jumped on it." He bent over the dead
pig. "See? One, two, three. Three bullet-holes. It couldn't have
lasted much longer."

"It could have lasted long enough to kill me."

Sam laughed. "Just like you. Always exaggerating." He
examined my shirt, and the flesh beneath. "Just a rip and a graze.
I suppose you reckon that's just about a fatal wound, eh?"

"I didn't say that. I just said it could have done me a lot more
damage. If you hadn't jumped on it."

But it was no use. He'd spoilt it all. I didn't want to believe
him. I desperately wanted to believe he'd saved my life. Because
Sam owed me something and I didn't like him being in debt to
me.

I happened to be walking along the riverside by myself that
day. It wasn't at all unusual for me to wander the riverside by
myself in those days. I don't mind telling you I was a pretty
moody kid when I was younger, and I didn't have too many
friends. Partly on account of my father being a teacher; other
kids at school distrusted me. Also I lost my temper easy, and

15

slammed into kids if they argued with me. Really slammed them, I mean. I once broke a boy's nose, and another time twisted a boy's arm till it snapped. Naturally I was supposed to be a problem child. I knew all about that because I listened near the living-room door when my parents talked about me.

"He's just slow to settle in this town," my father would say.

"He's had more than two years," my mother said. "Nearly three. Anyway most children are quick to accept a change of scene."

"But you can see he still hates the place. I know he misses the sea, for one thing. You can always notice the difference in him whenever we go off to the coast for a holiday. And he's always worse than ever when we get back."

"That doesn't explain anything. Why does he still hate it here? That's what we have to ask ourselves. And why isn't he like other children? Why doesn't he have friends?"

"I don't know. It beats me. I agree he's not very well balanced. Or adjusted to his age, rather."

"And whose fault is that?" my mother asked.

"All right, all right. So I forced the pace too early. But I had Derek reading and writing before he was four, remember. It didn't affect him much, one way or the other."

Derek, by the way, is my older – my only – brother. He's up at university these days, a lecturer. I'll get round to telling about him later.

"Derek was different, Frank," my mother replied, "and you know it. You really didn't force the pace with Derek. Even when he was three years old, he was two years ahead of other children his age."

"All right," my father said, "so Derek was different. He was naturally bright. And Nick's not, I suppose."

"You suppose? I should have thought it was glaringly obvious."

"It's true I've been slow to accept it."

"Well, you'll have to."

"It's unreasonable, really, that there should be such a difference – the same home, the same parents."

"Are you trying to argue with a fact?"

"Not at all. I'm simply saying that it's a mystery."

"There's such a gap between Derek and Nick anyway. Nick's virtually an only child, you know."

"Beryl, you talk alarming nonsense sometimes. Really. Wasn't Derek an only child? Before Nick was born? What the hell has that got to do with it anyway?"

"I don't know. It's just that Derek never *looked* like an only child. Nick does, all the time. You don't watch him. I do. He's painfully lonely. You should see the way he potters round the house, playing by himself all day. Inventing his own games. It breaks my heart if I watch him for too long. He never seems to have had a real friend of his own age. He just can't cope with other people—with anything."

Well, to tell the truth I felt pretty damn sorry for myself after hearing all that. But not too sorry. What they didn't know was that I had a friend. Perhaps not my own age, exactly, because sometimes he could be pretty well any age. He was always floating round, when I went for a walk anywhere, and we held some great old conversations when there were no other people about. That was the point. We had to be by ourselves to have these conversations. Tanny just wouldn't talk otherwise. No one else knew about him. We had some pretty interesting talks about different things – about Te Ika, for instance, and all the dozy people who lived there. He wouldn't tell me his name, so in the end I invented one. The thing about Tanny that really surprised me was that he could remind me of all sorts of things in my life that I'd forgotten. "You shouldn't do that," he'd say. "Remember what happened to you before?"

"What happened before?" I'd ask, and then he'd tell me.

"Well, that's interesting," I'd say. "Fancy that."

"So don't say I didn't warn you," Tanny said. "Because I did."

"All right. I'll remember now."

And I usually did remember. It's hard to say just where I first met Tanny. Probably along the riverbank somewhere, in the bush, or when I was scrambling around hills near Te Ika. When I first spoke to him, anyway, I realized he'd already been around some time. After a while he even started coming home with me. Now and then my mother would overhear something, and ask who I thought I was talking to in my bedroom. If that happened Tanny would clear off, fast, and not be back for a day or two. He told me I shouldn't ever listen to what my parents were saying about me. "It never does you any good," he said.

"You're quite right," I'd say, as I strained to listen to what my father was saying.

"Aren't you going to take any notice of my advice?"

"Of course I am. Just shut up for a moment, though. I can't hear what they're saying."

And Tanny would shoot off in a huff.

"Give him time, Beryl," my father said. "Just give him time. Love and affection's the thing. I can see I might have made a mistake with Nick. Time will tell. He might settle down."

"But he's not normal, Frank. Surely you can see that. Look at all this aggression that springs out. These fights he gets into. Other children have learned to give him a wide berth. He's just not normal."

Frankly I couldn't tell you who won that argument, if anyone did. I mean I just got bored with the whole thing, and wandered back to my bedroom.

I suppose it couldn't have been long after that when I was walking along the riverbank by myself. I was looking forward to a quiet yarn with Tanny. And I came to the swimming pool where these two little Maori kids were blubbering. It seemed Sam had been teaching them to swim, and had scared hell out of them by not coming up after a dive into the pool. These two tiny kids didn't have a clue about what they should do. They just stood there looking at each other and howling. But they managed to tell me what had happened, and I guessed Sam must have hit his head on a snag or rock after his dive. I sent one kid running off for help. Then I stripped off my shirt and dived in. I didn't have any reason to hesitate. About the one thing I could do well, in those days, was swim. I don't even remember anyone ever having to teach me.

The pool was deep in the centre. I dived down and down,

pumping myself through the watery green sunlight. Thin spouts of mud turned lazily, and an old man eel twisted away in front of my face. The bottom of the pool was murky, and it was hard to see anything except old sunken logs and boulders streaming with slime. I went up, took a deep breath, and kicked myself down again. This time I saw Sam, all right. After he hit his head, he'd become tangled in the branches of an old tree. This was off towards the side of the pool, where it was shallower and where I should have looked in the first place. His brown body bumped back and forward with the current of the river. His black hair drifted all over his face. He looked sound asleep, as if he'd decided on a quiet nap in the underwater quiet. I started untangling him. My pale arms looked shimmery against his dark skin as I shifted him and tugged. Drifting pebbles and dead wood clicked and snapped against my eardrums and my lungs were near bursting. Then he came free and floated soft and helpless in my arms. Dragging him, I kicked up to the surface, where we arrived with an explosion of water. I'd never tasted air so sweet. I couldn't breathe enough of it down. A crowd had collected, people were running from everywhere, and one of those kids on the bank was still blubbing his head off. Puffing and blowing like a grandfather seal, I pulled Sam to the bank and then sat on him, like I'd once been shown, to push the water out of his lungs. To tell the truth I didn't think I had a show in hell. I'd never seen anyone deader. But I kept at it, pumping his lungs and shooing other people away. I mean, what else could I do?

Then water dribbled from one side of his mouth. He actually spluttered. I was aching all over, but I didn't stop until I'd squeezed all the water out. I really knew I'd won when his eyes flicked open and closed again. He didn't seem to see anything much. All the same, he was alive. I just keeled over quietly. I noticed that people were covering us with blankets, carrying us both off somewhere. I wasn't terribly interested.

So I didn't have my yarn with Tanny that afternoon, or any afternoon afterwards. I never really caught up with him again.

Of course there was a great fuss about the affair, including a screed in the *Gazette*. It didn't amount to much, though. It wasn't as if I'd been brave or anything like that. It had all just been a matter of me coming along at the right moment. But I must say things did improve at home. My father looked at me with new interest and my mother kept weeping quietly; I couldn't see the point, really. I heard her say to my father, "I thank God, I really do."

For what? For damn near drowning Sam?

With one thing and another, it seemed I had some friends after all. But they didn't fool me much. I mean they wouldn't have come near me if I hadn't had my name printed in the paper. Actually the *Gazette* invented these friends. Some reporter chased round trying to get kids I hardly knew to say things about me. So they said things like "I always knew Nick was a good swimmer." Or "Nick's my very best friend. He's always rescuing kids."

The liars.

The bloody liars, if you don't mind me saying so. It made me feel sick and ugly in the stomach to read what they said. I made a point of bashing their noses and banging their heads together when I got back to school. Boy, I can tell you I wouldn't have had one of them for a friend if you'd paid me a thousand quid or more. I've got principles.

I did finish up with one friend, though.

I was taken round to meet Sam Waikai's parents and they made a tremendous fuss of me. Sam's father was old and wrinkled, and hobbled round on a carved walking stick. His mother was huge, as fat as a house, all sort of overflowing from her tight spotty dress, and she almost crushed me to death in her great arms. She wailed and wept and kissed me till my face was dripping. They had a big family, but most of the children had left home. Sam was their youngest. So you couldn't blame them, really, for getting so excited about Sam nearly drowning.

To tell the truth, I never thought I'd get out of their house that day. For a while there it seemed they intended to keep me, along with Sam. They just didn't want to let me go home. And the fact is I didn't mind too much, either. They made me feel at home, they really did. I was bulging with food and drink by the time they finished with me. As well as dripping with those kisses. Mrs Waikai kept up the kissing all afternoon. You'd have thought we were in a marathon or something. To tell the truth I think kissing is a pretty soppy business, even when my mother does it, but with Mrs Waikai I didn't mind too much. She wasn't kissing me just because I'd made a rash promise to behave myself in future; that was my mother's usual reason. It was Mrs Waikai's way of showing she was happy. She couldn't talk, half the time, because her throat was so full of things she couldn't manage to say. So she kissed and wept instead.

"Remember," she said, "this is your place now. You come out here and see us whenever you like, when you're playing with Samuel."

She had it fixed in her head, you see, that Sam and me were friends and had always been friends. Nothing could shift the idea, though neither of us tried very hard. Sam was pretty quiet, all round, that day. He wasn't surly, exactly, though he could be fairly surly if he liked. It's just that he didn't seem too happy about me getting all the attention, as if I was the one who had come back from the dead.

"Your folks won't mind you coming here to see us, will they?" Mrs Waikai asked.

I didn't think about that for a second. "No," I said. "They won't mind at all."

"Good," she said. "So this is your other home now. Remember that. And come here whenever you want. I don't know why Samuel didn't bring you here before. Why didn't you come before?"

"I don't know," I said. "I never thought of coming, I suppose." I kept my tongue hard in my cheek.

"Well, don't forget in future. And if there's ever anything you want, ever any way I can help you, you've only got to ask." She took Sam's shoulder in one big hand, mine in the other, and steered us together. "Because," she went on, "you're the boy who saved my Samuel." She still had our shoulders firmly. "And I want you both to promise me something right now. I want you

21

to promise that you'll both always look after each other. Like brothers. Promise?"

We both promised as she wept over us.

After a while Sam and I went outside and mooched round. We didn't have anything to say to each other, much. The Waikai place was a small patch of swampy Maori land just outside Te Ika. A couple of cows grazed, and there was a big garden. The Waipa river ran nearby and there were great limestone cliffs, dotted with toe toe feathers and topped with scrub, behind the place. I'd only seen it from the road before, the old house and the garden. Just as I'd almost only ever seen Sam from a distance, across the other side of a classroom. Or from the sideline of a football field; Sam was a fairly smart football player, and I was strictly a spectator. I doubt if I'd ever talked to Sam more than twice in three years at that school. In a way, I felt pretty sorry for Sam. For having me suddenly on his hands, I mean. It was pretty tough being told he had to act like a brother towards someone he hardly knew, and probably didn't like anyway. I was fairly embarrassed by the whole situation, to tell the truth, but I couldn't see any way of getting out of it without hurting Mrs Waikai. After we grew bored with wandering round the section and having nothing to say, we went back to the house and Sam fetched out a football. He kicked it in my direction and I managed to catch it.

"Try a dropkick," he told me.

I kicked the ball, but it didn't go very high.

"That's a punt," Sam said. "Don't you know the difference between a dropkick and a punt?"

I didn't, so he explained the difference. After a dozen attempts I produced a reasonable dropkick. "Now let's see how you take a pass on the run," he said. We jogged over a paddock and then he flicked the ball to me, fast. I dropped it. "I can see you've got a lot to learn," he said. "Anyone who can swim as well as you can ought to be able to handle a rugby ball." We played around with the ball for some time, since it gave us something to talk about, and when Sam finally grew impatient with my mishandling and bad passes he went into the house and fetched his brother's rifle. He asked if I'd done any shooting, and I told him I hadn't. I'd never handled a rifle at all.

"Never?" Sam said, astonished.

"My parents don't believe in them," I said. "I mean, I didn't even get toy guns for Christmas or anything."

"Well," Sam said. "I can see you got a lot to learn, all right."

He told me he often went shooting with his brothers. Lately he'd even been allowed to go off by himself with a ·22, and he sometimes came home with a rabbit or hare for dinner. He took me down to the back of the Waikai section, under the cliffs, where he fixed up a jam-tin target on a fence-post. He walked back about thirty yards, pumped a bullet into the spout of the gun, and fired. The tin whanged off the post with a hole shot neatly through the middle. He propped the target up again and asked if I'd like a try. I couldn't have seemed especially keen. Because Sam said, "Don't worry. A ·22 hasn't got any kick."

I took the rifle cautiously, as if it was likely to blow up in my face, and shoved it awkwardly against my shoulder. Sam showed me how to line up the sight, and I pressed the trigger. The jam-tin stayed exactly where it was, but a chip flew off the post underneath. "Not bad for a first shot," Sam announced. "A bit of practice and you'll bowl that tin, no trouble. It's just a matter of getting your eye in."

My fourth shot clipped the side of the tin. I felt pretty smart. We pot-shotted a while longer, and then wandered back to the house. Sam didn't find it so much of an effort to talk to me now.

"Don't worry," he said. "You'll come right. You got a reasonable eye. Not everyone could have hit that target fourth shot. Starting right from scratch, I mean."

"You think so?" I said.

"I know so. I seen some people who couldn't of hit an elephant at five yards."

He wasn't exactly heaping praise on me, but I couldn't help dancing with happiness inside myself. When we reached the house we found Mrs Waikai waiting for us, beaming, out on the veranda. I must still have been looking fairly pleased with myself, because she said, "You look like you've been having a good time."

"I have," I answered. "A really good time."

"I can see you and Samuel get on well together," she said. "I could see it the moment you walked in here this afternoon." She grabbed both our shoulders again. "I feel like you're both my own boys. My own sons."

With that fierce grip on our shoulders, there wasn't much we could say in reply. I felt embarrassed on Sam's behalf. This brother business could go too far; I mean he had enough real brothers without having a dozy pakeha thrown in too. I tried to flash Sam a quick grin, to show him he wasn't really stuck with me, but he only shifted his solemn eyes away from mine. I felt pretty stupid, left with that grin on my face; I got rid of it fast and tried to concentrate on what Mrs Waikai was telling us.

"You must always remember that promise you made me this afternoon," she said. "Always. Because that's the way I want to remember you. Like you are today. Young and happy, with all your lives ahead."

She slapped a kiss to right and left, to my face and Sam's.

"Come on now," she said. "Get moving."

She bulldozed us inside. The table was loaded down with food again. A keg had been opened, and a dozen glasses were being filled at a time. Relatives and friends from miles around had called in for some celebration. Of course I had to be introduced to all the people there, one by one, and my hand soon ached with heavy handshakes. Some of the really old Maori women, with *moko* tattooed on their chins and shark-tooth necklaces around their wrinkled necks, didn't shake hands with me; they rubbed noses in the old Maori fashion instead. I couldn't have stood too much of that, though; my nose would have got raw. I didn't need to look in a mirror to know it was getting very shiny. Some of the people in the room were jabbering away in Maori, others were going flat out in English. Sam scurried round filling glasses and passing out food. When I was finished with being a guest of honour, I helped him; he handled the beer, since he had more experience at that job, and I handled the food. As the celebration went on, with the noise threatening to split the house down the middle, Mrs Waikai seemed to grow above it all, above everyone; I'd never realized she was so huge. She was really tremendous, there was no one in the room to touch her for size. She'd changed out of her spotty dress and was all in dark like the other old Maori women, dark dress and dark headscarf; she stood in the middle of the room, waving her huge arms, pointing with her fat fingers, ticking off some people, cheeking others, and laughing and crying with anyone who wanted to laugh or cry. She seemed to get herself involved with everyone. When some of the young men pushed out into the kitchen to tell stories, she joined them there for a while; when a girl who'd just lost her husband in an accident burst into tears, Mrs Waikai wept too, and then helped the girl into a bedroom where she could recover. With tears still large and shiny on her face, Mrs Waikai came back into the living room and called some singing. Four guitars appeared from nowhere, feet were stamping, hands clapping; groups formed around the room, to harmonize, with Mrs Waikai conducting. When one of the old men grew obstreperous, and leapt into a haka, eyes rolling and tongue protruding, Mrs Waikai applauded and then quickly made him sit down again.

"Too much of that and you'll be in bed again, Uncle Tahu," she said. "Remember what the doctor told you?"

"He just said no more beer," Uncle Tahu argued.

"And no more hakas, either," Mrs Waikai said. "At your age."

But when younger people swirled out to dance in the empty space at the centre of the room, she laughed and clapped and urged them on till they fell back into their seats exhausted. Soon I realized it was time for me to leave. I'd promised my parents to be home before dark. When Mrs Waikai had a spare moment, I plucked at her sleeve and told her I was going.

"So soon?" she said.

"I promised."

"If you promised your folks, then you must keep your promise. You're a good boy, Nick. I can see that." She turned and waved an arm to quieten the singing. "Listen, everybody," she announced, "Nick has to go."

Then the guitars were playing again and people were singing that I was a jolly good fellow. I was hoisted on to someone's shoulders, while everyone sang for me, and my face blazed with embarrassment.

When I left finally, I was so loaded down with things to take home – kumara, watermelon and sweetcorn – that Matthew had to run it over to our place on the back of his truck. I sat up in the cab, feeling pretty much like a conqueror with all my booty, while the Waikais and their friends stood around farewelling me.

After I got home with all that stuff, I found I was still on a fuss there, too. That was one of the nights when my mother went around having quiet weeps. I must say I was fairly relieved that there was no more kissing involved. I'd had quite enough for one day. At one stage my father decided to have a man-to-man talk to me. I don't know what about, exactly, because he didn't get very far. And I was distracted from what he did manage to say by all the trouble he had lighting his pipe. He struck one match after another, but he just couldn't seem to get the confounded tobacco alight, and he coughed and spluttered as if he was coming down with influenza. He muttered something about not having been the best of fathers, all things considered, but he didn't make the point of this very clear. Also he wanted me to know he meant well. I got pretty impatient with all this and he must have seen that I was, after a while.

"Well, it doesn't matter, Nick," he grunted finally. "We're both very proud of you. That's all. That's all I want to say, really."

I couldn't help feeling disappointed. I'd thought he was going to tell me something important. About the facts of life and such-like; I found some of that stuff pretty interesting.

I went off to bed feeling sad that night, what with one thing and another. I knew I wouldn't have another day like it in my life again. And I hadn't missed a single day at school, either.

Coming out of the classroom at lunch the next day, Sam pushed through a crowd of kids to ask if I'd like a kick around on the football field. I said I wouldn't mind. I was pleased to be asked, and surprised too; I'd made up my mind that he intended he forget me as fast as he could. I wasn't much excited about rugby, to tell the truth, but if it interested him, that was all right by me. Later that year when Sam was made captain of the school first fifteen, he wangled me into it, too, and I don't mind boasting that we made a pretty fierce combination in the back-line. We often practised on the quiet, just the two of us, and Sam gave me some very useful hints about the game. This was in a paddock behind his home. I took to spending most weekends and school holidays over at his place, and often ate and slept there instead of going home. Sometimes Matthew took us off into the bush on hunting trips and later, when we were thought to be old and responsible enough, Sam and I went off by ourselves. My parents were very good about this; at least they didn't complain much. Now and then, as I dashed out of the house in the direction of the Waikai family, my mother would call me back and say, "Don't you think you could spare us a little more time, Nick? We are your parents, after all. We never see much of you these days."

But my father would argue from the background, "Leave him alone, Beryl. Let him sort things out for himself. It's natural that he wants to spend time with someone his own age. It's only reasonable."

"I suppose you're right," my mother sighed. "But all the same, we are his parents –"

"A few months ago you were complaining that he didn't have a friend."

"You're right," she said. "I'm sorry." She put a hand on my shoulder. "Well, at least try to get home early, Nick. Before dark."

Not that there weren't some awkward moments. I often put my foot in it. There was the day I asked, "Why don't we have a party?"

My father peered at me above his reading glasses. "A party?" he said, not sure he heard right.

"Yes. Lots of people and beer and food and everything. Everyone laughing and crying and singing. Why don't we ever have one?"

"What on earth's got into the child?" my mother said.

My father shook his head in astonishment.

"It wouldn't hurt once in a while," I argued. "I mean you might enjoy yourselves."

"People laughing and crying and singing?" my mother asked. "Do you know what you're talking about? Do you? People being sick in the bathroom and breaking furniture and fighting over the flowerbeds, more likely."

"You see, Nick," my father said earnestly, "your mother and I have been to one or two parties like that. Earlier in our lives. We even threw one or two parties ourselves once, in my student days. Perhaps not quite as violent as your mother suggests. But rowdy enough. We're really a little too old for that sort of thing now."

"Too old?" I said, thinking of Mrs Waikai.

"Of course. One grows up. One learns to accept one's age." He seemed to have pretty well convinced himself he was in a wheelchair already.

"I see," I said, backing out fast. "Well, I really wasn't suggesting we have one. I was just wondering why we didn't, that's all."

"I hope you're not being a nuisance over at the Waikais," my mother said. "Perhaps you should be spending a little more time with your own family."

If I was a nuisance over at the Waikai place, then Mrs Waikai was a pretty convincing actor. She always seemed pleased to see me. I knew I wasn't a nuisance as far as she was concerned. All the same, though, I had this uneasy feeling about Sam. Say I hadn't rescued him from the river that day, would we ever have been friends? Would he have wasted his time coaching me for football, or teaching me to shoot? I couldn't make up my mind. I still can't, really. I mean I knew how I felt about Sam, all right. And Mrs Waikai knew too. If Sam happened to be away somewhere when I arrived over at the Waikai place, she liked to talk to me, to sit out on the veranda beside me in the sun and tell me all she hoped for Sam. Sam was going to be different from her other sons; he wasn't going to finish up driving a truck, felling timber, shearing sheep or farming. Sam was going to be educated, really educated. She was going to see that he finished school, and she hoped he would go on to university. "That's why I'm glad he's got a friend like you," she said. "A schoolteacher's son. You've been brought up to appreciate the value of education."

Well, I couldn't argue with that, really. I mean it was absolutely true that I was a schoolteacher's son.

"I know you can make Sam appreciate the value of education too," she went on. "And I know you will. You're just like one of the family now, you love Sam just like the rest of us. I know."

I can't say I really knew what she was going on about; not then. "Yes," I muttered, embarrassed by her hand on my shoulder, "Sam and me are pretty good friends, all right."

But I couldn't help thinking we were friends only because he felt in debt to me. Or because she'd made him feel in debt to me. That might sound silly, but I'm not so sure. And that's why he spoilt everything that Saturday, when the boar rolled over me. He made out that he didn't do anything, really, and that the boar would have died anyway.

We could have started off even. He would have paid his debt. Perhaps things would have been different after. Or perhaps we would have been friends just the same, real friends. The thing is I'll never know. Say it is true that Sam was only friendly because he felt in debt to me? I often think about this, and I sit looking into nothing.

We got back to camp in a good mood. Soon our fire blazed and an opossum stew bubbled. We hoped the pig would keep fresh till Monday. Sam wrapped the carcass in cool green leaves and stowed it away in a place which would be shady during the day.

It was black in the bush by the time the stew cooked. Except for the firelight trembling red on trunk and leaf. Whenever we moved huge shadows flapped up and down the trees. After we'd eaten we moved closer to the fire for warmth. We tossed potatoes among the cinders and dug them out when they were baked crisp. Apart from the crackle of the fire and a lonely morepork which seemed to want to join us, there wasn't a sound in the bush. If we stopped talking for a moment, we could almost feel the silence and the dark. When I moved still closer to the fire, Sam started singing his twisted-up version of that old nursery rhyme:

Little Nickie Flinders
Sat among the cinders
Warming his pretty little toes

Sam was the only person who could get away with that kind of cheek. I've always been sensitive about my name. When I was very young some kids called me Cinders. Cinders Flinders. I bashed them, of course. Some were even cheeky enough to call me Polly, Polly Flinders. I bashed them even harder. I had to do a fair amount of bashing when I was younger on account of my name. Mainly to preserve my dignity. But I let Sam get away with it. Because he was my friend, that's why. He knew he could call me Cinders, or Polly, or any damn thing he liked. But he didn't, often. There were just a few times, like that one, when he couldn't resist the temptation to fool around with my name.

Little Nickie Flinders
Sat among the cinders
Warming his pretty little toes

It was true enough. I was almost in the cinders, and I was warming my toes.

After a while we spread our sleeping bags close to the fire and went to sleep. Or at least Sam went to sleep. I lay awake listening to that old morepork hoot, wishing Sam had really saved me from the boar. It was just my bad luck we'd got three shots into it first.

When I did go to sleep, I had a bad dream. I had this potty-chair, the one I'd seen in the farmhouse. I didn't know why I was carrying it, and I didn't know what to do with it. There was a great crowd of people round, grinning and pointing at me and shaking with laughter. While I wandered between them with this stupid potty-chair. I didn't want to put it down anywhere

where people were going to look at it and laugh. I knew that would be wrong. So it seemed as if I would just have to keep on carrying it, and let them laugh at me instead. I hated that potty-chair, I really did. But I was stuck with it.

"Won't anyone help me?" I cried. "Won't *anyone*?"

The damn thing was growing heavier all the time, as if it was made of iron or something.

No one offered to help. Everyone was more interested in looking and laughing.

I started raging and swearing at them all. I wanted to swing my fist into their grinning faces. But I couldn't have done that without putting down the potty-chair, where they'd make fun of it. I hoisted it up on my shoulder and staggered along while they laughed and mocked me. I started falling over and getting up again with my knees cut and bruised.

"Won't *anyone* help?" I cried again.

The next time I fell, I woke up. In a very sour mood, I can tell you.

Chapter Four

SAM WAS OUT OF HIS SLEEPING BAG AND BENDING OVER me. The sky was filled with grey and pink, the bush was damp and shiny, and our fire was almost out. He had his hand on my shoulder.

"What's the matter with you?" he said.

"Nothing." I wasn't in the mood for conversation.

"You were groaning your head off."

"No law against that," I argued.

"You scared hell out of me. I thought you were being murdered."

"I think I was." I tried to recollect the dream.

"I don't mind you having nightmares, just so long as you don't groan in my ear. I woke up thinking it must be the end of the world."

"It felt like it. In the dream."

It was no use going back to sleep with dawn in the sky. We built up the fire, finished off the stew for breakfast, swilled down weak tea, and rolled our sleeping bags. I felt cold, and shivered whenever I moved away from the fire. I was still awfully shaky after that dream. I'd have felt better, for once, if I'd woken up in my own bed at home, with the church bells ringing for Sunday morning. The bush didn't seem at all friendly now. The tall trees, all dripping with silver dew, rose chilly and remote above our heads. The sky grew red with sunrise.

It was a pity I had to bring my bad dream up here. I was sure that was why the bush had turned unfriendly. Usually I managed to leave ugly things behind.

"It might be a good day," Sam said, "so long as you don't get scared of any more little baby pigs."

Sam's idea was to work right back into the hills, in a seaward direction. We followed a faint track as far as it went, then we just bush-crashed. We explored gullies and clambered along ridges. The bush warmed up quickly. It was the first really hot day of spring.

By noon we hadn't seen a thing. We pulled off our boots, dangled our feet in a cold creek, and ate the last of the sausages. They weren't very satisfying.

"It stands to reason," Sam said, "there must be something in this bush somewhere."

"Yes," I agreed. "Us. That's about all." My stomach rumbled emptily. I still had some chocolate, but I decided to keep it in reserve. At least we had our pig to show for the weekend. We wouldn't go home empty-handed, so I didn't feel too guilty.

"Let's try that hill," Sam said after a while. He pointed west. But he really didn't need to point it out. It was the only hill worth mentioning. It stood at the end of the long, narrow valley through which our creek ran. Tall thin limestone crags like cathedral spires rose each side of the flattened summit.

"All right," I said. "I'm game. If there's nothing up there, we'll pack it in."

"It's going to take us the rest of the day to work that hill over anyway."

Jumping from boulder to boulder and splashing along the bank, we followed the creek up. Around one twist in the creek we came to a fantastic display of bush-clematis. The white flowers, all shimmering with sunlight, dripped from every tree in sight.

I said to Sam it was worth the whole trip just to see that. To tell the truth I forgot my bad dream, even.

"*Pua wananga*," Sam said. "That's the old Maori name for those flowers. It was supposed to be sacred. Pick some, if you like."

"There wasn't a tapu on it?" I asked.

"Not that I know," Sam said. "But I suppose if it was sacred, there might have been a tapu."

I'd never been able to make up my mind whether Sam took tapu seriously or not. Anyway he didn't touch the flowers. And after some thought, I didn't either.

33

"I might pick some on the way back," I said, postponing the decision.

We started moving up steep ground. It was tough all the way. I'd never seen bush so dense and tangled. Probably no one else had been fool enough to struggle through it in a thousand years, if ever. In places we had to crawl on our stomachs. A deer would have heard us from two hundred yards off, and we wouldn't have seen a pig in front of our noses. It was pointless hunting without dogs in that kind of bush. But I glimpsed big limestone cliffs ahead, and guessed the ground might clear.

We pushed up to a ridge. Looking back, we could see all the way down the valley we'd travelled. There wasn't a building or cleared acre in sight, nothing but bush and hill for miles. Bush and hill and great lumps of limestone, all creepered and plumed. Here and there creeks and waterfalls shone. The sun was really fierce. Sweat dripped stinging into my eyes.

Sam ploughed on ahead. Now and then, when the ground levelled off, we stopped and circled quietly. But we didn't see or hear anything. It must have been about mid-afternoon by the time we reached the top of the hill. There was quite a view. Though the sea was really still miles off, it seemed near enough for me to fling a stone and make a splash. Not that I had the energy, anyway; we collapsed on a great smooth rock and lay there, panting. A stiff breeze cooled us. The sky was huge. We shared it only with a slowly circling hawk.

"You take one side of the hill," Sam said, "and I'll take the other. We'll meet back here in half an hour. Let's hope we see something."

We split up. I took the seaward side of the hill. It was all limestone ledges, like descending steps, with quite a scramble from step to step. It might have been a stairway to the sky for some giant, some immense god. Clumps of toe toe clung here and there and, in more level places, clusters of miro and nikau. This side didn't look at all promising except for goats. No sooner did I have that thought than something white flashed away in front of me. I fired. I must have caught the goat in mid-stride, for it swayed out over the ledge and then tumbled a couple of

34

hundred feet into the bush below. A sheer fluke. I hadn't even seen it properly. I didn't plan to chase after it; the damn thing could stay down there. I just hoped it had died quickly, before it fell.

To tell the truth, I was angry. Angry at myself for killing so pointlessly. Probably that goat had been perfectly happy and at home on the hill. It belonged there, in that high wild place, and certainly had more right there than me. Then I had to come and blast hell out of it. Why? Why did I have to shoot it, to kill it? Just to show I was human? If I'd known how to write out my resignation from the human race, I'd have done it on the spot, don't worry. The pig, the day before, was different. It was him or me, and it was almost me. A stag was different too. It was his bushcraft against mine, his cunning against mine, and besides there was food involved. I'd broken my own rule, not to kill unless for food, and I felt sick and ugly inside.

I slid down to the next ledge and saw it was the last. Strictly speaking it wasn't another ledge at all, but the brink of a two-hundred-foot bluff or cliff. So I walked along it cautiously. I pushed through some scrub, watching where I placed my feet, and then found myself not in a clear space, but in a cave. The entrance was almost concealed by growth. I'd been so concerned with watching my step that the cave had grown around me before I knew it.

Fright kicked like a great foot in my stomach. The cave was filled with tumbled bones. Leg bones, thigh bones, ribs and human skulls. Yellowy in the light and patchy here and there with moss, jutting up at wild angles, they seemed to cascade out of the dripping dark at the back of the cave, to flow right to my feet. It was an old Maori burial cave, that was certain, and I'd walked right into it.

Tapu? For a moment I didn't even think of tapu, I was so surprised. But I backed out of there, fast. As I came out of the scrub I heard a voice behind me. It was Sam, of course, breathless.

"Heard your shot. What was it?"

For a moment I couldn't understand him. I'd forgotten the goat.

"Just take a look through there," I said shakily.

Pebbles and loose rock clattered away as he scrambled past me and pushed through the scrub. As he vanished I realized I'd made a mistake. Tapu. Of course. It was no way to find out whether Sam took tapu seriously or not.

I was just going to call him back when a thought stopped me. Why not get my own back? I mean, he'd laughed at me when I went into that farmhouse. It was my turn to laugh at him. So I didn't call him back. I didn't tell him there was a burial cave behind the scrub.

For a few moments there was nothing but the cracking sound he made through the scrub. Then I heard him yell. He must have fled, terrified. Because then there was a crash and another yell.

And Sam was over the side.

Chapter Five

THE SILENCE ROLLED IN LIKE THICK MUD AND FILLED up where his yells had been. His yells, and that faint scraping crash when he hit the bottom.

I dived through the scrub to see where he'd gone over. I found the place easy enough. It was only four or five feet from the mouth of the cave to the edge of the cliff. The bushes were still trembling where he'd hurtled through.

I leaned over the edge but I couldn't see a damn thing. Except bush, the tops of tall trees. I slung the rifle on my back, grabbed a creeper, and lowered myself over the edge of the cliff. It seemed the quickest way down.

"Sam?" I called. "You all right?"

Silence.

We'd be laughing about it later on, of course. We'd laughed about things like this before. We'd both have a great story to tell. About the day Sam went over the cliff.

"Sam?" I called.

Nothing. Nothing at all.

I seemed to be trembling. So badly, for a moment, that I couldn't make my body do what I wanted. But I held tight to myself and slid down the cliff a few yards at a time, grabbing at whatever vegetation there was to grab.

I yelled for Sam until my voice started to crack.

Then I was sliding, bumping, and there was nothing to grab. Actually I just sort of watched myself start falling. It seemed to happen very slowly. By that time I didn't care too much, really. It was the quickest way down, all right. No doubt about that.

Things began colliding with me. Rocks and trees bounced me back and forward like a football, then dumped me hard. Everything sang. When the singing quietened, I looked round and saw Sam about five yards away. At least I saw his boots.

37

The rest of him was hidden. My aim hadn't been too bad at all. I could have dropped fifty yards away. By the look of the sky it was late afternoon already.

The thing was I couldn't move very well. I had this pain in my chest. Every time I moved, something grated and hurt inside. Then there was my leg. I didn't need to be a medical genius to work out that some bone was broken. If I lay quite still it wasn't so bad. I wished I could get the noises out of my head, though. They really bothered me.

Of course, I couldn't stay still for long. Not when I found I couldn't get an answer from Sam. One way and another, I got myself over to him. If it wasn't my chest hurting, it was my leg. And those damn noises. I mean, I think it took me a fair while to get those five yards. I kept passing out and waking up again. By the time I reached him, anyway, it was just about dark.

He was crumpled and quiet though he made a sound like a groan now and then. Once, before it got really dark, he opened his eyes and looked at me. That was all. Just looked. But he knew who I was, all right. I could tell. He looked at me for a long time. His eyes were huge and bright.

"It's all right," I said. "We'll be all right. We've just got to hang on, that's all. Someone will come."

Someone? I thought about that. It was Sunday night. We weren't expected home till late Monday. Matthew would wait in his truck for us till dark, or after dark. Then he would drive back to Te Ika to raise search parties. It would be Tuesday morning, at least, before anyone even began to get near us.

I didn't say that to Sam though. I just tried to make his head more comfortable. It was back at an awkward angle. His eyes were closed again.

The bush was getting cold. Everything was getting cold. I didn't have a dog's show of lighting a fire. I'd done all the moving round I was likely to do. I lay there beside Sam and wished I had something to cover him with. I knew he ought to be covered. But all I could do was hold him gently, and keep on holding him, while he slept and made those strange faint sounds, like faraway groans, in his throat. I couldn't do much, but I could give him my warmth for as long as that lasted. After a while I saw the moon riding between the trees. But a long way off, like through the wrong end of a telescope, and getting farther away.

Then it was morning and I was still holding Sam. I really wasn't hungry and thirsty, but I felt I ought to be. I remembered the chocolate in my pocket and fetched it out.

"Something to eat," I said to Sam. "Have some."

He showed no sign of waking up.

"That's right," I said. "Sleep it off. We'll be all right. If we just hang on."

His eyelids were quite still. He must have stopped groaning sometime in the night.

"Sam?" I said. "Where does it hurt? Would it help if I shifted you round a bit?"

He didn't seem to know where he hurt. Or if he knew, he didn't plan to say.

"All right," I said. "Sleep it off."

The chocolate made me thirsty, so I sucked some dew from a fern-frond. Then I thought Sam might need some moisture in his mouth too. I reached out to pluck him a frond, and the noises in my head went off with a hell of a bang.

It was evening, pretty dark already, and I was surprised to find my head still attached to my shoulders. I reached out for Sam's face.

"We'll be all right soon," I announced.

For a moment his face didn't seem to be there; I seemed to be on my own, talking to nothing.

"Sam?" I said. "Sam?"

Then I found his face. He was terribly cold. Colder than me, and I was shivering all over. I felt as weak and stupid as a baby, and now I wanted to cry like a baby. I wished Sam would talk to me. I wished someone, anyone, would talk to me. But there was just the black bush, the dew on my face, and the moonlit sky. I lay looking up at the sky, watching rags of cloud float past the moon, wondering how the hell I could ever stop myself shivering.

39

I told myself to think of things. To think of anything. Anything but Sam, in fact. Anything that might make me feel better and keep me alive.

It was hard. Too damn hard. It was much easier to think about being dead. My parents would be upset, of course. They were going to be damn sorry for a lot of the things they'd said to me.

That thought actually made me feel better, on the whole. But it didn't stop me shivering.

Then there was my brother Derek. He would come down from Auckland for the funeral. I could just imagine him getting off the train in his best dark suit, all ready to console my parents. He'd know how to handle the whole business. He'd know exactly what to say. He was pretty good with words. I mean it was his business, he had a vested interest in using them.

I could almost hear him saying something like, "Nick was an active, healthy boy. He wasn't cut out for the intellectual life. He liked taking risks."

No, that didn't seem quite right. I mean anyone who could write essays with titles like *Tradition and the Mission: T. S. Eliot's Embryonic Dichotomy* really ought to be able to say something more original. I mean that really was the title of one of his essays; I worried about it because I thought dichotomy meant something indecent. But it turned out to have nothing to do with T. S. Eliot's sex life at all. Derek looked at me with pity when I raised this point. His essays always had good titles, like *W. B. Yeats: the Transcendent Paradox*. I thought that was awfully clever too, when he explained it. I'm glad, on the whole, that my parents produced one brilliant child. They worked so hard at it, I mean. And they were thrilled to pieces when he published his first book of poems. You might have struck it somewhere – *Islands in Uncertain Seas* by D. K. Flinders. To tell the truth I didn't like it too much. It was full of this sad stuff. Derek brooding here, and Derek brooding there. Derek looking at mountains, Derek looking at bush, Derek looking at sea, and Derek feeling awfully lonely and depressed about being a New Zealander, away from the centre of the universe. I suppose that's England or something; I know he's breaking his neck to get over there. I can't help being prejudiced when I talk about Derek, I know I'm not really fair. I mean it's not his fault he doesn't like the things he writes about. Everyone else writes about those things, and about how shocking it is to be a New Zealander, so I suppose it would put Derek in a pretty embarrassing position if he didn't do it too.

I wouldn't have minded right then, though, if Derek had come along to talk to me. I could have given him a pretty fair idea of what it felt like to be in the bush, for example. We could have had a great old yarn under that cliff, Derek and me. With Sam there beside us.

Of course I can't be fair to Derek. Not after he wrote that poem

> *half-naked and savage*
> *my brother gallops through green*
> *native here as the webbed weka*
> *unambiguous in its lacklustre swamp*
> *nesting in shreds of pioneer purpose. . . .*

That's what he said about me. How would you like to be called a savage, and compared with a dozy old weka? That's why I can't be fair to Derek, really. I could just imagine the sort of elegy he'd write about me. For my brother Nicholas, dead in the bush. It would probably make his name, and get into all the New Zealand anthologies.

But I'd have been glad to see his face, all the same.

Anyone's face.

God's, even.

I looked up at the sky and hoped He might take the hint. I'd have had one or two things to tell Him too.

It was certainly getting to be a damn long night. Light rain swished into the trees above my head, and after a while I felt it dripping cold on my face. The moon clouded, everything grew darker.

I thought of Grandfather Flinders. I suppose I'd been on the brink of thinking about him all the time really. I certainly couldn't have thought of anyone better. He could have given me tons of advice. Not that he was actually around to give me the advice, but all the same the idea of him bucked me up.

He knew the bush, all right. No one had kept count of all the farms he hacked out of the bush. He was one of the first white men to go into the King Country to farm after the Maori wars. It was still pretty wild when he went in, and for a long time it had been forbidden territory to the pakeha. The Maori king ruled there, and as a matter of fact Sam Waikai's great-grandfather had been an adviser to the Maori king.

But that wasn't the important thing. The really important thing, which I was remembering now, was that Grandfather Flinders once lay four days and four nights in the bush with a broken thigh. Some friendly Maoris found him in the end.

I concentrated on that for a while. If I didn't have God, I at least had Grandfather Flinders. I concentrated until the world began to shift this way and that, faster and faster, bumping and rolling. I hung on to Sam. I still wished he hadn't laughed at me back at the farmhouse. Then I would have stopped him before he went full tilt into the burial cave. That damn potty-chair. I should have known it meant trouble. I couldn't get it out of my mind. What a dozy sort of thing to think about when you're dying.

The first thing I thought was that Sam was wrong after all. We weren't the only ones shooting in these hills. I must have been only half-awake, but I heard the shots all right. One, two, three.

And one, two, three again.

Then I realized that though it was bright day, morning or afternoon, we weren't in our camp. We were lying smashed about at the foot of a cliff, and I hadn't been having a nightmare. It was real. We'd been there two nights, and a day or more.

I managed to fasten my hands on my rifle, though. Then I let rip. I seemed to smash hell out of the bush with my three shots. Each time I pressed the trigger and worked the bolt, my chest caught fire.

Blasted leaves came drifting down.

42

One, two, three again. Their shots; they'd heard me.

I wondered how many more shots I would have to fire. Actually they sounded quite close already. As if they were on top of the hill behind us.

I waited until I thought I heard a voice in the distance. I fired one shot, and then the bolt clicked home on nothing. The magazine was empty. Well, they'd have to make do with the one shot. I had a try at yelling, but I didn't have much voice left. I didn't have much of anything left. I let the rifle fall. Then I turned to say something to Sam. Actually I never got further than opening my mouth.

For a while it seemed just the noises in my head again. But when I opened my eyes I saw it was the search party. They were trampling and scrambling in from all directions. One look was enough. I closed my eyes.

I didn't have much to say, on the whole. I let them do what they liked. I must say they were all terribly gentle. Except for the brandy. One of them poured a nip down my throat and my stomach kicked it right back up again. A hand was washing my face. Someone was saying, "Don't worry, son. She'll be right."

"Be careful with him, won't you?" I said.

They were lifting me tenderly on to some stretcher. They were all awfully nice.

"Poor little bugger," someone said. "What's he going on about now?"

"His mate," someone else said. "He's going on about his mate. Poor little sod. He doesn't know."

They just didn't seem to understand me at all. There were voices everywhere. It was hard to sort them out.

"Everything's under control now," a deep, dark voice said. "Don't worry yourself. Don't get excited."

Actually he sounded more excited than me. Later I heard that when they found me I had Sam's head nestled in my arms. I don't know why this should have thrown them into such a great panic.

"Easy now," this deep, dark, kindly voice said, as they carried me through the bush. "Watch you don't bump the young fellow." I heard someone up ahead, slashing a track.

At the time I didn't understand why they were in such a hurry to get me out of that place. But they thought I was off my rocker, you see. They thought I didn't know Sam was dead.

Chapter Six

I COULDN'T TELL YOU HOW LONG I SPENT IN HOSPITAL.
I wasn't passionately interested in counting days and anyway
at the beginning the days just flowed together with the nights
so it was hard to tell one from the other. Now and then I tried
to raise my head for a breath of air and a look around. There was
a long window, there were two chairs; there was a door which
swung quietly shut. There were people in white, always people
in white. The whiteness hurt my eyes. Everyone spoke softly;
people said much the same things. Except the doctor. He was
the only one who spoke loudly. I suppose he had a right to.
Actually it is only because he spoke loudly that I remember what
he said. At a guess I would say it was about three or four days
after I was carried into the hospital; he sounded very angry.

"And whose bright idea was this?" he said. "To put him in
this, of all rooms? Isn't there someone in this hospital with a
sense of tact?"

I couldn't imagine what he was raging about. His voice had
woken me up.

"Just listen to it," he went on. "Just listen. Virtually right
beneath his window. Do you think that's likely to help his
recovery? Do you?"

It was then I became aware that I could hear something apart
from his voice. A steady rising, falling noise that you had to
listen to carefully for a while so that you could pick out the
separate sounds of weeping and wailing.

"But all the rooms with this ward overlook the Maori meeting
house," the sister said. "They're all the same."

"Then shift him out of a room," the doctor said. "Put him
into the main ward. He doesn't need a room to himself any
more."

There was a white flurry of nurses around me, and a squeaking

45

of wheels as my bed was rolled over polished lino floors. Around a corner, down a long passage, windows and doors streaming past. Anyone would have thought I was some speedway ace, the way they zipped me through the hospital; I'm sure they broke all records for the movement of patients that day.

Which only goes to show, I suppose, that the doctor should have kept his big mouth shut. If he hadn't got angry with the sister and woken me up, I wouldn't have heard the tangi. I wouldn't have known they were burying Sam. In any case it was pretty pointless trying to hide it from me; why shouldn't I be allowed to know? Dead are always buried; buried or cremated or entombed or dumped in caves or some damn thing. Was I supposed to imagine Sam an exception?

Apart from that, the days were all much the same. I might have been in hospital three weeks or three months, for all I knew. The thing I couldn't understand was why they were so slow bringing me up for trial. I knew they were getting ready for this; I could tell by their damn stupid questions. My parents seemed to make a point of not asking about what had happened. But the other patients asked, all right, and some of the nurses too. The ward sister was on my side, though, and put them right. I overheard her telling one patient that I was a bad case of shock, on top of everything else; and I had to be left alone. You can't imagine the stupid questions I was asked. Wasn't I lonely? Wasn't I afraid? Didn't I pray?

This last question, to be fair, came from a minister of religion. He sat on the edge of my bed, swinging a leg as he tried to yarn to me. He was very young and amiable. "Didn't you feel the need to pray to God when you were alone up there in the bush?" he asked.

I didn't like to disappoint him. He was in business with God, after all.

"I wouldn't have minded a yarn with anyone," I admitted. "Providing they showed some interest in talking to me."

"It was up to you to make the first move, surely."

"Why?"

It was entirely the wrong thing to say. He took ten or fifteen

46

minutes to explain why. He talked so fast his words jumbled and all I could hear was God, God, God.

"If you want to know the truth," I said, "He doesn't interest me passionately."

"Come now," he said gently. And smiled. "We're all God's creatures."

"That's our bad luck, then."

"Bad luck?"

"He ought to accept some responsibility. But it looks like He can get away with pretty well anything. It seems to me He's got no sense of responsibility at all." It was something that had been worrying me for a while, as a matter of fact. I started telling him about this book I read. About how all these Jews were stuffed into cattle wagons and taken to the gas chambers, little kids and old women and all.

The minister blinked. "Are you suggesting He was responsible?"

"No. I just mean He should have called a stop to the world, to the human race, right then. And He would have, if he'd had the slightest sense of responsibility. Anyone else would have called the whole thing off out of common decency. But it looks like He hasn't got the common decency."

"He loves us, Nick."

"That's great. Just great."

"But He does love us, Nick. He sent His only son to die for us."

"I don't see what's so great about that either. A lot of people have sent their sons off to die, some way or other."

"You're a very strange boy, Nick," he said. "A very strange boy. Where do you pick up these ideas?"

He talked as if a boy of my age shouldn't really know about the Jews or anything. He talked as if I shouldn't go around with my eyes open. The more he rambled on, the more I grew suspicious. I knew what he was getting round to, all right. He was just softening me up.

"All right," I said. "So go on. Go on and ask me."

"Ask you what, Nick?" His eyebrows lifted in surprise.

47

"You know what I mean. You know what I mean, all right."

"I don't, Nick. Really."

"You don't fool me a minute. Who sent you here?"

"I don't understand you, Nick."

"Go on and ask me. Go on."

He started looking very harassed, and swung round and caught the eye of the sister. She'd been keeping an eye on us both. But she was in it too. I knew what they were up to. They were both terribly nervous, all the same. I suppose it was because I'd started yelling.

"Ask me why I killed Sam Waikai," I shouted. "Go on."

"Nick, please," he said.

"Nick, please," the sister said, running.

"You haven't got the guts," I cried. "You haven't got the guts to ask a perfectly simple question."

There were nurses running and screens going up around my bed. I saw the needle, just for a moment, and felt the prick in my arm.

But I knew what was going on, all right. I knew for certain a few days later when the policeman came tramping down the ward, looking too damn friendly for his own good. It was Sergeant Crimmins; I'd seen him often enough around town. His boots thudded and squeaked up to my bed. He drew up a chair, with an amiable smile in my direction, and planted his big clumsy helmet down on my locker.

"Well, now, Nick," he said, "how are we today?"

"You've got to warn me first."

"Warn you?" His smile hung like something forgotten on his face.

"Warn me that anything I say can be taken down and used as evidence against me."

He frowned, then laughed.

"What's so funny?" I asked.

"You." He sat there burbling stupidly. "You must be feeling better, Nick. A whole lot better."

"All right, then. Where are the handcuffs?"

"Handcuffs?"

48

"You need them, don't you?"

"You're a real card, boy. A real card." But he didn't seem too sure about that, because he stopped grinning and chuckling. "Well look, Nick, to be perfectly serious I must ask you a few questions. It won't take more than a few minutes. I don't want to tire you. After these questions I'll go away and prepare a statement for you to sign. All quite simple. We need the statement for the inquest, you see. They've decided to go ahead and hold it without you. But we need this statement first."

"Well, you'd better warn me, hadn't you? Before you start." He wasn't going to pull a swifty on me.

I could see the sister standing near, pretending to be interested in another patient. She had her nervous look again.

"But there's no question of that, son. No question of warning you. Not for something like this."

At last he actually seemed to see that I was serious. Frowning again, he said, "Have you got something to tell me, Nick? Something you specially want to say?"

"Warn me first."

He sighed. "All right, I warn you. God knows why."

"That's no way to do it. Do it decently."

He took a deep breath. "I must warn you, Nicholas Flinders, that anything you say may be taken down and used as evidence against you."

"That's more like it. I'll give you evidence, all right. All you want. The first thing I want to say is I'm guilty."

"Great," he said. "What of? Stealing fruit from the Jackson orchard last year? Shooting an insulator off a telephone pole? Everyone's guilty of something, Nick. I'm just not interested at the moment, unless there's something very special you want to tell me. Is there?"

"Of course there is. About how I killed Sam Waikai. That's what I'm guilty of."

He sat up stiffly and looked at me in a very strange way. "And how did you kill him, Nick?" he said, his voice soft.

"I shot him, of course."

"Shot him, did you?" He was very matter of fact. "Well,

49

now." He sighed, and put his thick hands together, as if he was praying, and leaned over towards me. "And why did you shoot him, Nick?" Then his lips dropped shut, tight.

"Because he laughed at me. That's why. Because he made me feel ridiculous. Because he made me feel guilty. I just couldn't help it. When he jumped out in front of me, up there on the side of the hill, I just couldn't help it. I just fired without even thinking. And he went over the side. I got him first shot. And he went over the side."

"Nick, are you sure you're remembering this right?"

"Of course I am. I got him first shot. Then he went over. I felt sorry about it afterwards, though. I mean he was probably perfectly happy till I came along. He belonged. I didn't."

Sergeant Crimmins shook his head slowly. He didn't look at all happy, and no wonder. He'd had one murder case lately, and that was bad enough. He swivelled round on his chair and nodded to the sister. He looked pretty shaky.

"What's wrong?" I said. "Are you frightened I might shoot you too?"

Screens started going up round my bed again. Sergeant Crimmins breathed with a wheezy sound.

"Look," he said, "we'd better get all this straight, Nick."

"I just want to know when I'm coming up for trial. That's all."

"There's no question of you going on trial, son."

"Why? Do you think I'm going to die or something?"

"No, son. Not at all."

"I've just told you I'm guilty. Isn't that good enough for you?"

He was sweating now, and mopping his face.

"I'm here about the inquest, Nick. I'm just here to get a statement. That's all."

"There's generally an inquest before a murder trial, isn't there?"

He made a groaning sound. I'd got him there, all right.

"Look, son. The fact is – and you know it well enough – the fact is you didn't shoot Sam Waikai. You hear me? You didn't shoot him."

"Are you trying to tell me my own business?"

Against me he just didn't have a show.

"You're not remembering right. You've been all confused. We all understand. But you're still confused."

"It strikes me you're pretty confused," I said. "What the hell do you know about it anyway?" I thought that was a pretty curly question too.

"I was there, Nick. I was one of the search party that found you and Sam. I can even remember talking to you up there."

I recalled his voice suddenly. Deep, dark, kindly.

"And I'll tell you something else, son. I'll tell you something for a fact. You couldn't have shot Sam Waikai."

"Why not?"

"Well, because you were both great friends, for one thing. So I've been told."

"What does that prove?" He wasn't very smart, Sergeant Crimmins. I could see he needed to be taught a thing or two. "People who like each other sometimes kill each other. Have you ever read Oscar Wilde?"

"No, son. And I don't think you should have either, at your age."

"If you want to know, I think Oscar Wilde is just about the greatest writer who ever lived."

"Well, now. That's very interesting, son. Very interesting indeed." But he didn't look too interested. He closed his eyes in fact. I could have sworn he was praying.

"Do you know what he said? Each man kills the thing he loves. That's what he said."

It didn't seem to make much impression on Sergeant Crimmins, and I was disappointed. I mean we could have had a great old yarn about Oscar Wilde. But he obviously wasn't in the mood for it at all. The fact is I've been looking for years for someone I can talk to about Oscar Wilde. Some people giggle, other people sniff. Derek sniffs, for example. Not that he's actually bothered to read Oscar Wilde. He doesn't need to; he already knows what to think about Wilde. I admit I'm a retarded reader. I mean I actually have to read something before I can express an opinion. Listening to Derek I realize there are great advantages in an education. Apart from being able to hunt embryonic dichotomies and transcendent paradoxes, I mean. Still, Oscar knew what he was talking about, all right. Each man kills the thing he loves. I mean it explained everything all of a sudden.

"That's very interesting too," Sergeant Crimmins sighed. "But you didn't shoot Sam Waikai, son."

"No?" I got very cool.

"No. Because for another thing, Sam wasn't shot. You hear me, Nick? Sam wasn't shot."

I sat puzzling over that for a while. I couldn't make sense of what he said. I was getting itchy under my plaster again.

"Bullets leave holes, Nick. A bullet fired at a man leaves a hole in a man. But I suppose you know that."

He was trying to be sarcastic. With that deep, dark, kindly voice. I hadn't been able to remember a thing about that search party till now. The last thing I'd been able to remember was seeing Sam in front of me, by the edge of the cliff. And I lifted my rifle, without thinking, and fired. I could even remember his eyes after I fired, before he fell. Because he looked at me long and sad, unblinking, as if he was unable to believe it. I felt sick and ugly, but it was too late, there was nothing I could do. Then he toppled over.

I tried to get Sergeant Crimmins into focus. But things were pounding away in my head again.

"Can you hear what I'm saying, Nick?" he asked.

The sister was bent over him, whispering. A nurse came through the screens with a mask over her face, and she carried a needle in one of those little antiseptic bowls.

"Don't try any of your damn truth drugs on me," I yelled. "I know all about those. I'm not ignorant. I've read books."

I was trembling or shivering, hot and cold, and my throat was tight, choking, and I could hardly get the words out. "If you want to know the truth," I said, "it was that potty-chair. That's the truth. But don't use any drugs on me." But they had me trapped in that plaster and I couldn't do anything about the needle anyway.

Sergeant Crimmins loomed over me and put his hand on the side of my face. "Don't worry, son. I'm going now. I'll leave you to think about what I told you. I might see you tomorrow." He turned away to the sister and began talking to her. "Oscar Wilde, for God's sake," was all I heard.

For there was a gentle roaring in my ears like the sea. And I was diving into it, diving down. As deep, deep as I could go.

I slept most of the next day. When I woke, sometime in the afternoon, the first thing I saw was that big black helmet sitting on my locker again. Then Sergeant Crimmins' fat, grinning face.

"Hello, Nick," he said. "How are we today?"

"We're terrible. By myself I might be all right, though."

But I couldn't dislike him, I really couldn't. They had screens all round my bed already, though I hadn't even started yelling yet. A nurse put her head round a screen and asked would we like a cup of tea.

"Thanks," Sergeant Crimmins said. "I think we're both going to need it. Don't you think so, Nick?" He flicked out a notebook and studied it while the nurse fetched the tea. "Now let's see where we got yesterday. Ah yes. We didn't get very far, did we?"

The nurse arrived with the tea. He sucked and slurped at his cup, and smacked his lips. Then he glanced at his notebook again. Today he was obviously going to be all professional. But if he thought he was going to impress me with that notebook, he had another think coming.

"As a matter of fact, Nick, we only seemed to have cleared up one thing. That you didn't shoot Sam Waikai."

I was silent, so he had another go at his tea. It was amazing the variety of noises he could produce from a single cup of tea, all up and down the scale.

"I take it you withdraw your plea of guilty," he said.

"I think that's my business."

He was prepared to be patient today, terribly patient. "Look,

53

Nick, I'm going to tell you what I know already. Then I'm going to tell you what I *think* happened. All right?"

It certainly suited me, if he planned to do all the talking.

"In the first place, then. You and Sam went shooting on Labour weekend. Right? Right. We know that for certain. You went up there Friday night and camped in the bush. Right? Right. We know that because we found your camp. On Saturday you seem to have shot a pig and a couple of possums. We found the pig and the possum skins. It looks like you spent Saturday night in your camp too. Then you went shooting farther back into the hills. Right? Right."

"You know more about it than I do," I said, and tried my lukewarm tea.

"Now I'll start from the other end of that weekend. We found you and Sam under a cliff. We also found a dead goat nearby. I'll put these things together and tell you what I think happened. Someone shot that goat up on the side of the hill. You or Sam, one or other of you. My guess is that whoever it was started down the face after the goat—to finish it off perhaps, make sure it was dead. Then whoever it was got into difficulties, got trapped on a ledge. The other one tried to rescue him. But you both misjudged and fell down into the bush. How's that?"

He seemed very satisfied with himself. He certainly made the whole thing sound reasonable. I mean I could almost believe it myself.

"It sounds good," I admitted.

"That's the stuff," he said cheerfully. "Now we're really getting somewhere." He wrote something into his notebook. "We've got to straighten out the story a bit. We're not exactly out of the bush yet, are we?"

"No," I agreed. I only needed to close my eyes, to tell the truth, and I was in the bush again, strangling on supplejack. He was certainly right about that.

"It's just a question of getting a few particulars now. For example, who shot the goat?"

"I did." I would have said it to please him, even if I hadn't.

"Then you started off down the face."

"I suppose I must have."

"Then you got trapped on the face somehow, and Sam saw you were in difficulties. He tried to rescue you. He came down the face towards you. And – " He paused and looked at me, astonished. "What's wrong? What are you looking at me like that for?"

"You've got it right," I told him enthusiastically. "That's just what happened, all right. Why didn't I remember before?"

Sergeant Crimmins had become rather uncertain of himself again; now he looked quite bucked up. "So Sam tried to rescue you," he said.

"It was nothing unusual," I said. "We were always getting each other out of scrapes. The first time I met Sam, as a matter of fact, I rescued him from the river. You could say we were just evening up."

"Really?" He looked at his notebook, but he didn't write anything down. "When was this?"

"Years ago. When we were just kids."

"I see. So it's not really relevant."

I felt depressed. "No. I don't suppose so."

"Right. Well, we'd better get this straight and I won't bother you any more for the time being. Sam came down the face to try and rescue you. But when he tried, you both lost your footing on the face. And fell down together."

"I suppose if we both fell, we must have fallen down together." This was a very fine point, of course, but I was in the mood for fine points now. "Mustn't we?"

But he was busy scribbling in his notebook. My fine point went floating out the window into the sunny day.

After a while he looked up. "So Sam lost his life trying to save you," he said. "How's that?"

"That's fine," I agreed. "That's just what you ought to say."

But he only gave me a queer look, and went on writing. I could tell he was tired of the whole thing now. He wanted to get it over with, and no more funny business.

"Are you sure you understand?" he asked. "I said Sam lost his life trying to save you."

"Of course he did," I agreed.

I was tired suddenly, and wanted to see the last of that note-book. For I'd begun to see that I could fool everybody but myself, and if I couldn't fool myself there was no point. No point in it at all. When Sam died I lost all hope of ever evening up with him. He'd stayed in debt to me, and I would never know whether or not he really liked me. No lie I told, no yarn I spun about his death, would ever make me feel any better about it. Nothing could. Not even anything Mrs Waikai had to say. I could just imagine what she'd say, and I couldn't stand the thought of facing her again. Even if I told her how I happened to send Sam walking into that burial cave, not a specially brotherly thing to do, she wouldn't say anything to me that wasn't gentle with love. Perhaps that was the trouble, why I was afraid.

A couple of days later Sergeant Crimmins came back with a long, typewritten statement for me to sign. It was all very clever, and had a lot of words I'd never have thought of. He'd certainly had a great old time with his dictionary. He didn't mention Oscar Wilde, though, or any of that stuff. I signed the statement, we shook hands over it, and he stayed just long enough to accept the offer of another cup of tea.

Chapter Seven

I LEFT HOSPITAL WITH MY FRACTURED RIBS MORE OR less healed and part of my leg still in plaster. To tell the truth I wasn't too enthusiastic about going home. I'd only just learned to cope with everything and everyone in the hospital. People had caught on to the idea of not bothering me. Now I had to start out all over again.

I rode home through Te Ika with my father, looking out at the tight houses in the tight streets. It was a bright Saturday, with people mostly outside in their gardens, among their clipped shrubs and tidy flower-beds and goldfish ponds and plaster gnomes. If you want to know the truth, everything looked just too neat and happy. If I saw a scene like that in a movie I would know something big and bad was building up: a massacre or flood or earthquake or landslide or something. I sneaked a quick look up at the hills above the town, just in case. But they looked quite tame, with sheep grazing here and there, and a faint heat-haze. They didn't look at all sinister, and they certainly weren't going to fall. In the movies you can always tell by the theme music. It gets low and spooky and warns you about what is going to happen. Well, I didn't have any theme music to keep me company on the ride home; I just had this trembling feeling inside me, which was a kind of unpleasant music in a way. It was certainly spooky, and left me unhappy. Men mowed lawns and trimmed hedges or drank beer and read their race guides. Kids played cricket, or squealed around on trolleys and scooters. Housewives fussed and washed, and sheets flapped and flashed white and crisp under the hot blue summer sky.

Perhaps everything looked too solid. Perhaps that was the trouble. The houses, the shops, the movie house, the post office, the railway station. Sometimes it's hard for me to believe that Te Ika was just swamp and wild bush seventy years ago.

Only the telephone and power poles looked brittle with the heat, likely to snap at any moment. The pale road shimmered, and spots of dark asphalt bubbled here and there. "It's going to be a long summer, Nick," my father told me. "That's what the old Maoris say. The cabbage trees flowered early this year. That's how they're supposed to tell." He actually thought he was cheering me up. Summer, and the fact that I couldn't swim while my leg was in plaster, was going to drive me mad. Sam and I always had our best times in summer, swimming or floating down the river and over rapids on canoes or rafts. What use was summer now?

We rattled over the Bailey Bridge that had survived a dozen floods since the river swept away the old bridge. The water gleamed below, between green trailing willows, and Maori kids splashed and swam. The silver birches down our street, which should have been bright with new leaf, looked dusty and half-dead. I hobbled up our front path, my father helping, while my mother came weepily down the steps of the house to meet me. She pecked at the side of my face a couple of times.

"We thought we'd never get you home again," she said. The tears made snail-tracks down the side of her face. "We thought we'd never have our Nick back."

I wished I was about a million miles away from home, from Te Ika, somewhere where no one would ever know me.

"And here you are," she said. "At last. Home again. I can't believe it." She pecked at my face again. She seemed to think she was likely to hurt my leg or something if she kissed too hard.

Then someone in smart black tapered trousers and open-neck shirt appeared on our veranda. Derek. Casual and grinning, with his hands in his pockets.

"Hello, Buster," he said. "Been having fun again?" He tried the breezy approach, which really didn't suit him.

"Derek came down for the weekend," my mother explained. "So you'd have a real homecoming."

It was that, all right. My mouth ached with my smile, and my face felt like hard enamel that might split suddenly. I was strange, they were strange, the house was strange, but I knew I was expected to join in the game of pretending that everything was all right again, everything was the same. I wished I could throw a yelling fit to get out of it. But I'd stopped throwing those a good while back. After I signed Sergeant Crimmins' statement as a matter of fact. All I could think of was that Sam wasn't hobbling up to his front door. Mrs Waikai wasn't wailing and weeping over him, kissing him till he dripped, after his return from hospital. His father wasn't waiting quietly in the background. His big brother Matthew wasn't standing, grinning by the front doorway of the house. That was for certain.

"This heat bothering you, Nick?" my father asked.

"You feel all right?" my mother said.

"He's gone very pale." That was Derek, I could tell.

They were all grabbing hold of me and looking anxious, for some reason.

"Of course I'm all right," I said as I keeled over into their arms. I'd only been wishing for a yelling fit. And I got something better, a faint. I just felt weak and, as my eyes closed, that black bush swooped down, tangling, and gathered me up. Boy, I went about a million miles all right. I couldn't complain about that.

Then I was sitting in a chair, my head back, and my mother was sponging my face. Derek and my father were going round in circles. "It's this heat, that's the trouble," my father kept saying. "This confounded heat."

"It's all been too much for him," my mother said. That cold water was certainly sweet on my face.

Things slowed down after a while. I found the way to hold the world steady was to concentrate on something. On a veranda-post, say, or a shrub in the garden. One thing at a time. Otherwise everything was likely to crack down the middle, and let the bush swoop in again. It was quite a responsibility, actually, to keep Te Ika in one piece. The place didn't seem quite so solid after all.

My mother vanished, and then Derek sat by me and tried to make conversation. "What does it feel like to be famous again?" he asked.

I couldn't understand what he was talking about. So I didn't have anything to say.

"One thing will probably make you happy," my father announced. "No more school for you this year. It's almost finished."

My mother appeared in front of me again with a cool orange drink. "Sip this," she instructed. "Then off to bed, Nick."

Actually I couldn't think of a better place to be. They couldn't get me to bed fast enough, for my liking.

I suppose it was only a few days later when my mother came into the bedroom for a yarn. She carried a big bowl filled with apples, bananas and oranges. I liked the look of the oranges especially; my mouth was dry. She placed the bowl beside my bed.

"Mrs Waikai dropped this fruit round this morning," she said. "While you were asleep. I offered to wake you up. But she said no, she'd be quite happy to see you when you tell me you're ready to see her, she'd be quite happy to wait."

I didn't say anything. I'd just started to reach out for an orange, as a matter of fact.

"What's wrong?" she said.

"Nothing."

"You'll have to see her sometime, Nick. I can't keep putting her off, you know. She tried her hardest to see you while you were in hospital. If I explained once, I explained a dozen times about the doctor not wanting you to be overwhelmed by visitors."

I didn't have anything to say about that, either.

"She goes on all the time about how you're her boy too now that Sam's gone. Really, Nick, if you don't help me I don't know how I'm going to cope with her. I really don't. Can't you help, just a little bit? Can't you say you're ready to see her?"

I concentrated on a spot in the middle of the ceiling this time. The wallpaper was no good. It tended to swim, and float inwards.

"Another thing, Nick. You must spend more time out of bed.

60

You can't stay there all day. The doctor's quite insistent. You've got to get some exercise."

She sighed.

"Are you listening to me, Nick?"

I'd worn out that spot, so I tried another off to the side. The ceiling still looked fairly firm. I had this bedroom pretty well taped from all angles.

"You must make more use of your leg, Nick. You've got to get out and around a bit. Please, Nick. You must try to help your mother."

The sounds of summer droned in my window, cicadas and lawnmowers and bumble bees. She was still sighing and going on. Expecting me to say something.

"Nick, I know you've had a bad time. We all know you've had a bad time. But you have to help yourself now. You hear? We can't do everything for you. You have to help yourself."

A golden thought for the summer. I had to help myself. Even the ceiling started to look shaky now. I switched from those spots to a thin beam of sunlight which made a small bright patch on my dressing table. It stayed very steady, though it stood to reason it wouldn't last long.

She gave a last sigh and rose. I seemed to be hearing a tremendous amount of sighing these days. "Is there anything you want, Nick?"

"Yes. I want you to take that bowl of fruit away."

I could say that fast.

"Nick, please."

"You asked me if I wanted anything. Well, that's what I want. You to take that bowl of fruit away. I don't want to have to look at it."

One thing I like about my mother, she doesn't argue with me. Not when she sees I've really made my mind up. She went out with the fruit all right.

Derek came down from the city again for a weekend. At some stage, when he'd given up trying to talk to me, he had a great old argument with my parents. Not a noisy one, though; they spoke quietly so I wouldn't hear. Possibly they thought I was asleep anyway; I usually slept most of the day. They were sitting in deckchairs in a shady part of the back garden which normally would have been safe enough, far enough away from my bedroom. What they didn't allow for was a very warm still day, and all the doors and windows being open to the slightest sound. Also they probably didn't allow for my mother raising her voice at a certain moment in the conversation.

"Homosexuality?" my mother said. "Derek, really. Not in this house."

"Look, mother, you really must get it out of your head that homosexuality means dirty old men. Homosexual attachments of some kind or other, not necessarily physical at all, are common among young people in adolescence."

"Where did you learn all this? Who taught you all this?"

"It's common knowledge these days."

"I don't see what's common knowledge about it. *I*'ve never heard of it. Nor, I daresay, has your father."

My father coughed delicately. To show he was there, I suppose. "Beryl, I think you should be fair and give Derek a chance. He might have something, for all we know. At least he can offer an explanation about Nick, which is more than we can. He might be talking good sense."

"Good sense? I've never heard anything so awful. I don't see how you can sit there, Frank, and listen to him. He's trying to tell us, don't you understand, that we've reared a – " She couldn't bring herself to say the word again. "All these years, in this house."

"Derek's not saying anything of the kind. He's just offering an explanation. A psychological explanation. He sounds perfectly reasonable."

"And who gave him Oscar Wilde to read? That's what I'd like to know."

"You know as well as I do that with all his outdoor interests Nick might have stopped reading altogether if it hadn't been for Oscar Wilde's stories. He's lost interest in all his old books, and unless it's something he's forced to read at school, he seldom picks up a new one. I've been quite encouraged by the fact that Nick can still read for his own enjoyment. Anyway there's nothing wrong with Wilde as a writer. As a man, perhaps. But as a writer he can be delightful."

Then Derek chipped in again. "You see, mother. That's what I mean. Oscar Wilde and dirty old men. That's all the word means to you."

"Do you think I'm going to sit quietly listening to all kinds of filth about Nick?"

Derek sounded very patient. "No, mother. You must get this idea of filth out of your head. I've explained to you that it's something fairly normal among adolescents. It's certainly nothing to panic about. The truth is that, when we're young, we often go through some sort of homosexual phase."

"I certainly didn't." My mother sniffed. "And I'm certain your father didn't. Did you, Frank?"

"Well," my father said uneasily. "Not that I recall."

"There you are, Derek," my mother said with satisfaction. "I positively refuse to believe that the world's so different now. I just can't credit that the world's gone stark raving homosexual in the last thirty or forty years."

"I'm not saying it has," Derek went on. "Of course we don't always recognize homosexuality as such. Crushes on school-teachers of the same sex, intense friendships with young people the same age, and suchlike things. We grow out of it, and we never give these things a second thought. But the fact is that most of us, at sometime or other, have survived some homo-sexual experience."

"What's this got to do with Nick?" my mother said.

"Well, mother," Derek said, with a sigh deep enough to equal any I'd heard lately, "I think it may have a good deal to do with his present condition. If my guess about this friendship is right – and you agree that he did have an intense friendship with Sam Waikai – then the point is that Nick hasn't had a chance to grow out of it in the normal way. That's the danger, you see. He's liable to develop a fixation about this friendship. All the signs are there already. His listlessness. His reluctance to leave bed.

63

His refusal to talk about anything important, or to see people outside the family. You asked me to come down here this weekend to see if I could interest him in the world again. Well, let me tell you it's been a hopeless task. All the signs –"

"My God," my mother said. "What are you telling me? What *are* you trying to tell me, Derek?"

"I'm not trying to tell you anything. I'm just suggesting. Suggesting a good reason for Nick's condition. And suggesting that mere physical attention might not be enough for Nick. That's all."

"Then what are we supposed to do?" my father asked, very reasonably. "That we aren't doing already?"

Derek was silent for a few moments, then he gave a thoughtful cough and said, "Understand him. That's the first thing. Understanding first. Then all the rest of what he needs, affection, love, patience, will follow."

"What's he getting now, if he's not getting those things?" my mother objected.

"He must have understanding," Derek said.

"Do you think a psychiatrist might help?" my father asked.

"Derek," my mother said firmly, "I think this conversation has gone quite far enough. I just won't have it, you hear? Not in this house."

"But you have it, mother. You have it already. And you'll just have to – "

Well, to tell the truth I'd heard enough. I wasn't going to have it either, all that crappy stuff. People weren't going to say I took Sam up into the bush for all kinds of dirt. I picked up a book and slammed it right into the window. It was Oscar Wilde, as a matter of fact. The broken glass went tinkling everywhere. That shut them up pretty smartly, I can tell you. If you want to make a really satisfying sound, if you want to show you're really disgusted, try heaving a solid book through glass. There's nothing better.

Anyway I didn't hear anything more from them. They must have thought I'd been sleeping through all that crappy stuff.

Through all that dirt of Derek's. They must have got a damn big fright when they heard I was awake.

Later in the day my father came into my bedroom grim-faced. He spent quite a while clearing up broken glass and pasting some temporary cardboard over the shattered window. Then he went out to clear glass out of the flower bed by my window. He came back inside carrying the Oscar Wilde book.

"No," I said. "You can get rid of that. I'm not interested in stories any more. Take it away and burn it. Or something."

Chapter Eight

OF COURSE I DIDN'T KNOW, ALL THAT TIME, THAT I HAD been in the newspapers. When Derek asked me what it felt like to be famous again, I really didn't know what he was talking about. I didn't know till quite a while after I was taken home.

One day I got tired of my mother telling me I ought to be on my feet more. For the sake of peace, I did an experimental five-minute hobble round the house. Just to show I could do it if I liked. I started trembling after a while, but on the whole it wasn't too bad. My parents had the idea they ought to ignore me while I hobbled round. So they ignored me. My father was sitting out in the shade of the veranda, reading, and my mother was cooking in the kitchen. My father said "Good day, Nick," and went on reading. My mother said "How nice to see you, Nick," and went on cooking. All very psychological.

I got back to my room feeling pretty shot. But I decided there were probably worse things in the world than walking. I felt reasonably happy for all the effort. I could count on at least a couple of days of peace now, before my mother started agitating about exercise again.

I sat puffing and blowing on the stool beside my desk. My schoolbooks were stacked there, just as they had been when I left for the Labour weekend shooting trip. There was even some unfinished homework. I opened a drawer idly, and then I found these clippings. Obviously my mother had saved them, thinking I might be interested. Probably I wasn't meant to read them until I was well again.

There were pictures among all the words. A recent photo of me in school uniform, and a three-year-old snap of Sam. I looked sour. Sam was grinning. It was the wrong way round, somehow. 15-YEAR OLD BOY'S LONELY FORTY-HOUR VIGIL BESIDE DEAD FRIEND IN BUSH COUNTRY, said one headline. HARDENED

BUSHMEN WEEP AT TRAGIC FIND, said another beneath. There was a photograph of the search party coming out of the bush with two stretchers. On one of the stretchers I could just distinguish my own face; the other was covered. Words jumped up at me.

When searchers reached him, young Nicholas Flinders, himself injured and weak from shock and exposure, expressed only concern for the welfare of his companion. "Look after Sam," he instructed them.

Because of his condition the boy, a Te Ika schoolteacher's son, was unable to give a coherent account of the tragedy. He appeared unaware that his companion had been dead for at least 24 hours.

Searchers described him as "the pluckiest . . .

I didn't read any more. I couldn't stand the thought of how many friends might have been invented for me this time. I was just shoving the whole lot back when my eye caught the other clippings. The ones of the inquest. MAORI YOUTH GAVE LIFE SAVING FRIEND, said the heading.

A young Maori lost his life while trying to save a pakeha friend trapped on a cliff-face during a Labour weekend shooting trip. This was revealed yesterday at an inquest into the death of . . .

I couldn't get back to bed quickly enough. But I admit the clippings did explain a lot of things. The way people looked at me in the hospital, for instance, and the stupid questions they asked. It also explained all that rowdy business about Grandfather Flinders.

The first thing was his telegram. I heard my parents discussing it. And arguing.

"Be reasonable, Beryl," my father said. "We've put him off twice already."

"Well, we couldn't have him seeing Nick in hospital. You know that, surely."

"But Nick's not in hospital. He's home now. He's on the mend. There wouldn't be any harm in letting the old man come for a couple of days."

"What good is it going to do Nick?"

"What harm is it going to do him? You might look at it that way."

"And why does he want to see Nick, anyway? Explain that, if you can."

"I don't know any more than you do. He just wants to see his grandson. That's all. That's all it amounts to. It's reasonable enough."

"He's never taken any interest in his sons, let alone his grandsons. Unless he's wanted something out of one, of course. Look at the way he's always treated you. And the way he treated Derek, when Derek went to see him."

Derek had taken his freshly printed book of poems out to Grandfather Flinders' place on the outskirts of Auckland. It was going to be a big presentation, because one of the poems was dedicated to Grandfather Flinders. In fact it was about him, more or less.

> *You who shared the land's eager rape*
> *Opening valleys like thighs*
> *Through passionate days which rang with blade*
> *Stripping green garments*
> *Through sensual nights which sang with flame*
> *To lie your head on a blackened breast.*

and a lot more of the same. Well, the old boy wasn't too much impressed by this poem, and I don't blame him. He instructed Derek to get hold of a garden fork, and made him dig potatoes all day.

"You've never liked my father. Let's be honest about it."

"I've never noticed any great affection on your part either."

That seemed to floor my father for a minute. There was a sad silence, then he said, "Well, he's my father. I can't get away from that, can I? I owe him something."

"What, exactly?" my mother said.

"Loyalty," my father said. "A little loyalty."

"Loyalty. I hate that word. That's been your father's trouble all his life. His sons have all been loyal. And it's made him even more unbearable. He's just become more and more arrogant and

68

stupid. You all ought to be ashamed of yourselves, all the Flinders boys. You could have put him in his place years ago. But no, you've let him go his own sweet way. And let him make the name Flinders a laughing stock right through the country."

"Come, now. You're exaggerating. It's not been that bad."

"Hasn't it just? Your memory must be failing. You weren't saying that a couple of years ago, I remember. You said you couldn't look people in the eye at the time of his last court case. Not with his name in the papers every day. You flinched every time people asked if you were some relative. Now go on, try and deny it. Just try."

"Now look, Beryl – "

"Go on. Just try. I'm listening."

I could tell that things were going badly for my father. Nothing made him more miserable than Grandfather Flinders' court cases. Particularly when they were reported prominently in the newspapers for their comedy value. Not that Grandfather Flinders was a lawyer. But he thought he knew everything about law, all right, and he hadn't stopped suing people, for defamation and breaches of contract and suchlike things, all his life. He didn't waste money hiring lawyers; he believed they were all incompetent parasites anyway. He conducted his own cases, and his cross-examinations were quite spectacular. He learned his law sitting in smoky little huts in the bush, and I suppose that's why he was called a bush-lawyer. It all started when some contractor failed to take delivery of a thousand of his sheep during a drought; they died of thirst. He sued, and discovered he liked arguing in a court room. So when he wasn't farming, he was having a court case. It was just his way of relaxing. He discovered he could have a case over just about anything.

Even when he shifted up to Auckland and more or less retired, he didn't stop. There was always someone to sue. The local council, a drainage board or a land agent. And the government too, of course. He'd sued the government five times and won twice. The newspapers liked Grandfather Flinders and he liked the newspapers. That was the worst thing. And if any of his sons got into trouble, Grandfather Flinders rushed to defend them. Like Uncle Harry, for instance; he got pulled up for speeding once, and normally might have got away with a fine of three or four pounds. He finished up paying ten pounds, plus court costs for a whole day of Grandfather Flinders' defence.

Only one thing made my father more miserable than these court cases, and that was being reminded of the time Grandfather Flinders stood for Parliament. He started campaigning as an independent a year before the elections, and held meetings in small country towns. My father had the humiliating job of ringing a bell to announce a meeting. He was very young then, still in short pants. Grandfather Flinders made him march up and down the main street ringing this bell. When a big enough crowd gathered, Grandfather Flinders would mount a small ladder and begin denouncing all the people present as congenital idiots unfit for the vote. He never promised anything, except a Royal Commission into his own grievances, at these meetings. He just insisted that his listeners were ignorant, deluded, stupid and ridiculous. I mean it didn't get him a terrible lot of votes, that sort of thing. My father said it was a puzzle to him why Grandfather Flinders wasn't lynched. He says he still has nightmares, sometimes, about ringing that bell.

"I'm still listening," my mother said. "I don't notice that you've got much to say for yourself."

"Beryl, we've been through all this before."

"Well, don't talk to me about loyalty again. Not where he's concerned. A lot of good it's done him. And you."

"All right. So you can't stand my father. You've made that perfectly clear. Well, what do you want me to do? Tell him again that he's not to come?"

"I don't want him in the house. You know what it's been like before."

"This is different. He's not coming to see me. He wants to see Nick."

"Then tell him Nick's still sick."

"That excuse is going to get a bit thin."

"Nick's still not well. That's obvious."

"The doctor seems happy enough."

70

"You know I'm not talking about his physical condition."

"But – "

At that stage one or other of them decided to slam the kitchen door. Their voices became muffled. Anyway I gathered Grandfather Flinders wouldn't be coming. I can't say I cared much. He would probably only want to ask stupid questions like everyone else who wanted to see me. To tell the truth I didn't get on too well with Grandfather Flinders, anyway. Whenever I saw him I always seemed to do the wrong thing, and he would call me an idiot, another miserable idiot in a family of bloody idiots. Like the time when we visited his place in Auckland, and he sent me up a tree to chase down an opossum which had been a nuisance to his chickens. First he said I was a lily-livered coward, because I didn't grab the thing right away. Then when I tried to grab it he said I was a hare-brained dolt because I'd got close enough to get my eyes scratched out. I couldn't win, either way, and no one ever won an argument with Grandfather Flinders. Except Grandmother Flinders, and she had her own special ways.

I lay there thinking of what new names he might invent for me and started feeling sleepy again. I was still catching up on my sleep. The hotter the days, the more I slept. There seemed to be no end to the sleep I needed. I could drift off any time, just about. So long as I didn't think of anything, that was the main thing. To stop myself thinking about Grandfather Flinders, for example, I resorted to my special technique.

First I gently closed my eyes. That was the easy part. Then I tried to imagine myself floating. After a while I was floating. First I floated out of bed, the sheet falling away, and then I floated out the window. I hovered above the house, looking down. I saw the red corrugated roof, the crazy-paved footpath, my father's pet native shrubs, my mother's hydrangeas, the neatly clipped lawn. I got a bit higher and saw the other houses scattered round our street, and the cabbage trees growing along the creek near our house. Still rising, I saw all of Te Ika soon, the gleaming river and the dusty roads, the tiny rooftops shiny with sun under the dry bony hills where dead bleached trees

71

lay among split pinnacles of limestone. I saw how the hills and wild bush crowded round Te Ika, how small and patchy the farms were. I was really zooming up now. Soon the hills and mountains and bush seemed to have swallowed Te Ika up altogether, and I couldn't see a sign of life at all. I was so high I was looking at all the North Island of New Zealand, and the South Island too, and it was all the same green wild colour, in a blue wild sea. I felt happy at last. Almost happy enough to go back again, because it didn't seem possible that anyone lived down there.

But I never did start back, which would have been interesting, because by that time I was asleep.

That was my special technique. Thinking about nothing was the important thing, all right. I was getting pretty good at that business.

There was one thing I couldn't quite manage, though. The dreams.

The sun glittered in a million places through the wet leaves, the dangling creeper, the beards of fungus. This old lady, dressed all in black, came pushing through the foliage, searching and calling. It was Mrs Waikai, of course.

"Samuel?" she called. "Where are you, Samuel?"

I couldn't help her no matter how hard I tried. Mostly she just looked through me.

"Samuel?" she called. "Where are you, Samuel?"

I remembered, and ran. I ran till my chest hammered and my body ached. And I brought back to her the only thing I could find, that potty-chair.

"Samuel?" she said.

I placed the potty-chair down in front of her. "It's all I have," I said. "It's all I can find."

"Samuel?" she said, seeing me at last. "Samuel?"

Then I knew I was Sam. She crushed me in her fat arms, and her lips were all over my face. But I wasn't Sam after all, and I only wanted to die.

I was sitting on the veranda with my father. It seemed to be just after breakfast. My father was reading a book, the sky was bright, but something was wrong. Then I twigged it. The moon was shining in the sky, not the sun. An enormous silver moon. I pointed this out to my father, and he looked at me over the top of his reading glasses.

"Well, that's reasonable, son," he said. "That's reasonable, isn't it?" He went back to his book.

It didn't seem to be a very big point to argue about. The moon appeared to be doing a perfectly good job up there. If it satisfied my father, I supposed it was all right. My mother came out on the veranda and said what a beautiful morning. She didn't seem to think the moon was unusual either.

She even went so far as to say it was hot. I didn't say anything.

Derek came walking up the front path. I was starting to feel something horrible might happen, as a matter of fact, and I was quite relieved to see it was only Derek. He wasn't wearing anything to speak of, but then neither were my mother and father.

"It's psychological," Derek said. "It's only a phase. We all go through it."

"Indeed," my mother said, "and who is we?"

"I think we should listen to Derek," my father said. "He might have something to say."

"I have nothing to say," Derek said.

"That's reasonable," I said. "That's reasonable, isn't it?"

My father gave me a queer look, but I began reading the morning paper which was spread across my knees. I came to the report of the inquest. It turned out to be more interesting than I thought. *This was revealed yesterday at the inquest into the death of Nicholas Flinders, aged 15 years, a resident of Te Ika.*

"Did you see this?" I asked, and passed the paper over to my father. He inspected the report for a moment.

"Well?" he said. "What's wrong?"

"Nothing," I said. "It's just about me. That's all."

"That's reasonable," he said.

"That's psychological," Derek said.

"Not in this house," my mother said.

"But that's the moon up there," I announced.

"We know," they all said.

Chapter Nine

I WOKE EARLY ONE MORNING THINKING OF THUNDER. But it was just someone banging and bellowing and swearing at the front door. I heard my parents tumbling out of bed and struggling into their dressing gowns. "But we told him," my mother was crying, "if we told him once, we told him a dozen times. We made it quite plain he wasn't to come."

"You didn't really expect him to take any notice, did you?" my father said breathlessly as they charged through the house to stop the noise.

Then they had the front door open and Grandfather Flinders came clumping into the house. Neighbours woken by the noise too must have had a great old squiz between their curtains that morning.

"Thank Christ someone in my ridiculous family has turned out all right," he boomed. "Where is he? Where the hell is the boy?"

"Nick's still very ill," I heard my mother say. "He's not to be upset or disturbed. The doctor says —"

"Bloody nonsense. That's all they ever say. Don't talk to me about them bastards. I've had a gutsful of doctors in my time. There's only one thing they want, and that's everyone in the country busy dying on social security. Where is he? Where is that bloody boy?"

"Please," my mother said. "Please. I must insist. I really must. I can't have you seeing Nick."

"God almighty," he roared, "I've come a hundred miles to see him."

"I can't help that," my mother said. She hurried down the passage, reached into my room, grabbed the door and pulled it tight. I guessed she was standing on the other side, a human barricade. "I can't help that at all. We warned you not to come."

74

His voice sounded like rusty old iron. "I been waiting two months to see the young bugger. All I get told is he's sick. He probably is too. Sick with woman's fuss and doctor's bullshit. If this keeps up he'll probably be good for nothing but the knacker's yard. Now, where is he? I've waited two months and come a hundred miles. Do you think I'm going to stand here and listen to what some miserable idiot swine of a doctor says?"

There seemed to be some sort of tussle outside my door. I guessed my father was trying to hold on to Grandfather Flinders.

"Now listen, Dad," he said. "Just hold your horses and relax. Let's all relax. I think a cup of tea would be in order, Beryl."

"You against me too, are you?" Grandfather Flinders shouted. "I might have known it. My own son. My own bloody son. You're all against me, you bastards."

"Now, Dad, don't start flying off the handle. Let's all just relax. Let's have a quiet cup of tea and talk about this thing reasonably, shall we?"

"Expect me to be reasonable, do you? That's lovely. Bloody lovely. After two months and a hundred miles, and I'm not allowed to see that boy. Let me remind you that that boy in there is a Flinders. You hear that? A bloody Flinders."

"All right, Dad, so he's a Flinders."

"And he's my grandson, you hear? My grandson. Are you going to stand there and tell me to my face that I can't see him?"

More tussling and scraping. "Please," my mother said, "Frank, do something, please."

"Take orders from her, do you? So that's what it's all about. Castrated by apron strings. Like every other man in this country. Lovely. Are you a man or a neuter? My own son. No loyalty, nothing. Lovely. Bloody lovely."

"I can't stand it," my mother cried. "Him and his foul mouth. I can't stand it, Frank. Do something, you hear?"

"Look, Dad, this is getting us all nowhere. Let's hold off for a minute. I suppose you must have come down on the newspaper bus. Anyway I suppose you must be feeling tired after all that travelling. Aren't you? You must be. I think we should let Nick finish his night's rest. I suggest we go into the kitchen. I've got

75

a bottle of brandy there. You look as if you could do with a nip."

"Brandy, did you say?"

"That's right, Dad."

"Brandy, eh?"

"Come on, Dad. Have a nip. That'll put you on your feet again. Come on, through here."

"First time I ever been offered brandy the moment I arrived in this house, by God. Damned if I won't try a nip, as a matter of fact."

The tussling had stopped. Grandfather Flinders' feet banged away into the kitchen. Chairs scraped. Glasses rattled. My mother filled a kettle and clanged it on to the stove. I hobbled to my door and opened it slightly so I could hear better.

"How was the journey, Dad?"

"All right. What do you expect? Great stuff, that. Great stuff. Nothing to beat the pure grape."

A bottle tinkled against a glass. It sounded as if Grandfather Flinders was on to his second nip already.

"By God, yes," he said. "Great stuff. How is that brat in there?"

"A lot better than he was when they brought him out of the bush. That's about all I can say. He's mended nicely."

"Great stuff. Lead in your pencil, son. Cheers."

"Now, Dad, how about a cup of tea?"

"Tea be buggered. I'm here on business."

"What business?"

"Flinders business, son. Flinders business. Great stuff. You could get a lot more in that glass, by the way. That's it. Don't let your hand tremble. That's the main thing. Flinders business, son. That's why I'm down here. Now are you still telling me I can't see that boy?"

"We'll have to talk about this, Dad. We'll have to talk about this very seriously. And reasonably. Now how about that cup of tea?"

Apart from clanking cups and saucers significantly, my mother had kept very quiet. I thought she might have decided to let my father handle everything. But then she said, "You can discuss what you like, all you like, as seriously and reasonably as you like. Just so long as there's no question of anyone upsetting or disturbing Nick."

"No one's planning to upset or disturb him, Beryl," my father said. He sounded as if he had things pretty well under control. "Dad's just paying us a friendly visit. Isn't that right, Dad?"

"Call it what you bloody like. It's all the same either way, as the old cow said to the bull. It doesn't make a hell of a lot of difference to me. Just so long as I have a yarn with Nick."

"That's all you want, Dad? A yarn with Nick?"

"Look," my mother said, "I must make it quite clear that –"

"Beryl," my father said, "be patient. We're all being quite reasonable. He just wants a yarn with Nick. That's all."

"How's your eyesight, son?" Grandfather Flinders asked.

"Not so bad, thanks Dad. I have to wear glasses for reading these days."

"Well, I wish you'd stick them on your bloody nose. There's been an empty glass sitting here in front of me for the last five minutes."

"Sorry, Dad." My father sounded more and more like a naughty, repentant boy.

"Great stuff. No doubt about it. Well, I'll be right to see Nick any minute now. Thank God someone in my family turned out all right. I been losing hope. You know that? I been losing hope for years. I couldn't believe the seed would all go bad. A man's got to have some faith. A man's got to hang on to something."

"I suppose so, Dad."

"What do you mean, you suppose so? Of course a man does. What the hell happened to my family, anyway? That's what I want to know. None of you turned out much good. Hardly an ounce of guts among the lot of you. Did the depression knock the stuffing out of you? Was that it? Did you all shrivel up with the first cold wind? You all look shrivelled to me anyway. Shrivelled and half-dead. You wouldn't believe it now, but men were men in this country once. It was a man's country. Now the women have taken over."

"Yes, Dad. You might be right."

"What do you mean, I might be right? I know I'm right."
He slammed down his glass. "Now where's Nick?"

"He might have gone back to sleep. Let's hope so anyway.
How about that cup of tea now, Dad? Then we can talk about
this thing. As a matter of fact, we have great problems with
Nick. We have trouble getting him to move around. It's all we
can do to get him out of the bedroom. He's never moved away
from the house. He doesn't want to see anyone. He doesn't want
to do anything much except brood."

"Is that right, eh? The lazy little bastard. I'll soon fix that."

"You'll fix nothing of the kind," my mother said.

"We'll see about that," Grandfather Flinders announced. His
chair scraped back and his feet clumped. "Let me see the young
swine. Just let me see him."

"Now, Beryl," my father said, "it can't do any harm. Not for
a minute or two. Let's not all fight about it again."

"Where *is* your loyalty?" my mother said. "Is it to me and
Nick? Or is it to him? Just let me get this clear."

"You're unreasonable," my father said. "You're being quite
unreasonable, Beryl."

"That's the worst thing you can say about anyone, isn't it?"

"Let's not say things we might regret later."

"You plan to let him go into Nick's room, don't you? You
planned it all along. That's it, isn't it?"

Grandfather Flinders didn't wait for them to settle the
argument. He strode through the house and then my door
banged open wide.

Chapter Ten

HE HAD A HUGE OLD BROAD-BRIMMED HAT STUCK sideways on his head. That was the first thing I noticed. That hat, and then his greasy baggy old herringbone trousers, the unbuttoned waistcoat with the watch-chain drooping, the bright check shirt also unbuttoned with the tie loose and askew, the crumpled shiny black suit-jacket with sleeves too short to cover his old bony wrists. His hobnailed boots were cracked and the colour of dried mud. A couple of fly-buttons were undone, and a torn race guide hung out of a jacket pocket. Grey hair brushed out where his shirt split over his chest. He looked as if he'd pretty well come straight from feeding his chickens and digging in his potato patch. Except for his twisted tie. Grandfather Flinders always put on his tie when he was going out anywhere. He only had the one. And there was hell to pay if he lost it, if Grandmother Flinders couldn't find it. He'd say how in Christ's name could anyone look decent without a tie.

He didn't look any older. He probably couldn't look any older, not even if he lived to be a hundred. His face would have gone well in a horror film. It was a great spidery tangle of lines and wrinkles with his fierce blue colour-blind eyes blazing out. He had a huge half-hooked nose, with a very bony bump in the middle, and his smile was filled with nicotiney stumps of teeth. He still had plenty of hair left, though; it straggled silvery from under his hat and curled around his big flappy ears. His face had always been dark with sun, so dark people sometimes mistook him for a Maori. He'd obviously had a shot at shaving before he left home, but there were neglected patches of grey bristles here and there about his chin.

"What's all this bull I been hearing about you?" he asked.

As he came across the room I could smell a variety of things, the brandy, pipe-tobacco smoke, home-made carbolic soap, and he'd certainly come straight from the chickens, all right.

"What do you mean?" I said.

"All this bull I been hearing about you. About you not getting up. And sitting here sulking. Is it true, you little poufter?"

My parents put their heads through the door. My mother looked very distressed, but my father looked as if he couldn't make up his mind one way or the other.

"Get the buggery out, will you?" he told them. "Can't you see I'm having a yarn with my grandson? This is going to be strictly private, between Nick and me. Clear out, you bloody fools, and leave me alone."

My father placed a hand on my mother's arm and they backed away, my mother looking even more distressed.

"And close the door," he instructed.

The door closed. There were mutterings on the other side.

"And don't listen, either," he bawled. "Damn spies." Their feet went reluctantly away to another part of the house. My mother's voice grew shrill again. "I warn you, Frank," she said. "I'm just warning you. If –"

"Now," said Grandfather Flinders, making himself comfortable on the edge of my bed, "now we better get down to business, fast. What the hell's the matter with you. Your leg still crook?"

"I can walk round on it. It's coming out of plaster tomorrow."

"You can walk round on it, eh? Then what's this about you brooding round the house all the time?"

"I still feel crook," I said.

"Bloody nonsense. You got nothing to feel crook about now. As far as I can see, you're still alive. Which is more than you can say for your cobber, the Maori fellow. You look a bit pale. That's all. Not enough sun. We can soon fix that. Why don't you walk round more?"

"Because people only want to talk to me."

"Naturally. Naturally people want to talk. It's all they're good for, some of them. Talking. You got to get used to that."

"And I get fed up with their stupid damn questions."

I could see I was going to get fed up with him fast too. He was like that minister, Sergeant Crimmins and Derek all rolled into one.

"Of course people ask bloody stupid questions, boy. Of course they do. You got to get used to that too. Statistically, ninety-seven point five per cent of the population is mentally deficient. I read that somewhere once, boy, and I never forgot it. It made a great impression on me. It explained a damn lot of things. You just got to make allowances for people, boy. They're not to blame for being mentally deficient. Naturally they ask stupid questions. Naturally."

"What about my father?" I asked.

"Of course he's not the full quid," he said. "Your grandmother's side of the family, of course. Your mother's eighteen bob in the pound too. As scatty as a fowl. Most women are. Your father's really an old woman anyway. Christ knows how I bred him."

"What about Derek?" That was a shrewd one. I'd got him there. Derek was the most brilliant of all his grandsons. "What about him?"

"Just a plain nut case. Beyond help, son. Anyone who starts seeing valleys like thighs is beyond human help, that's certain." He paused. "Now," he said, "who else is bothering you?"

I hesitated. "Well," I said, "there's Mrs Waikai, I suppose."

"Well, I don't know her, boy. But she's probably the same. Only one chance in forty of her not being the same. Poor woman."

"Someone's got to be all right, surely," I said. "Anyway, how do you know I'm sane?"

"I'm not saying you are. Anyway it's a pretty damn lonely business being sane in an insane world, boy."

"I don't feel terribly sane at the moment."

"That's a healthy sign. When someone admits it. Shows they know the difference."

He rose, hawked and spat out the window into my mother's hydrangeas. Then he sat down and rumbled his nose into a dirty scrap of handkerchief. I could see something important was coming. He cleared his throat too.

"All right," he said. "Tell me what you thought about. When you were lying up there in the bush."

"I don't know."

"Don't know?" he growled.

"I just don't remember," I said stubbornly.

"Who do you think you're fooling?"

"I don't want to fool anyone. I can't even fool myself."

"And you reckon you don't remember?"

"Maybe I just don't want to remember."

"Come on now. Try harder."

"All right," I said. "If you really want to know, I thought of you at one stage."

The remains of his teeth rose like yellow icebergs into his huge smile. "You did?" he said.

"You knew I did. That's why you asked me. I lay there wondering what you thought about when you were stuck in the bush with a broken thigh. What did you think about, anyway?"

His smile vanished. He took a badly charred pipe out of his pocket, stuck it in his mouth, then rolled a blob of black tobacco between his palms.

"I was wondering if anyone would remember to milk the cows. My bloody sons. Never could rely on any of them. All the lazy bastards ever wanted was to sit on their chuffs."

"Did they remember to milk them?" He'd forgotten the most important part of the story, as usual.

"Of course they forgot. They were too busy haring through the bush looking for me. They pretended they actually wanted to find me, the lying whores. But your grandmother remembered to milk them. A fine figure of a woman in those days, your grandmother. I mean she had a fine figure when she wasn't breeding. She was in calf a hell of a lot of the time." He put a match carefully to his poisonous looking tobacco, and vanished behind dense smoke. "Quite a girl," he said to me from the other side of the smoke, "quite a girl she was though. They don't make women like that any more."

"Were you in love with her?" I asked. This was one point I felt I ought to get straight. Also it stopped him asking questions about me. But he emerged fiercely from the smoke looking as if I'd stung him.

"Mind your own bloody business," he roared. "What's it got to do with you, you young prick?"

"You're asking me a lot of very personal questions. I thought I'd ask you one too."

"Never mind what I did to your grandmother. It's none of your business."

"I wasn't asking what you did to her. I was asking were you in love with her."

"Same thing, boy, same thing. So just keep your mouth shut about that, and you and me will get on better. You hear?"

"Well," I said, "since we're on the subject, you might as well hear the latest news. According to Derek, I'm queer."

It was beautiful to see Grandfather Flinders' face. He really sat up and listened. "What's that, boy? What's that?"

"Derek says I'm a queer. He says I got a fixation."

"And what in Christ's name is that?"

"A queer thing. Something psychological."

"Shit a brick," he said.

"He thinks he knows all about it. I heard him telling Mum and Dad how I must have got up to all sorts of dirty sex stuff with Sam Waikai in the bush."

His face bulged, and he looked likely to split a couple of veins. "Well, I'm stuffed. Did he say that? Did he?"

"He pretty well came right out and said that. Oscar Wilde and dirty old men, that's what he talked about. I heard him."

"No wonder you're crook. No bloody wonder. By Christ, wait till I lay my hands on that sneaky, uneducated little whore. I'll fix him. I'll wash his mouth out with carbolic. The little shit, I'll teach him a lesson for talking dirty."

One thing I decided about Grandfather Flinders, he was on my side all right. But I couldn't help grinning at the thought of him cleaning out Derek's mouth.

He put another match to his pipe. "Now tell me," he said, as smoke poured round the bed again, "you still feeling crook?"

"I don't know."

"You feel a little better, anyway?"

"I suppose I do, come to think of it."

"Of course you do. What you need, boy, is a holiday with your grandfather. You and me could get on well together. That's why I came down to see you. To take you back with me. Now what do you say?"

I had a vision of myself climbing aboard the next train out of Te Ika. I couldn't think of anything that would suit me better. "Great," I said.

"Good. We'll fix it up then." My bedsprings sighed with relief as he stood up. "I'll fix it up with your parents right now."

"I don't know what they'll say."

"What does it matter? It's up to you and me, isn't it? See you later."

He left the bedroom, streamers of smoke tangling behind him, and banged my door shut. I heard him traipse through the house calling out to my parents. Then there was a terrible kefuffle. I only heard scraps of it.

"I won't hear of it," my mother said. "And I'm not going to stand here and be abused. You understand, Frank. I always thought this was my house –"

"Now, now," my father said, "now, now."

"Well, I'm buggered," Grandfather Flinders said. "I never cease to be amazed at what goes on in this world. I never cease –"

"You hear me, Frank? Either he goes or I go. I will not stand here and endure this abuse. You must make your choice, and make it now. Your father or me."

"Look, Dad," my father said, "it's no use us getting all upset –"

"Damn me, I believe you're going to turn me out. My son. My own bloody son. Who reared you? That's what I want to know. Who brought you into this world, eh? It wasn't this woman here. I can tell you that right now."

"But, Dad –"

"And there's no question of Nick going off with him," my mother said. "No question of that at all. Just make that clear to him, Frank. I wouldn't tolerate it for a minute. Think of what he'd do to Nick."

She was beginning to sob. But not because of Grandfather Flinders. Because of me. I realized that suddenly. She cared about me, she really did. I started shivering. And I wished, after all, that Grandfather Flinders would clear off and leave us in peace. Perhaps he did make me feel better, but I didn't want him round if this was going to happen. I mean I didn't get on too badly with my parents, on the whole, and they did their best. They weren't to blame for the world. They weren't really to blame for me, either. I could see that, all right. If you want to know the truth, I can get pretty damn fond of my parents at times. And sometimes I can feel so sorry for them, the things they miss, the fun they've never had, the things that have gone wrong in their lives, I can get a lump like a rock in my throat. Grandfather Flinders was one of the things that had gone wrong in their lives. I could see that, all right, and that was why I'd rather he cleared off. Only the trouble was I also wanted to get out of Te Ika now; I wanted to clear off with him. All these things clanged together in my mind like a hundred bells and I shivered. I hadn't felt worse since I was up in the bush.

More kefuffle. Then slamming doors, banging, tramping, swearing, a final yell and a final slam. "My God," my father said. There was a long trembling silence, and then the house seemed to settle. "My God," he said again. "He's gone. He's gone, Beryl. Really gone. We've done it this time. Really done it. We've actually turned him out. You hear me, Beryl? We've actually turned him out of our house this time." He sounded as though he was in tears.

"Nonsense," my mother said, but she didn't sound too sure of herself either. "Nonsense. He walked out himself."

"The hell he did. We turned him out, Beryl. We actually turned my father out. Out of his son's house."

"Then it's about time. That's all I can say."

"But he came to see Nick. That's the point. He came to see his

85

grandson. He's an old man and it was important to him. Don't you understand? He came because he really cares about Nick."

"He came to interfere."

"But he didn't mean harm. He probably came with the best of intentions, but we just didn't give him a chance. What have we done? Turned him out. That's all we've done."

"We didn't turn him out. We simply stood up to him. That's all. It's about time one of his sons stood up to him. You ought to be proud of being the first. I only hope he takes the hint and stays away from us now."

"Beryl, you don't know what you're saying. You don't know what we're doing."

"I know what I'm doing, all right. And I've been dying to do it for twenty-five years or more. Believe me."

But Grandfather Flinders knew what he was doing too. I heard a rap on the new pane of glass my father had puttied into the bedroom window. There he was, his big boots in the flower bed outside, stalks and petals bruised and scattered round him, peering in at me and grinning in a twisted sort of way.

"Go away," I said. "Go away before they see you. There'll only be more trouble." But it was all I could do to say that, just about, the way I was feeling.

"Hey," he said, "aren't you coming home with me?"

"My leg's in plaster."

"Well, when it's out of plaster, then."

"I'll think about it," I promised.

"Think about it? What the hell do you mean? You were keen a few minutes ago."

"It depends on how they are."

I wished he wasn't so persistent. I could still hear their voices snapping and cracking in the other part of the house. This was the way Grandfather Flinders always left his sons' homes. In uproar. Arguments blazed away for hours, sometimes days, after he left.

"What's it got to do with them?" he asked.

"Because I don't want to hurt or upset them too much. That's all."

"Nonsense. They're enjoying themselves. Both of them. Listen."

I listened. It really sounded a lot of fun. They were hysterical with all the fun they were having. My mother was threatening to walk out forever. My father sounded about ready to shoot himself.

"They're both getting a great old kick out of it," he went on. "Your mother enjoyed chucking me out at last. And your father loves beating his breast. Don't take it too serious. You ought to hear your grandmother and me sometimes."

"No thanks."

"Well," he said finally, "I'd better see about a train home. You'll be coming up to see me, won't you?"

He tramped off. The sobbing and shouting died away in the other part of the house. After a while I heard birds singing round the cabbage trees over by the creek, and then kids skidding along the footpath on scooters. One thing about it, you always remembered any day that Grandfather Flinders turned up. Also you learned to appreciate peace and quiet.

My mother came into the room with breakfast on a tray. Her eyes were quite dry.

"Don't forget your exercise today," she said. "And, by the way, I saw Mrs Waikai in the street yesterday."

I didn't have anything to say. My mother hesitated for a moment.

"Nick, listen to me. She's coming over on Saturday. I'm sorry, Nick. I had to tell a lie. I just couldn't put her off any longer. I told her that you'd said you were ready to see her now."

"You what?"

"I told her you said you were ready to see her. Nick, you must understand. This couldn't go on. And she understands, Nick, she really does. But she says you mustn't feel guilty."

"Who says I feel guilty?"

"No one does. Mrs Waikai just said you shouldn't, that's all. Anyway there's no need to talk about it now. I just wanted to tell you that she's coming over on Saturday."

I did a quick calculation. My plaster was to come off on

Thursday, so today must be Wednesday. I had exactly three days to think about what I was going to say to Mrs Waikai. Three days to prepare to go back into a part of my life that already seemed as dead and distant as Sam.

"Nick, I know I've asked you this before. But is there anyone else you'd like to see?"

"Anyone else?"

"Any friends," she said hopefully.

"I told you there isn't anyone else. And don't start inventing them for me, please."

"All right, Nick. Please yourself."

She was very careful not to say anything about Grandfather Flinders, though she did sniff the air a couple of times, as if she could still smell him, before she left the room.

"Friends," I said into my breakfast. "Friends, for God's sake."

After breakfast I heard my father snipping away at a hedge. Eventually he came into the bedroom, sweaty and flushed, not looking altogether the happiest man in the world.

"We want you to ignore anything that happened this morning, Nick," he said. "Just erase it from your mind."

I wish he hadn't started in on it. My mother had the right idea. To talk about something else.

"All right," I said, "so nothing happened this morning. Grandfather Flinders didn't come."

"That's the idea," he agreed.

He actually had a shot at smiling, but he wasn't spectacularly successful.

After he left the room I lay looking at the wall, thinking about what he'd said. "Erase it from my mind, for God's sake," I said finally.

Then I realized, for the first time, that I was actually talking to myself. Again. The way things were, my old friend Tanny was probably all set for a reappearance.

"You keep away," I said aloud, just in case. "You were just a figment of my imagination. Anyway I grew out of you. Boys my age don't have invisible friends."

88

I could almost hear him laugh, somewhere in my head, and then I knew I was really afraid.

The doctor arrived on schedule the next day. The son of old Doctor MacFarlane, who drank himself out of practice, he was very efficient. He chipped and peeled off the plaster, and there was my leg all in one piece. But so pale and shrivelled it seemed to belong to someone else.

"I hope you'll give it plenty of use, Nick," he said. "Walk around on it as much as you like. The more the better."

"You never know," I joked, "I might even try a stroll up to Auckland."

Perhaps my parents overheard, or perhaps he passed the remark back to them. Anyway later in the day my mother said, "Nicholas, there's just one thing we should perhaps clear up. There's absolutely no question of you visiting Grandfather Flinders."

Chapter Eleven

I GOT UP TO AUCKLAND BEFORE DARK ON FRIDAY NIGHT.
I only needed one look at the traffic raging through the city
in the rush-hour, then I took off through the suburbs fast. I
found Grandfather Flinders digging up potatoes in the cool
evening. He was wearing the same check shirt, and his unbuttoned black waistcoat. His tie was gone, though. He had a
red handkerchief knotted round his neck. "Here," he said, and
handed me the garden fork, "make yourself useful. Turn up a
few more." He mopped his face. "Been a scorcher of a day. A
bloody scorcher. You certainly took your time about coming,
didn't you? Where is your grandmother? Where is that woman?
She seen you yet?"

I hadn't had time to get my pack off my back, let alone search
out Grandmother Flinders. She was feeding food scraps to the
chickens. When Grandfather Flinders called her, she came
wandering ghostly out of the dusk. "Who is it?" she said.
"Who's there? Oh dear me, it's you Nick. Oh dear me." She
dropped her scrap-bowl with a bang, and flew at me like an old
thin bird. Her face felt soapy smooth against mine as she
hugged and kissed. "Nick, Nick," she kept saying, "are you
better now?"

"For God's sake," Grandfather Flinders growled, "give the
boy a chance to get his breath."

"I don't see that you're giving him any time." She grabbed
the garden fork from my hands and held it up. "What's the boy
doing with this?"

"Digging spuds. Giving his old grandfather a hand. That's
what he's doing with it."

She threw down the garden fork in disgust, not even listening
to him, and hugged me again with her thin arms. There wasn't
much to Grandmother Flinders, but that didn't stop her over-

whelming me. But I felt pretty damn glad to see her again. To tell the truth, I'd always liked her a whole lot more than Grandfather Flinders. The old boy could be a constant pain in the neck, but Grandmother Flinders never was. Besides, she could keep him in his place, and sometimes even stop him being a pain in the neck. No one else could.

"Oh dear me," she said. "You sure you're all right? Sure?"

"I'm fine."

"You're thin, Nick," she said, the pot calling the kettle black. "Terribly thin. You're going to need a lot of building up." She meant porridge. She claimed to have built all her children up on smoky, burnt bush porridge. "Come on inside. You need something to eat, I'm sure."

"I knew I'd never get those bloody spuds dug," Grandfather Flinders said. "I might have known."

"You've had all day," she said. "If you'd dug them this morning, instead of looking for golf balls, we'd be a whole lot better off."

"Never mind," he said, "I got you to help me get them off to market now, haven't I, Nick?"

"Leave Nick alone," she said. "If you think you're going to have this poor sick child dig potatoes while you laze round the golf links, Hubert Flinders, you've got another think coming."

The golf links were not far from their house. One of his chief money-making hobbies was collecting lost balls from the scrub at the edge of the fairways. Often he grabbed them before the owners had even had time to start looking. And any little kids who tried to muscle in on his business were scared off pretty fast. He could be a fairly fearsome sight when he charged through the scrub. He sold the balls at the clubhouse, sometimes to the original owners; he called the money his brandy and betting fund. If the racehorses gave him a bad time, or his brandy supply got low, he became frantic in his search for lost balls. I knew all about this because he'd had me scratching around for balls in the scrub often enough before. He used to pay me a penny a ball, and then sell them at two or three shillings each. Sometimes I made sixpence a day. He paid me this grudgingly while putting a pound or more into his fund.

While the old boy grumbled into the evening, I limped into the house with Grandmother Flinders. She sat me down in the living room and then bustled off into the kitchen. I really felt at home. For one thing, their place had a special smell. A pretty old and musty smell, but nice and familiar too. You knew where you were, right away, when you stepped into their place. It was the only place I could really call home; my parents lived in town after town before we finally arrived in Te Ika, and even there we shifted from house to house before they settled on one in particular. I suppose we hadn't had time to develop a special smell; anyway even at the best of times I'd never felt specially at home in Te Ika. Here it was different though. Just that ancient smell told me. It reminded me of all the times in my life, all the different stages in my growing, when I'd been brought here to see my grandparents. Of course there were plenty of familiar things to see too. The lace curtains, the dark old wallpaper patterned with harps and ivy, the velvet chairs bumpy with broken springs, the worn sheepskin rugs on the floor, the mantelpiece jammed with knick-knacks, the old rifle on the wall and the decrepit stag's head. There were photographs pretty well everywhere. Grandfather Flinders, the champion axeman, in a black singlet beside a chopped log. Grandfather Flinders, the crack shot, sitting on a huge tusker. One of those slab huts with corrugated iron chimneys in the bush, and eleven ragged kids, six boys and five girls, standing outside; my father hadn't been born at that stage. But by the look of Grandmother Flinders, who was in the photograph too, he was well on the way. My great-grandfather's big homestead up north; that picture was getting pretty faded now. I suppose someone in our family might still have owned it, if it hadn't been for my great-grandfather's fondness for booze and racehorses. It was a very painful story. There were also one or two photographs of Grandmother Flinders when she was young; she looked fairly terrific, even in her ancient clothes, and far too sexy for the daughter of a Presbyterian minister. You could certainly see why Grandfather

Flinders had gone soft on her anyway. Not that he looked too ugly himself, when he was younger. He was there again and again. The hunter, the fisherman, the axeman, the runner. And the handsome ball of muscle who was once a personal bodyguard to George V when he toured New Zealand before he was crowned. Most of the other photos were of daughters and sons. My father at his graduation ceremony, for example. Or wartime photographs of other sons in army uniform. There was a Military Cross hanging by Uncle Fred's; he hadn't come back from the war. He was working in a punishment squad, digging latrines for being absent without leave, when the Germans made a surprise attack. He finished off ten Germans before he was shot himself. Grandfather Flinders quite liked telling this story. He said it showed what a bit of healthy discipline could do for a man.

He didn't tell, though, about how he locked himself up in his room for a week after the news about Uncle Fred came; or how he nearly refused to go and collect the medal. And personally I still can't see the value of digging latrines in wartime.

Uncle Fred, his youngest and favourite son, died years before I came along. But one of my earliest memories was of Grandfather Flinders haranguing his other sons, saying what an example of spirit Fred should be to them. The war must have already been way in the past, because I was born in 1947. I don't suppose that was a particularly important or marvellous year; anyway I've never heard anyone speak of it. And I certainly don't recall a damn thing about it myself. But I do recall that Grandfather Flinders was still holding forth about Fred some time after I was born. So he really must have been fairly fond of Fred. "Fred was game for anything, he liked taking risks," I can remember him saying.

"He liked sucking up a lot of booze too," someone muttered.

"Who's contradicting me?" Grandfather Flinders demanded, glaring round his sons. "Who the hell is contradicting me?"

No one owned up; no one was game enough. When Grandfather Flinders collected his sons round him, something he liked to do regularly, he always had a few light lumps of wood stacked conveniently by his chair; he could throw these very accurately to settle a family argument, or stop someone contradicting.

Sitting there with these ancient memories in my head, I jumped in my seat when Grandmother Flinders twittered back into the living room. There was a pleasant smell of something cooking in the kitchen. "Nick, Nick," she said. "Dear me, I've only just thought about it. Your parents."

"I sent them a telegram on my way. After my first ride."

"Your first ride?"

"I hitch-hiked."

"Hitch-hiked? You walked all that way? On that leg?"

"Hitch-hiking isn't hiking. I didn't walk too far, don't worry. My first ride took me to the middle of a town, so I sent a telegram from there. I could only afford thirteen words. I just said where I was going and for them not to worry. And I sent my love. I could just afford to say love too."

She looked alarmed. "You mean you left without telling them?"

"Of course I did. It wasn't any use telling them. They'd only have stopped me coming. After all that wrangle on Wednesday morning."

"Wednesday morning? Oh dear me, don't tell me Hubert's been at it again."

She always called him Hubert when she was angry with him. It put him in his place. True, it was his real name, but he liked to forget it, and his friends, people the same age, called him Barney. She called him Barney too, when she wasn't angry.

"Was it that bad?" she asked.

I nodded and lowered my eyes. "It was pretty bad this time."

"I should have known. He'd hardly gone to Te Ika before he was back again. The old devil. He never said a word."

"I suppose I shouldn't be telling you," I said. "Perhaps you'd better not tell him I told you."

She ignored me and went to the door and called, "Hubert, Hubert, where are you? Hubert?"

But old Hubert was probably too busy hiding himself somewhere on the section. Perhaps in the privy. As soon as he heard

94

her call his name in a sharp tone of voice, he would guess that the whole story had come out. And he'd take cover. The privy was his usual retreat. Or the chicken house. He could spend hours in both places studying racehorse form by candlelight if Grandmother Flinders happened to be angry about something.

When she got a grim silence for an answer, she turned from the door. "The old devil. I should have known. Well, we'd better let Frank and Beryl know you've arrived safely. They'll be worried to death."

"At least they must know where I am. I suppose they guessed even before they got my telegram. When they found my bed empty this morning."

"What did you come for, then? If you knew they weren't going to like it?"

I didn't want to talk about that. "I just had to come. That's all."

"Not that we aren't glad to see you, Nick." And to show me she came over and gave me a healthy smacker on the cheek. "But you shouldn't really have come if it was going to upset them."

"I just had to," I said stubbornly. It was ridiculous the way she reminded me of Mrs Waikai. They weren't at all alike.

"Well, you're better. That's the main thing." She'd decided to take what she called a large view of the whole business, so I knew I was all right. Certainly she had no intention of letting me go, sending me back. "I'll just phone through a telegram to say you're all right. And to let them know *I'm* looking after you, not Hubert. But just wait till I get my hands on Hubert. Honestly, Nick, that man gets worse with age."

She went to the phone and in a voice that seemed to be suddenly shaky and old sent through the message. It was a pretty antique telephone, but Hubert refused to touch the thing at all. He said the confounded machine was likely to give a man an electric shock. It was all right for Grandmother Flinders to take the risk, though. If he wanted to put a bet on a racehorse she had to ring it through for him.

When she finished with the phone she fetched my dinner, a

95

thick slab of steak with chips and four fried eggs. She looked very satisfied when I polished everything off. I'd been starving on rabbity salads and things for two months.

"That's the boy," she said. "We'll have you fit in no time." She meant fat; fit and fat were the same to her. "There was quite a bit about you even in the Auckland papers, you know."

I really didn't want to go into all that again. "Yes," I said.

"We were awfully worried at the time. That you might be more hurt than the papers said. The papers never get things right. Who was this friend of yours? This Maori boy?"

"Just a kid I knew. We knocked round together."

"It's so sad, the whole business. I suppose you miss him."

"I suppose I do."

"But you'll make new friends, Nick."

"Yes," I said. "Of course."

"You look terribly pale. And tired suddenly. In fact, you're not looking very well at all. What you need, Nick, is plenty of building up and plenty of sleep. I'll go and make up your bed."

When she left the room, old Hubert came creeping in. He'd been studying horse form somewhere, all right. He had a race guide in his hands. "Switch on that confounded machine for me, boy," he said.

He meant the radio. He never touched the radio or electric light switches himself.

I turned the radio on, and a Friday night sports programme came up. An announcer discussed the next day's racing fixtures and named the horses which had been scratched. While he listened, Hubert marked things up in his race guide with a blue pencil. When the programme was finished he looked at me sadly. "Don't tell her too much. That's been my principle all through life. Too much of anything isn't good for her."

"I'll try to remember," I promised.

"You and me, we might have some private things to talk about. Things we don't want to get back to her."

"Like what?"

"Like something I'm planning to talk to you about."

"Can't you tell me now?"

"No," he said firmly. "I got other problems right now. And here's one of them."

Grandmother Flinders came into the room. "Hubert," she said, "have you been upsetting Frank and Beryl again? Come on. Tell me the truth. Have you?"

He just sat there, rubbing his dry old lips together and looking down at his big thick hands.

"Hubert," she said, "tell me the truth. Have you been up to your old tricks again?"

He fetched his pipe from a pocket and stuck it defiantly in his mouth. "I haven't been up to anything," he said.

"No?"

"No." He struck a match. When he was hidden by enough smoke, he went on, "I just went to see them. But I wasn't welcome. That's all. Anyone who says any different is a damn fool of a liar."

"Didn't you appreciate that they had a sick child in the house?"

"Balls," he said. "Absolute balls."

"Hubert, please watch your –"

"I'll tell you what he's sick of. Sick of old women and that bloody idiot swine of a brother."

"Hubert, you're not answering my question. Apart from not watching your language. And you're not telling the truth. Nick, it's time you went off to bed. An early night will do you good."

I stood up.

"And switch that damn machine off before you go," Hubert said. "It's either one thing or the other, and I can't switch her off."

Chapter Twelve

THE THING I LIKED ABOUT LIVING WITH THEM WAS THAT
I could walk round anywhere without people looking at me,
without meeting people I knew, and without getting stupid
questions. That was the best thing. I couldn't have done that at
Te Ika. Not that their suburb didn't remind me of Te Ika in
some ways. When Hubert first planted himself down here near
Auckland, it was a fairly bare stretch of land. It was also the last
land he was ever likely to own. He'd gone through about
twenty farms in the King Country and elsewhere by that time.
He had a knack for shifting while the going was good, so before
he ruined one place he always managed to buy another. Grandmother Flinders said he was a kind of King Midas in reverse,
everything he touched turned to mud. But it wasn't true here.
When he settled for this land it was all scrubby and swampy, but
he cleared the scrub and drained the swamp and milked a few
cows for town supply and stabled racehorses for one or two
trainers he knew. He also planted pine trees which were now
over fifty feet tall. He built the house with pit-sawn kauri and
broke a collar-bone when sliding off the corrugated iron he was
hammering on to the roof. There was hardly another house in
sight in those days. Hubert thought he was keeping Auckland
at a distance. But it turned out that actually Auckland was just
keeping Hubert at a distance, till it was ready. And it wasn't long
coming. First a couple of factories went up about a mile along
the road. The next thing houses were popping up here and there
around his land. Surveyors came to peg out new streets, and the
rates shot up. Hubert hung on to his land as long as he could
until the rates forced him to sell, acre by acre. He also sold off
his cows, one by one, while carpenters hammered, bricklayers
clattered and cement-mixers churned. He had court cases in all
directions at this time; he even sued one builder for making

enough racket to turn his last two cows dry. He sued some for trespass, others for blocking his view. He was also prosecuted himself for obscene language, for aggravated assault, and for behaving in a menacing fashion with a loaded firearm. When it was all over, anyway, his straggling old house with peeling weatherboards sat there among neat new homes on quarter acre sections. He still had about two acres of land which he wouldn't sell at any price. But the land he had left really wasn't up to much. It ran back behind the house. There was about an acre for his potato patch and his chickens. The rest was a broken clay bank covered with scrub, gorse and ragwort; it was a mystery why he hung on to it, because it only brought him trouble. The local council accused him of growing noxious weeds there, and now and then reluctantly took him to court. They didn't seem to like the court cases anywhere near as much as he did. Hubert said it was the principle of the thing, he had a moral right to grow what he liked there, even noxious weeds. He would denounce the council as a collection of power-drunk maniacs and have the court in uproar over the injustice he suffered. But it did look, sometimes, as if he might be cultivating the weeds deliberately so he could have the court cases. Because the fact is he did attack the other growth, the scrub, with a slasher from time to time. No one saw any point in this, except that it kept him fit, because he only let it grow again.

Anyway the district wasn't too different from Te Ika now, except that it was supposed to be part of Auckland city. The streets weren't rough and stony any more; they were sealed. Shrubs grew beside the concrete footpaths, and there were trellis fences, hedges and concrete walls in front of the houses. There were all sorts of bright flowers and creepers and vegetable patches and farty banana trees where you'd have seen only grass, cows, fences and old Hubert's pine trees before; almost all his trees, except on his land, had been felled. The houses were mostly clean and bright with regular coats of paint, venetian blinds hung in the front windows, television aerials jutted from the corrugated rooftops, plaster gnomes and rabbits squatted round goldfish ponds, and lawnmowers rattled all weekend. Hubert took a scythe to the long grass tangling round his house just once a year. He said he'd never made a religion out of grass and he wasn't going to start now, even if it was his misfortune to be born in a country which was only good for growing grass. A kindly neighbour, keen on keeping the tone of the neighbourhood up, and property values too, once offered to lend Hubert his motor-mower; that was another assault case. Apart from the lawnmowers, which were steadily becoming more motorized and noisy, the only sound you heard regularly was babies crying. You could hear them almost any time of day. And see their nappies flashing bright on spinning clotheslines.

The best thing about their place was that it was less than a mile from the sea, an easy walk. My leg got all the exercise it needed. First walking down to the beach, then swimming, and walking home. I soon lost my limp and I spent ages on that beach. It was a pleasant place, a small tidal bay with pohutukawa, kowhai and puriri thick on the cliffs around. Most houses were hidden in the bush and if you struck the beach early enough in the morning it could be very peaceful. Later in the day the place was noisy with people, speedboats and transistor radios. I hadn't realized before just how much I'd really been missing the sea. When I first went to Te Ika I was hungry for it, as a matter of fact, so hungry I thought I'd starve and waste away. But the Waipa river did seem to make up for it, after a while. The Waipa and Sam, who I found in the river. I suppose that was the turning point, that day I pulled Sam Waikai out of the Waipa. Because I wasn't specially hungry for the sea any more, and Te Ika didn't seem so bad to me after all, even if it was inland. Besides, there was the bush. Sam introduced me to the bush. I hadn't really known the bush, or lived in it, before I went to Te Ika. With Sam, the bush and the river, I thought I'd forgotten the sea; I told myself I didn't care about it one way or the other. But now I realized I'd been kidding myself, to some extent. There was nothing quite like the sea. I could float in it for hours while the sun warmed my face. Then I swam lazily back to shore, threw myself down into warm sand and dozed off. Sometimes I fished from rocks, turning browner all the time. Grandmother Flinders certainly couldn't complain about my colour for long.

Not that there weren't some bad moments at the beginning. It was a while before I shook off Te Ika. The first few nights I usually woke up to find the light on and Grandmother Flinders bending over me.

"What's wrong, Nick, what's the trouble?"

"Nothing," I said, though I was trembling.

"You were yelling your head off. Was it a bad dream?"

"I can't remember," I lied. I was sweating with relief. I wasn't in the bush any more. I wasn't helping Mrs Waikai search for Sam.

"Dear me," she said. "It's your stomach. You need more lining on your stomach." She rushed away for a mug of hot sweet milk. And in the morning I had to face a mountain of porridge and a great heap of fried eggs. Hubert and I would sit eating away for the best part of an hour.

Then there was Derek.

My parents must have had a long conference after I vanished and the telegrams arrived. Anyway my father didn't come up to fetch me home, as I half expected. Instead they rang Derek in Auckland and asked him to talk me into going home. Poor old Derek; I mean I can actually say poor old Derek these days, though I couldn't then. I was still pretty much afraid of him, he seemed to know so much.

He came out to see me that first Sunday. Luckily for Derek, because it was a Sunday Hubert was away supplementing his brandy and betting fund. I wasn't helping him for a couple of reasons. One, because Grandmother Flinders said he wasn't going to start dragging me everywhere the moment I arrived. Second, because I was still haggling over my future commission on lost golf balls. I reckoned I should get threepence a ball now that I was going on for sixteen. Hubert said bloody nonsense, in his day kids would have gone down on their knees for a penny a ball. As a result, apart from a spell on the beach early in the morning, I spent most of that Sunday yarning with Grandmother Flinders.

She liked yarning with me. There weren't too many people she could yarn with any more. The women around were mostly young and busy with husbands and babies and washing machines, and anyway there wasn't much profit in talking to a lonely old lady for hours. Not when there were things to be done. I didn't mind, though. I had all the time in the world to listen.

"Nick," she'd say, "stop me if I'm boring you."

"No," I'd say, "I'm interested. I really am."

And she'd go on, for example, about how she'd cooked over an open fire in those slab huts in the bush. The fireplaces were usually huge, about fifteen feet by ten, and she'd have a half dozen different things cooking over the flames. It wasn't so bad in winter, when there was frost or fog outside, but cooking over those fireplaces could be a pretty sweaty business in summer.

Then she'd tell me about how her kids were born. Some of this stuff could be pretty horrifying. About how Uncle Harry arrived prematurely in one of those huts, for example. Hubert was away at the time, and the other kids were too young to help. They simply stood around howling while she heaved in labour and produced Uncle Harry. Then there were the twins, Uncle Ed and Aunt Margaret; they'd been born in the fern by the side of a bush-track before she could get to hospital. Hubert had to leave her there, and ride off to get the doctor. She said she was surprised how they lived, in the end. But what really surprised me was how she'd lived through all that stuff. Boy, I know I wouldn't have.

Another thing, I know I wouldn't have stood old Hubert either. Looking after him should have been enough to kill anyone. The way he dragged her round from place to place, I mean, with that tribe of ragged kids getting bigger all the time. It sounded as if he hadn't cared about her, or them, at all. In fact I couldn't help saying something about him being selfish.

"No, Nick, not selfish," she said. "He wasn't selfish, really. Preoccupied perhaps. You see, he was always fighting with something. With the land, or with people. It's just he's a man who made his mind up very young not to let himself be used as a doormat by the world."

"So he used his own family as a doormat."

"It may seem like that to others, Nick," she said gently, "but it's not really so. At least it didn't seem so to us. You see, we understood him. Even if he never really understood us. He was a real man, Nick, and he wasn't afraid to stand up to the world. You couldn't help admiring him."

And you couldn't help wanting to give him a good kick in the behind, either. Even so many years, after. For all she said now, I was sure she must have felt that way at times.

"You mustn't mention to your grandfather that we've been talking about these things," she went on. "It would make him very unhappy."

The way I saw it, he should have had that coming long ago. It was probably too late now, but if someone had made him unhappy he might have woken up a bit and taken some responsibility. But he'd been able to get away with anything. That was the way it looked to me. I promised not to say anything, though, and I never did.

We were still sitting there yarning at the back of the house when Derek arrived. He looked fairly smart in jacket and tie. It was just a pity Derek had grown old so young; his hair had half vanished down the middle of his head, and his face was almost as unhappy as my father's. Grandmother Flinders kissed him. "How nice to see you, Derek dear," she said. "We don't see much of you at all these days."

No one said why.

He seemed pretty nervous until I explained that Hubert was away collecting golf balls. Then he was keen to get down to business, fast, in case the old boy came back. "I have one or two things I'd like to talk to you about urgently, Nick," he said.

Grandmother Flinders rose. "It's all right," she said, when I offered to help her inside. "You two boys can talk as much as you like. I'm going to have my afternoon nap. God bless, Derek. And do come to see us again soon."

She went off looking tired and trembly. She seemed to have

exhausted herself talking to me. There really wasn't much left of her at all.

Derek took a deep breath. "Now," he said, "what's all this about, Nick? You might tell me."

"I'm staying here. That's all it's about."

"You know, of course, that you've upset them terribly at home."

"I know. I'm sorry about that. I really am. I can't help it, though."

"This isn't going to help you, Nick. Staying here won't help you at all. You'll have to face up to things, you know."

"What things?"

"Your life. Everything. You just can't clear off. It solves nothing."

"I don't know what you're gabbling about. Who said I was trying to solve anything?"

"Please take me seriously, Nick."

"I am. That's why I can't understand this stuff about solving things. So far as I'm concerned, there's nothing to be solved."

He sighed.

"Nick, we all know it's very sad about Sam Waikai. But you're still alive. You understand? You've got to accept responsibility for yourself."

"That's the trouble. That's just what I've done. Accepted responsibility for myself."

"By running away? Come now, Nick, that's really not good enough. Why did you run away?"

"Because I wanted to be somewhere where people wouldn't know me. Where I wouldn't have to go nutty in a bedroom because people felt so sorry for me they wanted to ask stupid questions. What I like about Grandfather Flinders is he doesn't feel sorry for me. And I wanted to be somewhere where other people didn't make up my mind for me. Besides, I just wanted to swim in the sea for a while."

"Couldn't you have talked about this with Mum and Dad? They would have been quite agreeable to your staying with me in Auckland. I'm sure they would have. But your coming here makes for all sorts of family complications. It's like your saying, right out aloud, that your parents aren't good enough for you. That you prefer your grandparents. Can't you see that? Can't you see how it looks to other people?"

I couldn't, as a matter of fact. If people were dumb enough to look at things that way, then they were too dumb to worry about. "Anyway," I said, "there would have been far more family complications if I'd stayed back there. I can tell you that right now."

"What do you mean?"

"I've got more family now than you know about. And I just want a chance to make up my mind about it all."

"I don't understand, Nick. You mean these Maoris —"

"I mean Mrs Waikai. You wouldn't know about her. You see, she made Sam and me like brothers. And that makes me her son, in a way. As far as she's concerned I'm her boy now. She even tells Mum that. Mum doesn't take it seriously, of course."

"But surely you don't, Nick."

"I have to, don't I? If Mrs Waikai does."

"I don't see that at all."

"If you don't see that, then you can't see anything. You've been going on about responsibility. Well, that's what I mean. Someone's going to be hurt, whatever I do. Whatever way I turn."

"Nick, you mustn't let guilt run away with you. You must keep a sense of proportion."

"You don't understand. It was the same before. Except Sam was alive then, and it seemed more reasonable me going over there all the time. How's it going to look now?"

But Derek wasn't paying much attention. He was getting nervous again, and twitching looks over his shoulder in case Hubert was coming back. He seemed to get jumpy at the slightest sound. "Let's go for a walk, Nick," he said suddenly.

So we walked past the privy and the chicken-house down past the potato patch to the back of the section. It was cool under the pines, and the dry needles made hundreds of little snapping sounds under our feet.

"Look, Nick," he rambled on. "You mustn't think I don't understand. Because I do."

I didn't see why he should come and see me then. If he already understood. But I didn't say anything. I supposed he might as well talk himself out.

"You've got to understand, Nick, that at the moment your escape mechanism is operating. So you can't face up to the fundamental issues involved."

"My what is operating?"

"Your escape mechanism."

"That's pretty interesting," I said. "I didn't even know I had one."

"It's just a psychological process. We all have mental escape mechanisms."

"What's it like? Has it got gears and everything? I mean first, second, top and reverse?"

"In a manner of speaking, yes, I suppose it has." But he didn't seem too sure; he looked flustered. "Look, Nick, the really fundamental thing, to which you must face up, is your friendship with Sam Waikai. And you must face up to the fact that he's dead."

"I thought I'd already done a pretty good job of facing up to that. Back up there in the bush."

"Well, the point is that you mustn't start blaming yourself or anything like that. Though it's perfectly natural from a psychological point of view. At times like these you're liable to project free-floating guilt here there and everywhere. You must learn to recognize your friendship for what it was, and start again."

"Don't get on to that stuff again," I warned him.

"Nobody else can really help you, Nick. You must do it yourself."

"Then what in hell are you going on about?"

"I'm just pointing out that you can't do it by running away. That's all. You're only mentally avoiding fundamental issues."

He rambled on happily through this psychological stuff. He couldn't seem to get it straight in his head that I'd come up here because I wanted to. He was determined to make a hell of a big mystery out of it all.

"And I think you should go home, Nick. That's the main thing. They're in a terrible state about this back there. They rang me up on Friday night and again last night."

"I'm sorry about all that. I really am. But I can't go back right now."

"So that's your last word," he said. "Is it?"

"Tell them I'll come back when I'm ready."

"When will that be?"

"I just told you. When I'm ready." It was really terrible, the way he couldn't understand a simple thing like that. It's not that Derek's dull or anything. It's just that he's all complicated with knowing so much. "When I'm ready I'll have a shot at getting this mechanism thing into reverse."

"Anything else you want me to tell them?"

"Yes. That I'm feeling a whole lot better already. But I need a bit more time, that's all. Tell them I'll write a letter. I really will, I promise. And, while you're at it, you can tell them to give my love to Mrs Waikai. And to say I'm sorry I missed her before I left, but I'll see her as soon as I get back."

"Well, if that's all you've got to say –"

"I've had a damn lot to say as far as I can see."

Derek shot a swift look in the direction of the house. "Isn't that Grandfather Flinders arriving back?"

"That's him, all right."

"Look, Nick, I think I'll just dodge off across the back of the section."

"It's all right. He's dug all the potatoes he wants for the next week or two. I mean don't panic about him making you dig any."

He was in a terrible sweat. "It's not that. It's just that I've got people to see this afternoon. At a barbecue affair, on a beach near here. I'm late already."

At that moment Hubert was muddling round at the rear of the house. He hadn't seen us under the pine trees at the back of the section.

"I'll just call him over, if you like," I offered. "He'd be delighted to have a quick little yarn with you. He'd be awfully sorry to miss you."

"I'm going to be awfully sorry to miss him, because I really must leave. Really must. Give them both my love, Nick. Say I'm sorry I had to go."

He hared off, in his neat clothes and shiny shoes, up into the scrub and gorse and noxious weeds. He tried to look very cool, as if this was something he did every day, but he didn't look any too cool scrambling up a clay bank and through a barbed wire fence. Something ripped, either his pants or his jacket, but he was in too much of a hurry to notice. He looked back, once, and gave me a feeble grin as he waved goodbye. He was safe; Hubert still hadn't noticed him.

I walked slowly back to the house, kicking at pine cones. Hubert looked grumpy. I guessed it had been a bad day for the brandy and betting fund.

"Derek came," I said. I thought I might as well get it over with. He was bound to get into a fine old rage about Derek. "He had quite a bit to say. And he wanted me to go home."

"Did he now?" he said vaguely, studying one of his retrieved golf balls. It was in poor condition, and looked as if it would only fetch about a shilling. "And what else did he have to say?"

"I don't know. It was all too deep for me." I was feeling pretty tired, as a matter of fact, and didn't want to go into it all again.

"And you still reckon it's not enough," he said.

"What's not enough?"

"A penny a ball."

"No," I said. "It's not anywhere near enough."

"All right," he said. "We'll make it twopence."

Still grumpy, he marched off inside.

Chapter Thirteen

WITH FINDING GOLF BALLS, DIGGING THE GARDEN, listening to old Hubert, yarning with Grandmother Flinders, swimming and fishing, my days were fairly full. I went to bed tired every night. There were some days when Te Ika might just as well have been sunken under the sea, or swallowed up by the earth, for all it concerned me. I wrote a letter off to my parents, though, and got a long one in reply. It was from my father. He said he hoped things had turned out for the best, but still it would be better if I didn't stay away from home too long. After a while my mother wrote too. She kept off the subject of where I was staying, and just gave me a selection of Te Ika news. She hoped I would be home soon. In a PS she said Mrs Waikai called round at the house regularly for news of me, and sent her love. I wrote back and said, well, I expected I would be home sooner or later, but right now I was in the middle of a difficult situation.

I was telling the truth, as a matter of fact. I was in a difficult situation. Right in the middle; Hubert on one side, Grandmother Flinders on the other. They were getting pretty snaky with each other. Of course it had started up with me, and that was why I felt responsible and couldn't very well clear out. My leaving wouldn't have made any difference to the situation, not any more. It all started when they both wanted to tell me things, and one got jealous if the other took up too much of my time. Grandmother Flinders told me on the side I could do a lot of better things than listen to the ignorant rubbish Hubert talked. Hubert told me I shouldn't take too much notice of Grandmother Flinders and her stories, she was a clucky old hen at the best of times.

Before long they were at it good and proper.

So there I was, in the middle. In the house I had to act as a referee. And if they weren't speaking to each other, which was quite often, I carried messages between.

"I don't know how I lasted nearly sixty years with him," she said. "Tell him it's sausages for dinner."

"I should of cleared out long ago," he said. "Tell her I want breakfast at seven in the morning."

"Tell him to get his own breakfast," she said.

"And tell her to feed those sausages to the fowls," he said.

But she got his breakfast, and he ate the sausages. Things didn't fall to pieces altogether, not after sixty years. All the same, it could be bad enough at times. When I got tired of trying to straighten them out, of trying to make them see reason, I took off for the beach. After a while there I'd be fresh for refereeing again. I tried to make a fair division in the jobs I did for them, so there could be no disputes. If I went with him after lost golf balls one day, I'd spend the next day doing something for her. Like going up to the shops, or digging a new cabbage patch. This was intended to put an end to one of her grievances, because she maintained that, as far as Hubert was concerned, gardening began and ended with potatoes. She'd always had to grow other things herself. She'd been on to Hubert about a decent cabbage patch for the last ten years, but he preferred to harvest golf balls.

One thing that quietened Hubert down eventually was his new court case. The council was trying to stop him keeping poultry; they said there was a health danger, with all the flies, in a built-up area. Also there was a noise nuisance. The roosters woke the neighbourhood too early in the morning. There had been complaints, a lot of them, and the council was forced to do something. A health inspector came out to see Hubert, and was run off the section. So the council had to prosecute. Hubert cheered up immensely, and wandered round the house muttering his preliminary speech to the court. Since Grandmother Flinders wasn't very receptive, he rehearsed on me. "Your Honour," he said to me, "I ask you, sir, if this is the British justice for which our ancestors fought? Was it for this that men fought and died at Magna Carta?"

"Magna Carta wasn't a battle," I told him.

"Mind your own bloody business."

"Well, it wasn't," I insisted. "You'd better get your facts right. As far as I can see, Magna Carta was just an ordinary piece of blackmail."

"All right," he said, "was it for this that men fought and died through countless generations?"

"That's better," I agreed.

"Let me remind you, your Honour," he roared on, "that my grandfather was one of the first Europeans to settle in this country. In 1832, eight years before this country became a British colony –"

"I don't know that they'll be too fascinated with all that," I said. "I mean did he keep chickens or something? You might bring that in."

He ignored me.

"We put our sweat into this country, and our blood," he shouted. "And what has it come to now? Where is our heritage? Where are our brave dreams?" He paused and took a deep breath. "Where, your Honour? Where?"

He let me think about it.

"I'll tell you where," he went on. "In the clammy hands of bureaucrats. The undertakers of our heritage. The nightsoil men of our dreams. In the hands of health inspectors and such-like piddling shits and mugs –"

"I don't think you should get too abusive," I argued. "I mean I don't think it would go down too well if you called them all mugs."

"I'll call them what I bloody well like. With all due respect to your Honour."

He was getting so worked up that he'd started to sell himself the idea I was really the magistrate. I'd just come from the garden, as a matter of fact, all grubby and sweaty with the spade in my hands, when he caught me on the hop with this new version of his speech. I'd been going to put the spade away and then pay a quick visit to the privy. So I was listening with some strain, shifting from one foot to another.

"These mugs," he said, ignoring my objection, "where were

they when men, real men, were winning this land from the wilderness? Where were they?"

"They probably hadn't been born," I interrupted.

"Where were they when armies of men were winning this country's wealth from goldfields and gumfields?"

"I just told you. They probably hadn't been born."

"All right, your Honour, all right. So they hadn't been born. We'd of been a bloody sight better off if they'd never been born. That's what I'm saying."

"Silence in the court," I said. "Silence."

"Thank you, your Honour. Thank you. The question is this. What right have these idiot swine got to tell me what to do? Is this justice, British justice? Is this what we've fought and died for through countless generations?"

"I think you should get to the point," I said. "You ought to be talking about the poultry by now."

Besides, my bladder was getting pretty urgent.

"I haven't got to that part of my speech yet," he said. "I haven't nutted out what I'm going to say about the poultry."

"Well, you'd better work it out. Anyway, while you're thinking about it –"

I fled to the privy. Then I came back and put the spade away in the toolshed. Something there caught my eye. It was a curious thing, a sort of long thin sword, but with a handle like a spade. I'd seen it before and intended to ask about it. So I grabbed it, anything to distract from British justice and countless generations, and took it out of the shed.

"What's this?" I asked him.

"A gum-spear, boy. A gum-spear. Used to work with it on the gumfields."

He took hold of the spear and gave me a demonstration of how to use it when searching for kauri gum in the earth. It was interesting to see the technique. You stabbed it into the ground, where you guessed a kauri tree might have fallen and petrified thousands of years ago, and tried to find something hard. If you knew enough, you could tell just by the vibrations of the spear whether there was gum under the ground or not. Then you dug it out. By the time he'd finished demonstrating, he'd ripped up half the back yard with the spear. It was a pity I hadn't got him on to helping with the cabbage patch.

He stood there puffing and blowing; he'd forgotten his speech to the court entirely. "You get the idea, boy?"

"I think so."

"We ought to have a real try at it," he gasped, shaky with excitement. "You and me. There's still a bit of gum left up north. If you know where to look. There's gold, too, round Coromandel. If you know where to look."

"You mean we might go and look?"

"We ought to think about it, boy. I been meaning to talk to you about it. I think you and me ought to make a trip. Back to all the old places. Nothing to stop us, is there? Don't go mentioning this to your grandmother, though. This is strictly between you and me. Remember I told you we might have something private to talk about? Well, this is it. All right?"

"All right," I said. "When are we going?"

"Hold your horses, boy. We'll go in our own good time. No hurry."

"My school holidays don't go on forever. I have to go back to Te Ika sometime."

"Let all that look after itself. Just don't go telling your grandmother about it, that's all."

"We'll have to tell her about it sometime."

"But not just yet. You understand? Don't mention a damn thing to her. Otherwise she'll get all upset. Between you and me, I been planning this trip for the last ten years."

"Then why haven't you gone?"

"No one to go with, boy. That's one thing. Your grandmother wouldn't have it on. She won't move from this place. Not till she dies. That's what she says."

"All right," I said. "You've got someone to go with now."

But he wasn't listening. "Not till she dies," he repeated, and shook his head sadly. "That's what she says. She reckons she's had enough dragging round from place to place in her life. So she won't shift from here, ever."

"I don't blame her, exactly. Not from all I've heard."

"You mustn't think I don't love the stupid woman, Nick."

"I know."

"It's just we've never understood each other too well."

"I don't know about that. I think she's got you pretty well sized up."

"You do, eh? And what do you bloody know about it?"

"A fair bit."

It was about time I stood up to him.

"Well, you know too much then," he said, stalking off angrily. "Too bloody much, you hear?"

Chapter Fourteen

SOME DAYS GROWLED WITH THUNDERSTORMS, BUT MOST were fine. They passed by swiftly. Hubert and Grandmother Flinders began talking to each other again. It was a relief to stop refereeing and carrying messages. I swam and sunbathed and fished the odd snapper out of the harbour and wrote home again to say I was all right. The court case was postponed, and Hubert quit rehearsing his speech. But he still muttered about this trip, whenever he was alone with me.

"First we'll try the gum," he said. "Then we'll try the gold. Then we might head down the country a bit."

I began to understand what was going on in his head. This was exactly what he'd done more than sixty years before. After he left his family, when he was about twenty, he worked on the gumfields, then searched for gold around Coromandel. Finally he moved down country and somewhere on the way met Grandmother Flinders. He married her and took her off to his first bush-farm.

I understood something else too. He didn't really plan to make the trip.

It took me some time to realize that it was all just something to think about, to talk about. He would go on day after day planning it down to details and working himself up into a fine old state of excitement. That was the point, it was something he could look forward to. And perhaps having a secret, particularly a secret shared with me, made him feel one up on Grandmother Flinders. At times he probably even kidded himself into believing he would really make the trip one day. I don't know. All I knew, for sure, was that he was really as set in his ways as Grandmother Flinders, and it would take something like an earthquake to shift him from her and the house, his potato patch, the chickens and the lost golf balls. If he ever visited any of his family, as he'd visited us in Te Ika, he usually couldn't get back home fast enough.

I was disappointed when I realized all this, naturally. But I wasn't too upset, on the whole. I was more shaken up by something that happened down on the beach. Nothing was further from my mind than Te Ika that day. It was a still and sweaty Auckland afternoon with a great dark thunder cloud slowly lifting from the horizon. Against my principles I sloped off down to the beach. First, because it was too warm to sit at home; second, because the tide was in. If I'd only stuck to my principles about not going down to the beach when the place was crowded, I wouldn't have got into trouble.

There were yachts trembling on the windless sea, launches puttering, speedboats zooming; half Auckland seemed to be on the water or in the water. The shoreline was crowded with picnic parties, kids fighting and yelling and knocking down sandcastles, young lovers mooning round hand in hand with transistor radios. I cleared off to the rocks right at the end of the beach, where I had a fairly private sunbathing place between a couple of straggly old pohutukawas. I was lucky; it was still deserted, so I dumped my clothes and took off into the water.

That day I swam farther out into the harbour than I ever had before, past the most distant boat, and then I turned slowly back for the shore. Each day I made a point of swimming as far out as I could, and I got a great kick out of discovering I was a hundred yards better off than the day before. I climbed back on to the rocks and collapsed, closing my eyes against the sun. My heart was banging like a gun with the effort, and I tingled all over.

"Well," said this voice out of nowhere, "if it isn't Nick Flinders."

I had a sick feeling the moment I heard my own name. I knew it was Te Ika catching up with me at last. And not just Te Ika. My mind had been empty, really empty, and now I had things all over again: the bush, fern and creeper dripping with rain, and Sam beside me; the search party, the hospital, and Sergeant

Crimmins; my hot bedroom, the itchy plaster, and Derek talking dirt. There wasn't anything I didn't have again when I heard that voice, and my own name. I thought I'd finished with all those things. But they'd been there hiding in my mind all the time, just waiting for a chance to come back.

With this sick feeling, it was all I could do to open my eyes. That pleasant tingling of my body turned into shivering.

"You're certainly a long way from home," she said.

"You are too," I said, " if it comes to that."

"Everyone's been wondering about you," she said. "People have been saying lots of things."

"They can say what they like, for all I care."

It was Glenys Appleby, a girl in my class at school. She was a big girl, plump, and I'd heard other boys say old Glenys could be a lot of fun at school dances and, sometimes afterwards, on the riverbank. Right now she was giving a black bathing suit a pretty stretchy time. To tell the truth, I didn't have any opinion on the subject of whether Glenys Appleby was a lot of fun or not. I mean she didn't fascinate me too passionately. She had this long damp hair swishing round her bare shoulders, and these bright teeth, and I could see she'd done her share of sun-bathing this summer too.

She towered above me, her hands on her hips, grinning. She seemed a bit nervous and uncertain of herself, though; she kept flipping out her tongue, like a lizard's, to moisten the corners of her mouth.

"I hear you cleared off from home," she said. "Lucky old you."

"It's not true. I merely happen to be having an extended holiday here with my grandparents." I tried to summon up my dignity, but it seemed to be on extended holiday itself. "That's all."

"Well, that's better than nothing. I'm in tow with my parents. We've got a house up there." She pointed to somewhere up behind the beach. "For part of the school holidays."

"Well, there are worse beaches, I suppose." It was just my luck. Te Ika arriving right on my beach.

"Don't you like Auckland?"

"It's all right. I don't go into the city at all. I just stick round here."

"I'm going to live in Auckland when I leave school," she announced. "I've just decided, this holiday."

"Great," I said. "You're welcome to the place."

"I'm going to take a job as a secretary. In some big office."

"Great. I bet that'll be a lot of fun."

"Te Ika's too slow and sleepy. Nothing ever happens there."

"That's a matter of opinion," I told her.

"Are you arguing with me?"

"I haven't said a word."

"You sound argumentative. Once upon a time I thought you were a terribly quiet boy, Nick."

"I still am. When I'm left alone."

But she didn't take the hint. Out came that lizard's tongue again, flip, flip. Then she sat on the rocks beside me. She leaned back on her hands, her face to the sun, so that her hair swung shiny behind her shoulders and her legs were spread wide. Flip, flip, flip. It was very distracting.

"We were all awfully sorry about Sam," she said. "We know he was your best friend."

"He was a pretty good friend," I admitted, wishing to hell I could think of some way of shooting through on the conversation. The way she spoke, she made it seem like Sam was just any old friend.

"All the same," she went on, "I don't see why you should go off your rocker about everything."

"Who says I'm off my rocker?"

"Everyone says so. They say your brain was permanently damaged by your terrible experience."

"What do they know about it? It's my brain, isn't it?"

She shrugged carelessly and smiled at me. She could turn on the charm, all right. I mean she thought she looked pretty damn fascinating.

"I must say you don't look too nutty to me, though. You just look the same Nick Flinders."

"Well, I am pretty much the same. Sometimes I wish I wasn't."

"Are you going back to school?"

"When I feel like it. I'm in no passionate hurry."

"I don't blame you. School back in Te Ika doesn't amount to much. Not when you've been to a big city like Auckland."

I could see she was pretty sold on this Auckland stuff, all right. Another year or two and she'd be dressed in the height of fashion and clip-clipping up and down Queen Street, running messages for her boss. I suppose the idea of it seemed like paradise to her. In a way I envied her. I had nothing much to look forward to. No trips with Sam, not even that trip with Hubert any more.

"Well," I said, "I hope you make out all right in Auckland, anyway."

"I don't know," she confessed sadly. "Sometimes I think I haven't got a very good figure. I'm too fat."

I saw I was expected to say something consoling. "It's not too bad," I said, "as far as figures go. I mean it's probably a whole lot better than mine."

"Am I supposed to be flattered?" She didn't look at all happy. "Nick, you've got no idea about girls."

"I've got a fair idea."

"You're innocent," she sniffed. "That's your trouble."

"So what should I be? Guilty? That's the opposite of innocent, isn't it?"

She just looked puzzled. "I don't know what you mean."

"It's just I don't go in for all this moony stuff," I said. "Why should I, anyway?"

"You're scared of girls. I see that a mile off."

"That'll be the day. No girl ever scared me."

All the same, I felt queer watching that tongue flip between her bright teeth. It was hypnotizing me. I wished she would go away and leave me in peace. She and Te Ika. It didn't seem I'd ever get far enough away.

"All right," she said, "why don't you ever go to the school

dances? You and Sam never went. Other girls reckoned you were snobby. I reckon it was just you were scared."

"We had better things to do with our weekends. Anyway that stuff doesn't interest me a hell of a lot."

"You're scared of me right now," she persisted. "I can tell." She flopped her big fat legs glamorously around on the rocks. "You don't fool me for one second." But she was puzzled, she didn't seem too sure of herself at all.

"You're getting awfully boring on this subject. Can't you talk about something else?"

"What else is there?"

"Te Ika, for instance. What's going on back there?" I wasn't passionately interested in knowing, but at least it might give us something different to talk about.

"Nothing ever happens there. I told you that."

I started feeling trapped. Really trapped. I felt the sweat coming up like a moustache on my lip.

"You're the only interesting thing that happened all last year," she went on. "You and Sam. Didn't you know that, Nick? There was more talk about it than anything since those murders."

That was something else I thought I'd forgotten. Something else that had only been waiting to come back again. The murders. And walking into that empty house, down the gloomy passage, past the bloodstained bedrooms, into the dusty kitchen. My stomach turned over, remembering, but Glenys didn't seem to notice. Right now she was turning on the charm in a big way, and didn't have time to notice.

"You were a regular hero. Those pictures in the papers and everything."

"If people are stupid enough to believe that stuff, well it's their own fault for being so stupid."

"That's not very kind, Nick. You were a real pin-up boy for a few weeks. We couldn't wait for you to get back to school. But you didn't come. And then the new Elvis Presley film came along."

"Well," I said, "what do you know?" I was surprised, I really was. I mean I couldn't understand it. And I sat there with the sun growing hotter, my sweat sprouting everywhere, watching her puzzling face and flicking tongue. There were a lot of things in the world that still didn't add up, but I wasn't going to admit it to her. I planned to add them up for myself, when I got a chance.

"We talked for hours about how you must have felt lying there beside Sam, with him dead," she said. "I know it was morbid, but we couldn't help it."

"I wouldn't say it was morbid," I argued, trying to show I could be reasonable after all. "I'd be pretty interested in that kind of thing myself."

That more or less finished the subject. I mean it would have been all right if we'd quit talking and just relaxed in the sun for a while. The trouble was she couldn't keep still, she stayed fidgety. She seemed to think she was a failure if she couldn't keep me yapping.

"I don't mind telling you," she said, "the competition's still pretty keen back in Te Ika. You ought to know that. I tell you, there's a lot of girls back there who would like to be in my place right now."

"Who, for instance?"

"Well, Helen Fowler for one. Maggie Archer for another. And Christine Wentworth."

"That's very interesting," I said, still trying to be reasonable.

"They'll be maddeningly jealous. When I tell them I met you here."

"They sound maddeningly stupid to me."

"Never mind. I'll be able to prove that they're wrong. And that I'm right."

"About what?"

"About you being snobby. I always said you weren't. And you're not. But I'm right about you being scared. Because you are."

"Christ almighty," I said, "can't you leave that stuff alone?"

"All right," she said. "Go ahead. Go ahead and prove it."

"Prove what?"

"That you're not scared."

Boy, I've never seen anyone looking more scared than she was right then. She was about as nervous and twitchy as a cat.

"Go on. Prove it."

"What do you want? A fight or something?"

"A fight? Oh dear me," she giggled. "Oh dear me. Poor, poor Nick."

"Look," I said, "I'm not a hell of a lot interested in proving anything right now. I'm shooting through, if you don't mind. It's time I went home."

I stood up, and she stood up too. I discovered I was two or three inches taller than her, and that made me feel better.

"So you're running away again," she said. "Is that it?"

"Who said I was running away?"

"You ran away from Te Ika. Everyone knows that."

"I left Te Ika for a strictly personal reason."

"You ran away. Just like you're running away now. For the same reason, probably. I bet there was a girl."

"A girl?" I couldn't help thinking of Mrs Waikai, and I laughed. "Well, I must say you know a damn lot about nothing."

"All right, so why are you running away now?"

"Don't flatter yourself. I'm not running away. I'm just going home. I mean back to my grandparent's place."

"Because you're scared."

"Give it a bone, will you?"

Flip went the tongue. Flick, flash went the charm. She could turn it on, all right.

"Nick, don't get angry, please."

"Who said I was bloody well angry, for Christ's sake?"

"We could be friends, Nick."

"I bet. Great."

"We could be. You and me. We could have a lot of fun together. Round the beach here. And when we get back to Te Ika."

The really terrible thing was I started feeling sorry for her.

"What's wrong?" I said. "There are plenty of boys around here, aren't there?"

She studied her toes as she dipped her brown foot gently into a rock pool. "Not many. And there are a lot of girls with better figures."

"Well, that's really a terrible shame."

"One boy talked to me for a while yesterday. He asked me my age. And when I told him, he just walked off."

"That's a bit tough, I agree."

"So you see," she said sadly, "it's really not that much fun being here. I've been looking forward to this holiday for months. Now I just mess round here all day, bored stiff." She looked about ready to weep, but instead of weeping she put out her hand. I looked at this hand for a moment, then I realized I was supposed to grab it or something.

"Can't we be friends, Nick? Don't go home. Stay here a bit longer. Let's go for a walk together."

I decided I couldn't look at her hand forever. And I couldn't shoot through without reducing her to tears altogether. So I took hold of it. It wasn't bad as hands go, warm and soft with a cool place in the middle. It was amazing how she cheered up right away. It was even more amazing how tightly she held on to me.

"I don't suppose a walk would do me any harm," I said finally. "Where to?"

"Over to the Maori look-out. I haven't been there yet. I've only heard about it. I didn't want to go till someone showed me the place. But I haven't had anyone to go with."

"Well," I said, "let's go, then."

The Maori look-out was a point just beyond the western arm of the bay, a jagged and rock-strewn cliff patchy with native bush. A plantation of pines separated it from the actual beach. In the days when only Maoris lived here, on a hill-top *pa* behind the beach, they used the point to watch for enemy war-canoes travelling across the harbour. Scouts planted there would give warning of an attack. But according to one old legend which Grandmother Flinders told me, the *pa* was once surprised from the rear. Most men were slaughtered or taken slaves, and women and children were flung to their death from the look-out to the rocks below.

I told Glenys this yarn as we walked up through the pines. In the distance we could hear a speedboat roaring. A party of kids came whooping between the trees, but they left us alone as they plunged, skidding and rolling, back to the beach. The noise back there slowly faded. The pines had a pleasant dry musty smell and our feet pad-padded over the cool needles. Glenys clung to me, puffing, as the climb grew steep. After a while we came out of the pines into native scrub. A few big old pohutukawa stood around the cliff-edge. We looked down to where the sea smacked lightly on rocks.

"The legend says," I went on, "that on very quiet days you can hear the ghosts of the women and children moaning and sighing here."

Well, it was reasonably quiet. Glenys pretended to shiver, though we were out in the hot sun again.

"I don't think I like that story much," she announced, and held my hand even tighter.

"You must admit it's not a bad view, anyway."

The sea was silvery, and islands and headlands seemed to float shimmering in the heat.

"But you've spoiled it all for me now. Isn't there somewhere else we can walk?"

"All right." To tell the truth I felt a bit sick myself, looking down. Only it wasn't the legend. I didn't have a great head for heights any more. "We can walk along the cliffs a way. It's all still pretty much wilderness up here."

A couple of lovers came to stand quietly behind us. They didn't look down at the rocks. They just stood and said what a beautiful view, though actually they didn't take their sloppy eyes off each other. We moved on, ducking and scraping through the scrub, still holding hands. Glenys seemed happy again.

"I bet Helen Fowler would be jealous if she saw me now," she said. "Maggie Archer too."

"Why?"

"I told you, idiot. Because you're the big hero. Your picture in the paper and everything."

The scrub seemed to be getting thicker. We couldn't find a track.

"Hey," she said. "Slow down."

With all our bare flesh, we were getting pretty badly scratched about. But the point was that we weren't getting anywhere fast. I stopped and said, "Well, I suppose we might as well go back now."

I mean I'd done my duty. I'd taken her for a walk.

"Go back? What's wrong?"

"Nothing's wrong."

"You scared again?" She tugged at my hand, hard, as if it was a brake or something. We'd stopped in a patch of low fern. Rocks rose on each side. You could only just hear the sea.

"Look," I said, "if you don't shut up about that, I'll teach you a lesson."

"What sort of lesson, Nick?" She fluttered her eyes, big, and her tongue flicked round her lips. "What sort of lesson do you think you could teach me?"

"A lesson to keep your silly mouth shut."

It struck me that she really wasn't the only one around who should be taught a lesson. There was Derek too, only he wasn't here.

"Come on," she said. "You just try it." She grabbed at me playfully between the legs with her free hand, but only got a handful of my damp swimming togs. It was a near thing, though. And I saw what she was up to, all right. Her tongue was going as if she had me for dinner already. I slapped her hand away, got my other hand free, and bowled her over. As she collapsed into the fern, she grabbed me and I went over too. She seemed very excited about something and her arms and legs were going in all directions. I mean for a while I couldn't tell which was which. I gave her a couple of sharp smacks on the side of the head to keep her quiet and she looked so surprised she forgot to yell. She just panted, wild and shiny in the face, and kept trying to grab me. Her mouth was wide open and I could see that old tongue flashing round. She still really needed her lesson, so I biffed her again. That fixed her, to some extent. At least she yelled. But she managed to get me, all right, as we rolled over and over. She had hold of me with both hands and there was nothing I could do. Except yell too. She knew all the dirty tricks in fighting; I should have counted on that. It was painful, really painful, and I knew my end was near. She'd have me for a first course, no trouble. I didn't know I could be so weak. My breath jumped in my throat and I felt like melting butter inside. I mean there wasn't anything I could do and I could feel her hot tongue on my neck already.

"All right," I gasped. "Lay off. I give in. We're quits." But she took no notice.

And then it was all right.

It was the most curious thing that ever happened to me. One minute I was almost pleading for my life, the next I was winning again. I mean I knew, all of a sudden, that there was nothing to panic about. I had the advantage again and she didn't seem to know what she was letting herself in for. I just grew out of her clutch, and she was completely in my power. She beat about wildly and closed her eyes and moaned like an old cow. It didn't surprise me, particularly. I was past being surprised. I only biffed her once more, just to show her who was boss again, and then I got down to some fairly interesting close stuff. Little kicks of fright went right through her. I'd never seen anyone so wild and yet so helpless. But it was obvious she still had to be taught that lesson, good and proper, otherwise she'd start in on me being scared again. I intended to finish that for all time. But I must admit that, in teaching her a lesson, I learned quite a bit myself. I mean it was all fairly interesting, from my point of view.

"I bet Helen Fowler would be jealous if she saw you now," I said, trying to mimic her voice. "Maggie Archer too."

It didn't make much impression, though. I doubt if she even heard me. She certainly didn't reply. Her tongue lolled about like something dead in her mouth as she rolled around and sighed. It struck me that I might actually be killing her, and that scared hell out of me. I was even more scared a moment later, though, when I started shuddering myself and I just couldn't stop and a million tiny red lights jigged in my eyes. I wasn't only killing her, it looked like I was killing myself too. Then my eyes snapped shut and I was falling, falling, faster than light; but instead of rocks and trees banging me around at the bottom, there was just Glenys Appleby heaving like a whale, and the crushed fern, and the smell of her and me and the crushed fern. It seemed the luckiest escape I'd ever had. I couldn't feel anything broken, though I'd come down with an almighty thump. I just lay there getting my wind back and reflecting on my good luck. I seemed to be perfectly all right, after all.

I wondered if anyone round the Maori look-out had heard us. I supposed that, if they had, they'd just put the moaning and sighing down to those ancient Maori ghosts haunting the place.

But just in case there was someone investigating the noise, I stood up fast and pulled my togs on again. I'd lost them altogether during the infighting. Boy, I felt lucky to be alive. More than anything else I needed a good long swim in the sea before I got back to Grandmother Flinders. Glenys started fumbling with straps and things too.

"Just one thing," I said. "Before I forget."

Her lower lip trembled. "What's that?"

"You still reckon I'm scared?"

Her eyes grew huge and bright. She saw what I meant, all right.

She didn't say anything. Because she wouldn't admit, even now, that she'd been wrong. It was pretty disgusting, really. It was all I could do to say goodbye to her pleasantly.

I was glad about one thing, though. I'd certainly made Derek look a fool.

Chapter Fifteen

I WALKED HOME KNOWING FOR SURE THAT I'D FINISHED with that beach. Te Ika had taken the place over, as far as I was concerned. That great dark cloud dawdled on the horizon, but the sun was still shining, there was a thick blue haze over everything, and without wind the afternoon was stinking hot. The asphalt of the footpath scorched my bare feet, so I walked on the cool dry grass by the side of the road. I walked as fast as I could without running outright. I couldn't put a distance between myself and the beach, and Glenys, quickly enough. Not that I didn't feel sorry for her now. No, the trouble was she just happened to be there, on my beach. Now it was more hers than mine.

When I reached home I found Grandmother Flinders occupying some shade in the backyard. She sat tiny in the middle of the old wicker couch. Hubert wasn't to be seen. From the grim look on her face I guessed they'd been at it again and I wondered if he might be taking a breather down the section in the chickenhouse. I sat down beside her. To tell the truth, I felt pretty shot.

"Tell him it's not true, Nick," she said.

"Tell him what's not true?"

"That I've been propagandizing you."

"Who said you've been propagandizing me?"

"He does. Hubert."

"Well," I said, "that's a pretty stupid thing to say."

"Exactly. I tried to tell him it was stupid. But he insists that I've been deliberately turning you against him."

"I wouldn't worry about it. He's just got a bee in his bonnet."

But she was shaking, and near tears. This was unusual for her. It meant things were fairly serious.

"Just tell him, Nick. Just tell him it's not true."

"All right. I will."

"I'd never dream of turning you against your grandfather. You know that. You mean a lot to him, Nick. You know that too, don't you?"

"I haven't really thought about it."

"Well, it's true. At the moment he depends on you. Just be gentle with him, Nick. If he wants something, if he wants to do something, you just let him have his own way about it. That's the only answer. Otherwise he'll go on saying I'm turning you against him."

"I'll put a stop to that, all right," I said.

But my head was reeling, with the heat and other things; I'd really had more than enough for one day. I just couldn't think straight. I'd lost my beach, and it seemed if I wasn't careful I'd lose my grandparents too.

"I don't know where he's gone," she said. "He went off in a terrible temper. He actually said he'd just as soon you went home to Frank and Beryl now. At least there'd be some peace for an old man, he said." She paused. "That might be the best thing, Nick. For all of us. Don't you think?"

Now I knew for certain I'd had too much for one day.

"Besides," she went on, "they'll still be awfully worried about you. Anyway, perhaps you should think about it. For their sake too." She rose stiffly on her stick legs. Sometimes it was difficult to see how she held together. "Could you give me a hand inside, Nick? I'm not particularly strong today. I think it's time for my rest."

She put a trembling hand on my arm, and I helped her inside. We went through to the big bedroom she and Hubert shared. The afternoon sun was bright on the laced windows. "Remember," she said, as she eased herself slowly and painfully on to the bed, "just be reasonable with him. Fall in with his ideas. It's the only way. He'll come round again. He's still only a child, after all these years. I don't know how I've managed him. These days it just gets too much for me. Too much of a strain."

As she made herself comfortable, I hovered beside the bed, in case there was something she wanted.

"I thought he'd grow up," she said. "But he never did. A

child with the strength of ten grown men. That was what I thought when I met him. Did I ever tell you about that, Nick? He was a champion axeman then. It was a carnival by the river, tents everywhere and coloured pennants flying, girls in bright dresses and strong men bare to the waist. Barney was in a black singlet. His axe flashed in the sunlight when he struck at the logs. He was huge. There was no one could cut through an eighteen-inch log faster. The axe flashed, and his muscles rippled. He was as brown as old mahogany. He didn't look the sort of man who would need looking after. But he did, Nick, he did. Perhaps that is what has kept me alive so long, knowing I have to look after him."

"Well, you've looked after him pretty well, I must say. And all your children too."

"You think so, Nick? You really think so?" Her eyes quivered, and I knew she needed me to tell her that her life had been worthwhile.

"Of course. I don't know how you did it. No one does. All those years in the bush, dragging round from place to place, and everything."

Her eyes closed. There was actually a small smile on her face. She put out her old hands and fastened them both around one of mine. She held on tight, as if she was liable to drift away, while I stood by the bed. We were like that for some time, and we didn't speak. My legs felt empty. It seemed all my strength had gone. I tried some words in my mouth, but they didn't fit. My eyes wandered about the room. I saw the trunks under Hubert's bed where he kept all his papers and legal documents. And the black cash-box where he kept his brandy and betting fund. No one knew how much was in it, and only Hubert had a key. My eyes jigged from that to the old white china po, chipped and cracked in a hundred places; it looked about as ancient as Hubert himself. But it didn't look at all sorry for itself.

It was a moment before I realized she was speaking to me again. The words were so quiet and small; she barely whispered. "Nick," she said, "Nick, are you there?"

She actually still had hold of my hand, but I didn't point this out. She obviously wasn't the best today. I bent down towards her. "Yes," I said. "I'm here, all right."

"Nick, I'm worried. Who'll look after Barney if anything happens to me? None of the children will look after him. You know that. He's an impossible man to live with. Who'll look after him?"

"I'll look after him," I said. "I can switch the lights and radio on and off. Things like that."

"You promise?"

"I promise."

"And you'll try to keep him in order, try to stop him making too big a fool of himself?"

"Yes. I promise."

She was smiling peacefully again. Soon she was asleep. Her breathing grew quiet and even, and her hands slipped away from me. I arranged them neatly in front of her, straightened the bedcover, pulled down the blinds, took a last look round, and walked out of the room, shutting the door. One thing was certain, I felt better for having made her feel better; I'd almost recovered from Glenys and the beach. I mooched about the backyard for a while, thinking about everything and nothing, and then Hubert turned up. It was a race day, and obviously the horses had been giving him a bad time. He was ripping up a race guide in disgust and muttering angrily to himself as he came round the corner of the house. He saw me and stopped for a moment.

"You here?" he growled. "I thought you were down at the beach."

"No. I've finished with that place."

"Finished with it?"

"Too many people."

"Oh," he grunted. "So that's what it is. You fed up with life here? Is that it? You going home?"

"I hadn't thought about it. Going home, I mean. I suppose that's the logical thing though."

"Go home, then. Get the hell out. See if I care."

He stomped off towards the house. He was in a real mood.

"Where's your grandmother?" he called back over his shoulder.

"I put her to bed an hour or two ago. She's not very well."

I followed him into the house. He'd begun muttering to himself again. He muttered through the living room, down the passage, into the bedroom. The bedroom door closed and I heard him muttering on the other side. I thought I might as well make him a cup of tea. I went through into the kitchen, and put the kettle on to boil. I could still hear him muttering in the distance. It sounded as if he might actually be talking to Grandmother Flinders now. Then it stopped, quite suddenly. There was a long silence. The kettle boiled, and I set about making the tea. I arranged a cup and saucer on a small tray for Grandmother Flinders. She always instructed me not to let her sleep too long in the afternoons; she couldn't sleep at night otherwise.

Hubert usually banged around the house, so naturally I was surprised when he slunk quietly into the kitchen to stand beside me while I poured the tea. I hadn't even heard their bedroom door open and close. That was when I decided the horses had given him a really bad time. It looked as if one had actually kicked him in the face. His eyes were sunk, his mouth was loose, and he didn't seem to see me very clearly.

"Nick," he said in a crackly old voice.

"Yes?"

He seemed puzzled. Slow wheels seemed to be turning in his head. The house was absolutely quiet, apart from his breathing. Light came back into his eyes and he was looking at me, really looking.

"About that trip," he said.

One of his hands climbed up on to my shoulder. He gripped tight, and his fingers worked over my flesh and bone.

"What about it?" I said.

"I been thinking. I been thinking we ought to make that trip."

"All right," I said. "We can talk about it over this cup of tea. Here's yours." I placed a cup and saucer down beside him. "I'll just take this other one through for her."

"Hang on a minute," he said, and blocked my way.

132

"What's wrong?"

"Leave her sleep."

"But she always says –"

"It doesn't matter what she always says. Leave her sleep. We want to talk, don't we? We got to talk, you and me. Now or never, boy."

"All right," I said. I put down Grandmother Flinders' tray. "Talk away."

"Nothing much to talk about really," he decided. "It's just a question of are we going or not. Are we?"

"You mean right now?"

"That's what I mean, all right. You ready?"

I thought quickly. There wasn't anything to stop me. Te Ika had taken over my beach. If we were going to make the trip, this was my last chance for the time being; the school holidays would be over soon. But what about Grandmother Flinders? Then I remembered what she'd said. To fall in with whatever he said. For her sake.

"Yes," I said. "All right, I can be ready soon enough."

"Right. It's settled."

But he didn't make a move except to place his hand on my shoulder again. He looked deep into my face as if he was trying to see everything there. I could never be too sure of the old boy at the best of times. But right at that moment I knew he liked me. That he really did care about me after all. For I could have sworn he was going to cry when I said yes, and to make him that happy I'd have followed him anywhere, all the days of my life.

"I knew," was all he said.

"You knew what?"

"I knew you turned out all right."

He let go my shoulder at last, and we stayed looking at each other a few moments longer. Something was bothering me, though, something about the whole business. But I just didn't have time to think. I raced through to my room and heaved clothes into my pack. Then I rushed back to Hubert, the pack swinging from my shoulder, to help him get his gear together. But he was still standing where I'd left him, in the kitchen.

"Aren't you going to pack?" I asked.

"I got the clothes I'm standing up in. They been good enough the last ten years. They should last another ten."

"Well," I said, "we'd better wake her up and tell her we're off now."

That alarmed him. "Not on your sweet life, boy. She'd only stop us." He paused. "Look, I been thinking. While I'm getting ready, you use the telephone. Ring your Aunt Margaret and tell her to come over tonight. If you can't get her or she can't come, ring Aunt Esther. All right?"

"What's the point? We won't be here."

"Your grandmother will," he said slowly.

"I see. You mean she'll need looking after."

"That's it, boy. You got it. Their numbers are written over there, by the phone. Only don't say anything about us going away. Just tell them they got to come over. All right?"

"All right." I spent the next ten minutes on the phone. Aunt Margaret was out, so I left a message with one of my cousins. Aunt Esther was puzzled, but she wanted to know how I was, had I recovered from my terrible experience, and why was I staying over there anyway, and all right she'd come, it was a nuisance but she'd come, couldn't I explain what it was all about. I said I couldn't, really, I was just passing on the message; and I hung up.

While I was on the phone a mound of Hubert's things began to grow on the floor behind me. The gum-spear, the rifle from the wall, blankets, an oilskin overcoat, boots, a billy and a frying pan. Hubert was stuffing the smaller things into a sugar bag.

I thought of something else. A message to my parents. So I grabbed notepaper and a pen and wrote a quick letter, telling them I was off for a while, not to worry, and giving them my love. I sealed it into an envelope and wrote the address. I'd post it off first chance I got. Then something struck me. I turned to Hubert.

"Hey," I said, "you'd better write a letter too."

"A letter?"

"To her." I jerked my thumb in the direction of the bedroom. "Otherwise she's going to wake up and find us gone and not know where we are. Don't you see?"

He didn't seem to, for the moment. His face sagged.

"You just sit down and write it," I said. "Right now."

He left what he was doing, and walked slowly to the table.

"Here's the pen and paper," I went on. "Right here. All ready."

He stood there by the table and looked at me, then at the blank paper, as if he couldn't make sense of anything.

"I never written a letter to Beth," he said. "In my whole life."

"Well, you'd better start now. Give her your love and everything."

But he just stood there.

"For God's sake," I said, "do I have to write it too?"

"Well," he said, "why not?"

"You just sit down there. And write it." I took him by the shoulders and steered him down into the chair. I arranged the paper in front of him and fastened the pen in his fingers. He was as easy to manage as a child. "Dear Beth," I said. "Or, Dearest Beth. That's how you start. You carry on from there."

Dearest Beth he wrote, and stopped. Everything was very quiet. A clock ticked, bees hummed outside the window.

"Go on," I said.

The pen didn't move. He seemed frozen.

"What's wrong?"

"Nothing," he said. "It's just I haven't –"

"All right, then. Just say: Nick and me have gone off on a trip together."

The pen looked tiny, and likely to snap, in his huge old hand. He wrote spidery *Nick and me have gone off on a trip together*. He stopped again. He wasn't exactly frozen any more. His whole body was shaking with the effort of putting the words down.

I guessed it might be shyness, with me looking over his shoulder, so I moved away. "You write the rest," I said. "I'll carry on with your packing."

There was silence behind me.

135

I heaved a pair of old boots into the sugar bag. "Go on," I said. "Hurry up and get it written."

The pen scratched, and stopped.

"We haven't much time," I pointed out. "If we want to get moving before dark."

That seemed to do the trick. The pen began to scratch wildly. Five, ten minutes later he was writing just as furiously. He wrote and wrote, shaking his head and gritting his teeth and gripping the pen as if his life depended on it. It didn't seem he would ever stop. Sweat burst out on his forehead and dripped slowly down his nose where it hung in big drops before it splashed down on to the paper.

"Hey," I said at last, "isn't that about enough?"

But he didn't hear me. I had all his gear ready. The sound of the pen and the sweat going pit-pat pit-pat on the paper seemed to fill the quiet house.

"Just tell her everything's all right and that you really love her," I said. "That'll be enough." But when I went over to the table to stand beside him I realized he was telling her that already and a few other things besides. I only saw one or two lines:

Beth I always done my best and I know I never been up to much and I caused you a lot of heartache through the years while you stood by me against all them bastards who like bringing a man down to their own size but I never paid you the respect I should have which was your due and though this isn't the best time to say this just the same Beth I want you to know girl that I always . . .

I mean it didn't seem necessary to go into all that detail just because we were going on a trip. "Come on," I said. "There's no time now to write a book. Finish it off and sign it. We're all ready to go."

When he got up from the table finally, he seemed in a dream. After he sealed the envelope he groped round for his hat and took ages to knot a handkerchief round his neck and fasten up the legs of his trousers with string. Tired of waiting, I tidied up so that Grandmother Flinders would find things neat in the kitchen.

"Where's that letter?" I said. "I can't see it anywhere."

He thought a moment, then slowly produced it from his back pocket.

"She'll have a fat chance of reading it there," I said. I grabbed it from him. "Here. I'll put it beside her bed. So she'll find it first thing when she wakes up."

"Oh no you won't," he announced, grabbing it back from me. "I'll fix that. You just get yourself out the door. And fetch the axe. Don't forget the axe. That's important." The letter waving from his hand, he traipsed off to the bedroom and closed the door quietly. I dumped my pack outside the back door, and went to the toolshed to fetch the axe.

He was a long time getting out of the house and when he reached the back door finally he was breathing hard. He had his rifle slung over one shoulder, his sugar bag over the other. He thrust the gum-spear towards me, and I carried that with the axe. He'd obviously made a thorough raid on his brandy and betting fund while he was in the bedroom. Money bristled out of his jacket pockets.

"I'll look after some of that if you like," I offered.

"You just keep your thieving young hands off it," he roared, and I knew he was almost back to normal again. "At twopence a golf ball, you've robbed me enough this summer."

We walked down through the front gate, and it banged shut behind us. We hadn't gone a hundred yards along the road before people started looking queerly at us. Motorists slowed down to peer. We weren't something they saw every day of the week.

Afterwards I remembered something odd about that afternoon. He didn't look back at his place once. That dark cloud had made up its mind at last, and was half filling the sky. There was a rumble of thunder and a few fat drops of rain fell.

Chapter Sixteen

IT WAS NEAR NOON, HOT AND DUSTY. THE TRAFFIC
roared by. Cars seemed to speed up, rather than slow down, when
they saw us hitching. There must have been something about
us which didn't appeal to the drivers. Anyway there was a steady
swish-swish as they passed on their way north. It wasn't as if
Hubert made himself look pleasant, either. With his rifle on his
shoulder, he stood there spitting and swearing at each car as it
zoomed past. I was the one who had to thumb and smile.

The night before, we'd collected one good ride, in an empty
removal van, not long before dark. North of Auckland rain
raged back and forward across the land, and we spent the night
shivering under dripping pine trees. In the morning the sun
shone again and we picked up a ride in a cream-truck which had
dropped us where we were now, knee-high in dusty grass and
gorse on the roadside.

The trouble was that most cars were jammed with holiday-
makers. There wasn't space for the old boy and me, with all our
outlandish gear, even if they wanted to stop.

"The hell with them," Hubert said finally. "Let's swing the
billy again."

We retreated from the roadside to a creek which ran between
lichened boulders. I formed some small stones into a circle, and
heaped old rotten manuka sticks in the middle. Soon a fire
blazed. I filled the billy with water and fixed it over the flames.
When the water bubbled, Hubert threw a fistful of tea into the
billy.

"That's the way to make it," he instructed. "Good and black."
Then he tossed in some green manuka leaves for good measure.
"Always use a few of these too. Gives the tea some body. You
get the idea?"

"I think so."

"Good. I'll leave it to you in future."

We didn't notice the smart new Jaguar park near us. Anyway we were about twenty yards off the road and we'd been busy getting the tea brewed. Then I saw this dapper man in a blue suit emerging from scrub, fastening his fly. He noticed us about the same time. He had a skinny, shrivelled face and a thin moustache, and a feathered hat sat jauntily on his head. He looked more surprised than embarrassed. He thought a moment, then he wandered over.

"My God," he said. "It's been years."

Hubert looked him over with a frown. "Years since what?" he grunted.

But this fellow didn't hear the question. He half-closed his eyes and sniffed. "Just smell it, will you? Just smell it."

"Years since what?" Hubert repeated.

"Since I had a mug of billy tea. Just smell it, will you? Nothing to beat it. Billy tea boiled over manuka." He looked at us carefully, trying to size us both up. "You couldn't spare an old scrub-cutter a mugful, could you?"

Hubert studied his slick suit, then the parked Jaguar, in disbelief. His face said he'd never seen anyone less like a scrub-cutter in all his life. Nor had I. It seemed a pretty thin story.

"You're welcome," Hubert said, though it didn't sound like it. "But you'll have to use your own mug. If you got one. We need ours."

I suppose he thought that would finish the subject.

"It just so happens," the man said, all eager and excited, "that I've got a container in the car." He winked. "Usually I use it for something stronger."

He sloped off back to his car, through long grass and biddy-bid. He returned holding a glass, biddy-bid seeds all over his trousers. Pouring from the billy carefully, I filled the glass along with our two mugs. Then I dripped in some condensed milk.

Not worried about his smart suit, the man sat beside us in the dirt. He sniffed at his hot glass, smacked his lips, and then swallowed some tea. It was a wonder his mouth didn't blister.

"What a waste of thirty years," he said. He closed his eyes dreamily. "My God."

"Where'd you cut scrub?" Hubert said conversationally.

"All over. Wherever there was scrub to cut. I started when I was fifteen, sixteen. After the old man died and the farm was sold up."

"You must of come a long way since then." Hubert eyed the Jaguar again.

"A long way?" The man opened his eyes as if he'd only just seen us. He spat out of the side of his mouth. In disgust, it seemed. "You could call it that. A long way. But I wouldn't." He took another huge mouthful of the boiling tea and rolled it round thoughtfully before swallowing. "I come a very short way, really. I stopped off in Auckland, one trip, and took an easy job for the winter. That was my downfall, a soft job. It was just at the start of the depression. I finished up marrying the boss's daughter." He looked up at the sky, then at Hubert, then at me. "I mean it was either that, or starve. Either that, or a slave camp. You remember what it was like in the depression? All the single men being shipped off to relief camps? And she just fell into my lap like a rosy ripe apple. It was too easy. Do you blame me? I mean I got her in the family way, and that was that. And I married her. It was too easy. But do you blame me?" He looked at Hubert defiantly, as if he might, but Hubert just stared back and didn't say a word. "It was a small business back in those days. It grew fast with the war. We've even got branch offices now. And I been stuck in Auckland ever since. Son, you think you could spare some more tea? Thanks. Christ, it brings everything back – smelling it, tasting it again. Empty hills, scrub and bush as far as you could see. Night coming in, stars in the sky, manuka smoke drifting out of the tin chimney of our whare. Yarning with my mate. I had real mates in those days. Christ knows where they've gone now. I just didn't know what was good for me in those days. I tell you, I was a real young bull. I could do any job. Christ knows what I'm good for now. An office desk. That's about all. And Christ knows what I've got to show for all these years. A bitchy wife, a couple of spoiled kids. What's it all been for?"

"So you could sit here and enjoy a good brew," Hubert said. "Obviously."

"Well," the man said, "you might have something there, by God."

"There's worse troubles than marrying the boss's daughter," Hubert said. "Believe me."

"Well, you might have something there too. But I doubt it."

Hubert was actually starting to like the fellow. I could tell by the way he'd been looking him over. At first he'd been hostile and suspicious. Now he was quite gentle.

"Of course," he said, "not having married the boss's daughter myself, I'm not really in a position to argue. Fact is I never had a boss."

The man looked at Hubert in wonder. "No?"

"No. Never had a boss. Except the one I married." Hubert looked down into his empty mug as if he saw something strange there. Then he passed the mug to me and I filled it again.

We sat there for a long time while cars hummed on the highway, the day grew hotter, and a lonely hawk wheeled overhead in the sky.

"Know something?" the man said. "I hope you don't mind me saying this, but you remind me of my old man. He never worked for a boss in his life either. He just slaved himself into an early grave."

"That's the way it goes," Hubert agreed. "Sometimes."

The man looked uncomfortable. Finally he said, "Has it been worth it, though? Looking back, would you do it again?"

Hubert took a deep breath. "I'm buggered if I know," he said after a while. "Never thought about it before. I might. I think I would. Yes."

The man studied the earth and traced a pattern with a stick. He didn't look up. If he'd looked up, he would have seen Hubert's eyes were bleak.

"I was afraid you'd say that," he said at last. "I was bloody well afraid you'd say that."

"You can only take my word for it. Your father might say different. If he was around to say anything."

"No," the man said. "He wouldn't. Don't worry. I knew my old man, all right. You and him, you're alike. No doubt about it. But you're finished, people like you and him. Finished. You don't belong any more. You're a vanished, vanishing race. You hear? You're vanished. Gone. Dead."

"Don't get so bloody personal, man," Hubert roared. "What right have you got to kill me off at first aquaintance? Pull yourself together."

"Sorry," said a small voice. He took quite a while to pull himself together. Then he stopped drawing his elaborate pattern in the earth and threw the stick away. "Sorry. I really am." He paused. "You two going far?"

"A fair way," Hubert said vaguely.

"Mind if I come along?"

"Mind?" Hubert looked at that Jaguar again. "What do you think, Nick? Can we have him along?"

"I'll take you wherever you want to go," the man promised.

"It's all right by me," I said.

"Fact is," Hubert said, "we've done well for rides up to now. To tell the truth, we've been travelling a whole lot faster than we really want to go. We haven't had anywhere near enough time to study the countryside. That's why we took this breather here."

"Good idea," the man nodded. He pushed out his hand. "The name's Adamson, by the way. Adamson, Fred Adamson."

"Mine's Barney," Hubert said as he shook hands. He winked sidelong at me. "Barney Hubertson. And this is Nick, my youngest boy."

"Son?" Fred blinked in surprise.

"Why not? I'm not quite vanished yet."

"Congratulations," said Fred sadly. He became very thoughtful.

I was thoughtful too. I was trying to think of why Hubert should invent us a new surname. It was amazing what he'd do just for the hell of it.

"I'm just on the way up to a branch office," Fred said. "We've only just discovered that our senior salesman there has helped himself to a vacation in Australia."

"Did he tickle the peter?" Hubert asked.

"To the tune of two thousand quid. At least. That's the sort of thing I've got to worry about. It keeps me going, I can tell you. Christ." He mopped sweat from his face. "Will it ever end?"

A short way down the creek some figures appeared. For a moment one of them made me tingle from head to toe; it seemed to be someone I knew. Then I saw it was ridiculous. It wasn't anything like her. It was just an elderly Maori woman picking watercress. A couple of kids tagged along. They were filling a big flax kit as they worked their way up the creek. They hadn't seen us.

"Look at that," Fred said. "The Maoris have got the right idea. They know how to enjoy life, all right. Live off the land. Put your feet up and play a guitar. Why not? That's what I say."

"That's what they all say," Hubert growled. "That's what they all bloody say. I say balls. Absolute balls to that."

I stood up, but still pretty shaky in the knees. I emptied the billy into the fire and steam spouted from the cinders. Then I washed our mugs in the creek.

"Fun in life," Fred said. "And dignity. That's what they got. Look at that old girl."

"I don't see why they're supposed to have all the dignity," Hubert said. "And I don't know why they're supposed to have all the fun in life either. Would you say she'd had much fun in her life?"

Still arguing, they studied the old woman as she came closer. I didn't listen; I couldn't bear to listen. When I'd washed the mugs, I bent down to the water as if to wash my face. But really so the sound of the running water would drown out their words. The water ran clear and cool and fast, over thousands of thin smooth pebbles, hurrying towards mud and mangroves and sluggish, salty sea. I couldn't understand why it should hurry. I wasn't in the mood to reason with it, though.

By the time I turned back Hubert and Fred had given up their argument. Apparently they'd failed to settle it, and the old Maori woman was wandering back downstream with the kids following.

They talked about other things on the way north. It was a comfortable ride, even if we didn't cover a great distance. The trouble was that Fred wanted to stop, every thirty or forty miles, to swing the billy again. We bought some meat and barbecued it over a fire when night came. After the meal, they yarned about the old days while they finished a bottle of Fred's whisky. Then they started on Hubert's brandy. It was a fine, warm night with stars thick in the sky. Fred slept in his car. Hubert and I slept in a bivvy made of manuka and fern; there was just enough room for us both to crawl inside. Hubert snored and I took a long time to go to sleep. I seemed to have just gone off when I found Hubert shaking me awake and a faint light in my eyes. "Come on," he said. "Let's get moving."

It was still very early. No more than about five o'clock. I drawled blearily out of the bivvy and found Hubert all ready to go. "What about Fred?" I asked.

"What about him? He's all right. Sleeping like a baby. Come on."

"We leaving him?"

"Of course we are. It's the kindest thing we can do."

"Why?"

"Because he's enjoyed himself up to now. Another day or two and he'd only get itchy for his office desk again. We don't want to spoil it all for him, do we? Come on."

"Why'd you tell him our name was Hubertson?"

"I never tell anyone too much. On principle."

So we left Fred sleeping and hiked off down the road. There were brilliant streaks of red and gold among the long clouds swimming in the eastern sky. The morning was cool on my face.

Chapter Seventeen

ABOUT TEN O'CLOCK THAT MORNING WE WERE struggling down a clay road. The sea wasn't too far off. Crooked telephone poles and loose fences ran on each side of the road, and beyond the fences a few sad cows grazed on thin grass. Short fat hills scruffy with scrub rose all round, and cabbage trees made prickly silhouettes against the bright sky. We passed farmhouses now and then. They were either ancient places with huge verandas, half tumbled and unpainted, or new with fresh paint and no verandas. It was a quiet stretch of country. Only one car passed, in the wrong direction. As the heat thickened a haze grew over the hills. Then the hills began to change. As we got nearer the sea they became more like boulders than hills, great split boulders dumped clumsily out of the sky. A little vegetation clung to them, mostly toe toe with pale feathers drooping in the hot still day. A yellow dust kicked up round our feet as we walked.

"Not far now," Hubert said.

The road wound into scrub, then forked. In one direction it stayed wide. In the other, it narrowed; fern and gorse straggled over the edge. It didn't seem much used. There was hardly a tyre-track. Anyway we went in that direction; Hubert still hadn't told me where we were going. He simply promised me a surprise. He wasn't going any slower. His legs seemed to be jerking along at an even faster pace. The road – or track, now – dipped through a gully, then climbed. We topped a rise and looked down on a wild bright spread of coast. Surf made the shore hazy, but we saw sand, rock, sharp hills, silver creeks and patchy headlands.

"Down there," he said, haring away.

We left the scrub as we descended towards the sea. In its place was rough pasture, more brown than green, sprinkled with white sheep or red cattle. After a few hundred more yards he stopped and looked back, then waited for me; he pushed open a wooden gate and I followed. We were walking along what once had been a drive. There were tough, tall oaks and a line of elms. I glimpsed something pale in a clump of trees ahead. As we walked the trees divided, and I saw a house, a homestead; or what was left of it. Windblown wreckage lay around. Pieces of a rotted first-story veranda dangled. Windows were smashed. There was bracken and fern and young scrub where there had once been lawn. There was an old, fallen pine; it had clouted the house, knocking in one side, as it fell. Hubert was ten yards ahead now. Sunlight and shadow jumped in crazy patterns on his back as he strode between the trees. Then, about a dozen yards short of the place, he stopped. Just stopped and didn't move.

"There," he said.

"What?"

"There. That's where we began. You too. And don't forget it."

"Me? I've never seen it before."

"And nor has your father. But that doesn't matter. You have now." He stripped his gear, breathing hard, and unslung his rifle. "Nobody wants the place any more. They just use it for storing hay. See? Hay. That's all it's good for now."

I connected at last. That picture in the living room, and this place. I didn't even know, till that moment, the Flinders homestead still existed. No one had ever said anything. Well, the way it was now it might as well not have existed, I supposed; it didn't look anything like the grand old place shown in the picture. I wondered what held it up, if anything. Hubert was certainly right about one thing. It was a surprise.

"Well," I said, "it looks a good place to spend the night." I dropped my gear, and wondered where I'd said that recently. The sun was really hot now and shadow splashed like cool water on my face as I walked round the house and began to explore. There wasn't much to see. No one had lived in the place for thirty years, at a guess, and no Flinders for nearly fifty. Inside there was hardly a scrap of furniture left which wasn't rotted and collapsed; there was dust, thick dust, and hay. I left a neat track of footprints behind me as I went from one room to another, steering clear of shaky floorboards. I didn't give up until I made sure there was nothing to be seen except bending beams, cracking walls, tumbled fireplaces. I didn't know why I should feel disappointed. Perhaps it was because the place was hardly human any more. Soon it would be nothing but a shell where wind and rain could dance. Already one of the biggest rooms, part of the house which the falling pine had struck, had nothing but green leaves for a wall on two sides.

When I left the shade of the house, I found Hubert standing in exactly the same position, about a dozen yards off, stone still, eyes large and staring, his gear dumped at his feet. I knew that for him it was different; it couldn't help being different. For him it was probably solid again, the verandas all in one piece, the windows polished and shiny, the trees small and neat, the wide lawns green and clipped. He might even be seeing gardens bright with flowers, a fountain playing, ornamental ponds. For him the place was still human, all right. I wondered if he saw a small boy peer from the front door and then run helter-skelter down the steps, over the lawn and between the young English trees.

"I always wanted to come back," he said. "All these years. But I been afraid. Stupid. Crazy. What's there to be afraid of, eh? What's there to be bloody afraid of?" I didn't answer, so he said, "Bloody nothing. Nothing at all."

While he argued with himself I collected wood and boiled the billy. Later we dumped our gear inside the house and split up in search of food. I went down to the sea with fishing line and sugar bag, and Hubert took off into the hills with his rifle. I heard the whowwhowwhow of ricocheting shots while I hauled in a snapper; it sounded as if he was taking on an army. Whowwhow-whow again. He was bound to hit something in the end. Even if only a sheep. Then it was just whowwhow. It seemed his aim was improving, or perhaps he was just running out of ammunition. Then whow, and silence. He'd pumped enough shots into that hill to start a landslide; probably he was running for cover. I only caught the one fish. I filled the rest of the sugar bag with mussels from the rocks at low tide. I'd just got back to the house when Hubert came whooping in with a fair-size hare. I expected a pig shot full of holes, at least.

We didn't see a sign of anyone else around, all that day, except just after dusk when I spied a pair of headlights flashing on trees a short distance along the shore. I guessed lovers and didn't even bother to point the headlights out to Hubert. We sat in front of the old place, our campfire blazing, the light red and warm on our faces, while Hubert told me about his boyhood there. He really hadn't been much older than me when he set off to make his fortune on the gumfields. He went the day his drunken father tried to take a horsewhip to him; he knocked his father down and walked out. He'd never gone home again, never seen the place since. When he stopped talking, we heard the sea slopping on the beach, a morepork hooting from the scrub; the night was filled with the sound of insects. Moths wheeled over the flames and incinerated.

When the fire died we went into the house. We took Hubert's old bedroom, with the shattered walls on two sides, on the theory that it was the least likely to collapse on us now. The floor was well padded with hay, and we soon made ourselves comfortable.

A light breeze creaked through the place. Wood contracted, with small snapping sounds, after the heat of day. At times I imagined footsteps, and it took me a long time to go to sleep. Hubert seemed restless too. I heard him toss and turn, his blankets rustling over the hay. I dozed off for a minute or two and then I woke tingling. It wasn't ghostly footsteps. It was a long, strange, damp sound; if it was like anything, it was like wind through rainswept bush. Far away, then close; far away, then close. Coming and going like a heartbeat. For a minute I couldn't identify it at all. Then I knew. It was certainly a sound I'd never heard in my life before.

I didn't even know he could weep.

I tried to make up my mind what to do. I could ignore it, pretend to be asleep. Or I could go to him. It had to be one or the other, but I couldn't make up my mind. I thought I knew what he was weeping for, of course. For being a boy and every-thing. I supposed I might weep the same way when I was his age, if I lived that long. I might even weep for where I grew up in Te Ika. Though that, when I really thought about it, didn't seem too bloody likely.

I did nothing. I didn't want to intrude. He had his own reasons for weeping. It was his business, not mine. I waited till the weeping died down, till he seemed asleep. Then very quietly I crawled across to him and made sure he was well covered and comfortable.

Then the night began to get me too. I crawled back into my sleeping bag and lay there with my hands behind my head looking out at the new moonlight on the trees and the stars trembling in the sky. I had the sensation that if I moved, or breathed too loudly, the moon and stars might pop out and leave everything black. I lay still and tight. Even the smell of dry hay and dust seemed to vanish; I might have been right back in the bush beside Sam. Then it struck me that Hubert might be dying beside me like Sam, and there was no one near who could come to help. Suddenly I was sure. Hubert was dying and I was alone. The temperature seemed to drop; anyway my tears grew cold on my cheeks.

After a while I heard movement. It was Hubert crawling out of his blankets to see if I was comfortable. There was enough moonlight now for him to see my face plainly. He lay beside me and looked into my wide-open eyes. He didn't touch. We didn't speak. Then he sat up, making himself comfortable on the hay, and took my head and cradled it in his lap. That was all. That was how I finally went to sleep. When I woke in the early morning he was snoring under his blankets again. There were birds clucking and clanging outside, high in the old trees.

I slipped free of my sleeping bag, pulled on my swim togs, grabbed a towel and raced away from the house, down between the trees lining the old drive where Flinders' horses had clopped and Flinders' buggies bounced. Now there was nothing, not a horse, not a buggy; just me running, my hair floppy in the breeze, my feet thumping on the hard dry earth. The gate clacked shut behind me. I leapt across the road and skidded into scrub; I cleared a hump of land to look down at last on the morning sea.

Then I got a shock. I thought that whole stretch of beach would be empty. It was like a slap in the face to see someone in the surf, wading out on good strong legs; a girl. My heart pounded. Of course it wasn't; of course not. What would Glenys be doing here? Anyway this girl had pigtails; two pigtails dangling down the back of her neck.

But it took a while to convince myself, all the same, and the sea had lost its attraction anyway.

I spat at the morning and sat sulky in the cool flank of a sandhill. I trickled sand through my fingers and looked up and saw the girl bobbing in the swell beyond the breaker line. She didn't seem a particularly good swimmer. Then it struck me she must have come from somewhere. I looked along the shore and saw the tent which had risen in the night. There was a car parked beside it. So that explained the headlights flashing. There was no sign of anyone else round the tent.

When I looked back towards the girl in the sea, I couldn't see her; I guessed she was hidden by the breakers. I stood up for a clear view. I still couldn't see her. I counted thirty. No girl. I dropped my towel, stripped my shirt fast, and ran down the sand; I felt a good cold shock as I hit the water, then I struck out through the surf. It was a big surf, though there wasn't much wind; the water was red and shiny with the rising sun. I dived through breaker after breaker and rose gasping on the other side. I couldn't see her anywhere. I missed one wave; it did a tricky flicking swerve and dumped me. And dumped something on top of me. Something soft and hard, then soft and yielding. I grabbed, held on. Another wave roared down.

Then I was dragging her out of the surf like some giant fish. She was blind, her eyes screwed up, and choking and coughing; like a baby taking a fit. I got her to dry sand, dumped her down, sat on her and started to pump the water out. My speciality. Then I remembered the mouth-to-mouth technique.

Her eyes popped open right away.

"Christ," she said. "Christ almighty."

I leapt about five yards clear.

"Hell's bells," she said. "Where did you spring from?"

I kept my big mouth shut.

"Why didn't you leave me alone?" she growled. "I can't even drown myself in peace. Without getting sexually assaulted."

She stood up, dripping. Sand stuck thick to her back, the seat of her costume, and her legs.

"Well, that's that. Perhaps I really didn't want to, anyway. I don't know." She spat out the last bit of salt water, then looked at me. "Are you an idiot child or something? Don't you ever talk?"

"If I want to. Sometimes I don't want to." I turned my back and began to walk up the beach.

Feet thudded behind me. She grabbed my arm. She really would have been quite pleasant looking, if she'd given herself a chance. That is, her face wasn't bad to look at, and she had a pretty snub nose, slightly freckled, and quick bright eyes with fluttering lashes. Her unravelled pigtails were wild with water. She wasn't tall and thin, and she wasn't short and plump, but she was all right in all the usual places. Not that I was an expert in these things.

"Hey," she said. "Don't go racing off. I suppose I really ought to thank you. I mean, you weren't to know. Were you?"

"Don't mention it," I said. "The pleasure was all mine."

I tried to move off.

"Please." Her hand clung to my arm. "Won't you tell me your name?" She was like Glenys in one thing, all right. She could turn on the charm. But I knew all about that. I wasn't ignorant any more.

"My name's Nick," I said. "And if you want to know, I'm staying round here with my grandfather. It's been nice meeting you. Goodbye."

I walked up the sand, and she followed.

"You live on a farm?"

"Not exactly."

"I just wondered. You see, Michael said we'd have this place all to ourselves. He came here last year."

"Who's Michael?"

"My boy friend. If you could call him that. We only came last night."

"I know. I saw the lights." By now I'd reached my towel. I dried myself, then pulled on my shirt. "Well, I hope you have a good holiday." I turned away.

"Holiday?" she almost spat. "That's a laugh, by God. With that Simmons bitch along. It's been total war ever since we left Auckland. I know what they're up to, all right."

"Well," I said, "it's really none of my business. If you really want to drown yourself, you go right ahead. If I were you, though, I'd get further out beyond the breakers. You were coming in again when I caught you. I mean you weren't making a very decent job of it. In fact it was pretty half-hearted, if you ask me."

"What would you do," she said, "if a boy asked you along on a holiday, and then brought another girl along too?"

"I wouldn't do anything."

"If you were a girl, I mean."

"I'd say that would be pretty damn interesting."

"Oh, for Christ's sake. What's the use of talking?" She glared at me. "What do you know about the facts of life anyway? You're just a kid."

I started off again, one foot in front of the other. A thing like walking is awfully complicated if you come to think about it. All the balance involved.

"Nick," she called.

I didn't look back. I'd give her the facts of life, if she wasn't bloody careful.

"Nick," she called.

"Go to hell," I called back over my shoulder. "Where you belong, probably." Then I ran.

I cleared the road, flung open the gate, charged through the trees on the way to the house. I saw smoke. Hubert had a fire going for breakfast. The early sunlight was gentle among the trees and the smoke drifted slowly. I saw him moving up from the creek with a billy of water; first his hat, then his eyes, his pipe, his knotted handkerchief, his shoulders and huge old body. I'd never been quite so glad to see him before. I was still running. I didn't stop until I was quite close. When he saw me, I felt stupid. I stopped, breathless.

"What's wrong with you?" he asked.

"Nothing," I said. "I mean there was just someone down on the beach. That's all."

"Someone on the beach?"

"A girl."

A curious expression grew on his face. But he didn't say anything right away. He sucked at his pipe and shook his head thoughtfully.

"A girl, eh?"

"That's right."

"So you ran away."

He shook his head again sadly, and fixed the billy over the fire. "Nick, we ought to have a talk sometime, you and me." He grunted and coughed. "What was this girl doing?"

"Swimming. I mean, drowning. I pulled her out."

"Then you ran away?"

"Well, it wasn't quite as simple as that."

"But you ran away."

"All right," I said. "So would you."

"Don't jump to conclusions, boy. Never jump to conclusions in an argument."

"You weren't there. I was."

"What was this girl's name?"

"How do I know?"

"Sally," a voice said. She stepped out from behind a tree. She'd followed me. She looked so cool my cheeks blazed. She still glistened with water; she hadn't dried herself, and her wild hair dripped. "And I'd love a cup of tea, thanks. If you can spare one. I'm as dry and salty as old driftwood."

Hubert didn't say anything right off. He took his pipe from his mouth and thumbed back his hat as if to get a better view. He stared at her long and hard. "Well," he said finally. "And how do you do?" He still peered at her; I mean he was having a great old squiz. He seemed a little troubled or puzzled, though. "Nice to have you for company, Miss –"

"Miss nothing," she said. "Call me Sally." She looked at me. "God, I'm shivering. Could I borrow your towel a minute?"

I threw it at her. She used it briskly on her body and gave Hubert the glad eye again.

"I'm sorry to walk in on you like this," she announced. "But your grandson here pulled me out of the water this morning. When I got into difficulties. He didn't stay long enough to let me thank him properly."

The lying little bitch. But Hubert swallowed the story whole.

"Is that so?" he said. He put his pipe back in his mouth and shot a shrewd sideways look at me for a moment. "Well," he went on, "Nick's a great swimmer, all right. No doubt about that. He's just a little on the shy side, that's all."

"I really wanted to thank him. But he marched off. Stomp, stomp. Just like that. And when I called him, he ran. Very shy, I'd say."

They were talking about me as if I was something in a museum.

I turned my back on them and walked off to the house, to change out of my wet swim togs. I took my time about going back. I rolled up my sleeping bag in the hope that we'd be on the move again soon, and hung my swim togs out to dry. I could see them in the distance, sitting by the fire. Hubert was frying my snapper, and she was drinking tea. Out of my mug. She also had my towel draped about her shoulders. She was making herself at home, all right. I was too far away to hear what was being said, but I guessed Hubert was spinning some yarn about himself, and that she was oohing and aahing in all the right places. It was disgusting to see the way he played up to her. And the way she led him along.

She'd ruined everything. We'd been quite happy till she came along. We had the whole place to ourselves. Now she'd walked in and taken over. Sitting there with my mug, my towel, and about to eat my fish; and listening to some yarn that was probably meant for me. I decided not to go back to the fire after all. They could both go to hell, for all I cared.

I sat a good way off, on the fallen pine, and looked up at the sunlight on the trees and the birds drifting across the sky. In my time I've read books which tell me there's nothing like a bit of nature for putting peace back into the soul. Well, I don't know about that. I can tell you one thing, though. When I looked at nature that morning, had a really good look at it, I felt like getting a rifle and plugging every human being in sight, myself included. Because we were all a bloody mistake, that's why. Because it seemed to me that something had gone wrong with the world a long time back, and what went wrong was the first human being.

When I get off on my own, as I still like to do these days, out in the hills and bush, or on a huge lonely beach, I think about what a hell of a great place the world could have been if it was left to itself. We just aren't good enough for the place, if you see what I mean. There's one thing I like doing too, when I'm off on these trips, and that's looking up at the stars. The more I hear about it being unlikely that there's other human life in the solar system, or in the universe, the more relieved I feel. Take Mars. It gives me a good feeling to think about Mars, so wild and terrible and empty. I'd hate to think of it being fouled up by men and women. I think of all the wild empty beautiful places there must still be left in the universe, and I feel a great kick of wonder inside me. I'm glad that I've been born in the twentieth century, though, and not any later. Because I know everything will be fouled up sooner or later; there'll be french letters and twisted-up cigarette packets scattered on the moon, and broken bottles and bush fires on Mars. We'll bugger everything up by the time we're finished, that's sure. We were just the one wrong thing that happened in the world and in the universe.

But when I get thinking like this now, one thing does trouble me. Say there were no human beings; none at all. All right, so just imagine it, for a moment. Not a human footprint anywhere on the earth. The sea beating on empty beaches. The sun bright on the tangled trees. Birds thick in the sky. Mountains huge and snowy above the forest. Only the sound of animals and birds, wind and rain. Everything wild and empty, terrible and beautiful. Who would know that? Who would know what it was?

That's the point, you see. Something or Someone had to be able to see it all and know, and I suppose we were just the logical result.

But that morning I didn't go so far in my thinking; it's only lately I've gone so far. Anyway even the thought that we were just some logical result wouldn't have made me any happier about the human race that morning. I just sat there, at a distance, feeling murderous.

They didn't seem to notice me for a while. Then Sally saw me. "Hey," she called, "what are you doing over there?"

"Sitting," I said. "Looking."

"Why not sit and look over here?"

"I can do it quite well here, thanks."

"Snob," she said.

Then Hubert, who was fidgeting over the fire, stood up straight and looked at me. That curious, sad expression grew on his face again.

"Some more wood, Nick," he called.

It was just his stunt to fetch me over, but I couldn't argue. I took the axe, sliced some branches off a dead tree, and carried the wood back to the fire. I didn't hurry. It was obvious he didn't need any more. The billy had been boiling for some time, and the fish was almost all fried. When I dropped the wood, I didn't have any option but to sit down with them. I wore my neutral face. That is, I didn't give them the satisfaction of knowing what I felt about them both. Sally was talking away to Hubert again.

"So then you went off to the gumfields?" she said.

"That's right. No future here for me."

"There were gumfields all round here, weren't there?"

"That's right. Crawling with Dalmatians. Only they were called Austrians then. They came out in shiploads to dig the gum and make their fortunes. I don't know that many of them did."

"It must have been hard work."

"You could work your guts out for a week. Depending. But it was still better than working for a boss in town. That's why we did it."

"There must have been real men in those days."

"They were real men all right."

She was gazing up at him, her eyes stupid and shiny. One look at her made me fed up.

"I don't know where they are now," he said. "Dead, I expect."

"Not all of them." She just couldn't take her eyes off him.

"Most of them." He slapped the last fillet of snapper down on an enamel plate. "Well, there's breakfast. First in, first served."

"God knows," she said, "I've been looking long enough. A girl hasn't got a chance these days. To find a real man, I mean." She began chewing a fillet hungrily. Her mouth half-full, she went on, "Look at Michael."

"Michael?" Hubert looked up from his own fillet, and licked his fingers.

"My boy friend. I've been tramping round with him for all of a year. And why? God knows. He's as weak as water. He's never known his own mind for five minutes. And yet we've kept on. I mean I've kept on with him. Because I can't find anyone better, I suppose. But that's not the worst thing. The worst thing is, I love him. I do. So what the hell."

Hubert continued licking his fingers thoughtfully, but didn't say anything.

"I even let him break my heart," she said. "Crazy, isn't it?"

"What does this Michael do?" he said.

"He's an artist. An artist, for God's sake. Not that he earns a living from his paintings, of course. He teaches too. Takes art classes. That's the bitter end, as far as I'm concerned. Because who does he teach? Why, adoring women, naturally. He's even brought one of them along, this trip. A very delicate talent, he says; she needs to be nursed along. He says she's got all sorts of possibilities." She snorted in disgust, and then choked on a snapper bone. When she finished spluttering, she went on, "As if I don't know what sort of possibilities. And as for talent, I've probably got as much talent in my little toe. But I can tell you what she's got, all right. She's got a rich Daddy. And that's the one thing I haven't got. Me, I'm just a girl from the sticks. I milked cows until I was seventeen. And my father didn't even own a farm. He was a sharemilker. I was quite bright at school, though, and I got a scholarship to university. I lasted there a year or two, until I became too fascinated with sitting round in coffee bars instead of attending lectures. Then I met Michael. That was the end of me."

"You better put up a fight for him, if you really want him," said Hubert, chewing placidly.

"What do you think I've been doing?" she said. "But I didn't sleep at all last night, and this morning I was ready to give up fighting. For good. Then I happened to meet Nick. It's nice to meet people full of life." She flashed me a big smile.

"Nick's full of that, all right," Hubert said. He looked at me too. I was turning into a museum specimen again. Hubert had finished his tea, and I was really dry. I grabbed his mug and filled it from the bubbling billy.

"You're both so full of life," she went on, "you make me envious. I mean, I can see you both enjoy things."

Right then I was nearly busting with enjoyment. But to stop myself saying something nasty aloud, I took a quick swallow of tea. It was blazing hot. So I just spluttered slightly.

She stayed at least half an hour longer. I mooched off into the house, looking for something I might have missed seeing the day before; I didn't find anything new, of course, but it passed the time. Then I circled the house slowly. She and Hubert really had their heads close together now. I thought it was pretty appalling, particularly in view of the fact that Hubert was married to Grandmother Flinders. They were talking in very low voices and I couldn't hear what they were saying. They looked up in my direction now and then, so I guessed I must be coming into their conversation. They were probably scheming about how to get rid of me, so they could clear off together, the two of them. Not that I cared. I heaved a stick up into the trees, sent a dozen birds scattering in fright, and felt a pain in my gut. A trip into the scrub gave me some relief, but not much. When I got back she was standing up. Hubert beckoned me over to where they were sitting.

"Ah well," she said in a loud deliberate voice, "back to the battlefield again. Are you going to walk me home, Nick?"

I stood still and looked. I couldn't make up my mind whether she was serious.

"Come on, Nick," Hubert said. "See the lady home."

Lady. That was a joke.

So I had to walk her home. She crooked her arm invitingly as if I was supposed to put my arm through or something. I ignored it, anyway, and walked beside her, about four yards off. She was still giving me a pain in the gut. As we moved away from the house, down the drive, she said, "You don't know how lucky you are to have a fine old grandfather like that. He's a really wonderful old gentleman."

Gentleman. That was almost as big a joke as lady. They were certainly getting pretty inflated ideas about each other. I just wished she could have seen Hubert behaving in a menacing fashion with a loaded firearm, or chasing poor little kids who tried to get a share of the lost golf balls. We kept walking. Past the trees, through the gate.

"You look a big, bright boy for your age, Nick," she said.

I wondered why she should butter me up, but I refused to say anything.

"As a matter of fact," she went on, "it sounds to me as if all your family is pretty bright. Your brother too."

"Derek?" I smelt something strange right away. "Has he been talking to you about Derek?"

"Oh, he was just mentioned. In passing." She looked flustered, suddenly, as if I'd caught her out. "In connection with something. I forget what."

"Well, just don't talk to me about Derek," I said. "To tell the truth, I wouldn't care too much if I never saw him again."

"That's not a very nice way to talk about your brother."

"He hasn't got a very nice way of talking about me."

"I don't know. Derek sounds to me as if he might be very sensible."

"Sensible? Who's been telling you that?"

"Nobody's been telling me. I simply deduced it, myself."

I tried to think of something she might have been deducing it from, something Hubert might have told her. I couldn't think of anything at all. "I bet my grandfather didn't tell you Derek was sensible," I said, and held my breath.

"No. I rather gathered he hasn't a very high opinion of Derek either."

That eased my mind. To know that Hubert was still on my side. I could breathe again.

"Anyway," I said, "if you met Derek, you'd soon change your mind. I mean, he even looks odd these days. He's got this big long mournful face he's always had, only bigger and longer and more mournful now. His glasses are always sliding down his nose, and he looks at you over the top of them half the time. He's lost almost all his hair down the middle of his head already, and what's left comes out in a big bush on each side. I mean he looks weird, really, like he belongs to some strange religion or something."

"Well," she said. "After that description, I should be able to recognize him anywhere."

We'd crossed the road, and were over the sandhills and walking along the beach now. Waves banged up the sand and gulls, like blossoms blown in the wind, swerved and swooped upon a school of fish about a hundred yards out in the sea. There was a boat way out, a fishing trawler dark on the bright water. I could see the tent coming closer, growing bigger. I decided I'd walked her far enough.

"Well," I said, and stopped and turned, "I'd better go back now."

She grabbed my hand, fast, just swooped and grabbed before I had a chance to get away. Those fish out there probably had a better chance.

"Oh no, you're not. You're coming right along with me.

Dear Michael is probably wondering where fifty per cent of his harem's gone. You'll be my excuse, you see."

"No, I don't," I said. "I don't see."

She looked very thoughtful for a moment. "All right, I'll be honest with you then."

"You can be honest all you like, but I'm not going to be anybody's excuse. You better get that straight right now."

She took my shoulders with both hands and started to shake me.

"Look, just get this into your sweet head, will you? I've got to make the bastard jealous. If it's the last thing I do."

"You mean you want me –"

"Good boy. Full marks."

"Oh no, you don't. You're not going to come at that either." I tried to pull away, but she held tight.

"Please. Please, Nick. You'll be doing me a really great favour."

"You think I could ever make anyone jealous? Anyway, even if I could, I still wouldn't feel like it."

"Nick, it's really not much to ask. Please. I know you've been through a lot lately. All that terrible time in the bush and everything. But this isn't much. It really isn't. If you just come along with me and lounge round the camp a bit. That's all."

"So he's been telling you about that, has he?"

"About what?"

"That time in the bush." I took a deep breath, really angry now. "Anyway," I said, "that was nothing, that time in the bush. I've been through worse since then."

"Worse?"

"That's my business."

"All right, so it's your business. But just let me say something, Nick. You saved my life this morning, didn't you?"

"I haven't been able to make up my mind yet."

"Let's say you did. So won't you try to save it again?"

"You're making things difficult. Why can't you get my grandfather to help you out, anyway? He'd be delighted."

"Come on, Nick. This time you'd really save it. Really. You

shouldn't walk off and leave a job half-finished, you know. You really ought to do it properly."

"Well –" I was suddenly curious about this monster Michael. "Well, if you put it like that –"

"Good. I knew you would. I knew it." She planted a swift kiss on my cheek.

Chapter Eighteen

WE WALKED HAND IN HAND ALONG THE BEACH, around heaps of blackened seaweed and pale driftwood. Then we climbed up a sandbank to the tent. It was fairly well sheltered on each side by sandhills, and sat just above a fresh-water creek. Spinifex and lupin grew thick around, and the actual camp-site was shaded by a giant old pohutukawa. The car parked beside the tent wasn't much more than an old bomb. There was a transistor radio playing on its roof. Cooking gear, food, blankets and other unpacked odds and ends were strewn around, and an easel stood in the shade. Messing about the easel was a tall, thin young man with a little, pointed black beard attached to the end of his narrow face. He wore only shorts, and was barefoot. He didn't see us at first. The first to see us was the girl who was working over the camp-fire with a frying pan full of spitting sausages. She was very neatly dressed, with thin green slacks, nicely creased, and a matching green shirt, and a filmy blue scarf about her neck. She had a pale throat, and a very pale delicate face, and her long hair was glossy black. There certainly wasn't a single hair out of place. She looked too perfect to be sweating over a camp-fire. Anyway it looked as though the job was getting her down. She was red and flustered, and there was a faint smudge on her pale nose. Her eyes widened when she saw us through the smoke.

"Sally! We've been frightfully worried about you."

"I bet," Sally muttered. Sally seemed very tough to me now, with her snub freckled nose and pigtails.

The young man at the easel wheeled round and saw us both.

"Where the hell have you been? I hunted all along the beach."

"Well, you didn't look very hard. I've been with Nick here. Hello everybody, meet Nick."

We were still hand in hand. The young man gave me a pretty hostile stare.

"And where did you spring from? I didn't know anyone lived round here."

"This is Michael, Nick. I wouldn't let him bother you, though. He always asks fatuous questions. And this is Susan, Nick. Susan Simmons. Susan, as you see, is our cook this morning. I'm sure she's cooking an absolutely delightful breakfast, and I'm awfully sorry that I'm going to have to disappoint you, Susan. You see, I've had a marvellous breakfast already, Susan. Thanks to Nick. Fried fillets of fresh snapper. So please don't give me any of those ghastly sausages you're burning to a cinder. You and Michael will just have to manage them between you."

Susan smiled sweetly. "I'm sure Michael and I will manage to cope," she said.

"I'm sure you bloody will," Sally said. "And probably have."

"Now look here," Michael said, "I thought we agreed last night, no more bitchiness."

"I'm not being bitchy," Sally said. "Just making an observation." She let go my hand and waltzed over to the tent. "If you'll excuse me a moment, Nick, I'll change. While you're waiting, you might ask Michael to give you an art lesson. He's always on the lookout for pupils."

Michael didn't look too passionately taken with this idea. He watched Sally vanish into the tent, then looked at me, at Susan, then back at me again. I could see I irritated him, all right, and I supposed that was what Sally wanted. To tell the truth, I was on her side whether I liked it or not now. The question was, though, did I make him feel jealous? It didn't seem likely. Another question was, did I want to make him jealous anyway? He was a damn sight bigger than me.

"Mind you, he's pretty selective about pupils," Sally called from inside the tent. Her bathing suit came flying out. "I mean they're usually selected from the one sex. But he might be in the mood for variety these days. You never know."

I remembered Sally saying she wanted me just to lounge around the place a while. So I lounged; I sat down, uninvited, on the sand and tried to look comfortable. I wasn't any too comfortable, though. Not with Michael looking at me, and that Susan.

"You still haven't answered my question," he said. "Where do you spring from?"

"We're just camping round here, like you."

"A whole family?"

"No. Just me, and my grandfather. The two of us. That's all."

He grunted. "I might have known," he said to Susan. "I might have known we wouldn't have it all to ourselves this year. It was too good to last."

"You sound as if you own the place," I said.

He looked at me with sombre eyes. "Spiritually, yes, perhaps I do." He waved a hand in the general direction of discoloured cliffs topped by toe toe and cabbage trees. Razor-ridged hills, rising to a point like pyramids, stood beyond. "Since I've painted that scene a dozen times, I think my claim is just."

"Well, I'd just like to hear you tell my grandfather that."

"What's he got to do with it?"

"Because he did own this place. I mean his family. But not spiritually or whatever you like to call it. Really. They broke this land in from wilderness. All along this coast."

He didn't seem to like that thought at all.

"I can see," he said, "that you're too young to understand."

"That's a pretty crappy way of finishing a discussion."

"It is unfair of you, Michael," Susan agreed. "Nick's age shouldn't make any difference. I think Nick understands you, all right. He's just making the point that he's got a spiritual claim to this place too. It's not yours exclusively. That's all."

She gave me a consoling smile to show how much she understood. I decided she might be quite likeable after all. I was pleased with the way she took my side anyway. Michael seemed quite peeved.

"Was I saying it was mine exclusively?" he said, his beard bobbing up and down.

"Not exactly."

165

"Then please don't put words in my mouth," he scowled. "I'm quite capable of doing that myself, thanks."

"I can see that, Michael," she replied with a half-amused smile.

"And what are you getting at?" he said. His eyes flashed suspiciously.

"Michael, really. I'm not getting at anything. I'm just agreeing. Agreeing that you seem perfectly capable of putting your own words in your own mouth."

"Seem? What do you mean I *seem* perfectly capable? Are you implying that I'm not?"

"Oh dear," she said sadly. "Oh dear." Very slowly and methodically she began forking the blackened sausages from the frying pan on to a plate. There were smoke smudges all over her face now. "I think the safest thing is for me to say nothing, Michael. Really."

"Oh no," he said angrily. "You're not going to escape from this so easily. First of all you allege I claim exclusive possession of this place –"

"No, Michael. I didn't allege anything." She spoke very quietly and gently. "I just meant that you left the impression that you owned this place exclusively. You've talked like that ever since we left Auckland. It's always been *my* beach, *my* little corner of the country. I quite understand the way you feel. I think it's quite attractive, what little I've seen of this coast this morning. Perhaps I can even understand why you rather resent other people being here. You must admit you've been terribly possessive –"

"Just get this straight," he said. "I don't admit anything. To you or anyone. You hear? To you or anyone."

I supposed that I was anyone. He turned on me.

"And what are you still doing here?" he growled. "Who the hell invited you here, anyway?"

"Sally invited me," I said.

She was taking a long time to dress. Perhaps she felt she could enjoy the row more safely from inside the tent.

"Have a sausage, Nick," Susan said. She came round the

camp-fire and held the plate of sausages before me. I could see she was just trying to make me feel at home.

"Thanks," I said, "but I've eaten once this morning."

"Come on."

I didn't like disappointing her, she pleaded so much with her green eyes, so I took one.

"And what about me?" Michael said. "Don't I get any bloody breakfast, for God's sake?"

"I happen to be accustomed to serving guests first."

"And I happen to have paid perfectly good money for those sausages."

"All right," Susan said patiently.

"I certainly didn't pay for them to be eaten by every Tom, Dick and Harry who happens to be around this beach. Do you think I'm made of bloody money or something?"

"I'm sorry, Michael. I'll offer you the sausages first next time."

He snatched up three sausages and began chewing one feverishly. "I'm not asking to be served first. You're deliberately misunderstanding me. You hear that? Deliberately."

Susan sat down near me and looked miserably at the rest of her burnt, split sausages.

"Are you trying to make out that I'm uncouth?" Michael said. "That I've got no manners? Is that it?"

"Michael, that isn't true. You know it isn't."

"You're implying it, anyway. With that smug, superior look of yours."

Susan was near tears now. I felt sorry for her.

"I'm sorry if I look smug and superior. I really am."

"I had a perfectly legitimate grievance about the way you were handing out sausages to everyone round this beach. And you simply imply that it's bad manners."

Susan picked up the plate of sausages carefully, rose, walked over to Michael and set down the plate in front of him, like an offering. "There," she said. "You have the lot. For some reason I've lost my appetite."

"So I'm greedy, am I? Is that it, eh? By Christ, that's just about the bloody limit. I've had just about all I can take this morning, I'm telling you. Just about all I can take. First one runs off, without a word to anyone, and starts bringing juvenile delinquents back to the camp. The other one insults hell out of me over breakfast. Bloody women. Christ almighty. My day's ruined already. Ruined. Absolutely bloody ruined."

Susan didn't say anything; she turned her back on him. Then Sally appeared at last from the tent. She wore very brief shorts and suntop and had a smile on her face.

"Lovely day," she said cheerfully. She flipped a pair of dark glasses on to her snub nose.

"Shut up," Michael said savagely.

He picked up the plate of sausages and heaved them all over a sandhill.

"Dear me," Sally said. "Temper, temper."

"If you've got anything to say, don't say it to me," Michael told her. He indicated me. "Say it to your boy friend here. Just let me get on with my work. What a lovely way to start a holiday. God almighty."

Seagulls were diving for the sausages now, kicking up a terrible racket. It must have been a great day for them. Fish out in the sea, sausages on the sandhills. I decided I'd done enough lounging round. I hoped Sally was satisfied with the result.

"Well," I said casually as I stood up and looked at no one in particular, "I guess I'd better be shooting through. Thanks for the sausage."

Susan surprised me by speaking first. "Hold on, Nick. Wait for me. You'll show me round, won't you? I haven't had a chance to see anything of this coast yet. I'll just get my swimming costume and a towel." She hurried to the car and started ratting round inside.

"Hey," Sally said, "just a moment."

Susan pulled her head out of the car.

"Nick's with me," Sally said. "Don't you try to muscle in."

"I don't mind taking Susan for a walk," I said amiably.

I really thought Sally would like that. After all, I was under the impression she wanted Susan out of the way.

"That's rank treachery," Sally announced. "Rank treachery, Nick."

I stood there bewildered, wondering what was wrong with her. Michael just stood there, glaring at me, at Sally and Susan, at everything. Then he turned his back on us all and looked at his easel. I thought about making a run for it; then they could all spend the day happily snarling at each other.

"You promised me, Nick," Sally said. "Don't you remember? You promised me you'd take me for a walk."

It wasn't true, but of course I couldn't contradict her. Perhaps she was afraid of Michael now. Or perhaps she wanted to leave Michael and Susan together so they could peck each other to death. Well, that was hardly fair to Susan. I mean she'd stuck up for me, after all, and I rather liked her. All the same, I wished Hubert had walked Sally home. He would have known how to handle this situation. I felt really fed up.

"I suppose I could take you both for a walk," I said at last.

"Oh, Nick," was all Sally said, and she looked at me with big, hurt eyes.

"It's all right," Susan said sadly. "I won't muscle in. I'm sorry, Nick. I wasn't aware you had a prior engagement. Perhaps some other time."

I took a quick look at Michael. He was pretending not to hear.

"All right," I promised. "Some other time."

"Come on, Nick," Sally said, and we walked off together.

Chapter Nineteen

LOOKING BACK I WONDER WHAT IT WAS, EXACTLY, that Hubert told Sally about me that morning. While I mooched round sulkily and heaved a stick up into the trees, sending birds flying in fright up into the sky. Of course I have a fair idea. I know the bush was in it, and probably Sam. And somewhere Derek too. It didn't add up at the time, though. The only way I can make it add up is to remember what happened the rest of that day.

First Sally and I went back to the Flinders place and found Hubert. Sally told him we were going for a walk, and naturally she invited him along too.

"Thanks all the same," Hubert said. "But I think I'll just potter round here quietly by myself the rest of the day. I might get some more sleep. I've been short on it lately. Later on I might go after another rabbit." He waved his pipe at us. "You two shoot off."

I collected my fishing line, borrowed Hubert's for Sally, dropped them both in a sugar bag, and we set off leaving the old boy sprawled in the pleasant morning sunlight at the front of the tumbled house. His pipe smoked faintly in his mouth, and his eyes were closed; he was already nodding off gently.

We walked, all right. We must have walked from five to ten miles before that day was finished. We clambered over rocks, and left our wandering footprints over long deserted stretches of wet sand. We ate sea-eggs and mussels for lunch, and eventually found some drinkable fresh water beneath a flat terraced hill which had been a Maori *pa* site in old times. We fished for a while, off rocks while the tide was coming in, and Sally pulled in a small snapper; I caught two kahawai.

We hardly saw a sign of other human beings. A man, a Maori on horseback, high on a hillside whistling up his sheep-dog; that was about all. And the occasional boat, way out. The sky was huge, without a scrap of cloud. Heat shimmered off the white sand and burned the soles of our feet. After a while we took refuge in a small grove of pohutukawa between sandhills. We were both sunburned and sweaty, and badly needed to cool off. The thing was, though, we'd both left our towels and wet swim togs behind. The fact that we hadn't seen people made our decision easy.

"I hope you're not shy, Nick," Sally said.

"I got nothing to be shy about, much," I said. "Not any more."

She laughed brightly. "Of course, I'm forgetting again. Your being in hospital and everything. All those nurses manhandling you. Washing and shaving you. You soon get shyness knocked out of your system there."

It wasn't what I meant, really, but I let it pass. She'd made a fair enough try, and it showed she was pretty thoughtful, in a way; she was certainly trying to understand me.

To tell the truth, I'd started to like Sally quite a lot. Some girls just don't let you forget they're girls. Glenys Appleby, for instance. With Sally that day, I often forgot. She could have been a boy, just a mate like Sam, for all I thought about it. We brooded on much the same things, laughed at pretty much the same things. When she hauled in a fish, she didn't squeal madly and carry on about it. She was very quiet and matter of fact and she simply baited up her line and threw it out again. I supposed that having to milk cows till she was seventeen had probably done her a lot of good, one way and another. She didn't have ideas about herself being something special. So when we stripped off, scattering our clothes over pohutukawa roots, there wasn't any giggling nonsense about it. We simply ran naked down the sand together and dived in. I hit the sea first, and Sally was just a second behind. We splashed each other, and then competed to see who could ride a breaker furthest. There was just enough surf to make the competition interesting. We swam out, to catch the right breaker at the right moment, and then came skidding in, at a furious speed, right on the foaming crest of a dumper;

and then zoomed through the wild, tossing water till our bodies struck sand. And we'd lie there breathless arguing about who had travelled the furthest. Sometimes I think there's nothing in the world like riding surf. Nothing to beat it. When you flip yourself up on to a wave and ride that bucking water like you might a wild stallion, you could be a king or a god. The thing is to have no thought at all, though. The thing is to give yourself to the wave, so that you're nothing at all, not even a feather, so that you're just part of the wave, part of the sea, part of everything; the sky wheels, the sun explodes in your eyes, the water roars in your ears, and everything is white and silver, blue and green, and then you're flying, just flying, till you're dropped lightly to the sand. If you haven't given yourself, given yourself entirely, you're dumped. That's the sea's revenge. It has no mercy if you hold yourself back. If you're selfish, that is, and can't afford to give yourself. Or if you're afraid. And if you are like that, then you've got no hope of making friends with the sea; or with almost anything, for that matter. If you think you're something special, then you haven't a show in hell. I pity those people who need boards or boats to ride surf, who think their own bodies just aren't good enough. I pity them; I really do. For they'll never know that moment when you're nothing, nothing at all, and soaring in the joy of it, a king or a god.

When we left the surf, about an hour later, we had just enough strength to walk back up the sand to where we'd left our clothes. But we still had to dry ourselves, of course. We fell exhausted into a warm hollow between sandhills and the sun burned us browner. A light breeze off the sea had dropped, and the heat grew thicker.

"For a while there, this morning, I thought you didn't like me, Nick." she said drowsily. Then she lifted her head and gave me a slow grin.

"I don't suppose I did, much," I agreed. "Come to think of it, you didn't seem to like me much either."

"I think we've both gone sour on life," she said. "That's our problem, wouldn't you say, Nick?"

"I don't know. I got no opinion."

"I think it's true of both of us. At least, it was this morning. I'm a lot less sour on life now."

"Well, I'm glad about that. I mean I'm glad you've had a good time." I cradled my head back in my arms. My back was hot. It was about time I dried my other side, but I didn't move.

"And what about you, Nick?"

"I'm all right."

"But do you feel the same way?"

"I've had a good time, all right."

"That's not what I mean, really. I mean are you less sour on life?"

"I didn't say I was sour on life, did I?"

"Not exactly. But you know what I'm talking about, don't you?"

"To tell the truth," I grunted, "I don't."

"Come now, Nick. There should be no secrets between friends."

My arms, in which I nestled my face, made a kind of warm dark cave into which I could peer and dimly see thousands of sandgrains. I didn't bother counting them though.

"Are you listening to me, Nick?"

"I'm listening."

"I know you've been sour on life, Nick. Like me. And I think I know why."

"Then that's very bloody clever," I said.

I wanted to be back in the sea again, back on a breaker, with the spray roaring past my ears.

"I'm not so much older than you, Nick. Not so much wiser, either. So please don't be offended."

"That's enough of that."

"Don't be angry, Nick."

"I'm not angry. Just bloody shut up. That's all." I jumped to my feet, sand showering softly from my body, and stalked off to where our clothes lay jumbled in the shade.

Sally's feet slapped behind me. Then her hand fell tightly on my shoulder, and she spun me about. I didn't look at her. I refused to look at her. I looked past her face, up at the dry brown

173

hills, faintly terraced here and there, spotty with sheep and streaked with erosion.

"Don't be so damn stupid," she sighed. "You've still got so much to learn, Nick. Don't you want to know what I'm talking about?"

There was nothing else for it. So I biffed her across the side of the head. Just to prove that I did know. She went flying back into the sand, and lay there looking surprised and stupid. I've never seen anyone look so surprised. Her dark glasses dangled from one ear, then fell to the sand. She felt the side of her head tenderly.

"My God," she said. "Was that really necessary?"

"Just don't make out that I'm ignorant," I said. "I know all about it."

"About what? Using your fists? You're a positive menace."

She started getting up again. "And you'd better be careful," I warned. "I know all the tricks."

I watched her closely, in case she tried anything as she rose to her feet. But she didn't. I was surprised and, to tell the truth, a bit disappointed. That was when I realized I might have made a mistake.

"Do you mind telling me what that was for?" she asked, very calmly.

My face burned; I started to feel a fool. I bent down and fumbled round trying to find my clothes. I found it hard to see properly.

"What's the matter, Nick?" She moved closer to me.

"Nothing. Just leave me alone. That's all."

"Nick, you're not crying?"

"No. Just leave me alone. All you people. You're all the same." I must have started yelling, because I felt my voice crack, and some gulls flapped away in fright. Then I croaked, "I just want to be left alone."

"Oh Nick, Nick."

I bent down to look for my clothes again. But I still couldn't see very well.

"And I'm not bloody crying," I said.

I felt her hand fall lightly on my neck. "Please tell me what's going on, Nick. I'm as confused as you are."

"Nothing's going on. I'm just getting dressed. That's all. Stop trying to make me feel a fool. Cut it out, I'm warning you." I shoved her away. When she moved close again, I slung another punch at her. But this time she was ready. Quick on her feet, she ducked and grabbed my arm. Then, for some reason, I was lying flat on my back, spread-eagled on the sand. I felt like I'd run slap-bang into a goods train; all the wind had been knocked out of my body. I lay there puffing and croaking.

"Sorry, Nick. But you did ask for it, you know."

Through the haze I began to understand that she was sitting astride me. Wet strings of loosened pigtails swung round her face.

"I was quite an athlete once. Till I fell into bad company. I even took up judo for a while. It remains my only accomplishment."

"That's great," I said. "I might have known there were more dirty tricks than I knew about."

"How do you mean, more dirty tricks?"

"I had a different one played on me last time." I tried to heave myself up.

"Last time?"

"It's none of your business. If you don't mind, I want to get up. And get dressed."

"How do I know you aren't going to throw another punch at me?"

"You don't. So just let me up."

"Don't panic. Get your breath first."

"Get my breath? That's lovely. Very generous, after you've knocked it all out."

"And I'll do it again," she promised, "unless you tell me what this is all about. And about last time."

"You've got a long wait coming, then."

It seemed I was doomed to fight to mind my own business. I waited a moment, then said, "Look over there. Isn't that Michael coming?"

Her eyes widened, her head shot around, and I had her off balance at last. I heaved and she tumbled, all arms and legs. She recovered pretty smartly, though. As I got to my feet, she grabbed an ankle and brought me down again. So there we were, wrestling on the cool sand beneath the pohutukawa. The pace was fairly fast, and for a while it seemed touch and go who would win. I couldn't make up my mind whether she was laughing or crying, things became so confused. I felt vulnerable, because I still expected her to try the other trick. But she didn't. I began to understand that my weakness was also my strength at the same moment as I realized I would have to beat her the same way as I beat Glenys. There was really only one way of winning. Then I began to see that no one was winning, particularly. We weren't even wrestling in the ordinary way any more. It was all a damn sight more interesting than that business with Glenys, and that had been interesting enough. It wasn't quite like anything I'd known before, except perhaps riding a dumper in slow motion. Not that it was all easy by any means. I panicked for a moment, when I realized what was happening, and Sally seemed to see this.

"You're all right, aren't you, Nick?" Her hand ran up my neck into my hair. Then she pulled my head down into the hollow of her shoulder.

"I suppose I am. I haven't checked up lately."

"But you're comfortable?"

"I'm comfortable, all right."

"And not worried about anything?"

"Why should I be worried?"

"No reason. It just makes me feel better to know you're not."

I mean, we might have been walking together down the main street of Te Ika, instead of lying there under those trees, with the sun blazing beyond the shade, and the cool sand beneath us. She was moving all the time and when she moved, I moved too, so that after a while it was hard to tell who was moving; the movement didn't seem to belong to either of us. The whole business certainly had a lot in common with riding a wave. To get on balance you really had to give yourself, and that was trickier than it seemed at first.

"You see, Nick, it's still new for me too, in some ways. I said I wasn't much older than you, and not very much wiser. Well, it's true. I'm still a virgin, almost. A virgin once or twice removed, if that's possible."

I really couldn't make much sense of this at the time. It didn't seem to matter much though. I understood that she was re-assuring me, and that was the main thing. I also knew that I would look after Sally whatever happened. No one was going to hurt her again if I had anything to do with it. I was reflecting on this when I felt something give beneath me, like a wave snapping down on the sand, shooting me forward. I wasn't afraid, though, because I knew I wasn't alone. For a moment it was quite as wild as tumbling water, but I wasn't dumped. When the world grew round me again Sally was talking strange things into my ear.

It was all so different it seemed ridiculous. I didn't stand up, get dressed, and stalk away. In fact I was very reluctant to get up at all. I suppose we must have stayed there the best part of an hour. Then we took off into the water for a swim. After we climbed, dripping, out of the surf, we raced back and forward over the sand to dry ourselves. As we pulled on our clothes, Sally laughed. "What's the matter?" I asked.

"Just something I remember saying this morning," she said. "That I'd make Michael jealous. If it was the last thing I did." She sniffed cheerfully, and I saw she was both laughing and weeping. "Famous last words."

I decided I didn't know a damn thing, after all.

The sun sank as we walked back towards the Flinders beach; I think, in all fairness to Michael and anyone else who might claim the place spiritually, I can still call it the Flinders beach. Coolness came with sunset and dusk. We dawdled along the shore hand in hand. We saw smoke rising from a fire near the tent, and heard the transistor radio playing. Some news bulletin had just ended, and the announcer was chattering about weather and things. I decided I'd gone far enough, and stopped.

177

"Well," I said, "this is as far as I'll go. Good luck with Michael. He's not likely to beat you up or anything, is he?"

She laughed. "Look who's talking."

I could have sworn, when she said that, that I felt a cold hand on my shoulder and heard someone say, quite distinctly, "Nicholas Flinders." I looked around wildly; no one was there. It was all inside my head. Still tingling from the sound of my name, I decided I must be going mad.

"I'd better be getting back to my grandfather," I said hastily. "He'll be pretty worried about me, I suppose."

"Give him my love," she said. "And tell him what a good day I've had. No, tell him what a good day we've had. That's better."

The day was fading fast. There was flare after flare of brilliant red light beyond the hills, and the sea was copper and orange. Everything was marvellously still. Up on the hills cabbage trees stood in black silhouette against the inflamed sky. Everything below the hills was darkening, the beach, the dunes, the driftwood, the spinifex and lupin. There was only music from the transistor radio to disturb the quiet. I saw the firelight playing against the tent. Then I chilled, right through my sunburn. There was a figure standing by the tent, looking down. Michael, of course.

"Sally?" he called. "Is that you?"

He started moving down towards us. He was still thirty or forty yards away.

"Sally?" he called again.

I decided he could have been watching us for some time. Sally moved with fright when she heard his voice, but she still held on to my hand.

"I'll see you later, then," I said, trying to pull away.

"Don't run, Nick," she said. "Don't let him scare you."

I felt things lurch about in my stomach. "For God's sake," I said, "he's your boy friend, not mine."

But I stayed. I saw it would have been pretty undignified to clear off at that stage.

He arrived running and breathless. "Oh God, darling," he

178

began, "I've been so worried. I thought you might have been hurt on the rocks with the tide –" Then he seemed to see me for the first time, and stopped. He looked me up and down, and he looked Sally up and down. He said bitterly, "I suppose even cradle-snatchers deserve congratulations."

"You always put things so nicely," Sally said.

"You'll be happy to know Susan's cleared off. Back to Auckland. I ran her down to the main highway to catch a bus. She suddenly remembered she'd promised to spend a week with a friend at Lake Taupo."

Well, that just about finished things. It was all I needed to hear. I'd been a roaring success, all right.

"Very sad," Sally said, taking a deep breath, "for you, Michael. You know something? I think I might have liked Susan, given time. A great pity, really."

That seemed to cheer Michael up immensely. I couldn't make up my mind who was likely to get hit first, Sally or me. He just stood there, his arms hanging, as if even breathing was an effort.

After a while he looked at me. "And as for you –" he began, and seemed to choke.

"Leave Nick out of this," Sally said.

He looked me up and down again as if he was trying to make up his mind about something. "Your name," he said, "wouldn't be Flinders, by any chance?"

I thought about that.

"Yes," he went on, "five feet nine, brown hair, blue eyes, fresh complexion, strong build but may walk with slight limp. Presumed to be with grandfather. Sounds right, doesn't it?"

I felt that cold hand on my shoulder again.

"I don't know what you're talking about," I said. "If you really must know, my name's Adamson. I mean Hubertson."

I looked at Sally quickly. She had no expression on her face.

"And your grandfather's name wouldn't be Flinders too, would it?" Michael said.

Then, for some reason, I was running; running hard. I heard the beat of my feet over sand, spinifex, dirt road, grass and bracken and fern. The gate cracked shut behind me. I was in sight of the house, then in sight of Hubert squatted beside our campfire. I didn't stop running until I was right there beside him. I collapsed and tried to get my breath.

He just sighed.

"My God," he said. "And what are you bloody running away from this time?"

"Nothing." It made me feel safe again to see his old calm face there in the firelight.

"Well, you were moving at a powerful pace to get away from it, anyway."

"How would that fellow down there know our name?" I asked, still breathing hard.

"What fellow?"

"Michael, Sally's boy friend. How would he know our name was Flinders?"

Hubert brooded a moment. Then he rose to his feet, so that all six feet four inches of him was coloured quivering red in the firelight.

"Well," I said, "how would he know? And how would he know a description of me?"

But as soon as I spoke I knew the answer. I'd been too confused to think. Of course, that radio. News bulletins, weather forecasts, police messages.

Hubert didn't say anything, though. He was busy with something around the other side of the fire.

"You better eat something," he said.

"Eat something?" I said blankly.

"Fast. We're on the move again, Nick. You and me. We'll head off tonight."

"But how did he know? Would it be the police? The police broadcasting about us?"

"You fix the bedding, Nick. I'll pack all these things."

"Have we done something wrong? Why would the police be after us?"

"We mustn't forget the rifle," he said. "Or the gum-spear. They're both easy things to miss in the dark."

"You'd better tell me," I said. I felt like screaming.

"It's in that billy by the fire. Stewed rabbit. Should still be warm. Eat what you can, and throw the rest out."

"If it's the police, what have we done?"

"And your swimming togs are hanging in a tree beside the house. Easy to miss them too. You certainly took your time about coming home. Where you been all day?"

"We must have done something. Or you must have done something."

"Do you plan to sit there and yarn all bloody night? Or are you going to eat and help me pack?"

"What is it we've done, then? What is it?"

"It's the frying pan," he said. "And I'm shoving it in this bloody sugar bag. Are you going to eat that rabbit or not?"

I'd had enough. I rose, walked round the fire, grabbed his arm and held on hard.

"Are you going to listen to me?" I asked.

"I been listening, boy."

"Then what are the police on to us for?"

"It's not the police. Don't you see? It's someone who's been on to the police. To find us and bring us back."

"You mean like my mother," I said, "or Grandmother Flinders."

"That's it. Someone who doesn't want us to have this trip together. That's all it is. You better make up your bloody mind, boy, you want this trip or not?"

"Of course I do."

"Then we better shoot through tonight. If we're known round here, it's too risky to stay. Tomorrow we might have some bastard of a policeman calling."

"But you wrote her a letter," I said. "Before we left. You wrote Grandmother Flinders a letter. Telling her."

"So I did."

"Why should she get on to the police, then?"

"I didn't say she did, did I?"

"But I wrote Mum a letter too. Telling her all about it. And not to worry. You even posted it for me. Remember? That first

181

post office outside Auckland. Because I didn't have any money. She must have got it by now. So why should she worry?"

He shrugged.

"We'd better sit down," I said, "and write new ones. Before we leave. Telling them not to worry again, that we're all right. We can post them first chance we get."

"New letters?" he said. He didn't look too taken with the idea.

"We'll sit by the fire and write them. Right now, before we leave. Then they might call the police off."

I walked over to the house, hunted round in the dark for my pack, and felt out the pen and paper I'd put away carefully before we left home; I'd expected to write another letter to my parents eventually, but not so soon. I went back to the fire and handed the pen and paper to Hubert. "There," I said, "you can write yours while I finish off the rabbit stew."

He handed me the pen and paper right back again.

"You write all the letters you like, boy. Just leave me out of it. I've written mine."

"What do you mean, you've written yours?"

"I've written the only one I'm going to write Beth."

"If she's worried, you better write her another one."

"I only had the one letter to write her, boy, and I writ it. You won't get me scribbling another one. Not on your sweet bloody life."

"All right," I said, "if that's the way you feel. I just want you to know, though, that I'm going to the nearest police station first thing in the morning. If you don't write that letter. I'll get them to send her a message that we're all right."

His face twitched and his mouth sagged, but no words fell out for a while. At last he said, "You wouldn't do that to me, Nick. You wouldn't do that."

"Why not? If you don't write that letter, I got to get her a message somehow."

"All right, boy. All right. You got me over a bloody barrel now. I'll write you another letter."

"You're not writing a letter for *me*. You're writing it for *her*."

"All right, for her. Just so long as you don't go bringing no johns into it. Them bastards. They been keen to get their claws into me for years. Ever since I sued them for wrongful arrest. They never forgave me. I caused three resignations and collected five hundred quid."

"When was that?"

"Thirty years ago. A week later they arrested me again. For agitating among the unemployed and causing a breach of the peace. They never forget or forgive, them bastards. All I was doing was talking on a soap-box. That was in the depression when I was putting forward my plan to give the unemployed jobs at full pay building a bridge to Australia. So they could get the hell out of this country."

"But that'd be a twelve-hundred-mile bridge."

"So what? There were a hundred thousand unemployed. I didn't get anywhere with it, though. I was up against vested interests all the way."

"Against what?"

"Vested interests. The shipping lines."

"This isn't writing your letter," I said.

"Maybe not," he agreed, looking down at the pen and paper I'd replaced in his hands.

"I think you're trying to get out of it."

"I'll write it in my own good time."

"You'll write it now. While I'm eating." I began spooning lukewarm stew into my mouth. "Or else. Just remember, I been on pretty close terms with the police lately. Sergeant Crimmins down in Te Ika, he's not so bad. Almost a personal friend of mine."

The pen started working, fast. I guessed he had got as far as *Dearest Beth* when he took a deep breath and stopped.

"Get on with it," I said.

He was trying, no doubt about that. It was the pen that seemed stuck. He just couldn't seem to persuade it to move. The effort knotted tight all the lines and wrinkles in his face. And the flickering firelight showed me a little vein jumping at the side of his forehead.

"You'll feel better when you've written it," I told him. "I always feel better when I've got a letter out of my system."

True, that wasn't saying much, since I'd only written about four in my life. But I had to encourage him somehow. His whole body seemed to be fighting that pen. At last he looked up with miserable eyes. "I got nothing to bloody tell her," he said. "Nothing."

"Of course you have. About where you are, how you got here, what you've seen. All that stuff."

I filled my mouth with rabbit again. It was amazing the appetite I'd developed. I didn't give him any more advice. I left him to think the letter out for himself. It was too painful to watch him and see that little vein jumping with the effort. When I finished the stew I began tidying up round the camp and packing things. After a while I heard the pen scratch down a couple of words, so I knew things were going reasonably well. I fetched water from the creek and cleaned mugs and plates and billies. He still had his shoulder to the pen by the time I had everything packed and ready. But it was obvious he hadn't got very far.

There didn't seem much reason to hurry him, so I built up the fire and sat down, then lay back, with my hands behind my head, watching smoke and sparks drift up towards the stars. The moon had risen, and trees rose pale beyond the red glow of the fire. I had a lot to think about, one way and another, but it seems I didn't do too much thinking. One moment the world was red and silver and dark, and the next it was grey, all grey. Dawn was in the sky, a few flames flapped weakly over charred wood, and Hubert was still struggling with pen and paper. I wasn't cold; he'd covered me with a blanket after I'd fallen asleep, and pillowed my head with his jacket.

"Hey," I said, "you ought to have written a book by now."

He looked up. His eyes were bloodshot and weary. "A book?" he said, not understanding.

"How much have you written?"

He looked down at the paper and his lips moved silently as he counted slowly. "Nine lines," he said finally.

"Nine lines? You mean to tell me you've spent all night writing nine lines?"

It was ridiculous. I tried to shake the sleep out of my head, and the dream too. For the moment I still seemed to be in the dream which had woken me. A huge, fourteen-feet tall Michael and three enormous policemen had chased me across bleak land, murdering land with scraps of scrub, skeleton trees, and festering yellow sores of erosion. Until I saw the farmhouse up ahead with smashed windows and rusty roof. Michael's axe crashed behind me as I plunged through the front door. That was where the dream ended. I could still hear the sound of the falling axe.

"I could see you was tired," Hubert said, "so I decided to let you sleep before we shot through."

"I don't see the point in that." I got to my feet unsteadily. "Now you're tired. Besides, I still haven't written my letter."

"You'll have to write yours later on. We got to move now."

"We'd better. I dreamt that fellow Michael was after me. With three policemen." I didn't tell him the rest, but I could see he was pretty impressed, all right.

"And why should he be after you?" he said. "You got something on your mind?"

"I don't know what you mean."

Hubert looked down at his nine lines. He seemed to have cheered up considerably. "I suppose he wasn't too delighted by you staying out with Sally all that time yesterday," he said, and looked up with a twisted grin. "I do believe that, if I was Michael, I'd get the police too."

If he thought he was going to throw me into a panic, he had another think coming. Nobody was going to pull stunts on me any more. I went down to the creek and splashed my face with cold water. But I really didn't need cold water to wake me up. I was awake to pretty near everything now.

But I didn't care. Something had just clicked in my mind at last, and I had other things to think about. About just how much Glenys Appleby had told the police, for example.

Chapter Twenty

HUBERT YARNED ABOUT THE GUMFIELDS AS WE tramped along. He said the place where we were going was a great plateau of scrubland by the sea. A dry, dreary place, watered by a couple of creeks which dried out in summer, covered by thick manuka and a few stunted cabbage trees. It was hard clay country and once an army of men had camped there in whares and tents, men from every part of the world. Apart from the Dalmatians, he had known Californians, Frenchmen, Swedes, Danes and Germans. During the day they swarmed over the plateau, spades and spears flashing in the sun as they ripped and dug the gum from the tough earth. At dusk they sat outside their huts, scraping the gum clean for the buyers. Sometimes they sang as they scraped, sang the songs they knew from their homelands. When they sold their gum, there were often drunken fights; Hubert had seen a gum-thief speared to death in one of these fights. But most nights the camp quietened down early. A few voices could be heard for a while after the scraping finished, perhaps a lonely song. The lamps and fires would die, and in the darkness men muttered in their restless sleep, birds hooted, and the wind carried the sound of the sea.

We kept to back roads along the coast, or cut across country; Hubert said there was no point in showing ourselves on the highway. Anyway there had been no highway in his day, no roads at all. He'd hiked through bush and scrub, and along bullock tracks, to get to the gumfields. We got one ride from a Maori farmer driving a truck that was in pretty bad shape; some piece of the engine seemed to fall off every time we struck a bump in the road, and his brake was a piece of fencing wire.

"Gum Bay?" he said. "That's not so far. Just behind there." He pointed out a large, rocky hill just above the sea. "There's a track around the side. Walk about a mile."

186

He gave us a slice of wild pork to help us on our way. It seemed he didn't listen to the radio much, or to police messages.

We said goodbye and walked again. The track narrowed, so that it became nothing more than a ledge above the sea. On one side the hill rose steeply; on the other, waves pounded on rocks. Hubert strode ahead in great style, anxious for the first sight of Gum Bay. When he stopped, I came up behind him and looked over his shoulder.

"I might of known it," he said. "He's put us crook."

"What do you mean?" I asked. Because I could see a bay, all right. It was fairly sheltered, and the water was calm. There were holiday baches along the shore, and there was a small jetty where launches were tied. Beyond the beach the land lifted slightly. There were farms, neatly fenced, and farmhouses sitting in patches of pine.

"He's put us crook. That's not Gum Bay."

"Perhaps he meant the next bay down the coast," I suggested.

The track took us down to the shore, and we followed a seafront road past the holiday places. A few people sat on the beach in the late afternoon sun, but it was easy to tell the holidays were almost over. Most places were already empty. Then we came to the jetty. Just opposite was a store; some kids came out licking ice creams. We both saw the sign at the same time, *Gum Bay Store*.

Neither of us said a word for a moment. Then Hubert went out along the jetty, spat over into the water, and dumped his gear. He sat down and stared into his empty hands. I sat beside him in silence, my legs dangling above the water.

"Well, I'm damned," he said at last.

A man fishing from the jetty, with a silly striped holiday hat on his head, was looking us both over. I didn't like the look of the transistor radio which sat playing beside him.

"Can I help you people?" he asked. "I know pretty well everyone round here. Been coming for years."

Hubert didn't even hear the man.

"No," I said, "we're not looking for anyone, thanks."

"Sorry," he said in a friendly way, "but you two looked like you were looking for something."

"We were," I said. "But we're not going to find it."

We camped above Gum Bay that night, on the other side. Hubert fell asleep before he'd finished his mug of tea. He'd hardly spoken a word since the jetty. I covered him and then sat up quite a while longer, watching our fire burn low and listening to the sea. Hubert turned and groaned in his sleep. Sometimes he seemed to be talking to someone, but I couldn't make out the words. Anyway I doubted if he was talking to me.

Next morning we worked down the coast. I could see this was simply because Hubert didn't want to pass through Gum Bay again. We weren't heading anywhere in particular now. We walked easily, taking our time, and stopped often to swing the billy. It was a very broken coast, and sometimes it was a scramble to get around headlands. Either we climbed, or took a chance on getting round rocks at low tide. In the early afternoon we struck scrub country. It was steep, rugged land; there wasn't a house or road in sight.

"It could be worse," Hubert announced. He seemed to be coming to life again. At least he was talking to me. "It could be a lot worse."

A while later, after we'd explored the area, he said, "It's been well dug over. Perhaps three or four times. But we might be lucky. Just be careful you don't go falling down any old holes. You're likely to break your bloody neck round here." He paused. "Come over here."

I went to stand beside him. He pointed to a broken mound of earth.

"See that? That's the overturned root of an old kauri tree. It probably died ten, twenty thousand years ago. The shape's almost gone, it's been dug at, but you used to be able to tell from the shape which way the tree had fallen. That's the whole trick. When the tree was alive the gum collected up in the first branches. Maybe sixty or seventy feet up. First, you work out which way the tree has fallen. Then you pace out sixty feet and start digging. I'll take a guess. This way."

He began to pace through the scrub. I followed. He counted off twenty paces, then stopped.

"Not bad," he said, "considering. See where they've dug?"

We were looking down at a depression in the earth, an old trench. Hubert stabbed at the side of it with his gum-spear, but didn't make much impression; the clay was hard as brick.

"We might be lucky if we keep our eyes open," he said, "and find a few nuts. Gum-nuts. There might be a few scattered round."

After a few minutes of searching on our knees, Hubert came up with what looked like a small lump of clay. "We'll wash it down later," he said. "But that's gum, all right. Probably about all we're likely to find." He paused, then looked at me. "Here. You keep it." He flipped the nut into my hand. "It's yours. You'll be able to show your grandchildren."

I slipped it into my pocket and stood up, wondering about my grandchildren. I couldn't even imagine them. Then I noticed smoke drifting up from behind a ridge about five hundred yards away. We set off in that direction. "It could be just someone out shooting," Hubert said.

After we slid and splashed through a gully and a creek, we climbed the ridge and looked down on a bright garden in a dusty sea. A solidly-built hut stood at the centre of a large clearing. All the clearing was worked over carefully; vegetables grew by the hut, then fruit trees and terraces of grape vines. The hut itself was circled with flowers, and walls and roof were gripped by green creeper. There was no road, but a track wound away inland. The clearing covered about three acres of sheltered slope, and the manuka grew tall around.

While we stood on the ridge taking it all in and getting our breath, an old man with silver hair came out of the shack; he sat on his doorstep and lit his pipe. We started off down towards him. He didn't see us until we were about twenty yards away.

"You fullows shooting, eh?" He had a deep voice which seemed to fight each word he spoke. "You fullows not do yourself much good around here. No deer, no pig. Just the bunnies." His face was like old broken rock, very dark.

"No," I said. "We've been looking for gum."

His voice cracked with a laugh. "Too late," he said. "My God, yes. Too late. Me, I came forty year back. And I was too late. What you fullows think you find now?"

"Something that someone forgot," I told him.

"I found all that. I find all that long time back." He stood up and waved his pipe at us. "You fullows must get pretty tired looking for nothing. Take a seat, have a sit. I get you something to drink, eh? What you fullows like? You fullows guess I am bloody Dally from Dalmatia, eh? My English not too damn good. And I make Dally plonk, all right. My plonk here is not best, soil too sour, but is all right. You fullows like to try?"

"I'd say it'd be just the job," Hubert said, "for a dry throat like mine."

"My name Pat Radonovich. What you fullows call yourselves?"

Hubert eyed the radio aerial on the hut and invented a new name. We were certainly leaving an interesting trail.

"Well, you bloody fullows come too late, all right," Pat said. He went into the hut and returned with a half-gallon flagon of wine and three glasses. "Not in thirty years did I see anyone else come here looking for the gum. You fullows the first. Other fullows come shooting bunnies maybe, or get lost in the scrub. Nobody look for the gum any more. Only me here. Me, I see nobody for months if I don't go to town. Nobody bother me here, by God." He poured the wine carefully into the three glasses. Then he handed us each a glass.

"Let's see," Hubert said slowly, "forty years ago there'd still of been men down in Gum Bay."

"Not too many," Pat said. "One or two. Most gone. Off to city, farms, other places. Just a few stupid Dallies left forty years ago. All the good gum gone, mostly nuts left. And along comes me, Pat Radonovich, too late. Why you ask about Gum Bay? You know that place?"

"I did once," Hubert said. "Sixty years back."

A huge smile grew on Pat's face. "Well, by God. Is it to an old gum-man, an old digger, that I speak?"

Hubert nodded.

"Well, by God. Then it is a fine day for Pat Radonovich. A

great good fine day. For not in thirty years do I find such a man on my land. To talk to such man, I think sometimes I must talk to ghosts. Never in years to real man. Well, by God. Let me shake you by the hand, mister. Is a great good fine day."

He shook Hubert's hand fiercely. Then he spun around in a jerky little dance, grabbed the flagon, and slopped more wine into Hubert's glass. He didn't seem so concerned about spilling it now.

"We celebrate, mister. For it not so often two old digger men meet. What you say? We get drunk. By God, yes. Drunk to beat all the bands. Is real celebration tonight, by God."

They were on to their second glass of wine by the time I was on to my first. Soon they were laughing, shouting, and slapping each other on the back.

"And I tell you something, mister," Pat said. "Tomorrow in the morning is celebration again. We look for the gum together. Down in the swamp that only Pat knows is still the gum. Not too much. A little. Is there I dig when I am broken."

"Broken?" Hubert said.

"When I am broken, with no money for tobacco. When I have no vegetable or fruit to sell down in the town. Then you see me, Pat, hike off down to his swamp, his secret place, to fetch up some gum for sale. Is my pension, that gum, by God. Not to anyone do I tell about this swamp. Tonight we get drunk, mister, tomorrow we dig again the gum. Like is before, in old time. All right, eh?"

"All right," Hubert said. "But it's Nick here who ought to dig the gum. That's why I brought him."

Pat studied me. "Young fullow, eh? He want to dig the gum. Well, by God, we learn him to dig that bloody stuff. We learn him, you and me." He biffed me on the back cheerfully, and my wine spilt everywhere. I wasn't too unhappy about losing it, though. Sitting and sipping in the sun, I'd grown dizzy.

After a while I wandered off into the shade of the fruit trees. I found a place to rest and in a few minutes, after watching the sky sway back and forward, I was asleep.

When I woke, with a dry tongue and heavy head, the world

was dark. I wandered back to the hut. A hurricane lamp hissed inside the place, and the yellow light fell on Hubert and Pat where they still sat on the step. I smelled food cooking, which was a relief; I was starving. They'd almost finished the first half-gallon flagon, and another one stood ready at their feet. They didn't look at me when I turned up again; they probably hadn't even noticed that I'd gone. I pushed past them into the hut to see what was cooking and after a while, since they were still talking, helped myself to some food.

"Was after first big war," Pat was saying. "But always plenty little wars in my country. Always killing. One time my brother killed, another time my father. Next time maybe is me. Then I talk my mate Tony. He has cousin in New Zealand. This New Zealand good. No killing there, Tony's cousin say, good place to make money quick. Dig the gum, sell the gum, make money, buy land. So I ask Tony, what this gum is? From the tree he say, from the old tree dead in ground. Dig it, sell it, makes good varnish and lino. All the time Dalmatian boys go to New Zealand for the digging. So after the war is no more Dalmatia, only Yugoslavia. I think is probably more killing soon. I say Tony, we bugger off to this New Zealand quick. We dig this bloody gum and get rich. We get the boat and came quick, before is more killing. On the boat Tony sick. Too much in mountains, fighting in Austrian army, too long in snow. I nurse my mate, tell him all will be better, all. In New Zealand will be sun to shine, gum to dig, money to make. Tony just lie on his blanket and look at me. And spit, spit, cough. Then we get here. Tony still sick. We stand on top of boat and look over Auckland. Every man seem rich. Every man eat well, spend money. We walk round Auckland to find Tony's cousin. This cousin now a mean bastard. Too late, he say, you bloody fullows come too late. No more gum. Waste of time looking. He feed us scraps at the back of his restaurant, and offer us jobs. One pound a week he offer. Tony and me tell him get stuffed, and we clear off from Auckland to look for gum. Tony coughing worse now. We get to Gum Bay and find some Dalmatian fullows. Too late, they all say, all the gum gone, too late. You fullows bugger off back to town and get job. We don't go. Tony too sick. I build hut for him to rest, and in day I go off to look for gum. I find little, but is enough to buy food. One day I come home. Tony my mate is dead. I weep, I bury him. I get drunk too much. Is no more reason to stay in Gum Bay near other fullows. I shift down coast to look for more gum. To here. Is always just enough gum to buy food, never to get rich. But I stay. I build my hut, plant trees, grow fruit. Is all right. Sometimes I remember Tony. For him new country is only death. But is all right. I weep not for long. I grow my plants, I fish the sea, I shoot bunnies, I find little gum. Is all right for me. No more kill, kill. Is quiet, is peace. Nobody to bother Pat, nobody to put me in army. I listen the wind. I listen the sea. The sun shine, the rain blow. Warm days, cold days, is all same. All things over now, all things gone. Is quiet. Is peace."

Their heads were nodding by the time they started their second flagon of wine. I cleared a space on the floor of the hut and climbed into my sleeping bag. I listened to them talking, and watched the light of the hurricane lamp jumping over all the objects in the hut. There wasn't much furniture. A table, three chairs, two bunks built against the wall. The walls were pasted over with old newspapers. There were old calendars dating back to 1930. There was gum everywhere, in a hundred shapes. Gum carved into churches, ships, crucifixes and hearts. Almost every shelf in the hut was loaded with gum carvings. I supposed I ought to be thinking about gum, and about how I was supposed to find it in the morning, instead of about what Glenys Appleby and the police were likely to do to me between them. By rights I ought to have been the one getting drunk.

Hubert was in a bad way when I woke. His groans filled the hut. It was daylight, and he was in the lower bunk. I scrambled out of my sleeping bag to have a look at him. "God almighty," he roared, "how did I ever get like this?"

"Because you drank too much," I told him.

"Mind your own bloody business. Did I ask your opinion? Young prick, what right have you got to criticize?"

"All right," I said. "I don't know how you got like this. It's beyond me. I'm absolutely mystified." I fetched fresh water from Pat's raintank. Pat was still asleep in the top bunk. I splashed some of the water on to Hubert's face. He yelled.

"Christ, that's cold. What are you doing, drowning me?"

"I thought if I washed your face it might wake you up."

"Wake me up? I been trying to go to sleep, for God's sake."

He tried to lift himself up to fight me off, but fell back holding his head again. I washed his face gently.

"I thought you were supposed to be helping me," he said. "A great help you turned out to be. You hardly touched a drop of that damn wine. Left it all to me, and now you abuse me."

"I'm not abusing you. I never said a word."

"Don't contradict. You're always bloody contradicting. First of all you dodge drinking your share. Then you criticize me when an old man is at his weakest. Criticize, then argue. Always taking advantage. Here. Help me out of bed."

"I thought you said you wanted to sleep."

"There you go. Contradicting again. Are you going to help me out of bed or are you not?"

I helped him. He was shaky on his feet, and kept feeling his head to see if it was there. "God," he said. "Hammers and red-hot pitchforks." He staggered out to the raintank and drank a gallon of water.

The noise woke Pat. He hopped out of his bunk with a cheerful smile and bustled about getting breakfast. Afterwards we all sat on the front step of the hut drinking tea and studying the weather. It was another fine warm day. Then Pat stood up.

"Now," he said, "we look for the gum. Is best time, morning. Later too hot."

We set out. They went ahead yarning and I followed behind with spade and gum-spear. We walked about a mile through scrub country, following a creek-bed where only a thin muddy trickle of water ran. Eventually Pat led us to some damp low-lying ground covered thickly with fern. "Anywhere here is gum," he said. "In old days is mostly a lake. Diggers hurry to get rich quick, they leave it alone. But I drain it. Little bit every year. Until is no longer lake, but swamp. Underneath is gum."

They showed me how to use the spear. Then they made themselves comfortable up on a dry bank and lit their pipes. Pat produced a bottle of wine which they took turns at sucking. They watched and criticized while I prodded at the soft ground. I had to avoid the holes Pat had already dug. The spear kept striking stones and fern-root. The sun grew hotter. Sweat dripped stinging into my eyes, and my arms ached.

"Patience," Pat said. "Is all patience, boy."

"You're not trying deep enough," Hubert said. "Use the full length of the spear. And the strength God gave you."

So I stabbed and strained and sweated and wished I was swimming out in the cool sea. Sandflies nipped my neck, my ankles itched. I couldn't do anything that they didn't criticize. If I moved away, trying to get out of their sight, they shifted too and found another comfortable dry bank.

"He'd of starved, in the old days," Hubert said. "He'd of starved in a week, that boy. Hey, didn't you hear me telling you to use the full length of the spear?"

"You see Mate Yakich with spear in old days?" Pat asked.

"Mate Yakich? Ah, there was a man. I seen him, all right. I seen him split a young pine with his spear from forty yards off. He could of split a man, the same distance." Hubert paused. "Where's Mate now?"

"Dead. Ten years is he dead."

"The king of the gumfields. That's what they called him in my day. A giant of a man. Poor old Mate. He die in a bed?"

"In a bed, all right."

"Should of been a law against that."

"Then we drink to him," Pat said. He held the bottle high for a moment, then put it in his mouth. There was a gurgling sound. He passed the bottle to Hubert, who made the same sound.

"Hey, Nick," he called, "where's all the gum?"

I was crouched behind a clump of manuka, taking a breather.

"Nick, where are you?"

I could see them. They couldn't see me.

"Lazy young sod. He's cleared off. He couldn't take it, by God."

"Young fullows is soft," Pat agreed.

I made a real effort and stood up. I ignored them. I stripped off my wringing wet shirt and flung it away. Then I started spearing the earth again. I'd reached the stage where I wouldn't know a lump of kauri gum from a toffee apple, and I didn't care too much either.

"Got a heavy behind, that's his trouble," Hubert said.

"He is not doing so badly. Is just a young fullow."

"Then he ought to have more spring in his behind."

They were doing a great job of emptying Pat's bottle. My head was hot, my eyes sticky, my tongue and throat like sandpaper. A great holiday this had turned out to be. Marvellous. Nothing like sweating in a swamp while two boozing idiots criticized. The sandflies were swarming in for the feast now I'd stripped off my shirt. I'd given up slapping them away. What was I supposed to be doing, anyway? I was getting so bleary I found it hard to remember. I was pretty near ready to use the spear on either one of them.

"Patience," Pat called. "Is all patience, young fullow."

"You'd of starved," Hubert said.

Patience, starved. Patience, starved. Spring in my behind, Mate Yakich the king. Their words rattled back and forward in my mind as I worked over the swamp. Until I realized they were both strangely quiet. I stopped and looked back. They'd fallen asleep on the bank, the empty bottle shining in the sun between them. By the look of the sun it was almost noon.

I took my time and went my own sweet way, prodding here and there. At last I struck something that seemed to be neither stone nor fern-root, more like glass than anything. I fetched the spade and began to dig. I was so giddy I seemed to be floating, and digging suddenly wasn't any effort at all. Earth flew around me. Finally I turned up a lump of gum the size of two fists. I carried it carefully down to the creek and washed it gently clean. It came up very pale, almost transparent. Then I wrapped it in my sweaty shirt, picked up spade and spear, and went to wake them. It was very hard to wake them.

"What is time?" Pat said, bewildered.

"You find anything?" Hubert asked.

But I was already on my way back to the hut. When I got there I slopped some water down my throat. It tasted marvellously sweet. Then I unwrapped the gum from my shirt. It was even cleaner, and sat on Pat's table shining with my sweat.

"Is that all you got?" Hubert said, when he arrived. "Is that all?"

But I didn't care too much what they said.

Chapter Twenty-one

WHEN WE LEFT THE GUMFIELDS, WE TRAVELLED SOUTH through Auckland to the Coromandel peninsula. Neither of us was very happy about going through Auckland, but there was nothing else for it. It turned out to be quite safe anyway. We travelled by buses through the city, and no one recognized us. Perhaps Glenys had confessed to the police that it was her fault too, and they'd called off their search. And perhaps they hadn't. I had no way of knowing. Those people who eyed us for a while soon went on reading the evening paper and minding their own business. I watched the big buildings slide past, the liners and cargo boats docked at the waterfront, the big snarling lorries, the people clattering out of a thousand shops and offices. It was the noise that struck me most. I was nearly deafened. I wondered how people managed to stay alive and sane in all that racket. Yet Derek did. Well, he stayed alive anyway. And people like Glenys couldn't wait to get into the thick of it.

I was relieved when we started moving out of the city. I got a shock at one stage, though. A party of kids in school uniform boarded our bus. I'd lost track of time, and I hadn't realized the summer holidays were over. By rights I should have been back at school too, back in Te Ika. The thought was quite painful, but I couldn't understand why. I mean I'd cleared off from Te Ika in the beginning for a perfectly good reason. The thing was, though, I had to search for that reason in my mind now. And when I finally located it, beneath all the new things, it just seemed ridiculous. But one thing had led to another, and I was stuck now; there was just no going back. I watched those schoolkids enviously. They looked as if they didn't have a problem in the world. I felt like saying to Hubert, and almost did, "Look, I ought to be back in Te Ika now, back at school. I'm still just a kid, you know. But I can't go back now, even if I wanted to. I haven't even told you why."

Then I looked at him. He was half-asleep with the motion of the bus. His eyes were shut, and his head was fallen forward on his chest. He let out something between a snore and a sigh now and then. I shifted his head on to my shoulder so that he would be more comfortable. Then I knew that, even if I wasn't on the run from the police, I would still have stayed with him. So there was no point in telling him anything, really.

I was glad when those kids cleared out of the bus, noisy as birds, their schoolbags swinging. The bus rumbled on out of the city, and then we hitch-hiked to Coromandel.

We worked our way slowly along the peninsula. Above the sand and rocks of the shore and the narrow road rose high ranges covered in bush, hazy with heat. Streams burst suddenly out of the hillsides, tumbling in waterfalls, then sprawling to the sea on wide rocky beds. Everywhere we saw the wreckage of old gold mines, collapsed shafts, crumbling batteries, abandoned sluices. Most of these places were already half-hidden by creeper and fern. In a few years there would be nothing but overgrown cemeteries to show that thousands of men had once searched for gold there.

Hubert tried every creek. He tipped back his hat, fetched out the frying pan, crumbled a little moss carefully into it, and then dipped the pan into the side of the creek. He swirled gravel and water round, then gently shook the water out. Shaking his head, he'd say, "No colour. Nothing alluvial here. We'll try the next creek."

Off we'd go again.

"Don't hurry me, boy," he'd say. "Don't keep hurrying me. People gave up looking for gold here years ago. We can't expect to find it all in a bloody rush, can we? So don't hurry me, for Christ's sake. You're making me nervous."

"I'm not hurrying you."

"Hopping from one foot to another all the time. You can't keep still a moment. Just give me a chance."

He invented this, of course. Quite often I would just have

been relaxing on the sunny side of a creek while he searched for colour. Once he even woke me to inform me that I was making him nervous.

"But I was asleep," I argued.

"It doesn't matter. You ought to of been keeping an eye open."

"An eye open for what?"

"For anything," he said vaguely. "Here. Your turn." He threw me the frying pan. "Try up the other side of the creek. Take your time."

He lay down and went off to sleep himself.

I pottered round, dipping the pan and testing the gravel up and down the creek. I had the technique off pretty well. But having the technique didn't mean I was going to get colour. I crumbled the moss into the pan just the way he did, let the water flow in over it just the way he did. I did everything perfectly, except find gold. At first it didn't seem fair. But after a while I grew more patient and began to understand that, with a lot of things, you had to go through the motions whether there was something at the end or not; gold or something like it. It was a reasonable assumption that there was gold still to be found, so I went through the motions, looking for colour.

A couple of times I thought my patience had been rewarded, and I woke Hubert with a yell. He examined my discoveries with disgust. "Fool's gold," he snorted. He would explain that it was copper pyrites or golden mica before he went back to sleep.

So I kept going through the motions. I might have learned about fool's gold, but that didn't mean I knew anything about real gold, or that I would really know it when I found it.

One thing about gold, or looking for it, was that it certainly passed the time. The days skidded by. We camped in bivvies by a half-dozen creeks. Hubert left camp alone to buy provisions. He said it was better for me to keep out of the way. No one noticed an old man much. But people grew curious about an old man with a boy.

But of course we had to make an appearance together now and then, when we moved on to a new creek. There was only one road up the coast. At one place we stopped at a pub, just above a beach. I sat outside on a bench while Hubert bought a beer for himself, a lemonade for me. When he returned we sat silent for a while, watching the flat shiny sea, the gulls, and a boat trawling far out in the gulf. "No," he said finally. "It's no good."

"What isn't?"

"This hopping from creek to creek. Panning here. Panning there."

"No," I said. "I don't suppose it is."

So he was calling it quits. He was probably missing Grandmother Flinders. I was glad in a way. And sorry in another. I'd known the summer would have to come to an end sometime. I started planning out what I would do. First I'd see Hubert got safely back to Auckland, home to Grandmother Flinders. Then I'd clear off. Where? I didn't know yet. Anywhere but in the direction of Te Ika, that was certain. That was the only place where people knew me. Anywhere else I would be reasonably safe. A small pick-up truck stopped in front of us, kicking up a cloud of dust. As the dust settled a rangy farmer climbed out. He looked us over as he went through the door of the pub.

"No," Hubert said. "It's no good at all. We'll stick to one creek and work our way up into the ranges. That way, we might find something."

I was silent.

"You didn't think we was giving up, did you?" he said.

I studied my lemonade. "I wasn't sure," I said. "You mean we'll work our way up into the bush?"

"That's right. We'll just follow a creek up."

"I see."

"What's wrong?" He stared at me sideways, but I didn't look back at him.

"Nothing's wrong."

"You not keen about going bush? That it? You not so keen about the bush any more?"

"Excuse me," said a voice from the pub door.

We both looked up. It was the farmer. He leaned against the side of the doorway, tasting his beer.

"You pair wouldn't have the handle of Flinders, would you?" he asked. "Because if you do, the police are bloody curious about yous both. I don't know what you done, and I don't care much neither. I just know I'm getting bloody fed up with hearing about you on me wireless set, seeing you on me television, and reading about you in the paper. Why don't you give us all a bloody break and turn yourselves in?"

"I don't know what you're talking about," Hubert said.

"Break it down, Pop," said the farmer. "Don't you come the raw prawn with me."

"Flinders?" Hubert said. "Let's see, now. The name does have a familiar ring. I seem to have heard it somewhere."

"Look," said the farmer, "I'll be fair. Bloody fair, in the circumstances. I'll give the pair of yous ten minutes to make yourselves scarce. Then I'll do me duty as an honest, upright and sober citizen and mention to Bill Halloran that I seen you. He's the local john, in case you don't know. Ten minutes. There's a sporting chance. You might both of murdered someone, for all I bloody know. I might even be in danger of me life standing here. But I'll give you ten minutes start. Fair enough? I won't even look which way you go. Sorry about this, but I got a duty to meself to get some peace on me wireless set. Me cows are starting to go off their milk with hearing about you every morning. And I got a duty to Bill Halloran too. He's me cobber, and right now he's in crook with his bosses in Wellington on account of him being too lenient on the after-hours liquor trade round here. He needs a break, and you pair might be it. We don't want to lose Bill round here, he's the best bloody john we ever had. I'm just warning you, anyone in this district would do the same for Bill right now."

Hubert turned to me. "Nick," he said, "finish your lemonade. Ignore this gentleman here."

But the gentleman had walked back inside the pub. "Ten minutes," he said as he left.

"I suppose that could mean an hour round here," I said to Hubert. "But all the same –"

"It can't be the same one," Hubert said. "It can't be."

"What can't?"

"It can't be the same Halloran. He said that was the name, didn't he? Halloran?"

"That's right."

"It couldn't be the same one. Stands to reason."

"What are you talking about?"

"A john named Halloran. He ran me out of this place more than sixty years ago. At least I got out one jump ahead of him."

"What happened?"

"There was a fight. A man got badly hurt. Bloody near killed, in fact. The bastard deserved it. A sneaky little claim-jumper. Then this john named Halloran got on to me. He was a cobber of that man that was hurt. But I grabbed a horse and bolted off to the King country. I never seen this place again. Stands to reason, it can't be the same Halloran."

"Do you want to wait and find out? Ten minutes, that fellow said."

"It couldn't be. Could be his son, though."

"It could be," I said. "And you'll find out, all right, if you sit there much longer."

He seemed to wake up at last. He rose from the bench. "We better move," he said. "Get right out of here. That's what I had to do last time."

"What about the gold? And following a creek right up?"

"We'll forget about it. Like I had to forget about it last time. I might of struck it bloody rich. I'll never know now. We haven't got much time."

"Five minutes, by my calculation."

We shouldered our gear and started off along the road south. A Maori driving a cream lorry gave us our first ride. We dumped our gear into the back and climbed into the cab.

"You fullows going far?" the Maori said.

"King Country," Hubert said. It was the first I knew of it.

"I can give you a lift ten miles," the Maori said. "Far as the factory."

"Know where we can buy some horses?" Hubert asked.

"Horses?" The Maori looked at us in surprise. "You fullows want horses?"

"That's what I said."

"Well, I dunno. Funny thing you fullows want horses. I sell you a motor-bike, all right. Second hand. You don't want to buy a motor-bike?"

Hubert shook his head.

"You fullows fresh out of luck if you want to buy horses. Wait a moment, though. My cousin Ahu. Last thing I hear, a month back, was he selling his horse to buy a motor-bike. He always has a couple of horses hanging round his place. I dunno. Might still be there. Hard to sell a horse, these days. You might try old Ahu."

"How do we find him?"

"I take you there. Not too far." After a couple of miles he veered up a rough side road. "Old Ahu not the best lately. His wife die on him last year. Ahu never been the same since. No kids, you know. Ahu only been married one year when his wife die on him. My missus, she plan to give Ahu her next baby. To keep him company, so he won't be lonely. Give him something to think about anyway." We came to a small dusty farm beneath steep bush hills. Pigs and chickens were the only living things around the house. "This is Ahu's place. He don't farm in a big way. He shears, most of the year. More money in shearing other people's sheep, he says." He banged his hand down on the horn, and called through the cab window, "Hey, Ahu!"

After a while a sleepy-eyed man shambled out of the farm-house. "What's all the big fuss?" he asked.

"Got you a couple of customers. You want to make the big sale? These fullows want to buy horses."

"Horses?" Ahu said. "I don't want to buy any damn horses."

"These fullows don't want to sell them, Ahu. Want to buy them."

"Buy them?" Ahu looked interested for the first time. "Why didn't you say so?" He rubbed his eyes and took a good look at us. "You fullows want to buy horses?"

"That's right," Hubert said. "We want to buy them."

"Come right along," Ahu said. "This way, gentlemen."

We climbed from the cab and followed Ahu across to a paddock where two horses grazed. One was dark and lean. The other was grey and half-dead of old age. But it was a horse, all right. You couldn't argue about that. Hubert could argue about the price for the pair of them, though. Long before the argument finished Ahu's cousin had dumped our gear from the back of his lorry and driven off to the cream factory.

"It's dry discussion, gentlemen," Ahu said. "I think we better try some of my home brew. Should be just about right now. Last lot was no good. Didn't leave it long enough. Blew off the back of my head, damn near. Had a terrible time with my guts after. This lot should be all right, though."

Ahu fetched a dozen bottles and two jars of pickled mussels from inside the house. We learned about Ahu's history on this land, the history of his tribe back to the first canoe. We also learned a lot about his dead wife.

"About these horses," Hubert said, after a couple of hours.

"Horses?" Ahu said.

"These horses you want to sell."

"Not often you meet fullows who want to buy horses," Ahu said. "Nice to meet you fullows, though. How long you like to stay?"

"Stay?"

"Stay here with me. No use hurrying off. Not much of today left anyway."

There wasn't much of the beer and pickled mussels left, either.

"Stay a couple of weeks if you like," Ahu said, "if you fullows got nowhere to go. All the same to me. I don't see many people these days. I tell you something about those horses, anyway. Neither of them any bloody good. I wouldn't waste my money if I was you. Stay around here, with me, you might see some you like better sooner or later. Taihoa. Take your time. How about some more home brew? Did I tell you about that cousin of mine? That fullow who brought you here. Real young rascal, that fullow."

I started feeling desperate, and I was relieved when Hubert

finally offered the price Ahu had asked for the horses in the first place.

"You sure you fullows won't stay the night?" Ahu said.

"Thanks all the same," Hubert said, "but we got to be on the move."

After we saddled up, arranged our gear, said goodbye and cantered down the road, Hubert said, "We was lucky to get away. He would of kept us talking for a week. Terrible thing for a young fellow to lose his wife like that."

"He wasn't so young," I said, but he didn't appear to hear me. I was having trouble keeping my horse abreast of his. I had the half-dead one, of course.

"Terrible thing," Hubert said.

My horse had two speeds, slow and dead slow. I was soon falling behind.

"– fellow like that," I heard him mutter. He didn't notice that I was no longer quite with him. Soon I was trailing by about fifty yards. He was still talking away to himself.

When he finally noticed I was trailing, he pulled his horse over into a grove of trees. "We'll take a breather here," he announced. "Have a brew-up. When it's dark, we'll get on our way again. That's the story. Ride by dark, rest up in the day. No point in drawing attention to ourselves. Anyone seeing us at night will think we're just a pair of drovers on our way home. That Ahu said he did some droving. Gave it up on account of his wife. She was a fleeco in a shearing shed. They went in for shearing together."

"I know," I said. "I heard."

"Terrible thing," Hubert said.

I collected some sticks and lit a fire. Then I filled the billy from a creek.

"Something I should have told you," Hubert said. He looked thoughtful.

"What's that?"

"About that fellow I hurt in a fight. That yarn I told you back at the pub."

"Well, what about it?"

206

"I said he was a claim-jumper. Well, it was true in a way. I mean he did jump a claim. Only it wasn't gold, it was a girl. My girl."

I couldn't see what was so important about that.

"Looking back," he said, "I see I ought to be grateful to him. For stealing that girl."

"Why?"

"Because," he said, "I wouldn't of met Beth, would I?"

"No, I don't suppose you would," I said, and wondered.

Chapter Twenty-two

THE WILLOWS WERE BEGINNING TO YELLOW, AND there was a coolness in the evenings. The shortening days were still mainly fine, with sharp sudden rainstorms soon clearing; the blue hills rose up and quivered in the spectacular sunsets. We watched the sunsets, most fine evenings, from the steps of our whare. We made a point of getting through our evening meal quickly, so we could get outside with our mugs of tea and meditate on the big event. While the sun exploded, and beams of red spurted across the sky, Hubert yarned about his days in the bush country.

Mornings were silver, with thick dew glistening on grass and bush, mists rising from the river and tangling in the tallest trees. Between morning and evening was a huge space of time which we always managed to fill. We never saw anyone from one day to the next. For all we knew, there mightn't have been anyone else left alive in the world. There was just us, and sun and sky, river and bush. The bush rose on each side of the river from fern and toe toe to totara more than a hundred feet tall. It never seemed exactly the same colour. It had a different blend of greens for every hour of the day. The one thing that never changed was the sound of the river. We heard its distant rumble, as it raced through narrow gorges, all day and all night. At first I woke in the night, puzzled by the sound, but soon it became part of me, part of my life, just as the bush itself did.

It took us five days' riding to reach this place. We passed through the small town where Hubert first met Grandmother Flinders; it was still small, which seemed to relieve Hubert. The showgrounds by the river, where he won the wood-chopping competition, were still in much the same shape. We arrived there just after dawn and, after buying provisions, spent the rest of the morning sleeping on the outskirts of the town. Then we set off to find Hubert's first farm in the bush.

The truth is, we never found it.

It took us some time even to find the general direction. Roads criss-crossed, with confusing signposts, where there had been only horse-tracks in Hubert's day. One road led us into a pleasant valley, bright with grass, where sheep and cows wandered. A tractor puttered on a hillside, smoke drifted slowly from a gorse-fire. Farmhouses stood neat among pine shelter-belts and gardens.

"Now, where the hell would this be?" Hubert said, shifting back his hat and scratching his head.

Another road led us back into town again.

"I could of found my way round here blindfold once," he said. "When it was just a matter of crashing back and forward through bush. These bloody roads."

We wheeled our horses round, and tried again. We took a clay road which meandered some distance through second-growth, then bush; the land lifted steeply on both sides of the road.

"I think we're getting somewhere," Hubert said.

"I hope so." I watched dark clouds swarm across the sky.

The clay road became an overgrown track. We dismounted and led our horses as the bush grew tighter on each side.

At one stage Hubert stopped. "Still not keen on it, are you?"

"On what?"

"The bush. Still not too bloody shook on it, are you? I can tell."

The first rain flicked into our faces.

"I don't know what you're talking about," I said.

"Well," Hubert said. "We'll see."

The rain grew heavier. Water swirled along the track until it became more like a creek bed. We plodded on. It wasn't far off dark when we saw the whare on a slight rise ahead. It was an awkward construction of split logs and corrugated iron, with an easterly lean. There were willows and remnants of pasture around it; it seemed we had struck the edge of what had once been a sheep farm. Probably the place had been built by scrub-cutters; now it was just a place for shooters and trampers to rest up.

We stripped the horses and set them loose. Then we took shelter. Hubert stood in the doorway of the whare, rain still streaming down his face, and said, "We've missed it somewhere." He pointed up-river, in the direction of what seemed like a solid block of bush country. "My place was up there. Was, I said. Like one or two other places. I don't suppose there'd even be a building standing now. Well, it doesn't matter."

But his face said that it did matter. I left him to argue it out for himself, if he could. While he stood in the doorway and addressed the rain, I heaped up some wood, leftovers from the last occupant of the whare, and put a match to it in the big open fireplace. We were soon dry and warm. There were real bunks, our first since the gumfields, and after we'd eaten they tempted us to bed early. All round us, that night, was the countryside Hubert had watered with his sweat; all round us the bush grew again, as if he had never been.

"It does matter," I said aloud at one stage.

But Hubert was already asleep.

In the morning, with his hand on my shoulder, he watched the mists rise from the river as he had watched them rising fifty years before.

"At last," he said, "at last I've found a place that hasn't bloody changed."

He might have been beginning all over again, and I might have been Grandmother Flinders beside him. Hills burst through the mist, then distant mountains; fresh sunlight danced in the valleys below, with gleams of silver where creeks ran and water-falls streamed; gorges rose yellow, with pale tufts of toe toe. A hawk wandered across the sky. Birds chuckled and chimed, and beyond their morning din we heard the river rumbling out of the hills to plain and sea.

After breakfast Hubert lit his pipe. "Well," he announced, "we may as well make a start."

"A start?"

I watched him fetch the axe and heft it on to his shoulder. "Come on," he said.

He strode away from the whare. I followed him into the bush. It was thick, all right. Now and then he had to chop his way. He stopped at one big tree, then another. "No," he'd say. "Not this one." And he moved on. I tramped behind, still puzzled.

After a while we came to a rocky clearing where the dew still shone on moss and fern. A tough, solitary totara soared above our heads. Hubert studied it, then slapped it affectionately. "This'll do," he said.

"For what?" I asked, but he never really answered.

He planted the axe in my hands. He relit his pipe, and it jutted from his mouth at a determined angle. Then he nodded towards the tree. "Try that one for size," he said. "Take it easy, take your time. She's all yours."

I understood at last; I must have seemed pretty dim. I looked at the thin axe in my hands, then at the great tree rising against the sky. I guessed it had taken one or two hundred years, at least, to grow so tall. I remembered Sam telling me that totaras were once Maori heirlooms, handed down from generation to generation, from father to son, until they were large enough to fell for a canoe.

The more I looked at that tree, the more tiny and ridiculous I became, standing there with that stupid axe.

"Do I have to?" I said at last.

"Of course you have to," he growled. "You'll never know, otherwise."

"It's all right where it is. Can't we leave it? It's perfect the way it is. I don't want to hurt it." I let the head of the axe fall to the ground. Tiny stones clinked away. "Besides," I said, "it belongs here."

It seemed to me, in the sudden silence after I spoke, that he could have no answer to that one. Until he said, "And so do you."

I tried; I tried my hardest to get out of it. "But do I have to prove it?" I said.

"That's up to you," he announced, and looked away in the

general direction of the river. "I knocked over a few hundred in my day."

"But you had to," I said.

"And you don't have to," he answered. "That's the bloody point, you anaemic little squirt. *You don't have to.*"

I was shocked silent.

"You don't have to, so you won't," he raged on. "Yes, I might have known it. You'll grow up like everyone else, all right. I might of known I been wasting my time. You'll be able to sit your arse in an armchair and complain virtuously about the shocking bloody ballsup the pioneers made of this country. About how we wrecked and raped the place. Just like your bloody brother. All pure and good. Because you never had to."

There was nothing I could say.

"Here," he said. "Give me that axe. I'll show you a man."

I took up the axe again, but I didn't give it to him. I stepped over to the tree, feeling awkward on my feet. I took up my stance and raised the head of the axe.

"Feet a little wider," he said. "Axe a little higher."

I changed my balance.

"That's it," he said.

I hesitated. Everything was perfectly quiet and still. In that moment I couldn't hear bird, wind or river; I felt as though the whole land was holding its breath, ready to sigh. And as I swung my first blow, felt the tree shudder and creak, and heard the echo slam and bang back from the hills, I seemed to slice clean through that morning and every morning.

It took me the best part of an hour to finish what I had begun. Swinging the axe, I soon learned once more that the bush was nothing but trunk, leaf, branch and creeper; there was nothing the bush could do to me that I couldn't do to it. The totara leapt forward cleanly from my last blow, plunged, ricocheted along the ground with explosions of leaves and branches, and then like some great animal in pain crashed and slid thunderously down towards the river. The last leaf fluttered away, the dust settled. The bush became still again, and I became me; I heard a bird singing.

We were out shooting in the bush when the first big rain came. I'd noticed the clouds building darkly to the south, and had made a mental note that we ought to be getting back to the whare soon. I soon forgot this, though, when I heard a stag roar nearby. Hubert had been stalking silently ahead of me with the rifle. The roar froze us, coming from so near. I caught hold of his arm.

"Sam," I whispered. "Quick, Give it to me."

He looked at me queerly.

"What's the matter?" I whispered. "Hurry up. Give it to me."

Then I realized what I'd said, that I'd called him Sam. He didn't say anything, and I didn't say anything. He just biffed me lightly on the shoulder as he handed over the rifle.

I slid the bolt of the rifle home, and slipped lightly through undergrowth. I found the stag on the bank of a creek, just lowering its head to graze. I fired, once, and its head flew up; my second shot brought it down dead. We had fresh meat. While we skinned it and cut off the hindquarters, a strong wind sprang up and dark cloud filled the sky. Rain soon hid the hills; rain and blowing mist. We were drenched before we even started back. For a while, with the rain confusing us, we lost our sense of direction. The hindquarters began to weigh a ton. We were soaked and chilled for a good hour before we got back to the whare.

The next morning it was still raining. I fried venison steak over the open fire while Hubert lay on his bunk sneezing and spluttering. By evening he was worse. The day after he was running a high temperature, and on the third day he was delirious. Rain and wind boomed against the whare, draughts hissed through cracks in the walls. The mist seldom lifted. At best I could see twenty or thirty yards from the door of the whare.

I tried to keep him warm and comfortable. The open fire blazed day and night, and I made regular trips out into the rain to fetch more wood, which I heaped to dry beside the fire. I straightened his blankets, and refolded the jacket he used as a pillow, a dozen times a day. I fed him whatever his stomach could hold, like a baby, and cleaned up the mess he made in his bed. I washed his clothes, then, and hung them to dry. I bathed his burning face gently with cold water.

There wasn't much else I could do, except wait.

I stood at the door and watched the wind toss yellowing leaves from the willows around the whare. The leaves spun into clusters in the growing puddles of dark rainwater. Rain, rain, rain; it didn't seem it would ever end. It was probably raining on Te Ika too. The end of summer, the river flooded and full of debris. Raincoats to school, corridors and classrooms full of damp smells. Probably no one remembered me there now, not even Glenys Appleby; I'd soon be forgotten altogether. I supposed it was raining up north too, on the Flinders homestead, on the gumfields, on the places where we'd searched for gold. All the footprints we'd left in lonely places would be washed away now.

Hubert moaned. He was half-awake again, though his eyes were still closed. I washed his face and made him sip a mixture of condensed milk and brandy. It seemed to do him some good.

"The cows milked, Beth?" he asked.

"Yes, Barney," I said. "They're milked, all right."

"And the kids?" he asked. "Are they playing up? Don't be afraid to use the belt if they are. You got to be tough, girl."

"I've got them under control, Barney. Don't worry."

"Don't know what I'd do without you, girl. I really don't. You sure you're managing? You sure everything's all right?" His voice was just a feeble croak.

"Everything's all right. You just go back to sleep and stop worrying."

"You wouldn't ever leave me, would you, girl?"

"I'd never leave you, Barney. Never."

"And you really love me, girl?"

"I love you, Barney."

"Give us a kiss, girl."

I kissed him lightly on the forehead, and he drifted back to sleep again.

About noon on the seventh day a watery sun made its first

appearance beyond thinning cloud. It lit the streaks of white snow which had appeared on the highest hills. That afternoon Hubert was able to sit up again. The next day he was actually on his feet, a little shakily, and complaining about the quality of the food I served.

"We haven't got much food left," I told him. "I'm just making do with what we have. I'll have to go down to the town to get some provisions."

"All right," he said. "But don't be long. And don't go getting lost in the bloody bush again."

I started out early the following day, when I was sure he was perfectly all right, and could cook and fend for himself in the whare; I left him a good supply of firewood so he'd keep warm.

Our horses had grown tired of us and wandered off a long time back. So I walked down to the town. The bush track was muddy, almost a swamp in places. Creeks were still flooded, and I had to be careful fording them. It took me four or five hours to get down to the town. That left me just enough daylight to make the journey back. I went straight to the grocery store and provisioned up with sugar and flour, tea and vegetables, tins of meat and fish and fruit. My pack bulged. I hoisted it on my shoulder and marched out of the store. I'd gone about five yards when a hand fell heavily on my shoulder.

Chapter Twenty-three

I KNEW IT WAS OVER, THEN. I DIDN'T EVEN NEED TO turn and see who it was; I could guess. That heavy hand on my shoulder was something I'd dreamt about.

"Your name wouldn't be Flinders, would it?"

What was the use of lying? It was over, really over; everything had to come to an end.

I said my name would, as I turned. He didn't look a particularly athletic policeman, and he probably wouldn't have been very fast on his feet. I could have made a run for it. But I wasn't in the mood for that, either.

"You'd better come along with me," he said.

We walked along to the police station together. Town people stopped to gaze at us as we walked past. At the station he flipped off his helmet, pulled a chair up to his desk, and told me to drop my pack and sit down. Then he fell wearily into the well-cushioned chair behind his desk. I supposed that policemen got worn out quickly; this fellow was fairly young, but he looked as tired as old Sergeant Crimmins.

"Well," he said, "you've given us a great old run around, haven't you?"

I didn't have anything to say.

"First things first," he said. "Where's your grandfather?"

"That's his business," I said.

He fixed me with a deadly eye. "We know you went off with him," he said.

"That was a pretty smart piece of deduction. I bet it took a long time to work that out."

He rolled his eyes towards the ceiling. I've noticed policemen are pretty good on rolling their eyes. Sergeant Crimmins, for example; he could do it very neatly. This fellow didn't quite have the knack, but it was a fairly reasonable imitation of Sergeant Crimmins all the same. They don't use the Lord's name in vain, and they don't exactly pray either; they just roll their eyes towards heaven, as if even He might be putting a swifty across them. They don't miss a trick, those policemen, they like to cover a situation from all angles.

"Let's start at the beginning," he said. "I suppose you wouldn't mind a cup of tea, would you?"

They're usually pretty great on the tea too. I was ready to bet this fellow couldn't compete with Sergeant Crimmins' noises, though.

"I'll try one," I said, "that's if you're planning to swing the billy." I was fairly parched, to tell the truth. I'd been planning on a chocolate malted milk shake before I headed back into the bush.

He clumped off into the next room. A water-heater whistled, and he clattered round a bit; in the meantime, while he was out of the way, I again considered making a run for it, and wondered why I didn't. Then I knew the real reason. I was just too tired. Hubert had been too much of a responsibility. Besides, now that I looked at the situation squarely I realized that I would have to face up to that business about Glenys Appleby sooner or later, and accept what was coming to me; otherwise I'd be on the run for ever. I realized another thing too. There was no point in not telling them about Hubert; not now they'd caught me. In any case if he was left by himself up there in the whare, he'd only starve and go to pieces again.

The policeman came back into the room with a teapot, a milk-bottle, and cups and saucers all neatly arranged on a tray.

"I hope you've been thinking things over," he said. "If you're reasonable, you'll save us a lot of trouble. After all, it's not as if you're criminals. We've more important things to do." He began to pour the tea.

I sat quiet for a moment. "Would you mind saying that again?" I asked.

"I said it's not as if you're criminals. We've more important things to do."

"That's what I thought you said, all right." I became very thoughtful.

"Here's your tea," he said, and pushed cup and saucer towards me. "Sugar? You're just a straightforward case of missing persons. Though there's a suggestion of kidnapping, or contributing to the delinquency of a minor, as far as your grandfather is concerned."

I felt a giddy lightness right through my body. "Well, you can get that idea right out of your head. I went along with him of my own freewill."

"You're a minor, sonny jim. Minors don't have freewill."

"That's all you know."

"All right. We won't argue. Anyway it's not as if there's any charge that can be laid against your grandfather. He is your grandfather, after all. He may have misled you, but he hasn't really kidnapped you. A charge like that would be laughed right out of court."

"Who said he's been misleading me?"

"It's obvious."

That's another characteristic of policemen. They say "it's obvious" as if that's going to make it obvious.

"How is it obvious?"

"For one thing, you belong to your parents, not to him. For another thing, you should have been back at school a long time ago."

"But you were looking for us before I was due back at school," I said.

"Agreed," he sighed, and sipped his tea.

"Who got you chasing after us, anyway?" I asked. "My parents, or Grandmother Flinders?"

At that stage something strange happened. He put down his tea very gently; he seemed to be afraid he might drop the cup. Then he stared down at the blotter on his desk, as though he saw something unusual there.

"We thought you knew," he said at last, very quietly.

"Knew what?"

"About your grandmother."

218

"What are you talking about?"

He wasn't looking at me. He was tugging a file from a basket on his desk, then frowning at it.

"According to our information – what we've been told by your relatives and parents, that is – she died the day you and your grandfather cleared off."

"You're mad," I said faintly. "I saw her that day. I talked to her –"

Then my mouth dropped open and no words would come, no matter how I tried. Because I realized I hadn't seen her, not right before we left. Hubert had, though; he'd gone into their room, twice.

Things added up, at last; all kinds of things. Hubert going into the bedroom alone. That low grumbling voice. The sudden, long silence. The way he came out quietly, while I was making the tea, and gripped my shoulder. The look of his face, as if a horse had kicked him. The silence of that hot summer day, and his curious eyes.

There was hardly a thing that didn't add up. The phone call he asked me to make to Aunt Esther before we left, for example. She would have been the first to know; she would have phoned my parents, and probably the police. Yes, of course. And the way Hubert switched our names for the first person we met on the road. I began remembering other things in a rush, too, and felt dizzy. His weeping in the night, the way he brooded over that Ahu losing his wife.

The only thing that didn't fit, really, was the letter I'd made him write. When he knew she was dead, yet didn't want me to know. He could have pretended to write something, anything; he could have just scrawled a scrappy note to bluff me. But he'd gone about it as if she was still alive, as if she would really read all he wrote. All the things he wanted to tell her, had never told her, and could never tell her now. He sat there writing page after page with the sweat spouting off his face. It wasn't any wonder that he had nothing to say when I tried to make him write a second letter, when he spent all night over nine lines. He had nothing left. He'd said all he could say, forever.

I felt as if my brain would burst.

The policeman rose, and moved awkwardly round his desk. He put his hand on my shoulder, then he took a deep breath. "Sorry," he said. "I didn't realize –"

"It's all right," I tried to say. Perhaps he heard me.

"I mean I didn't intend to break the news so suddenly. I didn't know, I didn't realize I was breaking any news at all. Sorry."

"It's all right," I said. "It'll be perfectly all right. If you could just leave me alone. That's all. If you could just –"

But my voice wasn't functioning terribly well.

He left me alone, all right. He left the room altogether, and was gone perhaps ten minutes or an hour. I wasn't in a position to take much notice of time. I wasn't in a position to think straight about anything, much. I could remember, though. My memory was about the only thing that was functioning well. I was remembering things like the time Grandmother Flinders had flown at me, whirled me into her arms, when I arrived up in Auckland; like the way she bent over me when I woke calling out in the night. And other things, further back; I could smell the ancient smell of the house again.

"Feeling better?" he asked, when he came back into the room. "I'll brew you up some more tea. That should set you up on your feet again. I've been on the phone to your parents, by the way. They're looking forward to having you back tonight. As a matter of fact I promised to run you up there myself. They're very pleased to know you're in one piece."

"They must know I'm all right. I wrote them letters."

"Letters? I don't think they've been getting any letters. Not that we know of, and we'd have heard."

So he hadn't posted them. I might have known. I sat quiet, then said, "But what about my grandfather?"

"Well," he smiled, "I was coming round to that again."

"He's up there by himself in that whare. He's been sick."

"Whereabouts?"

I tried to explain.

"It's all right," he said. "I know the place. I had to go up there last year, to fetch out an injured stalker. We'll get your grandfather out, don't worry. First thing tomorrow morning. He'll be all right tonight?"

"I think so."

"I'll get a party up there, first thing. We'll carry him out, if necessary."

That was when I realized I had urgent things to do; I couldn't afford to mope any longer. I stood up and said, "If you don't mind, I'd sooner do without another cup of tea. I'd sooner get moving."

He looked surprised. "Whatever you like."

Everything began to move with a rush. We climbed into his car, the countryside flew past, and in just two hours we were cruising through the centre of Te Ika, and then down my street. Nothing had changed. Here, where it was warmer, the autumn leaves were still bright on the trees. It was a sunny afternoon, and schoolchildren were still dawdling home. It seemed that from the time we left the police station to the time we stopped at our gate I hadn't had time to get my breath. Then I was shaking his hand, thanking him, grabbing my pack and tumbling out of the car. "I won't stay for the reunion," he said, and sounded the horn to attract my parents.

As he drove off, they appeared on the veranda. My big, awkward father and my small, trembling mother. For a moment I just stood there off-balance, my pack weighting me down on one side. They looked at me, and I looked right back at them. My mother lifted a handkerchief to her eyes. It was like a signal. I started trudging up our front path, my head down. Then they raced to meet me. From the way my father approached, I expected he might be going to strike me at last. But his hand shot out just to grab the pack from me, as if I was still an invalid or something.

"Here," he said amiably. "I'll take that." He gave me a gentle shove towards my mother.

"Nick," she sobbed. "Nick, Nick. My boy." She clutched me, almost crushed me, and buried her head in my shoulder. I could feel the warm tears seeping through my shirt. "We thought we'd

221

lost you, Nick. We really did. We thought we'd lost you for good. Are you all right? Really all right?"

"I'm all right," I said. "I'm feeling fine." Then I found I was guiding her slowly up the path as if she, and not me, had been lost. I managed to get her up to the veranda, where I sat her down.

"There," I said. "Take it easy. It's all over now."

But it wasn't all over, not quite; things were still going in a rush. They were saying things, I was saying things, we were all saying things. What we all said added up to much the same, in the end. We were all saying sorry. For what? It's hard to say. For being ourselves, I suppose. My father was sorry for being the way he was, my mother was sorry for the way she was, I was sorry for the way I was; we were all sorry, yet there was nothing we could do about it. Nothing. I can see that now.

"You'll be going back to school, won't you, Nick?" she said anxiously.

She was actually asking me if I would.

"I'll have to give it some thought," I promised.

They took that very well, all things considered.

"And you'll tell us everything, Nick?" my father said.

I said I would, when I had a chance to get my breath. Right now I didn't have a chance. I had other business. They understood that too. They knew why I couldn't stay. I hardly needed to explain.

They stood there together on the veranda, holding on to each other, watching me sadly as I fled down the path. I looked back, once, and waved as I got up speed. Soon I was going so fast I went into sliding skids on the corners. On one blind corner I collected a kid I knew, and we both went flying. I didn't stop, though. I was about twenty yards down the road by the time he gathered enough breath to yell to his friends, "Hey, that's Nick Flinders!" On another corner I tripped on a kid's tricycle and pitched forward into gravel. I got up, my knees bloody, and kept going. My heart banged, my breath jerked in my throat, my feet hammered up and down. I took my old short-cut to the other side of town, hurdling a barbed wire fence in one leap, ducking through a hedge, splashing over a creek. Everything began to stream past as if it was underwater, houses, hedges, paddocks, people, paths, grass, gorse all in one steady flow. I had my second wind, all the pain and effort gone, so that I actually seemed to be floating. Floating along the old clay road that followed the river out of town. Hills drifted up in front of me, limestone hills sprinkled with toe toe and reddened with sunset; trees and long shadows passed in a swirl, and a light wind sent dead leaves spinning into my face. Puddles plipped and plopped beneath my pumping feet, and I heard the click of sliding stones. Everything was in a bright haze at that time of day and out of the haze, at last, swam the Waikai place. I didn't stop, even then. It seemed I might float on forever.

Mrs Waikai was out in front of the old house, waddling among the plants in her garden. She looked up as I pelted towards her, and as soon as I saw her face I knew she expected me; my mother must have warned her. She'd been waiting for the first sight of me, out there in her garden, in case I should come. In the red slanting sunset light she stood dark and solid, with a huge shadow, among the fiery green things. She was raising her arms, calling out towards the house.

"Look, look!" she cried. "It's my boy. My boy's come home."

Mr Waikai hobbled out on to the porch. Matthew appeared in the doorway. They'd been waiting too.

She swept me up with a great sigh. "My boy's come home," she said again. She was ruffling my hair, plucking at my skin to see if I was real, then weeping and kissing and almost carrying me up to the house like a child. Mr Waikai was hovering round with his toothless smile, and Matthew had a sly grin, winking at me when he got a chance. "He's home," she cried over and over again. "Back home." I couldn't tell any more whether she was sobbing or laughing, but it didn't matter; all I needed to understand was home, home, home. I could almost believe it at last.

I was there the next day, too, when Hubert arrived; I went

round to help prepare for his coming. But I was too late to be much help. Mrs Waikai already had a room prepared, the bed made, and a pot of soup bubbling on the stove. When the police car pulled up in front of the house, we watched Hubert thank the constable and shake hands. Then he turned to face us with a sheepish smile. I ran to help him up the path. Matthew collected his gear. Mrs Waikai was waiting for Hubert when we came up on to the front porch. "Welcome," was all she said.

"You're very kind to a stranger," Hubert said. He was so pleasant and polite he really surprised me. But he looked tired, old and tired, with the wrinkles sagging in his face.

"You're no stranger," Mrs Waikai said. "Not if you belong to my boy Nick."

So Hubert was home too. I'd kept my promise to Grand-mother Flinders.

Chapter Twenty-four

PEOPLE WHO SEE SOMETHING OF ME THESE DAYS SEEM to think I lead a complicated life. Having two families, two homes, I mean. They flatly refuse to believe me when I say there's really nothing complicated about it at all. Not as far as I'm concerned. I slip out of one house just as easily as I slip into the other. How many people can flip a coin to decide with which family they'll spend the night, or the weekend? Not many, I imagine. I simply can't see what's complicated about it. But I suppose it's all a question of taste. Not everyone would like to be a son in two families.

I will admit there was some confusion at first. I would tend to forget in which house I was expected for the evening meal. Then there was the matter of waking up in the morning to find I was in the wrong house for a change of clothes. My mother and Mrs Waikai sorted that out, eventually; they put their heads together and decided I would spend week-days at one place, weekends at the other. I still make the odd mistake, of course. And the whole thing still has one great advantage from my point of view. If I'm out of favour at one place, then I simply take off for the other. To tell the truth, though, this hasn't happened much lately. I'm never around long enough at one place for anyone to get tired of me. Then too I've found there's an improving intelligence system between the two places. If I'm out of favour at one, then I'm likely to be out of favour at the other too.

I can't pretend, either, that my parents were entirely happy at the beginning. Not even when I explained my responsibilities. But the fact that Grandfather Flinders already lived over with the Waikais made it simpler, and certainly made it look better in the eyes of other people in the town – which was something my mother worried about. She finally sighed and said, well, she supposed they'd almost lost me twice already. My father just said it was up to me to decide, it seemed a reasonable thing to him.

He usually walks over to the Waikai place at some time on a weekend to see Hubert. My mother seldom goes with him, unless she has some special reason to see Mrs Waikai. She hasn't forgiven Hubert, for taking me off, and I don't suppose she ever will. Everyone has some sore place in their lives, and that's mine, I suppose. Knowing she doesn't understand and never will.

Hubert and my father don't argue much now. They just yarn quietly together in the sun. Hubert's on his last lap and knows it. He hasn't much strength left after that trip with me. Mrs Waikai has him pretty much under control, but he has an ally in old Mr Waikai. When I see them sneaking off together, the moment her back is turned, I don't know who is leading who. They're pretty smart at salting away a bottle of brandy so she won't find it. They go along together to all the tangis and feasts and weddings and usually I have the job of leading them both home, which can be quite a business. Hubert has a new potato patch, right alongside Mr Waikai's kumara patch, and he hasn't given up his legal interests either. Mr Waikai represents his tribe at local meetings of the Maori Land Court, and Hubert now helps prepare Mr Waikai's speeches to the court. They have spent days discussing the arguments the court should hear. I've heard it said the court hasn't been the same since.

I suppose that's the one reasonably good thing I've done in my life, getting Hubert settled after Grandmother Flinders died. The chances are that I had to be successful at something. Statistically, I mean; statistically at least one thing I've done in my life ought to have come out right. And as for Grandmother Flinders' death, I don't expect the argument will ever be settled. Hubert himself won't refer to the subject. So there are only two viewpoints on the affair, my mother's and my father's. They've argued it out often enough, and questioned me, but neither will ever convince the other.

To my mother everything is perfectly obvious. "It was characteristic of him," she said. "To walk out like that, when she died. He's always been irresponsible, you can't deny it. The moment he saw she was dead, he walked out. Just like that. As if she hadn't given her life pandering to his every whim. He didn't even have the common decency to stay for the funeral. He walked out and left it to his children to manage the whole thing. He'd driven her to the grave and just couldn't accept responsibility. Or wouldn't. And you have the hide to sit there smugly and defend him."

"Just a moment," my father said calmly. "You're forgetting something."

"Forgetting what?"

"Nick."

"Nick? What on earth has Nick got to do with it?"

"Everything. He was there, remember."

"That's typical. Dragging in a mere child as an excuse."

"Look, let's be reasonable, Beryl. Dad's not used Nick as an excuse. He won't talk about the thing at all. And I'm not making Nick an excuse either. He's just a factor, a vital factor that must be taken into account when one considers this business."

"You won't allow that there's such a thing as common decency. Is that it?"

"Not at all."

"Then what else are we talking about? If we're not talking about common decency, what else is there to talk about?"

"A lot else."

"The man walked out on his wife when he found she was dead. Your own father. You can't deny it."

"I'm not denying it."

"Then what are you arguing about?"

"I'm not arguing."

"If you're not denying, not arguing, what are you doing?"

"Sitting here. Trying to reason this thing out quietly. It doesn't seem very difficult to me."

"Your own father," she said bitterly. "Your own –"

"Look, you don't know how much it might have cost him to walk out like that. I don't know either. What I do know is that when he went into that bedroom, and apparently found her dead, he had to make a choice. A choice between what you call common decency and – well, something else. He chose the something else. Because of Nick."

"There you go, dragging poor Nick into it again."

"I'm not dragging Nick into it. I don't have to. Because Nick's already there. Right in the centre of the whole thing."

"Most conveniently. If Nick wasn't there he'd have done exactly the same. It wouldn't have made a scrap of difference. It's so in character. To walk out on his wife as if – well, as if she was just one of his old dead cows. I don't suppose it ever struck him that she was a human being. The only time he ever really noticed her was when she didn't produce his meals on time. All those years."

"That's not quite true, Beryl. And you know it."

"All right. So it's not quite true. But it's almost true. I don't see the difference."

He sighed, and then used up half a box of matches trying to light his pipe. "Just try to look at it from his point of view for a moment. He went into that bedroom with Nick standing outside, in the kitchen, quite near. Nick told us that himself. Dad had to decide, right then, whether he was going to tell Nick or not. He knew quite well that Nick had almost gone over the edge about one recent death. He also knew that Nick had always been very attached to his grandmother. It might have struck him, mightn't it, that this new death might send Nick altogether over the edge? So what did he do? He postponed the decision. He thought of Nick, not himself. He charged off with Nick, to get Nick away from the place. A panic decision, perhaps. An instinctive choice. He wanted to protect Nick. That was all. Regardless of his own feelings. Given the same choice, given the same circumstances, what would you do?"

"Frank, are you trying to tell me you'd –"

"I'm not trying to tell you anything. I'm just trying to get you to see it from his point of view, at that moment when he had to make a choice."

"And I think you tell a wonderful story," my mother

said. "I think I'd almost believe it, if I didn't know your father."

So there it is. Perhaps there is something to be said for both viewpoints. Sometimes I think they are both right and both wrong. I can't be as sure of it all as they are. One thing I am sure of, though, is that it cost Hubert a lot either way. I think I've a right to judge that much. After all, I've as good as been Grandmother Flinders. They'll never know the half of it. I can't make my knowing add up into proving one right and the other wrong, and it doesn't matter. Just the knowing counts, and that can be a damn lonely business.

Matthew has asked me to be best man at his wedding. The wedding is coming off in a couple of weeks, as a matter of fact, in the Maori church which sits on a hill just outside Te Ika. When I argued that I was too young to be a best man, only sixteen, Matthew said age didn't have anything to do with it; and what the hell anyway, if I was going to be his brother, I'd better start acting like one and fall in with his ideas. Then I realized that if Sam was still here, he might have been best man; Sam or one of the older brothers up in the city. So I had to agree. Matthew and I have done some fishing and hunting together lately and he insists, though I don't really believe it, that marriage certainly isn't going to stop him going off with me for the odd weekend.

Strange how things go in pairs. Derek is supposed to be getting married sometime soon too. About the first we knew of it was a month or two back, when he arrived in Te Ika one weekend with his fiancée. He wrote ahead to say he was bringing her down, and my mother spent three days overturning and cleaning the house for the fascinating girl Derek said he was going to marry. I was bored with the whole business long before they arrived. My parents worked themselves up into a high old state; there's been nothing like it since Derek's first book of poems. He's just produced his second, by the way, and you'll find it in the bookshops if you're prepared to look hard enough. The title is pretty short and mysterious, *Absolutions* or *Convolu-*

tions, something like that; so mysterious that it escapes me for the moment. A lot of the things in it are still pretty mysterious too, if you ask me. There are the usual unambiguous seas and uncertain wekas, or perhaps I have it the wrong way round. Anyway you'll know it if you find it, because there's another poem there for me. I intend to give him my frank opinion of it one day. I don't plan to make him dig potatoes, though. I just want to give him a couple of days in the bush. In a note on the jacket of this book, he says he feels the collection marks the end of a certain stage in his development as a writer. Well, I hope so too. But he says he plans to turn more towards prose in the future, as a way of coming to terms with antipodean realities, whatever that means.

Anyway my parents worked themselves up into a fine old state, one way and another. Derek's short letter had been pretty miserly with information. He was so proud of himself he forgot even to mention the girl's name. So there was plenty of room for them to speculate on who the girl was, and what she would be like. To tell the truth, I got pretty fed up. Derek has a car now, a smart little Volkswagen, and when I heard it arrive at the front gate, that Saturday morning, and listened to my parents flapping through the house, I mentally tossed up whether I ought to clear off to the Waikai place. But that would have meant going down the front path and running into Derek anyway, so I compromised and went out to sun myself and Oscar Wilde in the backyard. There are a lot of little tricky, finicky bits in Oscar that I'm just beginning to get the hang of, these days. It was reasonably warm in the backyard, in fact damn warm for a late winter day, so I stripped off my shirt to get the best of the sun while I treated the commotion inside the house with disdain. I didn't see why I should be impressed by Derek picking up a permanent girl at last. Other people have done it years younger, before they've lost half their hair. And what's so great about getting married, anyway? It's something almost everyone does, sooner or later. I don't see why such a noise should be kicked up about it.

Sitting close to the back of the house in a little sheltered recess, my favourite sunning place, I could hear the voices inside, then feet banging this way and that, and into my bedroom. "Where's Nick?" I heard Derek ask.

"He was here just a moment ago," my mother said. "I can't imagine. Perhaps he's out the back. It's just like Nick to clear off when you're due to arrive. Have a look out there anyway. He can't be anywhere else."

More footsteps, close to the back of the house. First Derek's, then a pair of clipping heels. The back door opened. "Nick?" Derek called. He peered into the backyard, the sun gleaming on his bald patch, and then spied me over the top of his glasses. "Oh, there you are." He was half out the door, hanging on to someone's hand. "There's someone here I'd like you to meet. I don't believe I need to introduce you, though. I understand you've already met."

Then he stepped right out of the door and came towards me hand in hand with this girl. My stomach lurched over and my heart banged. She wasn't much changed, except that the two pigtails had become one long ponytail; she certainly had more than enough hair to make up for Derek's deficiency. "Hello, Nick," Sally said. "I see you're still sunbathing."

"Sally Waters," Derek said gravely, "Nicholas Flinders. Just to clear up the matter of surnames. I gather there was some confusion before."

"There was some confusion, all right," I managed to say.

I didn't have a chance to say much else, because my parents followed them out into the backyard. "It's such a beautiful morning," my mother said. "Why don't we have morning tea out here? Why, it's like the middle of summer. You'd never believe it was only August. Frank, you fetch the card table and set it up on the lawn. There, where Nick's lounging. Nicholas, can't you dress decently for one day of the year? Put your shirt on. It isn't decent."

"You just said it was a warm day," I pointed out.

"It's winter. People don't go with their shirts off in winter."

As I dragged my shirt back on, I grumbled, "I don't see why

it should be decent in summer, and indecent just because it's supposed to be winter."

"Don't argue, Nicholas," she said, which pretty much finished things. Actually I'd only been arguing so I wouldn't have to meet Sally's eyes, or say anything more to her.

With people coming and going, chairs and table being carried and set up, tea things chinking and chattering, and everyone invading my suntrap, I didn't have a chance to hear myself think. Why hadn't I arranged to go off with Matthew this weekend? Anything but this, anything. How much did Derek know, anyway? There's no doubt about it, your sins always catch up with you one day. It was going to be sheer bloody torture. As we all sat down to the table and my mother poured the tea, I still avoided Sally's eyes. I realized suddenly that this was probably what hell was going to be like, being skewered and grilled above tinkling teacups. Well, there was only one thing for it. I'd keep stuffing my mouth so full of cake and sandwiches I'd have an excuse not to talk.

Because I could see one thing clearly enough. I was going to be put in my place properly. I was just a kid again. Derek's kid brother. Probably Derek knew everything, everything that was to be known, and considered it all of very little importance. Well, to hell with him and Sally both; the sooner I got out of their sight the better. I hated their guts. I hated everyone's guts.

"Nicholas," my mother said, "would you please stop scowling and pass the sandwiches around?"

"Sandwiches?"

"Right there in front of you. What *is* the matter with you today?"

"Nothing, really. Just a small touch of heart failure."

My mother doesn't appreciate a lot of my jokes, and she certainly shows it. Actually, though, I almost wasn't kidding. My heart was still belting off like a fire alarm. I delicately passed the sandwiches around, keeping my eyes lowered.

"As we were saying –" Derek began.

"As who was saying?" my mother asked, smiling sweetly, anxious to join in.

"As I was saying, when you arrived on the scene and suggested we have tea out here –"

"Nicholas," my mother said, "do you really have to eat three sandwiches at a time? You're behaving like a half-starved savage."

I put two back. They were damn finicky things anyway.

"Did we miss something?" my father asked Derek gently.

"Yes. Well, you see, it's like this. Sally and Nick didn't need to be introduced. They've met once already."

"Oh?" my father said.

My mother blinked.

"And the funny thing is," Derek said, "we wouldn't have been here today, we wouldn't have been engaged, we probably wouldn't even have met, if she and Nick hadn't met first."

One thing about Derek, when he pours salt into a wound, he likes to do it by the bucketful.

"She met him up north," Derek went on, "when he was doing the gypsy act with his grandfather. She didn't know they were officially missing persons at the time, though. But someone up there recognized them from the police description on the radio, and they did a flit in the night. So she didn't see them again. Two or three months later, a few days after they were found, she overheard my name at a party we were both attending. So she walked up to me, introduced herself, and told me how she'd met my infamous brother."

"How strange," my mother said. "How very strange."

"And that," said Derek, "was how we met. Because of Nick." Then he looked at Sally with a sickening expression on his face. "Isn't that right, darling?" he said.

"Perfectly right," she agreed. "If it hadn't been for Nick, we'd never have met." I could feel the fond glance she threw in my direction, but I was busy studying the clouds above the eastern hills.

"Nicholas," my mother said, "will you please pass that plate around before you help yourself again?"

"Nick seems quite overwhelmed by it all," Derek announced.

I was overwhelmed, all right, but not in the way he meant. I was damn near drowned. I was deep in a dark green sea, among barnacled wrecks, and huge fish were nibbling at me with sharp teeth. A great old feast. Those sandwiches they were eating happened to be my flesh, that tea they were happily sipping was my blood. I tried to concentrate on clouds and hills again. You might as well fix your mind on something in your last moments.

"Well," my mother said, "it's pleasant to know, I suppose, that one good thing resulted from that whole dreadful business. I wouldn't have believed that anything good could possibly result from it. But there we are. It just goes to show. A fact is a fact. Isn't that right, Frank?"

"Perfectly true, dear," my father said. "We can't run away from the fact that something good came out of it in the end."

"Adversity always draws people together," she said. "I forget who first said that, but it's perfectly true. It seems to apply in this case, in some strange way. Something good always comes out of the bad."

The logic of this baffled me, entirely. Derek and Sally weren't contending with much adversity in order to draw together. Not if I knew anything about it. But I didn't know anything about it, I supposed. At least I wasn't meant to know anything about it; I was just a kid. Just a bloody kid, for God's sake.

"Nicholas doesn't appear to want any cake," my mother said. "Strange how his appetite comes and goes."

As if from a long way off, through the wrong end of a telescope, I saw that she was impatiently waggling a plate of something under my nose. I reached out about two miles and took a piece of it. I hoped it was nourishing. I was going to need a lot of nourishment, that was clear, if I ever hoped to get over this. A lot of building up.

"We're thinking about late January," Derek was saying. "We haven't made a firm date yet."

"A summer honeymoon," my mother said. "That'll be nice."

"That's the general idea," Derek said. "We'll have it when the Christmas holiday rush is over. We'll go camping up north,

234

probably. I don't know the region, but Sally assures me that at that time of year we should have a beach all to ourselves. Where did you say the place was, Sally?"

The cake had jammed in my throat, for some reason, but when I tried to wash the obstruction down with tea, the cup chattered against my teeth like a machine-gun, the tea went down the wrong way, I was awash as well as choking, and in my panic the cup crashed back on the saucer and sent hot tea slopping across my lap. Only my father seemed to notice, and he gave me a queer sideways look.

"That should be lovely," my mother was saying. "Really lovely. You're certainly choosing the right time of year. Your father and I had our honeymoon in spring. Remember, Frank? It rained for two solid weeks."

My father said he remembered, all right.

"Not that I believe we noticed the rain," my mother said daringly, with an awkward smile. Then she remembered I was still present and called herself to order; she coughed and the smile vanished. "Our cottage was really very snug and dry, you see."

I was still present, all right, but I wasn't paying much attention; at that moment I was quietly trying to mop the spilt tea from my lap and shirt-front with a balled handkerchief. It wasn't any use, though. The tea had soaked right through to the skin. It was distinctly hot and uncomfortable for a while. I pushed the damp handkerchief back into my pocket and decided I had better look as if I was taking an interest in the conversation again. If I hadn't been so off guard I wouldn't have looked straight up into Sally's face. She must have been trying vainly to catch my eye for some time. There was a faint, crinkly smile under her snub nose.

She gave me a huge, slow, careful wink.

No one else noticed; no one else was meant to notice. And I knew, then. I knew that I was wrong. Derek didn't know, didn't know anything at all. And wasn't going to know either, if I could help it; it would spoil everything if he knew. But that wasn't all Sally's wink told me, not by a long shot. She was telling me that, whatever the others thought, she knew damn well I wasn't a kid.

It seemed that whether I liked it or not, I was joined up with them now, with Derek and Sally, my mother and father; I was already right in the middle of their curious adult intrigues and mysteries. I hadn't even been given a chance to volunteer for the job, and I had no hope of backing out of it; I just had to make the best of it. I must say that, on the whole, it's going to be fairly interesting having Sally for a sister-in-law. All things considered, Derek couldn't have picked me a better one. Not if he tried for a hundred years. I'll be able to go to her with a lot of my problems; as a matter of fact I already do.

"By January," Derek was saying, "I ought to know about that scholarship. If I get it, we'll be off to England soon after, for two years. If not, well, it'll be back to the old annual grind in the lecture-room. But you know something? I don't care too much, one way or the other, any more. Not now I've got Sally."

A wonderful thing, love. No doubt about it. He had that expression on his face again as he looked across the tea-cups at Sally. Then he reached out and placed his hand over hers. It didn't strike me as sickening any more. It was just plain pathetic. I actually felt sorry for him. I didn't mean to feel superior, but I couldn't help it. I wondered if there was a country somewhere in the world with a custom about young brothers having the bride first. If there wasn't, perhaps I was starting off a new custom. The thought bucked me up quite a lot, and I felt like giving Derek some cheek again. Fair's fair; I mean he'd got Sally and I hadn't. I'd never had a show, really. I knew that, all right. So I burst out, "Don't forget to go over and see Grandfather Flinders. He'll want to offer you his congratulations. Especially when he sees your prospective bride."

Well, that wiped the expression off Derek's face pretty smartly. Perhaps the sandwiches were a bit heavy on his stomach or something, because he looked quite sick for a moment.

"Actually," he began, "we're not here for long and –"

"He's just across the other side of town. With that zippy little car of yours, you could be over there in five minutes."

"I'd love to," he said, "but –"

"It's all right. There aren't any potatoes to dig at the moment.

236

Anyway you haven't written a poem about him lately, have you?"

"No." His mouth closed and opened, as if he was about to say something, but then dropped shut again; something like a fish breathing its last.

"We really can't get out of it, Derek," Sally said. "Not that I want to get out of it anyway. I'd love to see the old chap again."

"There you are, Derek," I said. "You'll just have to go now. If Sally wants to. There's no getting out of it."

That pronouncement finished the subject. There was a silence, and my mother's ominous face was right at the centre of the silence.

"I don't know whether it was such a good idea," my father muttered.

"What's that?" my mother said.

"I don't know whether it was such a good idea. To have morning tea out here, I mean. That breeze has changed direction. It's quite nippy."

Anything to escape the thought of Hubert. In no time at all the tea things were clattering again, and we were moving inside. Derek still looked despondent, so as we walked into the house I did my best to cheer him up. I slapped him on the shoulder and said, "By the way, that's a very good idea of yours."

"What idea?" he asked miserably.

"About giving up poetry."

But it didn't help much, after all.

"You've got it all wrong," he told me. "I'm not giving it up. I'm just moving on to other things as well. That's all. I never said I was giving up poetry. I'm in the middle of a long sequence for Sally, as a matter of fact. Anyway I'm pleased you take such an interest in my work, Nick. It's really a great encouragement to me."

He turned his pained face to Sally. "If we're really going over there to see him," he said, "let's go and get it over with."

Well, if I couldn't cheer up Derek, at least Hubert could. It seemed, from what I heard later, that Hubert had been waiting for an excuse to crack a bottle of brandy. All in all, I suppose it

237

was a good thing I kept out of the way, for I might have confused Hubert. Anyway he was delighted to see Sally again. And he said he was pleased to congratulate any man who was good enough for Sally. He shook hands with Derek, biffed him on the shoulder, and forgave him everything, his poem and all, right there on the spot. Derek and Sally took a long time to get back from the Waikai place, and Derek dented his car against a lamp-post as he parked it outside our front gate. It didn't seem to trouble him much, though. I haven't seen Derek look happier in years. Perhaps there's even hope for my mother.

Actually I get along with Derek reasonably well these days. I put it down to the fact that Sally's done him a lot of good. But he maintains that we get along better because I'm more mature. Which I consider pretty much of an insult, for he's virtually saying right out that he didn't like me before. And I don't really think I'm that much different. Of course Sally has helped us get along better. She told me Derek was really very likeable, if one was prepared to be patient with him, and a brilliant writer besides. I suppose she meant she liked the sequence of poems he has written her. I'm glad he has pleased someone at last.

Incidentally, Sally took me aside that weekend, just before she left. She told me how she'd gone round to the Flinders' homestead, that morning Hubert and I shot through to the gumfields, to warn us that her friend Michael had just zoomed off to put a phone call through to the police. She and Michael had argued all night, and in the end Michael said he was going to put the police wise to her bloody criminal friends. He drove off to the nearest farmhouse, and she ran over to tell us.

"But there was no one there," she said. "Just the campfire. You must have left in a hurry, because you'd forgotten to douse it. And you couldn't have been gone very long. There were still a few bright cinders, a few wisps of smoke."

"We'd probably just left," I said. "We took a fair while to get away." I remembered, with a painful feeling in my chest, how Hubert had sat there all night long, while I slept, trying to write a letter to his dead wife.

"So I sat down," Sally said. "I just sat down and looked into the cinders while they faded. I seemed to lose track of time. It was a beautiful morning. The sun bright beyond the old trees, the dew shining on the grass. Everything marvellously still. Just the sound of birds, sea, and rustling leaves. I didn't even notice that the fire had gone out. I was still sitting there dreaming when the constable arrived. It was quite funny. He was so frustrated, I thought for a moment he was going to arrest me. Then I walked back to the camp, collected my gear, said goodbye to Michael, and hitch-hiked home to Auckland."

She hadn't seen Michael again after that morning. She said something else had gone out with our fire. She'd heard recently, though, that he'd taken himself off to Paris on some art fellowship. Well, it relieved me a little to know he'd had some good luck, after all that bad luck with his holidays. I certainly hope they teach him better manners in Paris, and not to go throwing his breakfast to the seagulls.

But all this is really by way of telling you that, after his visit with Sally, Derek came down to Te Ika again, in the school holidays. He wanted to take me back to Auckland with him, to stay with him.

"Just for a short holiday," Derek explained. "It'll do him good. I rather think Nick needs a break from Te Ika now and then."

A break from Te Ika? To tell the truth, it was the one thing I didn't need. I've grown to like Te Ika since I cleared off on my trip with Hubert. I'm not arguing that absence makes the heart grow fonder; you have to be fond if you want to become fonder. I wasn't really fond of this place before, but I am now. I often look around the place as if I own it. I suppose I had to find something as a result of that trip. The fact is I found Te Ika.

Some Sundays I climb high above the town, up the tall hills at the back of the Waikai place, and I sit down among the limestone outcrops and cabbage trees where everything is quiet and I have only grazing sheep for company. Far below I see the sparkle of the river, the sunlit houses strung along its green banks, the crooked streets, the school, the hospital, the Maori meeting house, and a faint puff of smoke from a shunting engine at the railway yards. Everything is peaceful under the hills. Then I feel not only as if I own the damn place; I feel as if I made it. I can almost tell myself that I've dug the gum, panned the gold and felled the forest to put those houses dreaming down below. And if I'm feeling guilty about wasting my time up there, because I have homework or some odd job waiting, well then I kid myself that I'm perfectly entitled to sit back, at some time in the week, to enjoy the fruit of my labour. It's always a good rest, anyway. Quite often, if the day is warm enough, I fall asleep up there and then wake to find the sun almost gone, the hills throwing huge evening shadows across the town, and the church bells chiming. And though my high patch of hill is still warm and bright, I feel cold and strange. I run wildly down the hill, leaping, skidding, tumbling, all in a hurry as if I might lose the town again.

Chapter Twenty-five

"YES," MY MOTHER SAID VAGUELY. "PERHAPS A SHORT break away would do Nick good."

"An excellent idea," said my father.

"Well, Nick," Derek asked, "what about it?"

"Is it Sally's idea or something?" I asked, suspicious.

"Sally's idea? Why should it be her idea? Of course it isn't. What's it got to do with her, anyway? I'm not married to her yet."

"I just thought it might be her idea. I mean, you haven't asked me to stay with you in Auckland before."

"Well, I'm asking you now."

"You absolutely sure it's your idea?"

"Absolutely positive. Why should it be anyone else's?"

I was convinced at last. Then I was so pleased that he really thought of me, really thought enough of me to travel all the way down from Auckland to invite me to stay with him, I couldn't do anything but say yes, right away, and start packing my bag. Derek stayed to lunch while I hunted out my toothbrush, and then we took off along the highway to Auckland. That trip really marks the beginning of my good relations with Derek. As we sped north, the small towns and farms and billboards flicking past, we yarned about almost everything. That is, I gave him my opinion on a lot of subjects. I really felt I was getting to know him at last, and that he was getting to know me. He asked me now and again about things I'd got up to with Hubert last summer, and sometimes he broke into such wild laughter that he almost lost control of the car and it swerved dangerously over the white line in the middle of the road.

"And how long did you stay on the gumfields?" he'd say.

"I don't know. I started losing track of time round then."

"And you really found some gum?"

"Really. I've got it up on a shelf in my room. A big, shiny lump of it. First-class quality, Pat said. Remind me to show it to you."

"Wonderful," he said. And then: "You didn't find any gold?"

"No. I'm pretty expert at looking for it, though."

That seemed to delight him.

"We probably would have found some," I went on, "if we'd stayed long enough. But we had to shoot through. Just like old Hubert had to, sixty years back. That was when we bought those horses. I think Hubert got his money's worth in home brew and pickled mussels that afternoon, before he got round to paying for the horses."

"Then you rode all the way south?"

"All the way."

"Wonderful," he said, chuckling to himself. "Wonderful."

He slapped his knee so hard that the car swerved out over the white line again. I mean it would have been pretty damn wonderful if we'd collected one of the big trucks zooming towards us on the other side of the road, so I tried to dodge the subject of last summer. He kept coming back to it, though, all the way to Auckland and through the city rush traffic, until I was just about a nervous wreck.

That was on the last Tuesday of the school holidays. I stayed in Derek's Auckland flat until the Sunday. In those five days I had plenty of time to get used to Auckland, since Derek lives pretty near in the middle of the place. The first couple of nights traffic noises woke me and I found myself too jittery to go back to sleep again. So I prowled round Derek's living-room like a lonely ghost, experimenting with his cigarettes and whisky; I had an idea that nicotine and alcohol might drug me off to sleep. To tell the truth they didn't have much effect, so then I switched off the lights in the living-room, flipped up the blind, and sat by the window. It could be reasonably interesting. Up in Auckland, they never turn out the street lights. I watched the constables plodding from doorway to doorway, and the police cars quietly patrolling. Sometimes there were lovers strolling home with lazy feet, or parties of Samoans and Maoris, once or twice with leis and guitars around their necks and coloured streamers twisted in their hair. There is an all-night pie-cart just opposite Derek's window, and a lot of the customers were drunk, so I saw one or two quite interesting fights. At first I had the hazy idea that it was all an entertainment put on for my special benefit, but it didn't look too entertaining for some of the people involved. Not when they were dragged off with bloody faces. When one fight started a short fat puffy-faced man, who didn't have anything to do with it, walked calmly away from the flying fists, and then threw a perfectly good bottle of whisky high in the air. When it crashed in the centre of the street, glass and dark liquid spraying everywhere, he yelled out what did it matter anyway, he'd never forget, never never bloody forget, we were all due for obliteration and damnation anyway and a good thing too; what did it matter, he'd never – Then he was away down the street, his words too faint to hear. I supposed the police might eventually pick him up, for yelling like that in the middle of the night; perhaps they might learn what he couldn't forget. I even looked in the newspaper, three days running, to see if anyone resembling him was up in court for being drunk and disorderly; I thought he might explain to the magistrate what he wanted to forget. But I didn't find anything about him. What he wanted to forget is still an almighty mystery to me. I don't mind admitting that it terrified me to see a man who needed to forget so badly that he actually wanted to get rid of the human race. It didn't help my sleep at all. I pulled the blind down, to wipe the scene from my mind, and had a shot at drugging myself again.

In the morning Derek gave me a queer look across the breakfast table. "Curious," he said. "If I didn't know better, I'd swear you were suffering from a hangover." He laughed as if it was funny.

Most mornings we yarned away an hour or so over the breakfast table and then, when Derek settled down to his writing desk, I went walking. I just about walked the legs off myself in those few days. Usually I wandered down to the waterfront first, where old men sunned themselves and fed seagulls, and leaning on a railing I looked across to the ships loading for Japan, America and England. Farther along, I saw the fishing boats puttering into the harbour, and fishermen mending their nets. Then I drifted back into the city, looking into the shops all the way up Queen Street and along Karangahape Road. I spent a lot of time in sports shops, wandering among displays of rods and rifles I couldn't afford to buy. I took an interest in all the construction work of course. There were buildings either being knocked down or knocked up wherever I went, bulldozers growling and welders striking blue sparks from girders. Sometimes I tried the museum as a way of passing time, and the art gallery. At least those places were quiet. Actually, though, I wasn't much troubled by noise after a while, I got too interested in things to notice noise.

Since I've come back to Te Ika, I've quite often talked about Auckland to various people, particularly to kids who think they know everything, and sometimes they've said to me, "Auckland? That's nothing. You ought to see London or New York." I don't see why I ought to; Auckland's quite enough for me. When people try to rattle me by disparaging Auckland that way, I'm damned if I don't start getting quite possessive about the place, much the same way as I get possessive about Te Ika. I don't mind admitting, though, that I had some bad moments, quite apart from that short fat puffy-faced man.

One day my legs were aching from hiking along concrete pavements and, Auckland being what it is, there wasn't a spare patch of land in sight where I could have swung the billy even if I'd wanted to, and had a billy. So I dropped off into a gloomy little shop decorated with pot-plants. I could see cakes on display and people sitting sipping at tables. I grabbed three cream-puffs and asked the girl behind the counter for a chocolate malted milk shake, a big one.

"No milk shakes," she sniffed.

"Well, a cup of tea, then," I said. "Anything."

"Russian tea?"

"What's that?" I asked.

"We have Russian tea and we have coffee," she said snootily.

She was that kind of girl who always has to be superior about something, even if only about serving a schoolkid from the country. "Make up your mind, please. There are other people waiting. There's a milk bar just along the road if you want milk shakes or ordinary tea."

She was just trying to humiliate me and I felt pretty humiliated, all right, with all those people waiting and watching behind me. But I had those three cream puffs in my hot hand, and I couldn't very well back out now.

"I'll have coffee, then," I said, thinking I was on fairly safe ground at last.

"Capuccino?" she said.

"Oh, for Christ's sake," I said, "give me any bloody thing."

As I carried my coffee and cream puffs away from the counter, reeling from the shock of how much it had cost me, I heard a woman mutter about the manners and language of schoolchildren these days. No wonder there was all this delinquency, she said, sparing the rod always spoilt the child. "Flog 'em," a man growled. "Flog first, last, and all ways. That's my motto."

Naturally I took off into the gloomiest possible corner of the place. That was when I noticed that several people at the tables were sipping fruit juice. The girl hadn't troubled herself to inform me that the place also sold fruit juice. I sat down at a vacant table spitting with temper, and it didn't improve things to find there was damn little cream in those expensive cream puffs. My coffee was lukewarm and tasted like leftovers.

My temper was still on the boil when a lean elderly distinguished-looking man cruised out of the gloom in my direction, nodded in a friendly way, and asked politely if he might share my table. His politeness and friendliness, and the way he treated me as an equal, certainly made me feel a lot better. "I haven't seen you lunching in here before," he said. "It's pleasant to see a new face."

"I haven't been in here before," I told him. "I'm just up from the country." At that moment I really didn't care who knew it; anyway I felt as if I was walking round in a pair of old muddy gumboots, straight from the cowshed. Particularly when I looked at all the smart women and slick men at the other tables.

"Just visiting, eh?" he said. "Well, well."

That gave us a great old start to the conversation; he wanted to know where I lived, what I intended to be, what my father did, and what I thought about life in general. We were still sitting there yarning when most of the other tables were emptied of the lunchtime crowd. He even fetched me a fruit juice from the counter, since I wasn't game to face that girl again, and insisted on paying for it himself. "I know how it is," he explained. "I remember being a boy. How well I do. Never enough pocket money."

"I'm always on a pretty tight ration," I admitted.

A short time later, while we were still yarning casually, three one-pound notes appeared magically on the table in front of me, beside my fruit juice. I stared at them in amazement, not quite believing they were real. "There," he said, "that should help with your little holiday up here, shouldn't it? You can buy yourself something really nice to take home. Go on. You take it."

"But I can't," I said. "Really. For one thing I don't know you. And –"

"Never mind," he said. "Put it down to memory. My memory. There is so much about my boyhood I seem to have forgotten. So much you've brought to life for me again. It's been a great pleasure for me, talking to you here today. Naturally I treasure many memories of boyhood and youth, but I realize now that I've treasured some at the expense of others. You've allowed me to possess the whole picture again. I think I can say safely that, for a little while, you've made me feel forty years younger. So please accept this, with thanks, from a grateful old man." He pushed the three notes a little nearer to me. "Please."

I looked at them, but couldn't bring myself to pick them up, no matter how my fingers itched; they would go a long way towards a new fishing rod. So, for a while, those notes just stayed there. They seemed to shimmer luminously. I couldn't say anything. My mouth was too dry, my tongue too thick.

"You've made me a gift," he explained. "The gift of life. You have that gift, boy, and you must be careful, very careful, how

246

you use it." He slid his hands back over his thin silvery hair and looked at me intensely. "In return I'm making you a gift. For anything you want. You see. That's all it is."

Suddenly everything was different. Suddenly he was pushing the notes into my hand, then holding my hand, and saying shakily, "You'll be good to an old man, won't you? You'll be kind to me, won't you? I know you won't let me down. I know you won't."

I only needed the one look at his sad hungry eyes, and I only caught the one glimpse of the snooty girl's face as the notes dropped behind me and I flashed past the counter on my way out of the place. I struck sunlight as though I'd never seen it before, and everything from the cars to the tallest buildings was solid and bright.

I stood there blinking and decided to get out of the city for a while; at least to the suburbs, to the old Flinders place. I'd been meaning to go out there since I arrived in Auckland, but I hadn't been able to face up to it, somehow. I sloped down town to the bus station, bought a ticket, and watched the big buildings of the city shrink behind. But I was really kidding myself; I wasn't leaving anything behind.

Hubert had never gone back. He sold up the old place, and arranged to have what he wanted sent down to Te Ika, after he moved in with the Waikais. Once more people didn't seem to understand him, but I thought I did. He just didn't want to look again into the emptiness where Grandmother Flinders had been. He'd gone through enough already; he must have looked long and hard into emptiness when he wrote those letters to bluff me.

I didn't stay there long. I stayed just long enough for the new people in the house to lift their curtains to see who was loitering outside their front gate. Then I moved on. The house already looked different. For one thing it shone with fresh paint. I supposed the musty, ancient smell inside was long gone. The lawns were mown, and the last of Hubert's pines had been felled. A tribe of children whooped in the back yard. And the back yard had shrunk to almost nothing. The section had been subdivided after Hubert sold up. There was a skeleton of a new house rising

247

where Hubert's potato patch and chicken run had been. And the old derelict bank, where Hubert's gorse and ragwort had blossomed, had just been ploughed flat by a bulldozer. In a waste of yellow sticky clay men were putting down foundations for still another house. Already there was almost nothing to show that Hubert had once lived there; already it was as though he had never been. On my way up to the cemetery I bought a bunch of flowers for Grandmother Flinders' grave.

Of course I saw something of Sally too. If she wasn't on the phone to Derek, she was calling round at his flat to cook us both a meal. She said Derek had been slowly dying of starvation in Auckland, until she met him, because he had no notion of how to feed himself. It seemed she virtually lived in his flat, looking after him, and I guessed she probably lived there altogether when I wasn't around. They were pretty circumspect in my presence, though. In fact they were so circumspect I started feeling more like an elderly parent than a young brother.

My third day in the city the three of us went off to the first night of a play which Derek had been commissioned to review. He and Sally had free tickets and he bought one for me because, he said, I had precious little chance of ever seeing a first night in Te Ika. In fact I had precious little chance of seeing a play, even. "It should be an education for you," he promised.

It was a real education, all right. Two people stood in front of us for the best part of three hours; that was all the play amounted to. A man and a woman talking. And talking. She washed dishes, or looked after babies or something; I didn't quite get the gist of her complaints about life, only that she didn't like it. She was stuck in one place, perhaps that was the trouble. The man, on the other hand, wandered round a lot. He was full of complaints too.

"I have never owned a refrigerator," he said sadly.

Just like that. It was tragic, really. If my heart didn't exactly ache for him, my behind certainly did; the seats seemed to be padded with old scrap iron. The moment I got into a reasonably restful position to go off to sleep, I started to get cramp in the leg. When I bent forward to massage my leg back to life, I cracked my head on the seat in front of me. In some ways I regretted I hadn't knocked myself out altogether; anything to stop that moaning in my ears. With my behind aching, my head throbbing and my leg cramped, I had a few complaints myself now, most of all that Derek had paid perfectly good money for my ticket. I sneaked a quick look at Derek and, since he didn't look the happiest, I assumed he was feeling the same way about that money.

That was where I was wrong, quite wrong. Right at that moment he was being moved and illuminated, according to the review he later wrote, and I had a sudden vision of Derek being shifted round and lit up like a Christmas tree. "Written with that marvellous French lucidity," he said, "this play is a delight and an experience not to be missed."

"What do you mean by lucidity?" I asked.

"Clarity," he said. "Transparency."

"What you mean is, then, that you heard those two up there on the stage complaining all right?"

"Well, yes. I suppose it comes to that. Yes, I suppose it does."

"Good," I said. "Just so long as I know."

I didn't argue with him about the play. After all it was his money, not mine. And I know he's way ahead of me in these things. But if he reckons hearing two people complain is an experience, as I know the word, then he's either misusing the English language, about which I'm not paid to be an expert, or he hasn't had an experience in his life. I still can't make up my mind one way or the other. Because I have to take into account that the word experience may actually mean different things to different people. Or the same thing, only different.

At least I learned one thing, that though we could talk to each other, in other ways Derek and I were still miles apart.

The morning after the play, the phone rang while Derek and I were yarning over our breakfast coffee. Derek took the call and, from the special sound in his voice, I guessed he was talking to Sally. "Goodbye, darling," he said finally, and came back to the breakfast table. "It was Sally," he announced. "She wants to meet you for lunch, if that's all right. Take you out to lunch, rather. I said I thought you'd be delighted. All right?"

"It sounds as if it's all arranged," I said.

"You can always ring her back."

"No. It doesn't matter."

Well, I had to meet Sally on a certain corner in Queen Street. I arrived there fifteen minutes early, dressed in my best long trousers, feeling about thirty years old. I even put on one of Derek's ties for the occasion. In the mirror I looked pretty smooth. And I felt pretty smooth too, until Sally arrived. She was mockered up to the nines and loaded with scent. She looked just too swish and glamorous. I felt about six years old again and was sure my knees were making a rattling sound.

"Hello, Nick. My, you are looking smart."

I mumbled something.

"Any particular place you'd like to go for lunch?"

That got my tongue working again. "Not really. But there's just one place where I don't want to go."

"Why's that?"

"I just had a couple of experiences there yesterday. That's all."

"Really? Well, you tell me if I start taking you to the wrong place."

The place where she took me wasn't a whole lot different. It was gloomy too, tangled with jungly pot-plants, and on all the tables there were farty little candles stuck in brown bottles which dripped with grease. It didn't look as if the grease had been cleaned off the bottles in years and, if that was someone's idea of cleanliness, I hated to think what the kitchen looked like. I lost my appetite right away. I couldn't make sense of the menu anyway. Finally Sally insisted on ordering something for me; I didn't want to embarrass her by saying I didn't want to eat at all. I know people have different standards of cleanliness, but it's not the time to point them out in the middle of a crowded restaurant.

"You're just picking at your food, Nick," Sally said after a while.

"I had a big breakfast, that's all."

"You mean Derek actually cooked you breakfast?"

"No. I cooked it. I'm pretty good at cooking these days. After

250

my trip with the old boy. I can cook a dozen different kinds of stew, for example. Not to speak of sausages."

Well, I could see I'd said the wrong thing, there. We both had a pretty vivid memory of one breakfast of sausages; a pretty vivid memory that brought back others. We fell silent, looking down at our food, picking away steadily. Sally was a great one to talk about appetite. She was eating about as much as a bird. But I could tell she had a lot on her mind, right then.

"It's all right," I said at last. "I don't want you to think I'm worrying about it."

She looked up with relief in her face. "You're not?"

"No. I got other things to worry about these days. Besides, I've got a girl friend."

"You have?" Her face shone with a smile. "That's wonderful, Nick. Really wonderful."

"I don't see what's so wonderful about it. Other people have girl friends. I mean it's nothing unique, is it?"

"I seem to have lost my head last summer. Lost all sense of proportion, that is. I've felt guilty ever since."

"I suppose I lost my head too," I said, "or something. I haven't quite worked it out." I hesitated, feeling I still hadn't reassured her enough. So I announced, "Part of the time, of course, I was really off my head. I know that now."

"I've been a different girl since, believe me," she went on. "Since that day I walked away from your campfire."

"Well," I said, "that's great. I only hope you're not too different, that's all."

"Why?"

"I don't want you to be too different. I suppose that's all it amounts to. I mean I think I've got a right to say that now. You'll soon be my sister, just about."

But when I looked at her, really looked at her, and didn't allow myself to be impressed by swish clothes and scent, I saw she wasn't that much different. I don't mean underneath; I knew all about underneath. I mean her eyes were still cheeky. I realized she would never be that much different, and the thought relieved me.

"I wouldn't say I was the same either," I explained. "But I hope I'm not ever too much different. I think that's what I mean."

"Let's shake on it, then," she said, offering her hand.

So we shook hands on the subject, fully agreed. Then our hands just lay there together on the table. I don't mind admitting that, despite all I'd said, I wasn't in a raging hurry to pull my hand away.

"That'll do for congratulations too," I said. "I never did congratulate you properly on the engagement. I want you to know I think you and Derek will make a great pair. I think you've done him a lot of good already."

Speaking like that, and holding her hand, I felt pretty much like a god; or at least like a father giving the bride away. So I went on recklessly, "I reckon that, between us, we ought to be able to straighten out Derek pretty well."

I was joking, of course, but Sally seemed to take me seriously.

"I'm glad you've said that, Nick," she told me quietly. "Because it's what I've been meaning to say. Or what I've been meaning to explain to you, rather."

"What's that?"

"How much Derek depends on you. You may not realize it, but he does, you know."

I felt as if my chair had been kicked from beneath me; anyway I came down with an almighty wallop. With my head still singing, I managed to say, "What's that again?"

"Derek depends on you."

"That's what I thought you said, all right."

And it was what someone else had said to me, not so long ago. Who? Then I remembered. Grandmother Flinders, talking about Hubert, saying he depended on me. What had I done to be depended on all over the place? It just wasn't fair.

"In his curious oblique way, he even recognizes it himself," Sally was saying. "He once told me, in passing, that you were his small window on reality."

"That's pretty damn insulting. I'm nobody's window."

"And on another occasion he said that you represent, for him, a small area of regret in his life; an area which he daily culti-vates."

"Well, he can go and cultivate somewhere else as far as I'm concerned."

"Nick," she pleaded, her hand tightening on mine, "it only means that he depends on you. That, one way and another, he needs you. All I'm asking is, well, if you'd be kind to him."

"There was an old man yesterday. He asked me to be kind to him too. That's what he asked. For me to be kind to him. But you know what he wanted, don't you? He wanted all of me."

"We're talking about different things, Nick."

"I'm not so sure. Not when I think about it."

"Really, Nick. You go on thinking about it, and I'm sure you'll see."

"I'll go on thinking, all right. Don't you worry about that."

"Because Derek needs you, it doesn't mean he doesn't love you. His need is just part of that love, that's all. Need is always part of love. And Derek does love you, believe me. He'd do any-thing for you."

"That old man might have loved me too, given time," I said. "He might have done anything for me too."

"I'm sure you'll see," she said firmly. "I'm sure it's only a matter of time. You must see the difference."

"I see the difference, all right. There's an old man and there's Derek. One's got dark hair, pretty thin on top I admit. The other's got silver hair. Derek wears glasses, the old man doesn't. That just about sums it up."

"Nick, if you go on and on like that you won't see, ever. Really. You just won't know."

"I just know something. I just know that for the moment I've got to keep all of me. If I start letting myself go, bit by bit, I won't have anything left that's any good at all."

"And what's the point?"

"What point?"

"The point of keeping all yourself, to yourself. What's the point of all this?"

"Because I might need it, that's all. I might need it, and I want to have it when I need it."

"Remarkable," she said. "For what?"

"I don't know yet. I don't –" I looked up into her face and remembered something and all the words in my head knocked together and collapsed with a tremendous clatter. Because there, right in front of me, sat Sally; that was all. I'd been sitting there like an idiot, talking to her as if she was another person altogether.

"Never mind," she said. "Don't work yourself up about it."

After a while I said weakly, "I'll work it all out. Just give me time. Then I'll tell you why."

"Well, don't worry about it too much. Not yet. There'll be time enough in your life to worry." She sighed. "Believe me."

A smile trembled on her face as if she was having trouble with it. But she managed to bring it under control in the end. I tried one too. She tossed her ponytail back and winked. It was amazing what a difference that wink made. I seemed to wake up, all of a sudden; I realized I was sitting in this Auckland restaurant holding hands with the prettiest girl in the place. It was a pity the place was too gloomy for people around to appreciate the fact. A pity there weren't any people from Te Ika there, either.

Then Sally looked at her watch with horror. "My God," she said. "The office. Just look at the time."

I raced Sally back to work through all the bumping elbows and sidestepping feet of Queen Street's lunch-hour crowds. We arrived breathless at her office building.

"Thanks a lot for the lunch," I said. "I really did appreciate it."

"The pleasure was all mine, Nick. Truly."

I wanted to leave her in the right state of mind, so I made one mighty final effort as the crowd rushed past us. "I meant all I said back there," I told her. "I really did. I've really almost forgotten that anything ever happened between us last summer."

"Bless you, Nick. I wish I had." She dropped a quick kiss on my forehead before she dashed up the steps into the office building.

I stood there looking into the blank space she left and tried to remember what her scent smelled like. I felt sure I would have split right down the middle, with a terrible tearing sound, if I'd had to tell that lie again.

Chapter Twenty-six

THE NIGHT BEFORE I LEFT AUCKLAND, THE SATURDAY night, Derek and Sally held their engagement party. That's where I met this character who's writing down this story for me; he's a friend of Derek's, or a sort of friendly enemy. I must say I was pretty apprehensive about the party. The thought of all these literary and artistic people, I mean. I couldn't see how I would fit in at all. Sally cooked us a scratch meal early, around six o'clock, and while the flat was straightened out, or should I say levelled out, in preparation for the party, I walked round shaking in my size-nine shoes. I had it pretty well fixed in my mind there would be a flat full of half-bald Dereks, all looking over their glasses wisely and making intellectual conversation.

"Well," said Sally, around seven o'clock. "That's got the decks cleared, at least. Now I'll get down to preparing the supper and get that out of the way. Nick, why don't you help Derek take the bottles out of the crates and arrange them on the bar?"

About seven-thirty there came the first knock on the door, and my first big surprise of the evening. Because when Derek answered the door, who stepped in but someone I hadn't seen since the sausages were thrown over the sandhills. As soon as I saw Susan I assumed there must be some terrible mistake.

"Hello, Nick," she said cheerfully, "how very nice to see you again." She put out her hand while I stood there staring. Derek didn't seem to see anything remarkable about her, though.

Nor did Sally. "You promised to come at seven to help with the supper," she called from the kitchen.

"Sorry, darling," Susan called back, "but things got in my way. You know how it is."

"I know how it is with you, all right," Sally said. "Muddle, muddle, muddle."

When Susan had shaken my hand she stripped off her glossy coat to show tight slacks, with vee-slits above the ankles, and an even tighter woolly blue jumper. Then she handed Derek the silver-capped bottle she had carried into the flat.

"My God," he said, "champagne."

"Strictly for you and Sally," she said, "not for the mob." She smiled. "You can toast your future with it after all the guests have gone. I'd put it away in a safe place if I were you."

"Don't worry about that," Derek said as he charged into the kitchen. "Hey, Sally, have a look at what Susan brought us." I heard him stand on a chair to put the bottle in a high place and then slam a cupboard door shut.

Now Susan was looking at me gravely, and I was looking everywhere but in her direction.

"You haven't had much to say, Nick. And you never did take me for that walk you promised along the beach."

All sorts of words crumbled in my mouth when I tried them for size. "That was your fault," I said finally. "You cleared off."

"What you lose on the swings you gain on the –" she began, and then stopped with an awkward smile. "Never mind, Nick. Perhaps some other time."

"Any time," I said, getting my courage back. "Any time as far as I'm concerned. You look as if you've been getting plenty of sun lately, anyway."

It was true. Her face, hands and ankles were dark with suntan. I noticed it particularly, when I looked at her, because in theory it was still the end of winter, or early spring. People had no right going round with suntan at that time of year. My mother would say it was indecent.

"Oh, that," she said, and studied one of her hands as if she'd only just noticed the tan. "That's the result of a trip up to the islands. I went there to paint, really, but I found Gauguin had been there before me. Finally I gave up, and made the best of the sun. It was pleasant while it lasted."

"Well," I said, "I wouldn't mind trying some of that sun myself."

Derek returned from the kitchen, and saved me from having

to make more conversation. "How was the trip, Sue?" he asked.

Then Sally called loudly from the kitchen, "Are you really going to help with the supper, or are you just going to talk about it? Don't tell me things are still getting in your way."

"No," Susan said, as she went into the kitchen. "Not things. Just your future brother-in-law. Blame him."

"Nick? Ignore him. He's a snare and a delusion, if ever there was one."

With Susan gone, I had a chance to collect myself and count my arms and legs. I managed to get things straightened out in the course of the evening, though. About Susan, I mean. She and Sally had met up again in the city, not long after their terrific one-day holiday together with Michael, and though they were fairly reserved with each other at first, they eventually compared notes, while getting merry and then sad at a party, and came to the conclusion that, minus Michael, they really liked each other after all. They started knocking round together, and Susan was at the party where Sally first met Derek. To give Michael all due credit, though, he was right about one thing and Sally wrong. Susan was supposed to be quite a talented artist after all. People were talking about her paintings, critics had liked what they'd seen of them, and Susan was just about to have her first one-woman exhibition. Which Derek predicted would be very exciting, though I admit that I take what he says with a half-pound of salt, after his review of that play.

By eight-thirty we were all sitting around the living room. The radiogram was playing, and there still hadn't been another knock at the door. "I've just had a frightful thought," Derek said gloomily. "Did we remember to invite anyone?"

Five minutes later fists began to hammer on the door and it didn't seem they would ever stop. The flat filled with the sound of banging feet, clinking bottles and beer-flagons, people shouting and joking, slapping Derek on the shoulder, kissing Sally, congratulating them over and over again. The radiogram played away unheard through all the racket. I was pretty much unheard too. I found a corner of the room where I wasn't likely to get trodden underfoot, and made up my mind not to shift.

At one stage Susan sidled over to me and whispered, "Don't let all these people intimidate you, Nick. Just remember that you've more right to be here than they have."

It was all right for her to talk. She was pretty popular, all things considered. Men would drop a kiss on Sally's cheek, and then give Susan their second look, as if they might try her too.

Still, I knew Susan meant well. "It's all right," I said. "I've been through worse than this."

I admit it may have sounded grim, the way I said it through clenched teeth, but I was holding tight to that corner. Pressure was growing, and I now had to consider the possibility that I might get slowly pounded to death against the wall.

"Cheer up," Susan laughed. "Look, I'll just go and fix myself a drink and then I'll sit with you."

She was a long time coming back, an hour or more. Too many other people, particularly men, appeared to think they were entitled to talk to her. She would escape one person, and then another would grab her. In the meantime I tried to amuse myself by watching other people at the party.

On the whole, I must say I was relieved to find so many of Derek's friends were healthy, normal-looking people. This Shadbolt character, for example, arrived in a party of four or five. I wouldn't say he looked exactly normal, but his friends did. One was about six feet four inches tall, a really husky fellow with fair hair, and he looked to me a pretty normal front-row rugby forward. Another one seemed just about as tough, slightly shorter and much bulkier, with oiled slicked-back black hair, and a really aggressive face; he looked like a pretty normal policeman. Then there was a really hairy fellow wearing a pair of oily trousers and a shirt torn open down the front which showed most of his chest and some of his stained singlet, and he appeared to have lost his shaving gear about ten days before; he looked as if he'd just come off a farm. They were followed into the flat by a short, stout, jowly fellow with very sad eyes who was carrying something that marked him out as different from them right away. They were all carrying beer-bottles and flagons; he carried a big crate of Coca-cola. Except for this one mournful fellow,

259

they all seemed fairly happy with themselves. This Shadbolt didn't look like anything in particular, or as if he'd come from anywhere; he wore black jeans and a red check shirt, his hair was half over his face and needed a pair of shears taken to it, and his gingery-blonde moustache drooped in a sort of sad Spanish way around the corners of his mouth. In fact I didn't take much notice of him, till later, because I was so pleased with all Derek's normal-looking friends.

Of course I was pretty much disillusioned before long. I got most of my information from Jim, the short jowly fellow, who installed himself in my corner with his crate of Coca-cola. I asked if he was a delivery man for the Coca-cola factory or something. He said no, he was just an ordinary postman, so I chalked up another point in favour of Derek's normal friends. Jim explained that he had to drink Coca-cola because he was an alcoholic. He offered me a bottle, and we sat there swigging away together. He really bucked me up, the way he yarned to me as if I was the only interesting person in the room, and he offered me small cigars which I smoked as soon as I was sure Derek wasn't looking; Derek had been complaining, after my sleepless nights, that he'd been going through an awful lot of cigarettes lately. After Jim and I had been talking for a while, I asked him about other people at the party. That was when I got disillusioned. That front-row rugby forward, for example, wrote pretty desperate novels about young boys who yell and scream at God, and whose mothers knock their fathers off. And the one with the oily slicked-back hair, the policeman-looking type, he really wasn't normal either; he wrote pretty frantic love poetry. I was almost right about one thing. That hairy fellow who looked as if he'd just come off the farm. Well, he hadn't come off a farm exactly, but he'd just come in from the bush country. The thing was, though, he was a writer too. He was a deer-culler when he wasn't writing about shooting deer, and about the hairy jokers who shoot them professionally for the Government. I've since learned that he's fairly famous, and that I really ought to have read his books. When people ask what he said to me that evening, I tell them he explained to me a technique for killing wild pigs with gelignite. What you do is, you cut open a potato and slip a detonator inside. Then you scatter a few of these potatoes in the bush where you know wild pigs are likely to roam. And you sit back and wait for the explosions. He reckoned you could collect any amount of wild pork that way. To tell the truth, I was pretty disgusted by this lazy man's way of hunting; it was just what you might expect from some literary friend of Derek's. Of course, I have to take into account that he might just have been telling a story. He'd been drinking a lot of beer.

Actually I was fairly merry myself, on that Coca-cola. Jim and I went through a half dozen bottles in no time. I grew very relaxed and wasn't much troubled by the noise, pushing and smoke any more. In fact I felt like quite an old hand at the party business, and I smiled amiably at everyone in sight. Jim was still talking. He really didn't need anyone to talk back at him. He just needed someone to listen. Without me saying a word, he argued his way from alcoholism to sex, from sex to religion, from religion to literature, from literature back to sex again. In between all these subjects, he quoted lines of poetry, and my suspicion grew. Finally I asked who had written the poetry. He said he had, of course.

It was a great sort of party, when even an ordinary alcoholic postman turned out to be a poet. I decided there just wasn't a normal person in the room after all.

Susan made her way back to me at last. "Hello, Nick," she said. "Oh, I see Jim's looking after you."

She glided away again to fix someone's drink. Well, I decided I wouldn't let that get me down. I wasn't going to let anything like that get me down again. If she preferred fixing some abnormal idiot's drink to talking with me, well that was just too damn bad. I wasn't going to worry about it.

"Drink up," Jim said. "Have another bottle."

"I'll try another one of those little cigars too," I said.

I felt pretty smooth. I was on top of everything and didn't give a damn about anyone. If people from Te Ika had seen me, they would certainly have sat up and taken notice. All things considered, I was moving in fairly elevated circles, among alcoholic postman poets, literary deer-shooters and beautiful green-eyed artists.

People started to dance wildly. It was rock 'n roll or twist or stomp, one of these new-fangled dances; I find it hard to keep up with these fashions. This Shadbolt was one of them, with his hair flying all over the place. There was a desperate look behind his huge black glasses as he tried to keep step with Sally, who seemed fairly expert. With that droopy moustache he seemed pretty much like a sad waltzing walrus. That was when I first took particular notice of him, and asked Jim about him. "He writes, too," Jim said, as if it was something normal. "He writes stories."

It was a relief when supper arrived. I don't mind admitting I moved fairly fast when all the supper was wheeled into the room. Sally's scratch meal at six o'clock had been very scratchy so far as my stomach was concerned, and I was starving. She'd made a better job of the supper, though. Everything was there from sausage rolls and oyster patties to cream puffs really loaded with cream. I worked my way through the lot systematically while the speeches were going on. It seemed to me a hell of a fuss for an engagement. I could see the point of the supper, all right, but not of the speeches. I found that if I kept my teeth working on asparagus rolls, I pretty well drowned out the sound of the speeches.

I was still there eating when the speeches and toasts were over and most people had turned their backs on the supper. I started feeling pretty conspicuous, so I made out that I was really helping Sally wheel the remains of the supper back into the kitchen.

When I got back to the living-room I realized I'd certainly paid a high price for supper. I'd been robbed of my corner. A man and a woman, both very intense, had taken it over and, on top of that, Jim had removed his crate of Coca-cola. It was quite a blow to find everything changed. I had a sense of insecurity.

Then I spied a vacant place on a couch, and moved in fast. It had a double advantage for me. It was next to Susan, and about two paces away from the new resting place of Jim's crate. The first advantage didn't amount to much though. Susan just smiled at me vaguely, and then went on talking to an elderly man with a very gentle face who sipped thoughtfully and delicately at a glass of sherry. Jim had pointed him out to me earlier as an art critic, and an editor of a very influential magazine, so in a way I understood her concern, particularly when I overhead he was interested in buying one of her paintings. People have to make a living somehow, even at parties.

I flogged a fresh bottle from Jim's crate without him noticing. flipped the cap off, and then discovered that my new place in the room had a disadvantage. It was right next to Derek and this Shadbolt having an argument. The radiogram was roaring, the dancers swung dangerous close to me, and to cap it all these two blasted my eardrums. Derek was saying Shadbolt's stories just didn't stand up to rigorous criticism. Shadbolt said what the hell was rigorous criticism anyway. Derek said literature was a serious responsible business these days, one had to be committed fully, there was no room for Shadbolt's irresponsibility. Shadbolt said where was the fun in that. Derek said he wasn't talking about fun. Shadbolt said exactly.

They might have gone on for hours like a pair of cut cats, but then Jim walked into the argument carrying his crate; he clung to it as if everyone else in the room was thirsting for his Cocacola. He said something to Derek ,which I didn't quite hear, but it seemed to upset Derek. My brother drew himself up to a great height and said angrily, "You don't have to be a postman to know all about life and literature." Which I thought pretty unfair, since Jim was an alcoholic too.

Anyway Jim soon backed out of the argument, still hugging his crate, with a despondent look on his face. He seemed to be feeling he wasn't wanted anywhere. The tall fair front-row forward took his place; in fact it was getting like a rugby scrum. I gave up listening to them and tried to overhear what Susan was saying to the elderly gentleman. I didn't like the idea of her getting too intimate with him, even if he was influential. She really didn't have to try so hard convincing him that he needed to buy a painting. Speaking for myself, I'd have just taken one look at her and bought a painting right off. But then I suppose everyone's not a sex maniac like me. Other people might want to have a look at the painting too.

To tell the truth, I couldn't understand much of what they were talking about. Between these two involved discussions, I felt left out of things. It was getting to be fairly much what I had feared the evening would be like. At this stage Shadbolt was explaining to Derek and the tall fellow, whose name was Ian, just why it was impossible to write a real novel in New Zealand. Without a coherent and developed society, he was saying, it was impossible to have a novel in the true sense.

"But I've written them," this fellow Ian said.

"Nonsense," Shadbolt said. "They're just inflated short stories."

"There you go, Maurice," Derek said. "Rationalizing again."

"What do you mean?"

"You can't write one, so then you claim nobody can. That's just like you. Rationalizing, rationalizing. All the time."

This seemed to depress Shadbolt, and I suppose that was when I started feeling sorry for him. He looked down at his beer in a melancholy way, then drank it down quickly, and without saying a word pushed between Derek and Ian and headed for the dancing. When next I saw him he was doing his waltzing walrus act with Sally again, but he didn't look any too damn happy about it at all.

About this stage I realized there was a limit to the Coca-cola my body could hold, so I fled from the living-room to find relief. With the queue at the bathroom door so enormous, I had a pretty painful time before I got back to the party. I might have known I would lose my place on the couch beside Susan. It was taken by a pretty impressive bored-looking fellow with a bushy moustache who kept tapping her knee, trying to distract her from conversation with the elderly gentleman. I thought he was pretty fresh, myself. And I was ready to bet the abnormal bastard only wanted to recite her some of his damn poems or something.

Well, I wasn't going to let that get me down. Nothing was going to get me down. I saw that the other couch in the room was just being vacated by a couple rising to dance; I pushed across the room and sat on it firmly as if it was a throne of gold or something. Anyway I wasn't going to let this place get away from me. Luckily I was again within reaching distance of Jim's Coca-cola crate, so I flogged another bottle. Jim had his back to me, and was talking very intensely to a sweetly smiling girl about God. From what I heard, it seemed that Jim and God had a pretty sad time together.

I didn't see anyone I could talk with, and to tell the truth I started feeling left out of things again. Then Shadbolt staggered away from the dancing, his face dripping with sweat. He asked no one in general if the place on the couch beside me was reserved for anyone in particular, and without waiting for an answer collapsed there, looking quite haggard. When he'd recovered his breath and mopped his face, he looked at me and said, "Enjoying yourself?"

I said I was, up to a point. I mean I sounded pretty cool, as though I was relieved about it being the last party of the week.

"Having a good holiday up here?" he asked. "Derek getting all the material from you he wants?"

Well, he seemed to know who I was, all right, even if he didn't seem to know what he was talking about. "What do you mean?" I said. It's best, I've found, to be careful with people who say lunatic things; they sometimes actually do turn out to be lunatics. So then I asked very slowly and distinctly, "What material are you talking about?"

"You know," he said, "for this novel Derek imagines he's going to write about you and your grandfather. I'm tired of hearing about it. I keep telling him he'll never write it if he talks about it so much. When I heard you were up here, I guessed he must really be going ahead with the thing at last."

The room seemed to travel outwards, and then back in again. "What's that?" I said faintly.

"My God," he said in alarm. "Don't tell me I've let the cat out of the bag. I naturally assumed you knew."

I took hold of the edge of the couch, as if that would steady the room.

"I didn't realize – " he began, and stopped. "I mean, well, I

265

simply didn't realize that you weren't to know about it. I naturally assumed –" He stopped again. "Well, it doesn't matter."

But it did matter. It explained everything. It explained Derek coming down to Te Ika to fetch me. It explained all those questions on the journey up to Auckland. And the way he yarned to me over breakfast in the mornings, before he went to his writing desk. While I walked the city, he probably sat at his desk making notes on all that I'd told him. I might have known it, I might have guessed.

Sally must have known. She must have known what was going on. Of course. The way she'd asked me to be kind to Derek. That was it. I could see what she meant now. She'd really been asking me to tell Derek everything, help him write his novel.

I stood up, feeling shaky in the knees. I had a few things to say to one or two people. I had quite a few things to say. And I was going to say them, and say them loudly, engagement party or no engagement party. I didn't care who heard what I was going to say.

Then Shadbolt grabbed my arm and jerked me back on to the couch with a bang. "Listen," he said. "You'd better promise me something right now. You'd better promise you won't say a word about this to Derek. That I told you, I mean. He'd never forgive me, never. I can see I've accidentally trespassed on to what is strictly family territory. Because I simply didn't realize, and I should have. Promise?"

Some words wobbled strangely out of my mouth. "Why should I?" I heard myself say. "Why should I promise?"

"Because he gives me bad enough reviews as it is. For one thing."

"That's a great reason," I said. "Really great."

"And because your brother and I have a rather precarious friendship anyway."

"That's another really great reason," I said. "I'm not promising anyone anything, not any more."

"Please, Nick," he said, and he went on and on.

I wasn't listening to him. I was listening to myself think. I found it hardest to forgive Sally; I might have expected it of Derek, somehow. I mean I should have known Derek was up to something; my own judgement was at fault. It was Sally I couldn't understand. That was the real betrayal. It was almost as if she'd gone for the police, instead of Michael, after the police description over the radio. I just couldn't believe it of her. The way she'd sat there, in that greasy restaurant, and asked me to be kind to Derek.

"You understand, Nick?" Shadbolt said, from a long way off. "Do you understand what I'm saying?"

I must have nodded my head, because he went right on talking, his voice further and further away.

Kind to Derek? That was great, really damn great. Well, I knew one thing for certain. Nobody was going to own all of me, not that way. I was nobody's window and nobody's cultivation. Nobody was going to get me like that, ever.

I had to be fair, though. Sally was in love with Derek. I was forgetting that. It struck me that love was to blame for a lot of crimes.

"Are you listening, Nick?" Shadbolt asked. "Do you understand?"

Again I must have nodded, because he went right on talking again. He could get very intense, believe me.

I could see it all; I could see just what Derek would do to me. Embryonic dichotomies, transcendent paradoxes, and all this dirty psychological stuff mixed up with antipodean realities. And before I knew it, that would be me, all that tricksy stuff; I'd be so fouled up I wouldn't know myself again. I wouldn't know myself, and I wouldn't own myself. Anyway Derek didn't know the half of it, he'd be bound to get everything wrong. He always had difficulty getting anything straight.

That was when I began to see light at last, in the distance.

"Now promise me, Nick," Shadbolt said, sweating again. "Promise me you won't tell Derek. Pretend to find out, some other way, but don't say your information came from me. All right?"

"All right," I said, after a while. "I'll promise."

"Good," he said, and mopped his face. "I thought you'd see reason, in the end." He looked fairly relieved, all round.

"I'll promise," I said, "on just one condition."

"What's that?" He blinked suddenly behind his glasses.

"That you write it all down for me," I told him.

"Write what down?" He started sweating again.

"All this stuff that Derek thinks he's got. I want you to write it all down just the way I tell you. No tricksy stuff."

"My God," was all he said.

"It's no use you telling me you can't do it, because I happen to have been told you write stories."

He was in a real sweat now. The dancing had been nothing.

"Besides," I went on, "I feel fairly sorry for you, if you must know. I mean I saw you get the worst of that argument with Derek. When he said you couldn't write a novel, so you only rationalized and said other people couldn't either. I heard all that."

"You did?" he said vaguely.

"Well, I'll tell you a novel, all right. Don't worry about that. All you got to do is write it down for me."

He sat there for a while, just looking. Looking into nothing, especially. "Derek would never forgive me," he said at last.

"It's one thing or the other," I told him. "You can take your choice. I'll promise not to tell Derek if you'll just write everything down for me. And if you don't write it down for me, someone else will."

I had him there, all right; I had him pinned down. He didn't have a hope of escaping, and I could see he knew it. Because he groaned.

"As far as I'm concerned all you writers are thieves," I went on sternly. "One's probably as bad as the other. I mean you're probably as bad as Derek. The way I see it, you've got this coming to you. You'd probably steal my character too, if you had half a chance. Well, I'm not going to be someone else's character. I'm going to be my own character." I took a deep breath. "How long will it take Derek to write his novel?"

He seemed to hear me, after a while.

"How long do you think?" I asked again.

"Derek's a very slow, patient worker," he said.

"I don't want to know all about that. I just want to know how long he'd take, that's all."

"It's hard to say. A year, two years. Perhaps even three."

"Good. That gives us time. More than enough. We could get it over with in just a week or two."

His mouth hung open long enough for me to count his missing teeth.

"You can come down to Te Ika," I said, "and I'll tell you something every day. Then you can write it down. It shouldn't take very long. Not more than three weeks, anyway."

"I think I need a drink," he said. "In fact I'm sure I do."

I saw him finish off one full glass while he was standing at the bar, and then he carried another full glass back with him. The beer didn't seem to do him any good though. He still looked pretty much stunned.

"All right?" I said.

He opened his mouth as if to say something, but he only put more beer into it. He didn't take very long with that glass, either.

"It's one thing or the other," I said. "You can take your choice."

"I should have got myself a bottle," he said, and went to the bar again. After he returned with the bottle, I said, "Did you hear what I told you? It's one thing or the –"

"I know," he said. "I heard."

"Well, you'd better make up your mind right now."

He filled his glass from the bottle. Then he drank all the beer in the glass down and seemed surprised by the fact that the glass was empty. "All right," he said at last. His voice was weak and distant.

"All right, what?" I said.

"I'll do it for you. I'll arrange to come down to Te Ika. I'll write it down for you, if that's what you want."

"That's the stuff," I said. "That's what I wanted to hear.

Cheer up. It won't be so bad. Not more than two or three weeks."

"Perhaps it would make a short story," he said sadly.

"Not a hope. You'd never get it all in."

"All what in?"

"All that I'm going to tell you. I told you, I plan to talk for a couple of weeks, at least."

He sighed, and poured from the bottle.

"Besides," I said, "whose idea is this anyway? Yours or mine?"

"Yours," he said. "I'm not arguing."

"Good. We'll get it all arranged then. It's only a question of us fixing a time. I'll let you know when its convenient for me."

"Convenient for *you*?" he said.

"Yes. Convenient for me. I'll tell you one thing, though. I won't be very long getting round to it. I'll let you know. I'll make sure of getting your address before I leave Auckland."

"Good," he said in that distant way again. He had been pouring the last beer from the bottle slowly and thoughtfully. "You do that. You let me know." He raised the brimming glass to his lips.

"If I were you," I warned him, pointing to the empty bottle, "I'd go easy on that stuff. You're liable to end your days drinking Coca-cola."

To tell the truth, I was feeling pretty perky again. I even looked across the room at Derek amiably, because I felt one up on him. It always makes me cheerful to know I'm one up on Derek. I also smiled pleasantly towards Sally again, as she danced around the room with that front-row forward novelist. It wasn't her fault she happened to be in love with Derek; it was easy to forgive her. I realized people were going home and the party had thinned down considerably. But more important, I noticed the place on the other couch beside Susan was empty. In fact there were places vacant on each side of her. Both the knee-tapper and the elderly gentleman had gone home. Susan caught my eye and smiled.

I decided right away there were more important things in life than literary conversation, so I excused myself to Shadbolt. "Don't worry," I promised, "you'll be hearing from me."

"I'm sure I will," he sighed, and headed off in the direction of the bar to find himself another bottle. He didn't seem at all receptive to friendly advice. He couldn't say I hadn't warned him though.

Before very long the party had thinned right down to five people; almost everyone had gone, and it was three o'clock in the morning. In the room were Derek and Sally, Susan and me. And Shadbolt, though he didn't really count; he was asleep. Sally studied him for a moment. "There always seems to be someone like that," she announced. "Someone sick in the bathroom or asleep on the floor."

To tell the truth, I was feeling fairly protective towards Shadbolt already; I mean I wasn't going to have people saying things about someone who was going to write down my story.

"He's all right," I said. "He could be worse."

"How could he be worse?" Sally demanded.

"Well, for example," I said, "he could be sick on the floor or asleep in the bathroom."

She didn't seem convinced. She fetched a couple of rugs to cover him, and put a cushion under his head. He looked very peaceful.

"Anyway," I went on, "He's had a fairly tough time tonight, one way and another."

"What do you mean?" Derek asked, shooting a sharp look at me.

Then I saw I had to be a little more crafty, if Derek wasn't to discover my plan. "Oh, you know," I said casually, "all that argument with you and that wild dancing with Sally."

"That shouldn't knock anyone out," Derek said. "Anyway, he was all right until an hour or two ago. I can't understand it. He didn't even seem to be drinking much. Not when I last noticed him."

"Then it's just amazing," I said. "Just amazing how people pass out, like that, all of a sudden. You just wouldn't credit it."

"Well," Sally said, changing the subject, "it was really very good of you to stay and help wash up, Sue. I take back all I said about you coming late to help with the supper."

"My God," Derek said. "That reminds me. I'd almost forgotten. That champagne." He charged off into the kitchen and came back waving the bottle.

"I really think strong black coffee would be more in order now," Sally said.

"No, damn it," Derek said. "Let's celebrate."

"We've celebrated," Sally sighed.

"Well, let's celebrate the end of the celebration. The fact that we didn't have a single fist fight at our engagement party, for example. And the fact that all our guests, but one, found their way home on their own feet. That's worth celebrating."

"Do we have to?"

"Besides," Susan chimed in, "I bought that champagne for you and Sally."

"All the more reason for sharing it with you, then," Derek announced. He looked at me. "And Nick too, if he'd like to try a small sip. You really should have been in bed long ago, Nick. Never mind. Sally and I are only going to get engaged once, thank God."

"I think I'd like to try a decent-size sip," I said. "I mean, I've never tasted it before. Besides, I'm pretty dry. All that Coca-cola. I feel dehydrated now."

"You'll have to be content with what I give you. I have to make sure you get home in fairly good condition tomorrow. You'll be bad enough as it is – with rings under your eyes probably. They'll wonder at home what on earth I've been doing to you."

Well, I could have made a pretty smart answer to that, all right. I mean about what he was doing to me, or trying to do. But I was in a strong enough position now to stay silent. I got a great kick, though, out of imagining the expression on his face when he read what I was going to tell Shadbolt to write down.

He worked away at the top of the bottle and the cork banged out like a ·303 in the bush. The champagne flew everywhere, thick and creamy.

"Glasses," Sally cried. "You idiot, Derek. You should have got glasses first." She fled to the kitchen.

To tell the truth, I wasn't too struck on drinking the stuff any more. As it spouted here and there, it looked pretty much like someone's shaving lather or something; anyway it didn't look very hygienic.

By the time Sally returned with four glasses there were various bubbly patches drying out on the carpet. Derek was studying the bottle sadly.

"Well, there's some left," he said. "About enough for a glass each, I should say. Enough for one toast."

Sally placed the four glasses on a low table and Derek poured from the bottle carefully, half-kneeling, as if he was performing some ancient rite. He certainly didn't spill another drop. "I think we should give Nick the first glass," he announced. "After all, he's the one person in this room who's got everything ahead of him."

As he looked over his glasses at me with that damn brotherly expression on his face, and handed me the champagne as if it was liquid gold or something, I felt like telling him I had a few things behind me too. But I didn't. I knew when not to ruin a celebration. Besides, he would find out, all right, and soon enough. I could just imagine his face when he read it, and how his glasses would fall down his nose in surprise.

When we all had champagne, Susan raised hers and said to Derek and Sally, "Well, here's to your happiness then. That's the general idea."

"I think we've had enough of that for one night," Sally said. She looked very tired. "Here's to your exhibition, Sue. Let's hope it's a great success."

"If we're all going to toast ourselves," Derek said, "we'd better not leave Nick out. Here's to Nick too."

We all drank. I decided the taste wasn't so bad after a while. I mean I'd certainly tasted worse than champagne. It sat on what was left of the Coca-cola in an interesting sort of way.

After we'd spent some time looking at the bubbles and drinking them down, Susan rose. "I think I'd better go," she said.

"It's been a long night. Not that I haven't enjoyed every minute." She glanced towards me. "And meeting you again, Nick."

I really appreciated her saying that, but I don't mind admitting I wasn't any too damn happy about seeing her leave. She walked across the room to fetch her coat. Then, about half way, she swivelled lightly on her feet and her green eyes flicked towards me again.

"You did promise me a walk along a beach once, Nick. Well, there's no beach within a mile of here. But do you think you could walk me home?"

Before I could speak, Sally announced, "That's a wonderful idea, Sue. Of course Nick will. It's not far, Nick. Only three or four blocks. Sue lives quite near, really."

"Nick would be delighted," Derek said. "A breath of fresh air would straighten him up nicely. Besides, it'll save me having to walk you home, Sue. This part of town really isn't the best at night, Nick. There are always a few queer customers hanging about the pie-cart over the road."

Well, I could have told him one or two things about the queer customers who hung round the pie-cart, but just then I was more interested in the way Derek and Sally were speaking for me. It was fascinating really. Not that I was prepared to object, but I did think I ought to have some say. After all it was me who was going to walk Susan home, not Derek or Sally.

At least Susan, anyway, was waiting to hear what I had to say. "Would it be any trouble to you, Nick?" she asked. "I could always get a taxi, of course. But I do like the walk."

"Don't bother about a taxi," I said. "It'll be no trouble, believe me." I shot across the room to help with her coat. "No trouble at all."

When we were ready to leave, I turned to face Derek and Sally. Derek was in the act of lighting a cigarette, and Sally was holding the four empty champagne glasses together like a posy of transparent flowers. "Well," I said casually. "See you later." I took Susan's arm.

Chapter Twenty-seven

OUTSIDE WE FOUND THE NIGHT WASN'T TOO COOL FOR A
pleasant walk. There were a few idlers around the pie-cart, but
no one looked really menacing. Susan pulled up the lapels of her
coat, half-hiding her face, and talked in a very low voice about
various subjects as we wandered along. I really mean wandered;
she seemed to like taking her time about a walk home. I found I
had to keep putting on my brakes to keep steady with her and,
whenever I slowed down, I started to drift. It was curious. I had
the same light, drifting sensation every time. As if I was sliding
along very cool smooth water, but upright on my two feet. It
didn't worry me. It was just interesting. The street lamps sprinkled strange watery spots of light through the trees which grew
along the pavement, and these lights floated over us as we walked
along. I found I was interested in that too, in the way we seemed
to be just gliding through this watery air, dark and light, light
and dark. Then in the way my head seemed to be floating
along, about forty inches above my shoulders. I found I was
interested in pretty near everything by the time that walk
finished, and it took a long time to finish.

When we reached Susan's door she looked into her handbag
for the key. "Well," she said, "you've been very kind, Nick."

"It's nothing," I said. "Really nothing." My words seemed to
drift out of my mouth, just like bubbles, with a faint popping
sound as they burst. "It's been a pleasure."

She gave me a strange look. "Are you all right, Nick? I mean
do you feel all right?"

"I feel absolutely terrific. I feel as if I could dance till tomorrow
night, and the night after."

"Dear me," she said, finding the key at last among the clutter
in her handbag. "That doesn't sound the best, Nick."

"What doesn't sound the best?"

"All this dancing you want to do."

"I could dance, all right. Don't worry about that."

"Perhaps I'd better straighten you up with a cup of black coffee," she said, opening the door. "I can't let you go off in this state. Come on in."

I swam down a gloomy passage behind Susan and surfaced in a gently lighted room. I found it was quite an interesting room, when I persuaded my eyes to study the place. It was low and very long, and of course there were paintings hanging almost everywhere. At one end of the room, near a big curtained window, stood an easel by itself; the bare space of floor around was spotted with bright paint. At the opposite end of the room stood an electric stove and a sinkbench littered with pots and pans and unwashed dishes and ashtrays. In between, in the middle of the room, the floor was covered with bright rugs and cushions. A bed was there, and a couch, a couple of armchairs and some shelves jammed with books. It was really three rooms in one. I hadn't seen anything like it before.

"What do you think of my studio?" she asked. "I must warn you I'm proud of it."

"I think it's pretty damn cosy," I said, prowling around. I spied Derek's latest book of poems lying open on a low table, and snapped it shut. "I wouldn't mind a place like this myself, except I don't do any painting."

I busied myself returning Derek to the bookshelf. I happened to notice a painting just above the bookshelf which looked familiar, though I'd never seen it before. Then I realized why. It was Sally, or at least the painting had Sally's general shape. I was about to say something complimentary, such as that Sally did almost look like that, nude, when I decided it might be wiser to hold my tongue.

"A pity I don't paint," I said, "come to think of it."

Susan threw off her coat and went to the sinkbench to make coffee. "Who knows?" she said, in a profound sort of voice. "You might, one day. You might paint, you might do anything, one day."

I flopped into the most comfortable armchair. "You're perfectly right," I told her. "I hadn't thought of it like that. I can do pretty near anything I damn well like, can't I?"

"Of course you can. And I think you probably will, Nick. I think you're strong-minded enough."

"I've got a pretty strong mind at the moment," I said. "Believe me. You haven't got anything to eat over there, have you?"

"You hungry still?"

"It doesn't matter if you haven't. I mean I just get like this at times. I want to nibble things. I suppose I must still be growing."

"Well," she said, "here's something to help with the growing." She tossed a packet of potato crisps at me. "Sorry if I sounded surprised. It was such a big supper."

I jammed my mouth full of crisps and decided they were certainly better than nothing. When the crackling subsided, I said, "I suppose I'll have all this growing over and done with in a couple of years. It's a pain in the neck, really. The sooner it's over the better."

"You won't feel like that when you're my age, Nick. You'll look back with regret on the time you were growing. And you'll wonder what on earth you did with your childhood."

"Well, I wonder right now," I said. "I really do. You've certainly got some weird and wonderful paintings here, haven't you?" I'd been studying them between crisps and conversation. "I mean they're certainly unusual, if you ask me. But then I don't know much. What's that one over there, for example?"

"A landscape."

"And that's the sun up there in the right hand corner?"

"That's the sun," she agreed.

"It's a pretty wild looking sun. But I suppose it might look like that at times. When I really think about it. What I mean is, it certainly doesn't look like the moon. When you look at that painting you can tell it's the sun, all right. You couldn't make a mistake."

"You like it?" she asked.

"Well, to be perfectly honest –"

"Don't worry about being polite, Nick. Just say yes or no."

"It's hard for me to say yes or no. I think I'd have to look at it for a while to make up my mind. I mean I'd have to get used to it."

"Fair enough," she said. "Then the best thing would be for you to have a chance to get used to it." She came from the sink-bench balancing two steaming cups of coffee. "You take it home with you."

"That painting?"

"Yes. That painting. You put it under your arm when you go. All right?"

"I haven't got a lot of money. You mean for me to borrow it or something?"

"No. It's yours, Nick. Yours. From this moment. Let's say it's a gift to celebrate our meeting again."

"Well," I said, "there's certainly a damn lot of celebration going on tonight, if you ask me. But you might want to sell that painting or something. I know there's some influential people wanting to buy your work."

"Let's say you've earned it, then. You walked me home to-night."

"You mean you give a painting to every boy who walks you home?"

"Hardly. But then not many boys walk me home. And it's not every night you walk me home, Nick. Tonight's very special."

"It's special, all right. As far as I'm concerned. But it's me who ought to be making the gift."

"But you have, Nick. That's the point. You've already made me a gift, the gift of your company."

"That's no gift, I'm telling you."

"Then let me be the judge, Nick."

To tell the truth, I was prepared to let her be pretty near anything she liked. She sat curled in an armchair opposite me, the coffee cooling on a low table between us. She didn't sit so far away that I couldn't smell her scent. I could have sworn it was the same as Sally's.

"All right," I said finally. "I admit you've pretty much sold me on the idea of taking that painting home. I think I'm starting to get quite fond of it already."

"You write and tell me when you've really made up your mind whether you like it."

"I will. Don't worry."

"Or come and tell me, next time you're in the city. You will come and see me again, won't you?"

"I'll do that too." The coffee was cool enough, so I started sipping it down. "I'll come and see you, all right. Any time."

"Good," she said. "So that's settled. And, remember, if there's ever any way I can help you, I'd only be too glad. Selfishly glad, in a way. You see, Nick, I had a very lonely childhood. I longed for a brother. But I was an only child. I never had a brother."

My coffee started going down the wrong way, and I choked and spluttered. No doubt about it, I was certainly collecting sisters thick and fast lately. When I'd recovered enough to get my voice into gear, I said, "I'll remember, all right, if I need any help. But you don't mind me coming even if I don't need help?"

"No, Nick. Not at all." She flashed a sweet sisterly smile. "I'll always be glad to see you."

I'd finished my coffee, so I didn't have much excuse for staying longer. When I stood, Susan uncurled from the chair and busied herself making a parcel of the painting. "I'm putting something else in with it," she announced.

"What's that?"

"A spare sketchbook of mine. You might be able to make some use of it. You said you might do anything you like one day. Well, you've got to try everything first, before you decide. You could do worse than begin with that sketchbook."

When the parcel was ready, I took hold of it clumsily. I was fairly clumsy, all round, working my way out the door with that parcel. Perhaps my eyes were clumsiest of all. I didn't know quite where to look with them. Whenever they got near Susan's face, and her steady green eyes, they veered away; I really didn't seem to have any say in the matter. And it wasn't as if I could look where I was going, either. My awkward feet collided with one side of the doorway.

"You sure you feel all right again, Nick?"

279

"I'm fine," I said. But I still didn't look at her. "I'd just better get home, that's all. I mean back to Derek's place. He's probably taken Sally home now, and is back wondering where I am. I really should get moving." I had another shot at getting out the door, but then Susan's voice stopped me.

"Aren't you forgetting something, Nick?"

It was pretty much what I'd been afraid of. I put my face back into the room for a brotherly or sisterly kiss; I wasn't sure who was meant to do what. And where, to tell the truth. Just when I made up my mind that it was up to me, and selected a free space on Susan's cheek, she made a quick decision and acted ahead of me. And she didn't choose my cheek or forehead; it wasn't too damn sisterly in that way. Her hair brushed against my face, and her arms went lightly around my neck; her face was cool and smooth, and her lips were gentle. I felt clumsier than ever, with my feet everywhere and my hands hanging on to that stupid parcel; but only for a moment. I felt pretty good after a moment. After a moment, with all that scent swimming round me, I decided I hadn't felt better in my life.

"There," she said. "Now home to Derek's, safe and sound. And don't drop the painting."

"I won't. Don't worry."

"I hope you really do feel all right. I mean, I hope you still don't want to dance till tomorrow night."

"No, not till tomorrow night. Just for the rest of my life." I waltzed down the passage with my painting.

"I'm not sure whether that's an improvement," she called. "Good night, Nick. And look after yourself."

"You look after yourself too," I called back as I leapt out into the night air. I seemed to just bounce my way home, from tree to tree, corner to corner, building to building; anyway I arrived there in no time. I considered a flying leap on to Derek's Volkswagen, where it was parked outside the flat, but decided the roof probably wouldn't stand it. As I flew up Derek's steps three at a time, I realized I could still feel Susan's sisterly kiss. I don't mind admitting I wasn't in any hurry to wipe it away.

I let myself into the flat quietly. It wasn't much changed.

Shadbolt was still asleep. All things considered, Derek had done a fairly effective job of disguising the fact that he hadn't taken Sally home. Her handbag was out of sight, for example. They'd forgotten just one important thing, though. Her coat still hung in the hall. His bedroom door was closed.

Well, I didn't blame them for shunting me off with Susan in such haste, and I could quite understand now why Susan had co-operated by keeping me away from the flat so long. She was a friend of theirs, after all.

It didn't worry me, though. Nothing worried me.

I placed my parcel down near the living-room door, where I would see it and remember to take it back with me to Te Ika next day, and then I walked softly across to my bedroom. I stripped off, slid into my pyjamas, dropped on to my bed. I couldn't go to sleep, though; I didn't have a hope. Bubbles still leapt and bounced and burst in my head. When I closed my eyes I could see them, all beautiful sizes and colours. I just had to tell someone how I felt, and it wasn't much use talking to Derek's shut bedroom door. Besides, I had so much on my mind. I jumped off the bed, went into the living-room again, and tried to wake Shadbolt. It was quite a job.

At last he groaned. "What's the matter?" he said in a thick voice.

"Nothing's the matter. That's the point. That's what I want to tell you. Everything's terrific."

"Good," he muttered. "Great." He seemed to want to go back to sleep again, so I shook him by the shoulder.

"What's the matter now?" he groaned again.

"I'll get everything fixed up," I said.

"What fixed up?"

"About you coming down to Te Ika. I'll get it all fixed up just as soon as I get back there. You can have my room over at the Waikai place. Mrs Waikai would love to have you. She's always glad to see my friends. Besides, I can talk to you over there. We can be pretty private. I'll fix it up so you can come down next week. The sooner the better."

"Good," he muttered. "Great."

This time he was really asleep, so I left him and went back to bed. To tell the truth, he hadn't been much help. At least I wasn't much less excited, and it seemed just as difficult to go to sleep. I put my hands behind my head, and looked up at the dark ceiling. My mind was still like bubbly, bouncing rubber. I admit that it had a lot to work on, one way and another. I couldn't help wondering when I would have a good excuse to get back to the city again. A lot certainly seemed to go on in the place. I should say I didn't have any really big ideas about Susan, though. I didn't plan to get hurt that way, not again.

I kept Shadbolt to his promise, all right. He's down in Te Ika right now, as a matter of fact. He's been here for the last seven weeks, getting it down. I admit that the job took a little longer than I thought. But, as I keep telling him when he moans about the time we're taking, he's got no right to complain; I'm telling him a novel, aren't I?

He has had some complaints, all right, about the last couple of chapters. About the party, I mean, and how I met him.

"But we can't put all this in," he said.

"Why can't we?"

"Because this kind of thing simply doesn't go into a novel," he said. "You just can't do it."

"Well, I'm doing it. I'm telling you to put it down with that trusty typewriter of yours. I want you to put everything down. Everything I tell you. Nothing left out. Who's telling this, anyway?"

"You are," he sighed. "But I really must insist. This sort of material simply doesn't go into novels. You can't tell about how the novel came to be written. Not in the novel itself. It's a convention."

"It doesn't sound like a convention to me. It sounds more like an excuse. You just don't want people to know how drunk you got at that party."

"And whose fault was it?" he asked.

"Are you saying it was mine? I warned you. You can't say I didn't."

"You hit a man over the head with a club and then you warn him not to fall in the river."

"There you are. More excuses. You know something? I think Derek's quite right in a lot of the things he says about you. You just don't stand up to rigorous criticism."

He rolled a clean sheet of paper grimly into his typewriter. "All right," he said. "Let's get on with it."

"I just want one thing cleared up," I told him. "I'm telling you this. You're writing it down. I don't want any funny business. Or any tricksy stuff. No transcendent paradoxes. No antipodean realities. Just remember."

"All right," he said. "All right."

"And everything's got to go in. The party too. Because that's all part of it. If I started leaving things out, because someone's feelings might be hurt, nothing would make sense. And it wouldn't be my story. When I've told it all to you, then I'll forget about it. And you'll have the novel I promised you. I don't care what you do with it, really. You can put your own name on it."

"All right," he said. "Where were we?"

"You were coming into the party," I said, "with all these normal-looking people."

He started typing with an expression of pain on his face. Sometimes he uses notebooks, sometimes the typewriter. For the party he used the typewriter. I had the impression he wanted to get it over with quickly. He groaned all the way through. You'd never have thought I was doing him a favour. Some people are just never damn grateful. For example, he keeps telling me about the long time he's been away from his wife and family. So I ask if he's got any complaints about Mrs Waikai's cooking. He says no, he just wants to see his wife and family again, that's all. He'd like them to know he was still alive. So I have to explain patiently that he can write them letters or make phone calls, I'm not keeping him prisoner, but he really shouldn't keep pestering me with complaints about his private life; it's really none of my business. "Besides," I tell him, "there's no more room for you in this novel."

"Thank God for that," he says.

"And I certainly can't spare any more space for stuff about your wife and family and the hard time you're having. Sorry, but there it is."

When I went over to the Waikai place this afternoon to tell him the last chapter, I found him asleep. He was fallen forward on a mess of notebooks and typewritten paper. There were cigarette butts everywhere, unwashed coffee cups, and the room was thick with smoke. I let some fresh air into the room, and revived him with a glass of old Hubert's brandy.

"It's no use," he said. "I simply can't go on."

"But we're right at the last chapter. You can't give up now."

He shook his head. "No. It's no use. I'm finished."

"Anyone would think you'd been working hard. You haven't a single blister on your hands, as far as I can see. You're just lazy, that's your trouble. Plain lazy. You haven't even bothered to shave yourself for six days."

"Four," he said. "Anyway the point is I really can't go on. Not any more. I need a good long rest. A holiday with my wife and kids."

"There you go again. I told you there's no more room for that stuff."

"I'll go up to Auckland to collect them. Then I'll take them to a beach."

"That's great," I said. "But we really can't go into that stuff. What are your kids' names, by the way?"

"Does it really matter?"

"Well, you might as well dedicate the book to them. I mean, they've had to do without their father for a fair while. And we might as well dedicate the book to someone. It's a what-do-you-call-it, one of those convention things. What about a foreword? Do novels have forewords?"

"Not usually."

"Well, we'll be unusual, then. We'll get Derek to write our foreword."

"My God," he said.*

"Isn't there another convention?" I asked. "I mean about saying everyone in the book is fictitious?"

"Well, that's up to you. You can say that if you like. I'm told it doesn't help much in a libel case though."

"Perhaps we'd better say it anyway. I mean it might look bad if we didn't. I'll leave that little detail to you. You can work out what to say. It'll be the one line in the book that's really your own."

"Thanks," he said. "Very decent of you."

I could see I'd got him interested again, so I said, "How about this last chapter? If we get that down, you'll be finished. You'll be able to clear off and see your wife and kids again. Don't you want to get it finished?"

"Finished?" he said. He looked down at the notebooks and typewritten paper everywhere. "I don't know how I'm going to put it all together. It's like a dog's breakfast."

"It *is* a dog's breakfast," I said. "That's the point. And this talk about breakfast reminds me. Before we get on to this last chapter, have you got anything handy I can eat?"

He tossed me an orange, and I peeled it as I started talking.

* I have declined to do so. In the circumstances I feel a brief footnote, rather than a foreword, would be appropriate. That this book in manuscript has come as a surprise to me should be evident enough to the most casual reader. Indeed it would be foolish for me to pretend otherwise. Thus I feel it would not be proper to append comments of a personal nature. Nor is it my intention to review the book (in any case an assessment of its place in New Zealand literature would be rather premature) other than to say that in my view, artlessness can no longer substitute for art. I hope I have not seemed unduly personal. My own interpretation of these events should be ready for publication within the next year. D. K. Flinders

Chapter Twenty-eight

TO TELL THE TRUTH, I REALIZE I CAN'T TELL THE TRUTH. Yes, I know I promised to tell the real truth. I said there was truth and real truth, and that I planned to tell the real truth. Well, the fact is that I've found it impossible. I've told the truth, I mean the facts, but I seem to be as far away from the real truth as ever. It's hard to explain why. Perhaps the real truth is something you can never really tell. Perhaps the truth is something you can know and tell, the real truth something you can only feel.

I'll put it like this. A science master of mine, who said he liked to make us think, once told us in class that there was really no such thing as cold, cool, warm or hot. There were only greater or lesser degrees of temperature at which human beings were comfortable or uncomfortable. So that is what the facts are, the truth is; greater or lesser degrees of temperature. But the real truth, the thing you feel, is that it's cold, cool, warm or hot. No one will ever convince me any differently. But all I can do is put down the facts, the truth, the degrees of temperature. It's really not up to me whether you feel cold, cool, warm or hot. It's your business, not mine. I know from experience that sometimes people will argue, for example, about whether a day is cool or warm. One person will say it's cool, another will say it's warm. There's no satisfying everyone. It's impossible. And perhaps, for the same reason, telling the real truth is impossible. Because the real truth is different for each person concerned. Or the same, only different. I can see I've learned something, but it appalls me when I realize just how much I've still got to learn.

I suppose you could argue that I really haven't learned much in the last year, that I've really only picked up a lot of useless information. It's true, in a way. I can dig gum in a country that is just about skinned out of gum. I can search for gold in a country that's fresh out of gold. And I can fell native trees in a country where people are busy replanting them. That reminds me of something, actually; of my father. He came into the house from his garden the other day in a tearing temper. He demanded to know what the hell I was doing, planting a huge bloody weed right in the middle of his garden. So I had to explain that it wasn't a huge bloody weed, it was a baby totara. That pacified him. It's still there, flourishing among his vegetables, but I plan to plant it on some hillside when it's ready. It's not much, I know, but it's the least I can do.

But I do think I learned something last summer. I don't think my head is entirely filled with useless information. I know some things for certain. I know, for example, that if I'm ever going to find anything, like on the day I searched for gum, then I'm probably going to find it when everyone else has gone to sleep on the job. And I know that when I find something, whatever it is, it's going to shine with my sweat. Because there's no other way. I know something else too. I know that I've got to go through the motions whether there's any colour at the end or not. It's just as important knowing how to go through the motions, without too much fuss, as actually finding the gold. In fact it's more important knowing how to go through the motions; because if you don't know, you're unlikely to strike any gold. Gold in any shape or form. This helps me to be very philosophical about things like going to school, for example. Or behaving like everyone else around me; getting out of bed at roughly the same time, going back to bed at roughly the same time, eating three meals a day, and all the rest. By doing this I keep everyone around me happy. There's no real difficulty in going through the motions. The trick is to know that you're going through motions, and not kid yourself. And not kid yourself either that you're actually going to strike gold at the end. It might be a matter of faith and it might just be a matter of luck, good luck or bad, and I've realized it's no use worrying hell out of myself about it, because there's nothing I can do. I haven't a dog's show of fixing the human race. Anyway what if we knew, for certain, that there was always going to be colour at the end? It wouldn't be very damn interesting.

I suppose that, strictly speaking, I learned something else last summer. Well, I don't plan to speak too strictly. I don't plan to go into that side of things. My mother would agree, anyway. She thinks I'm too young. Too young even to take Glenys Appleby out on Saturday nights. "Taking girls out at sixteen," she said, "it was unheard of in my day."

My father said he felt that as parents they mustn't be unreasonable, times changed, and maturity for better or worse came earlier these days. So I was allowed, in the end, to take Glenys out. It's really much like everything else. I'm going through the motions quite happily. Other boys have girl friends at sixteen, though possibly they don't have such an interesting history as Glenys has with me. To tell the truth, we don't get up to much. We get on all right together. That's what it amounts to. On Saturday nights we go to a movie, or a school dance, and I walk her home afterwards. I admit that we can get up to some interesting business on the walk home through the dark town, particularly on the riverbank. But never too much of it. I think old Glenys got the fright of her life last summer, and she certainly hasn't been the same since. She still talks about going to Auckland, though, and all that stuff; and I'm ready to agree I talk about it myself these days. Which reminds me that I still haven't written that letter I promised Susan, about whether I finally like her painting or not. I have it hanging in my bedroom, though my mother says how I manage to sleep with that monstrosity above my head is beyond her. I often sit and study it, and I still can't make up my mind. One thing about that painting, though. She's got the sun right; I've made up my mind absolutely about that. You would never mistake it for the moon, not in two thousand years. I suppose if she's got that right, she's probably got everything else in the painting right, but I wouldn't know for certain. I mean I'm no expert, and don't pretend to be. So I sit and look at that painting and wonder if I've really misunderstood, if I'm confused, if I'm really meant to like it in the ordinary way. I will say one thing, it's an experience. I wouldn't argue about that. Perhaps I'm not so far apart from Derek after all. And perhaps I'll write to Susan in a day or two and tell her that though I don't know yet whether I like her painting, it's certainly an experience. She might be pleased. She's probably wondering why I haven't written. I don't mind telling you that Glenys is as inquisitive as hell about my green-eyed artist friend up in Auckland; I was silly enough to mention Susan one day when I was trying to impress Glenys about my trip to the city. Glenys wasn't too much taken with the idea that Susan was only a kind of sister, and that the painting she gave me was just a sisterly gift. "What other sisterly things did she give you?" Glenys wanted to know. So I've learned, from bitter experience, to keep my mouth shut on certain subjects.

I suppose Glenys is really not a great deal different. It's just that she's quieter. I'm quieter myself, if it comes to that. And, incidentally, she simply won't talk about what happened on top of that cliff last summer. It seems that, as far as she's concerned, it just never happened at all. When we met again after my return to Te Ika, and started getting involved to the extent of knocking round together on Saturday nights, I did raise the subject with the idea of apologizing to her for everything. It was only decent that I should apologize. So I muttered away, tripping over words, trying to explain.

"I simply don't know what you're talking about," she said. "Do you know? Because I don't. And I don't think I want to know, either, thank you very much."

"You're unreasonable," I said, and thought how much I sounded like my father.

"Of course I am. I'm unreasonable and I'm ignorant. And if you don't mind, I want to stay ignorant. I don't know what you're talking about, and I don't care."

"But you were there," I said. "You were involved. That's the point. That's why I'm apologizing to you."

"Well, you can go and apologize to someone else," she said. "It's none of my business."

"Who else can I apologize to?"

"That's your business."

"That's great," I said. "Really great. Thanks for nothing."

"Besides," she said, "can't we talk about something more interesting?"

For a while, then, I really wondered if I hadn't just dreamed her and the whole thing; if she hadn't just been part of my madness or concussion, whatever it was. But she was too solid for a dream. There's no doubt about that.

It was Friday. The Friday before Labour weekend, cooler than last year's, but reasonably fine. Matthew drove me out of Te Ika, into the country, and dropped me at the foot of Murdering Valley. I mean it's actually got that name now. After two years everyone calls it Murdering Valley. I suppose the name will eventually be written into maps. It's not as if it's an especially unusual name in New Zealand. There was once a Murderers' Bay, until people living there decided the name might frighten off tourists, and I'm told there's a place called Murdering Beach in the south. But I suppose if you hunt hard enough around the country you can find every kind of name – there's even a place called Young Nick's Head, though needless to say it has nothing to do with me.

Anyway Te Ika has a Murdering Valley now.

I collected my pack from the rear of the truck, and told Matthew I'd see him in the same place Monday.

"You sure you want to be alone?" he asked.

"Absolutely sure," I told him, though I was afraid I might be hurting his feelings. "Just for a couple of days."

"And you sure you don't want my rifle?" he asked, pointing to the place where it hung in the cab of the truck. "You never know, you might just see something."

"I'm positive I don't want it," I said, and hoisted the pack on to my shoulder. "Well, I'd better get moving. I'll see you here Monday."

"I'll be waiting," Matthew promised. "Have a good Labour weekend."

"I will," I said, though I didn't believe it. "You too. And don't drink too much. You're going to be a respectable married man soon. You'd better get in training."

Matthew grinned sheepishly, put the truck into gear, waved goodbye, and rolled off down the road. In a moment he had vanished behind a corner, and there was just his dust settling. I was alone, completely alone for the first time in nearly a year, and I stood still for a while, as the dust drifted away, in the pale sunlight and silence of the countryside. When the last faint rumble of the truck faded, there was hardly a thing to be heard. Not even a bird singing. I could hear my own breathing, and the distinct rustle of my clothes when I moved at last, and then the click of stones and swish of grass beneath my feet as I walked off the road and cut across country. I adjusted my pack for comfort, so that it shaped into my back. There really wasn't much in it. Food for the weekend, groundsheets and sleeping bag, a change of clothes, a tomahawk and billy. I also carried the sketchbook Susan had given me. I hadn't made any use of it yet and, since I wasn't carrying a rifle, I thought this weekend might be as good a time as any to start.

The valley was changed this year. There wasn't a sheep to be seen. They'd all been rounded up at last, and taken away. Legally the land belonged to the boys, even though they'd murdered their parents and sisters, but it wasn't likely they'd ever want to come back to claim it. When they were released from borstal or gaol or mental hospital, wherever they were now, they would go off some place else and make a new start. It stood to reason they'd never want to come back here. And who else would want the land? Already the high ridges, each side of the valley, were untidy with scrub and second growth. The lower slopes were bright with blooming broom and gorse gone wild. The eroded slopes didn't look in any better shape. In fact, here and there the land had collapsed even more in a welter of upthrown clods and sliding clay. I supposed that in fifty years time all the scars would be pretty well hidden by growth, and no stranger would ever guess there had been a farm in the valley. And when people heard the name, Murdering Valley, they would probably think it dated back to the time of the Maori wars; it wouldn't mean a thing to them, or make them feel strange in the knees.

I was following the path Sam and I had taken at this time, on this day, last year. I stepped carefully across a creek, and climbed through a slack and rusty barbed-wire fence. The fences were almost shot; another year or two and they'd be collapsed. Actually the grass looked as if it would last longer. Here and there were patches of fresh spring green.

Then the farmhouse appeared at last, on a rise just ahead, exactly as it had appeared to us last year. I was tempted, as Sam had been, to go off in a different direction, to go wide of the place. But there was no going back now. I had to face it. There wasn't any wind, so there was no steady banging of loose roofing iron. The smelly water-tank had stopped dripping. Probably it had rusted right through. It was amazing how much I'd begun to remember. Almost all the odd scraps of metal, petrol drums and fencing wire, had vanished beneath long, wild grass.

My feet creaked up the steps on to the veranda. The silence was thick all around that place. Even my smallest movement sounded like gunshot. I slipped the pack from my shoulders, so quietly it seemed I was afraid of waking the dead, and then I noticed something new. Bottles, broken glass, everywhere. All over the veranda, in the passage. The front door had been ripped off its hinges, and all the windows were smashed now. The place looked as if it had been used for a wild midnight party, probably after some Saturday night dance in Te Ika. Whoever it was, anyway, had certainly hurried the place towards ruin. I felt so sick in the stomach I almost didn't go inside, afraid of what else I might find. But there wasn't much else, apart from a patch or two of dried vomit, more broken bottles, cigarette-butts and a few screwed-up packets, and a french letter in a bedroom doorway. It was a wonder they hadn't burned down the place, to finish the job. It would have been cleaner, at least.

My feet crunched slowly along the passage. Then I was in the dim kitchen. There the scene was much the same. It must have been a big party; they'd used every room in the place. I didn't turn and flee back down the passage as I had last year, though. Because my eyes were some time finding what I expected to see, in all that new clutter. But the potty-chair was there, all right, overturned in a corner. Probably it had been a big joke. Kicked around, perhaps even used, before being tossed into the corner. Certainly it was chipped in one or two fresh places. It wasn't fair. That was the dirtiest thing of all, as far as I was concerned. I wasn't afraid of the thing again. I didn't need to be. It actually seemed to have shrunk; anyway it didn't seem to be anywhere near so big as I remembered. I pulled it out of the corner, into a patch of better light, where I could study it. Then I knew I couldn't just walk out and leave it sitting there. I couldn't leave the thing to be kicked around for a joke at another party.

I picked it up and carried it back down the passage, to the place on the veranda where I'd left my pack. Sam wasn't sitting out there, waiting and laughing, this time. There was no one to laugh, no one in miles, and yet I couldn't help feeling ridiculous as I started off, pack on my shoulders, with that potty-chair hanging from the hand where my rifle should have been. It was a relief to get clear of the stink of the farmhouse. But I hadn't left it behind altogether. The potty-chair smelt of fresh urine. They had used it, that way, as a joke. Not that the smell bothered me for long. I found a small creek flowing down from the hills and, where the clear water sprawled out on a stony bed, just below the bush, I washed the potty-chair clean. So clean it didn't have the faintest smell any more. Then the puzzle was what to do with the thing. I couldn't make up my mind, so I hung on to it as I crossed the creek and entered the bush. It was even more ridiculous, and awkward, as I carried it along the narrow, overgrown bush track which Sam and I had used last year. It caught in branches and bush lawyer, and I felt like dumping the thing then and there, but I didn't. I didn't want it to be kicked aside with a laugh by the next person using the track. I suppose that was what it amounted to.

Anyway, after a while I didn't notice its inconvenience. The bush was clean, with fresh raindrops still shivering on the sharp bright leaves, and pungent with the smells of growth and decay. It didn't seem gloomy, even in the shade, though trees towered above me, lemon-coloured at their topmost branches by the last of the sun. And the coolness didn't chill me. It simply told me where I was, and welcome. My breathing was sure and even. It seemed I hadn't breathed so easily in a long time. I heard birds now, bellbirds chiming in the distance, and the odd fantail skittered away through leaves as I crashed steadily deeper into the bush. I'd lost the track, or the track had given out, but I thought I knew my direction. I stopped now and then, and listened. For a while there was nothing. Then at least I heard the faint sound of water. Swerving here and there to avoid the thickest growth, following the sound of water, I came to the place, by the tinkling limestone spring, where we'd camped last year. The sun was gone altogether now, even from the tops of the tallest trees, and in the bush darkness was coming fast. There was hardly a thing to show we'd once camped there, not a scrap of paper, and the flattened fern was tall again. There was just a faint scorched place where our fire had burned. I soon lit a new fire, and swung the billy, and settled back to eat my cold food. I didn't feel like cooking, since I wasn't far from sleep. After drinking my mug of hot tea, I stretched out a groundsheet, then my sleeping bag, on the fern beside the fire. On my back, I watched the flames tossing light up into the branches, among the shadowy leaves. I was asleep long before the fire burned low.

In the morning I woke to clear sky, and sunlight among the leaves, with all the old excitement of a new day in my body. After breakfast, I pushed a couple of chocolate bars in my pocket and spent most of that Saturday simply wandering. I learned more than I expected to learn. I thought I'd forgotten most things about that last Labour weekend, and I suppose I had, in a way. It's just that memories are never really lost, even if you don't own them any more. Anyway there was hardly a rock or a clearing, a dip in the land or a twist in the bush, which didn't own something of mine, and give it gently back to me. It was this gentleness which surprised me most. Because nothing hurt, not any more. All the pain had been drained away and there, in the same old colours, was the place where we'd shot our opossums, then the high clearing where I'd dozed, and the patch of bush where the young pig charged and our rifles cracked. Each memory was given back clean again, washed bright by a winter's rain and dried by a spring sun, and fresh and crackling in my mind.

It was dusk by the time I found my way back to camp. The first thing I noticed was that stupid potty-chair, still sitting near my sleeping bag, and I remembered that I had to do something with it. But I didn't have time now to worry about the thing. I hurried to build my fire, cook a quick meal, and get back to bed again. I was tired after all the day's tramping; I'd crashed through the bush in slow circles finding some of the places, and I'd certainly walked miles further than I had last year. I thought I smelled dampness in the air, and I wasn't wrong. Shortly before I went to bed, the first drops of rain smacked down on the leaves above my head, and made faint hissing sounds as they dripped into the campfire. I covered the sleeping bag with my extra groundsheet before I climbed into it, and though my face was soon wet, my body was warm and tight. I fell asleep with the slow rain cooling my face.

In the morning it was still raining. Moisture had leaked into my sleeping bag and crept in chilly patches through my clothes. Dense mist hovered in the tops of the tallest trees and it was hard, in the grey rainy light, to tell whether the sun had risen.

Everything was sodden or damp and I didn't have a dry scrap of paper to start a fire. I hunted out my change of clothes from the pack, and then I found Susan's sketchbook. It was just what I needed. I ripped it into pieces to start quite a healthy fire. It was a pity in a way, I thought as I warmed myself and drank hot tea, but Susan certainly wouldn't be able to complain that I hadn't made use of it. While my sleeping bag and damp clothes steamed dry beside the fire, I wondered if I was going to spend the whole day sheltering.

Finally I decided that was the last way I'd spend the day. When I had my gear fairly dry, I rolled clothes inside the sleeping bag, the sleeping bag inside groundsheets, and tucked everything into a dry hollow beneath an overhanging rock. I placed a little food for the day in the pack, swung it on my shoulder, and started off. As I did, I kicked against something. I looked down and saw the potty-chair. The damn thing was starting to haunt me again, and it seemed I'd never be rid of it unless I did something soon. So I grabbed it up and carried it along with me.

It was true the mist was lightening, the rain too, but that didn't stop me getting wet again, and the mist hadn't broken up enough for me to see my direction clearly. I blundered up two dead-end gullies before I began to get anywhere. The bush was noisy with dripping water, and I was showered and soaked before I'd gone fifty yards. By the time I'd backed out of those gullies there was just a faint silvering of sun behind the mist. The mist itself was starting to fray and lift in slow shreds. I followed a creek, steep slopes of bush on each side, and I thought I knew where I was at last. The last of the rain dribbled out of the sky, then it stopped altogether. Not that it made much difference to me right away. I still shivered. The creek was cold enough, too, when I crossed it to find more level ground for walking. I misjudged my footing on a slippery rock, and then I had to wade knee-deep. Well, a little more dampness was neither here nor there. I certainly couldn't get any colder.

So when the sun appeared, at last, it was like a golden gift. Each tree, each separate rainswept leaf and frond of fern, as high as I could see, tingled with light. There wasn't a thing that didn't shine or sparkle. It was like some huge celebration. The sun didn't have much warmth, not yet, but it was certainly a relief to know it was still there. Everything was clearing fast and up ahead I saw the giant hill, with limestone crags rising each side like cathedral spires, and I knew for certain I was moving in the right direction.

A bend in the creek brought me in sight of something more dazzling than the gleam of sunlight on green. The white, pure white, of the bush clematis shone everywhere. It was even more spectacular this year. The sight struck me still, and I was given back something else that was mine. After a while I moved forward slowly, until the clematis was bright all around, and found a rock in the sunlight where I could rest. Then it struck me that I could take home a root or two of clematis for my mother's garden. It wouldn't be as if I was destroying it, and the bush certainly wouldn't miss a couple of roots. Sacred or not, there were enough flowers here, where no one ever saw them. Anyway, to my way of thinking the bush still owed me a thing or two. I hunted some vines to their roots, removed them gently and stowed them in my pack. I hoped they would keep.

I started out again. Then I realized my hand was empty. I'd forgotten something. I turned back and found that potty-chair sitting there, a tiny throne, among the clematis. It still wasn't the right place for the thing, somehow. Not out there in the open. I felt now that it should be hidden away somewhere, hidden away for good and ever. Not dropped casually. Swinging it in my hand, I started up towards the giant hill. I hummed a bright, jingly tune to keep up my courage, then whistled it, as I tramped along; I told myself I felt fine. Until I realized that the tune had changed, and that for some time I'd been whistling the tune of the old nursery rhyme, the one Sam sang with the twisted-up words, a sly grin on his face:

> *Little Nickie Flinders*
> *Sat among the cinders*
> *Warming his pretty little toes*

I put a stop to that, smartly, and the silence seemed to roll out, flat and thick, all around. Anyway I soon didn't have much breath to spare for whistling. I was starting to climb, and the ground grew steeper with every step. Before long I was four hundred feet above the creek, and still climbing. I could look back down the valley, and see the miles I had covered since first light. Steam rose from the bush, but I wasn't any drier; I was freshly showered by tree or fern with every yard I moved.

I took an easier, slower route up the hill. I had more time to spare than we had last year. All the same, I judged by the sun that it was about noon when I reached the summit breathless. The sun was really hot now, but there was a wild, leaping wind in my face. My clothes began to steam as I lay against a rock and got my breath back. I didn't stay long up there in the wind. I started making my way down the other side of the hill, the sheltered side, over the descending limestone ledges. I slid and scrambled and grabbed at fern and scrub to ease my way from ledge to ledge. I don't mind admitting that I was pretty careful this time.

Then I came to the ledge that I remembered, the last and the widest. No goat leapt out in front of me. But there was the same patch of scrub and toe toe, with the tapu cave hidden beyond. I didn't go any farther. I needed the sun, and near the scrub was a warm golden pool of light where I could dry myself out. My boots and socks came off first. Then I stripped off my clothes, piece by piece, and wrung out the water. I placed everything to catch the sun, stringing the clothes out over the scrub until it looked like a Maori washday.

The distance I had travelled caught up with me at last, and I collapsed exhausted on the mossy rocks. The sun couldn't have been kinder to me, and it certainly couldn't have been much warmer. Soon it was too warm, and I remembered I was thirsty. I listened for water, and thought I heard a spring not far away, beyond the scrub, perhaps on the same ledge. As I rose to look for the water I saw my old enemy the potty-chair again, dumped beside my pack. At last I knew what I could do, had to do, with the thing. I wanted to get rid of it for good and ever, and now was my chance. I sighed, snatched the thing up and walked carefully along the ledge. The scrub was prickly on my naked flesh and the toe toe feathery and gentle. The cave opened before me, and in the broken sunlight I saw the bones and old skulls scattered.

No one had seen the place, or touched it, since Sam and I saw it; not even the party which had searched for us. Perhaps Sam and I were the only people who had seen inside the cave in a couple of hundred years or more. There could hardly have been a safer place anywhere in the world. I held my breath as I moved into the cave, for the tapu was something I could almost feel on my body, like the sudden cold of the place, and my bare feet brushed against one or two chilly bones. I placed the potty-chair down in a free space on the cave floor and then backed slowly out.

To feel sunlight on my body again was a relief. I took a deep breath.

Yet it still didn't seem enough. There seemed something unfinished about the whole thing. Then I remembered. I went back through the scrub and toe toe, opened my pack and fetched out the roots of clematis. Te Ika wasn't going to see them flower after all. I carried them to the cave, hunted for some soil near the mouth, loosened it up a little, and then bedded each root down securely. It might take root there, and it mightn't. There was no way of telling, and I'm not such an expert in these things. But there seemed enough chance that it might. One thing was certain, if it did take root and tangle its white flowers everywhere, there was no better way of concealing the cave altogether.

By the time I finished that job I was thirstier than ever, so I hunted for the spring I was sure I'd heard. My guess wasn't too bad. It was there all right, on the same ledge, just a yard or two beyond the cave. It flowed out of the side of the hill into a limestone basin, and dripped away over the ledge. I knew its position, so close to the burial cave, would make it tapu water. But I didn't let that worry me any more. I felt pretty tapu myself now. I buried my face in the water, so that its marvellous coolness tingled into my flesh and eyes, and then I drank until my thirst was gone.

I went back to where my clothes were drying, and found the afternoon sun warmer than ever. By its position in the sky I knew it was at this time, last year, that I had made my descent to this ledge, shot the goat, and found the cave. At this time Sam followed me, went crashing through the scrub, and saw the cave.

I sat there in the sunlight, waiting, and closed my eyes. But nothing happened. The minutes passed, the sun moved lower in the sky, perhaps an hour was gone. And nothing happened, nothing at all. What had I expected? I didn't even know any more. I just knew I had to be here, that was all. Birds sang, but nothing moved. The tall trees below me had stopped tossing and surging, for even the wind was quiet. The hazy bush climbed away over ragged foothills below, straggling down to the sea. Beyond the coast the sea was bright to the horizon. On the other side, not quite hidden by the side of the hill, rose the whitened volcanoes, one showing just a tall wisp of smoke in the still air.

The spring sunlight was browning me, but not burning. I relaxed at last and gave new places of my body to the sun. Looking dreamily out upon hills, bush, sea and coast and volcanoes, I wondered how the first people felt when they saw such a wild, terrible, strange place. The first Maoris or Polynesians. Except that they weren't called anything then, because it was long before they had to have a name for themselves. They were just people, just men. It wasn't any wonder they had to invent huge gods to stalk around the place; it must have seemed a place made for gods. Huge wild gods that could storm and trample, exploding the bodies of men into the air, or flinging them far away into the terrible loneliness of the sea. When I came to think about it, I saw that in any place like this, made for gods, human beings were bound to be disappointing. They didn't have a chance, really. They were bound to seem small and grubby with their little boxy houses, goldfish ponds, billboards, beer bottles, transistor radios and television sets; even with their poetry. They just couldn't help themselves.

All the same, as I lay back in the sun and closed my eyes, I couldn't help wishing that one of those old gods, if he was still around and had time to spare, would speak to me, say just a word. I grew drowsy. Then it seemed that something did happen. It seemed that someone actually spoke to me. I jerked upright into sitting position again, and I realized it was just my memory playing tricks. It was Pat I heard again, Pat Radonovich's voice I remembered. "All things over now, all things gone," he said. "Is quiet. Is peace." And that was all, all I had.

When I woke, the sea was even more brilliant with the descending sun. I wasn't cold, but I dressed because it was time to move, time to make my way back. I could feel the tanned warmth of myself beneath the clothes, and I knew it was a warmth I would carry with me all the way back to my camp, then out of the bush, through Murdering Valley, down to where Matthew would be waiting for me at the roadside.

But I still wasn't in a hurry to leave. I had no worry about finding my way back, even in the dark. I might lose my direction but I'd always find my way back sooner or later. I ate food from my pack and drank again from the spring. As I pottered about on that ledge, I began clicking together memories of all that had happened to me in the last year, clicking them together like beads on a string. Sometimes it seemed to me they all made some kind of sense; sometimes it didn't. Finally I decided they must add up to something. It stood to reason. So I swung my lightened pack on to my shoulders and, before I set off, did the one thing I was still afraid of doing. I moved close to the crumbled edge of the limestone and looked down to where we had fallen among the tangled trees.

I admit I didn't go too close to the edge, though. One fall like that is enough.

MAURICE SHADBOLT

MAURICE SHADBOLT was born in Auckland, New Zealand, in 1932. He has worked as a director of documentary films and more recently as a free-lance journalist. Assignments have taken him through the Soviet Union, Eastern and Western Europe, China, Southeast Asia and the Pacific Islands. He began writing seriously in 1955, and since that time his stories have been published in several countries and many languages; his first volume of stories, *The New Zealanders,* was published in the United States in 1961, and his second, *Summer Fires and Winter Country,* is shortly to appear. The winner of a number of literary awards and fellowships, he is also the author of a major book on New Zealand with the distinguished photographer Brian Brake. He lives with his wife and two sons in a house surrounded by native New Zealand bush above a subtropical tidal estuary near Auckland.

BKM #4

94   96 04 10
11   1   1   1